A Plus Size Diva
Who Ya Wit': The Beginning

OCT --- 2014

A Plus Size Diva
Who Ya Wit': The Beginning

Brenda Hampton

www.urbanbooks.net

Urban Books, LLC
97 N18th Street
Wyandanch, NY 11798

A Plus Size Diva Who Ya Wit': The Beginning

ISBN 13: 978-1-60162-426-0
ISBN 10: 1-60162-426-3

First Trade Paperback Printing October 2014
Printed in the United States of America

10 9 8 7 6 5 4 3 2 1

Distributed by Kensington Publishing Corp.
Submit Wholesale Orders to:
Kensington Publishing Corp.
C/O Penguin Group (USA) Inc.
Attention: Order Processing
405 Murray Hill Parkway
East Rutherford, NJ 07073-2316
Phone: 1-800-526-0275
Fax: 1-800-227-9604

Chapter One

I hated my job, but as bad as the economy was, I was pleased to have one. My boss, Mr. Wright, sometimes made me want to splash hot black coffee in his face, but other times he was cool to work for. I'd worked as his administrative assistant for thirteen years, and even though other opportunities at St. Louis Community College became available from time to time, I had somehow got complacent. Maybe because I knew the grass wasn't always greener in another department. I'd heard complaints from other administrative assistants who despised their bosses, so dealing with Mr. Wright just had to do.

Then again, maybe it was just me. I turned forty last month; my son, Latrel, left for college this year; I'd been packing on the pounds; and my divorce from Reggie was recently finalized. Needless to say, things were tough. Never in my wildest dreams had I predicted our marriage would end up as it had. We were high school sweethearts and had planned a life together forever. When Latrel was born, I was the happiest woman in the world. He and his father were very close, and over the years, they'd gotten even closer. So close that when Reggie started seeing another woman, Latrel knew about it but didn't say a word. I suspected that something was up, and when I would look Latrel in the eyes, I could tell he was hiding something.

He was so anxious to go away to college, and moving away from home had become his priority. I hated to put him in the middle of what was transpiring between me and his father, but I couldn't help but feel betrayed by both of them. Reggie's and my marriage was on shaky ground for at least the last four years we were together. His late nights at the office and constant trips out of town always brought about many arguments. It wasn't until I saw the infamous lipstick on the collar that I suspected something was up. I finally questioned him about my suspicions, and his response was quite surprising. He came clean, admitting that he had fallen out of love with me and wanted his freedom.

To this day, I have flashbacks of that dreadful day, and even though it went down as one of the worst days of my life, I appreciated his honesty. No doubt, it was time to call it quits. We hung in there for another three months, but as soon as Latrel left for college, Reggie went his way and I went mine. I still loved my ex-husband, but for him to renege on our vows as he did, I lost a lot of respect for him.

I was sitting at my desk, eating M&M'S, daydreaming about my failed marriage, and attempting to type a letter for Mr. Wright that had to get distributed today. My fingers weren't moving fast enough for him. When I heard him yell my name, my eyes rolled to the back of my head. I picked up my cup of coffee, and instead of taking it into his office with me, I sipped from the cup, smiling about my devious thoughts of tossing the coffee at him. I then placed the cup on my desk and straightened my gray fitted skirt, which was glued to my healthy curves. I flattened the wrinkles on the front and made sure that the silver buttons were buttoned on my rosy red blouse, which squeezed my size forty double Ds. Sometimes Mr. Wright complained about my attire. To him, as a full-figured woman, I dressed too sexily, bringing unwarranted attention. And if anyone stopped at my desk to pay me a compliment, that was a distraction.

I considered myself a beautiful forty-year-old woman. I was confident about myself, and even though my breasts weren't as perky as they'd been before and *some* cellulite was visible on my thighs, there wasn't much for me to complain about. The problem was I had an addiction to sweets! Sweet addiction or not, my body was well proportioned, and what kind of man didn't want a woman with meat on her bones? Reggie had never had any complaints, but I had a feeling he traded me in for a woman who was half my size and age.

I slid my feet into the gray, three-inch stilettos underneath my desk and made my way into Mr. Wright's office. He rubbed his wrinkled face up and down, massaging it with pressure. His cold blue eyes looked me over, and a deep sigh followed as he extended his hand.

"Have a seat, Desa Rae."

I took a seat in the leather chair that sat in front of his messy desk. Papers were scattered everywhere, and his phone was buried somewhere underneath. I had attempted to organize Mr. Wright's office for him, but he was a serious pack rat. He hated to throw away anything, and consequently, some of the papers on his desk had started to turn yellow. I turned my eyes to the six smashed cigarettes in his ashtray. His office had a smoky smell, which someone had tried to cover with cheap Glade garden spray. I figured that since he'd been under pressure, I was about to get an earful. I then looked at the round clock on his wall and saw that I was ten minutes away from taking my lunch. Obviously, he needed to hurry up with whatever he wanted to discuss.

Mr. Wright peeled the black-framed glasses away from his face and then combed his fingers through his layered salt-and-pepper hair. "I need a vacation," he said, then yawned. "And when I get back, maybe my secretary . . . uh . . . administrative assistant will have all my letters typed for me, my office will be spotless, and I'll never be late for an appointment, because she remembered to tell me."

I had been through enough in my personal life. Mr. Wright adding to my misery wasn't going to benefit him in any way. No, I hadn't been giving this job my all, but he knew about my divorce from Reggie. He knew that my son had gone away to college. Yet it seemed as if Mr. Wright wasn't willing to cut me any slack.

I repositioned myself in the chair and crossed one of my moisturized legs over the other. It was best that I kept quiet. If I didn't have anything nice to say, I wasn't going to say anything at all. I turned my attention to my chipped fingernail and thought about how badly I needed a manicure.

"Desa Rae," Mr. Wright said with a high-pitched voice. "are you with me, or is your mind floating somewhere else?"

With a blank expression on my face, I gave Mr. Wright my attention. "You asked me to take a seat, so I did. You haven't required anything else of me, so I assumed my job was to just listen."

He threw his hand back and looked at his watch. "It's almost lunchtime. Would you mind bringing me a bagel sandwich with turkey, ham, and cheese? The deli shop on the corner has awesome sandwiches. You should get you one too."

"My car really needs to be washed, so I planned to stop by a car wash. If you allow me a bit more time, I'll stop by the deli to get our sandwiches."

"I'll allow you an extra fifteen minutes," he said, then handed me a Post-it notepad. "Here's a list of things I need you to take care of before the day ends. It's not much, but if you have any questions about my requests, you can reach me by cell phone. After lunch, I'm leaving to spend the day with my wife. Today is our thirty-first anniversary, and I've made special plans for us. Before you go to lunch, if you could call the florist and have some flowers delivered to my house, I would appreciate it."

I skimmed the Post-it note, which specified a minimal number of things for me to do, including finishing the letter I'd been working on already. Mr. Wright had even drawn a smiley face on the Post-it, encouraging me to have a great day. I smiled and held out my hand. He looked at it inquisitively.

"What is it?" he asked. "You want more work to do?"

"Happy anniversary, but I need money for your bagel sandwich. You don't think I can walk in there and get it for free, do you?"

He chuckled and reached in his back pocket. "You're a fly young woman who should be able to get whatever you want for free." He pulled a ten-dollar bill out of his busted wallet, and as he did so, his credit cards fell out and so did his driver's license. I reached for the license, holding it in my hand.

"At your age, Mr. Wright, what do you know about a woman being fly? Your grandkids aren't encouraging you to be hip, are they?"

"My grandkids are all a mess. They say I'm too old-fashioned, but I'm set in my ways. I'm appalled that they listen to rap music, and they drink and smoke too much pot. I can't tell you the last time I saw any of them read a book, and my youngest grandchild, Katie, she's adapted a new Goth look. What's going on with these kids today, Desa Rae? It wasn't like that when I was growing up."

I stood up, wiggling my hips a bit so my skirt could drop to knee-length level. "Those days are long gone. Things have changed. The best thing we can do for our children is be there for them."

He stood up too. His black slacks squeezed his waistline, and his pot belly hung over his leather belt, which was there to keep everything intact.

"Well, I'm not quite ready to accept this change yet. I'd love people to get back to their conservative values and start doing what's right for this country."

I felt our conversation turning political, so I kept my mouth shut and followed behind him as he made his way to the door.

"I'm going to the men's room. Don't forget about my wife's flowers, and I'll see you when you get back with lunch."

Mr. Wright flat-footedly walked away, and I sat at my desk to call the florist. After I had a dozen roses sent to Mrs. Wright, I called to wish her a happy anniversary. She was one of the nicest women I'd ever met. I hated to admit it, but her husband was pretty darn nice too. Coming clean, I admitted to myself that I was the one with an attitude problem.

The long line at the car wash made me very impatient. The workers were engaged in horseplay and seemed so darn unprofessional. One worker was on his cell phone, cussing at his girlfriend, and another was arguing with a white man about some spots the worker had missed inside his car. Lil Wayne's "Lollipop" was thumping through the loudspeakers, and when I saw two females who had climbed out of their cars and were twerking, I was in disbelief. The attention they got delayed the workers even more. And after seeing numerous people waiting in line too, I was embarrassed. The hot sun was baking my body, and my wet silk blouse was starting to stick to my skin. I stood close to my car and reached inside for my glasses to protect my eyes from the sun's bright glare. As soon as

I covered my eyes, my cell phone buzzed. I looked to see who it was, and it was Reggie. The last thing I needed was to hear his voice, so I let the call go straight to voice mail.

"Sucker," I mumbled, tossing the phone inside my tiny purse. I tucked it underneath my arm, then abruptly walked inside the car wash waiting room to speak to a manager.

"Can I help you?" asked the man behind the counter.

"May I speak to the manager?"

"Can I ask what for?"

I forced a fake smile. "I prefer to speak to the manager about my concerns, if you don't mind."

The man twisted his thick, crusty lips and walked away from the counter. Moments later, he returned and asked me to take a seat.

"The manager ain't here, but I got somebody else you can talk to."

I cut my eyes at him and wouldn't dare take a seat in any of the blue chairs, which had stains all over them. I could have easily gone somewhere else, but this place was close to my job. My Lincoln MKS needed a cleaning right here and now. Time definitely wasn't on my side. I knew that Mr. Wright was eagerly awaiting his bagel sandwich.

I gazed out the smudged window at four black men and two white men in dark blue jumpsuits, sitting around, doing nothing. The line with people waiting had gotten longer, and some people were starting to leave. I shook my head at one of the workers who had the audacity to look inside the waiting room and blow me a kiss. My middle finger trembled by my side. I surely thought about lifting it so he could see it. My "Don't mess with me" expression said it all, but it wasn't enough to keep the man from coming inside.

"Is there somethin' I can help you wit'?" he asked as he walked through the door.

I looked at the name stitched on his jumpsuit. "Bud, I don't think so. You look as if you're too busy to help anyone."

"I'm on my break, but for a scrumptious-lookin' cookie like you, I'll—"

"Please don't do me any favors," I snapped. "There are people out there who've been waiting and waiting on your services. This is ridiculous. I can't believe I'm standing here, trying to coach you about doing your job."

Bud's eyes damn near popped out of his head. "Another angry black woman," he spat. "Y'all need to cut *us* some slack. I offered to help, but you don't want it. You'd rather stand there wit' yo' sexy, bitter self and attack me."

My brows quickly shot up. This man didn't know anything about me to call me bitter. And his "angry black woman" comment had hit a major nerve. My index finger rose. I was about to tell Bud to kiss me where the sun didn't shine. Instead, I was interrupted by someone clearing his throat. My head snapped to the side, and I saw an extremely attractive young man standing close to me. He immediately reminded me of Lance Gross, and all that dark chocolate was quite breathtaking. Due to the dirty blue jumpsuit he had on, he wasn't as clean-cut as Lance Gross, but his smooth skin and "Lure me into your bedroom" hooded brown eyes nearly swept my feet out from underneath me. His thin mustache was trimmed to perfection, and so was the minimal hair that adorned his chin. I hurried to gather myself, and when he turned toward Bud, I listened in.

"Are you finished with yo' break yet?" he asked.

"Almost. I just came inside to see if I could help this lady. She seems upset about somethin', but I'm not sure what's up."

I looked at the name stitched on Mr. Sexy's jumpsuit. "Roc, are you the manager?"

Roc shrugged, as if he didn't give a damn about my concerns. "Not. But I'm in charge of things around here right now. What's up?"

I rolled my eyes and released a sigh of frustration. All I wanted was a car wash. Instead, I had yummy and dummy standing there as if I'd done something wrong. I tightened my lips to keep quiet and made my way to the door. Roc rushed up behind me.

"Did I say somethin' wrong?" he asked.

I kept on moving. My long hair was bouncing, and my brisk walk implied that I would never, ever visit this place again. When I got to my car, I got inside and slammed the door. Roc stood there, with a confused expression on his face, and while rubbing his coal-black, neatly lined waves, he squinted from the bright sun. I put my car in reverse but couldn't go anywhere, because another car was behind me. I hit the horn with my hand and couldn't believe how upset I was.

"Damn it!" I yelled.

Roc stepped up to my car and squatted as he looked at me through the lowered window.

"Are you havin' a postal moment or what? Maybe I should back away from the car, in case I get shot. You too dope to be as angry as you are. If I've done anything to upset you, hey, my bad."

I took a deep breath to calm myself. I'd been overreacting to a lot of things lately, but that was to be expected. I zeroed in on his straight, pearly white teeth.

"Look," I said with frustration in my eyes. "All I want is my car washed. Is that asking too much? I'm on my lunch break, and I have thirty-five minutes left."

Roc backed away from the door. "Come on. Get out of the car. I'll personally take care of you."

That was music to my ears, so I exited the car and let Roc get in.

"No offense," I said. "But your jumpsuit is kind of dirty. My seats are off-white and I'd hate for them to get any dirtier."

Roc pointed to his chest. "I thought that's why you were here. Ain't it my job to clean the outside and inside of yo' car?"

"True. But you have grease on your jumpsuit. Right at your midsection."

Roc looked down, but it wasn't at his midsection. "Thanks for noticin'," he said, then winked.

He got out of my car, standing tall in front of me. He reached for his jumpsuit zipper, and our eyes were in a deadlock as he slid the zipper down, past the hump I'd already noticed. I felt so ashamed for getting myself worked up over a young man like him, but his sexiness was hard to ignore. He kicked off his black steel-toe boots, and the jumpsuit came off next. Underneath, he sported a white wife beater and jeans that hung low on his nicely cut midsection. His arms were muscle packed, and he had tattoos on both of them. How dare I stand there, gazing at him as if I hadn't eaten any chocolate all day?

"If you don't mind, I'm going inside to suck up the air conditioner. Please come get me when you're finished."

Roc nodded. I made my way back inside, swaying my noticeable hips from side to side. I got a few whistles, and even though they were from Bud, I didn't mind.

As Roc detailed the heck out of my car, I watched his every move through the window. His body was now dripping with beads of sweat, causing the thoughts in my head to become downright nasty. I visualized my light-skinned legs resting comfortably on his shoulders as he pumped hard inside of me. I gave him head, while he tongue tortured my tunnel in the sixty-nine position. Even Reggie couldn't do it like that. I smiled . . . Roc smiled. I assumed he liked it rough, but then again, his voice had a romantic pitch to it.

Yeah, he was a thug, but . . . how old was he? I thought about his age while biting my already chipped nail, trying to take back my outrageous thoughts. He had to be at least my son, Latrel's age or maybe a tad bit older. I couldn't quite understand my immediate attraction to him, but maybe it was due to me feeling so alone. I chalked it up to the fact that he was a handsome young man, one who was probably dating several attractive young women. Like the one with the petite figure who stood close by as he wiped my windshield. She wasn't giving him much breathing room. By the evil stares she gave him, I could tell there was an involvement. No doubt, the competition looked steep. If he was interested in women that small, I was way out of his league.

Roc tucked the dry wash rag into his front pocket and reached in his back pocket for his wallet. I saw him hand over several bills to the young woman, and afterward, she walked away. Once she sped off in her car, he looked inside the waiting room, focusing his eyes in my direction. I grinned, then took a glance at my watch. Time was not on my side, so I left the building and walked over to my car.

"I'm just about finished," Roc said, removing the rag from his pocket and turning it in circles on my windshield. "Feel free to inspect it."

I walked around my car, silently admitting that he had done a pretty good job. When I noticed a tiny speck of dried water on the trunk, I called him out on it.

"Oops," I said. "You forgot something."

He turned his attention to the trunk and looked at the dry water speck. "Are you serious?" He smiled and rubbed the tiny spot with a towel. "If you look hard enough, you might find more of those."

"I hope not. Besides, how much is this going to cost me? If there are spots on my car, then maybe you should consider offering me a discount."

He faced me and leaned his backside against the trunk. His arms were folded in front of him, and his bulging muscles were clearly on display.

"I usually don't offer people discounts, especially if the Roc personally takes care of them. But in this case, I got a better idea."

My hand went up to my hip. I felt the bullshit about to go down. "I'm almost afraid to ask about your idea."

"It's simple, Ma. What's yo' name?"

"Desa Rae. Why?"

"Because my real name is Rocky Dawson, Dez. Let me get yo' sevens so I can hit you up and take you to dinner. How about that?"

My eyes shifted to the ground, then connected with his. "Just for the hell of it, Mr. Rocky Dawson, how old are you? And by the way, my name is Desa Rae Jenkins, not Dez."

In slow motion, I watched his thick lips spit out the number. "Twenty-four." He stared at me. "How old are you?" he asked.

He was only five years older than my son! There was no way I could go there. "You know what? My age doesn't even matter. How much do I owe you?" I opened my purse, reaching for my wallet.

"The wash was on me. Now, to be fair, can you answer my question, or did you just realize that this young man may be too much for you to handle?"

I moved my bangs away from my sweaty forehead with my finger. Then I hurried to wrap up this conversation, which was going nowhere. "I'm forty, Roc. Thanks for the free wash, and you're right. You are too much for me to handle."

I headed to the driver's door and opened it. Once inside the car, I reached for my seat belt to strap myself in. Roc bent down to look in the window.

"Somehow I feel as if I got snubbed." He pulled the wet wife beater away from his chest and wiped some of the sweat from his face. "I've been out here sweatin' and slavin' like a Hebrew slave for you, and this is how you treat me? I see you got ghost when I told you my age, but if I told you I was thirty-one, would you believe me? Better yet, would it make a difference?"

I couldn't help but smile at his attempt. "No, it wouldn't make a difference."

"Why? Because you lied about yo' age? You know damn well you ain't forty. Thirty, maybe. Not forty."

"I have no reason to lie to you, and if I had time, I'd show you my driver's license. I don't, so you'll have to take my word for it. Now, if you don't mind, I really need to get going."

"Can't say I didn't try."

Roc shrugged and backed away from the car so I could drive off. I did just that, but I couldn't help but take another look at him in my rearview mirror. I licked my bottom lip, biting into it.

Damn, I thought. *If he were only ten . . . fifteen years older.*

Chapter Two

Latrel was coming home for the weekend, and as usual, Reggie and I had been arguing over where Latrel would stay. After our divorce, Reggie had to give up our three-bedroom, two-bathroom ranch-style home, which we'd lived in for years. I kept the house. Latrel had a decked-out bedroom in the basement, so it only made sense that he would agree to stay with me. The decision was his, but when he opted to stay with his father at his condo in Lake Saint Louis, I got upset.

"You don't love me, do you?" I asked with the phone pushed up to my ear.

"Mama, you know that ain't fair. I love you a lot. But I want to check out Dad's new place by the lake. You and I gon' hook up. Besides, I want you to meet my new girlfriend."

"Girlfriend? That was quick. Shouldn't you be focusing on school and your basketball career?"

"Trust me, I am. I get lonely sometimes, Mama. Tracie kind of been there for me."

My heart softened at the thought of him feeling alone. I definitely knew how that felt. "What time will you be here, and where is Tracie going to stay?"

"I'll be there around noon. Tracie is staying with me. I already talked to Dad about it, and he said it was cool."

"Oh, really? No wonder you don't want to stay with me. You knew darn well I wasn't going for it. If Tracie is coming with you, during the night, she can either stay with me or get a room at a hotel."

"That doesn't make any sense. I already told you I talked to Dad about it and he's cool. Why you over there trippin'?"

I was at work, so I definitely had to keep my cool. Latrel and Reggie were always going behind my back, making risky decisions. It drove me crazy. "I'm calling your father tonight, and we're going to discuss this. In the meantime, you'd better start making reservations at a hotel, or leave Tracie in her dorm room."

"This is crazy, Mama. Are you saying that you don't trust me?"

I slammed my hand on my desk and pulled the phone slightly away from my ear. After I was calm, I continued the conversation. "Tell me something, Latrel. Are you a virgin?"

"No. But what does that have to do with anything?"

"Strike one. Do you always use condoms?"

"S-s-sometimes. Mostly—"

"Strike two. Does Tracie take birth control pills?"

"I . . . I guess. I assume—"

"Strike three, my dear, and you're out! No, I do not trust you, and . . . and at what age did you lose your virginity? This is something completely new to me, but I'm sure your father knows all about it."

I could hear Latrel sigh over the phone.

"Huff and puff all you want to," I said. My feelings were hurt, and my eyes started to water. I felt so excluded from his life. "I have to go. Mr. Wright is calling me."

"Mama, please don't be upset with me. I can tell you're upset, but just know that I do my best. I'm not perfect, all right? I didn't tell you about my first time, because I was confused about what I was going through. I thought I was in love."

"But you felt comfortable enough to tell your father?"

"I didn't tell him until much, much later. And that's because he asked me. You never asked me until today. Today is when I told you the truth."

I swallowed hard, wiping a tear that had fallen down my cheek. I hadn't had those kinds of conversations with Latrel, and shame on me for putting all the blame on him. "I'll see you tomorrow, okay? I love you, and I look forward to meeting your girlfriend."

"Love you too, Mama. See you tomorrow."

I slowly laid the phone on the receiver and got back to work. Thank God it was Friday.

It was almost noon, and I was making lunch in the kitchen while running my mouth on the phone with my girlfriend Monica. We'd been friends for as long as I could remember. Monica had never been married, and she loved to live the single life. She had two children, a son, who was in his second year of college, and a daughter, who recently moved to California to pursue an acting career. Monica had done a good job raising her children as a single parent, but she was never pleased with their choices. I sat at the kitchen table, cracking up when she called her daughter, Jade, a joke.

"That's not nice, Monica. That girl is doing her best, and you should be proud of her."

"Oh, I'm very proud. But that doesn't mean she hasn't been working my nerves. That girl is rotten to the core. I don't know how she thinks she's going to gain her independence by moving to California."

"Well, it's a start. And you have no one but yourself to blame for spoiling those kids as much as you have."

"I couldn't agree with you more. Some parents are crushed when their children leave the nest, but me, girl, I've been on cloud nine. You know I've been traveling a lot. Getting out of this house, which I've been cooped up in for so long, makes me feel like a new woman. You should get your butt out of the house sometimes too. Life is too short, and you've got to let your hair down and cut loose."

"Eventually, I will. I'm just so out of touch. Being with Reggie for all those years was all I knew."

"I understand that, but Reggie isn't coming back anytime soon. You need to go out and meet people. Every time you go somewhere, you got men flocking all around you, but it's as if you look straight through them."

"I know, and at times, I'm a little confused by that. I'm not what society considers a fit woman, and even though Reggie never complained about my weight, I do think he wanted me to lose weight."

"Are you crazy? To hell with society. There is no doubt in my mind that Reggie was satisfied with your looks. Y'all just had other issues. You are blessed with curves that every woman should have, especially black women. I envy you, and don't you be over there trying to cut back on nothing. If you lose one single pound, I'll hurt you."

I laughed, knowing my best friend was right. My divorce from Reggie was about him not being able to get it together, not me.

"Okay, Monica, you got a point. I'm cool with my looks, but sometimes surprised by the attention I get."

"I'm glad you got my point, and as long as you keep that big ole booty in shape and that waistline perfected, you shouldn't have any problems meeting men."

"So, to hell with my brains, huh? Forget that I'm a wonderful woman who—"

"Yes, to hell with that for now. Most men aren't inter-ested in those kinds of things until they get to know you. Just make sure the inside, though, looks just as good as the outside."

We laughed but agreed. Monica continued on, trying to convince me to stop staying cooped up in the house. I told her I would think about going to a nightclub with her. Just as I was taking a homemade pepperoni pizza out of the oven, I heard the front door open. I stood with a big bright smile plastered on my face and waited for Latrel to follow the Italian aroma into the kitchen. When he stepped into the kitchen, as I expected, he was not alone. Reggie was with him, and so was a young white girl. I was frozen in time. My smile vanished, and my body felt as if cement had been poured over it. Monica was still running her mouth, and when she yelled my name, I snapped out of it.

"Girl, what's wrong with you?" she yelled. "Didn't you hear me?"

"I . . . I got to go. I think I've seen a ghost."

I hung up on Monica and wiped my saucy hands on my apron. Latrel was so taken aback by my comment that he took Tracie's hand and left the room. Reggie's self-righteous tail looked at me with a forehead full of thick wrinkles.

"You were way, way out of line. You need to go and apologize to your son and his girlfriend right now."

I ignored his demand and untied the apron straps at the back of my waist. "A white girl," I mumbled. "No, he didn't."

Reggie cleared his throat. I didn't have time to contemplate how good he looked. His masculine cologne permeated the kitchen, and he looked great in his casual attire, as he always did. He rocked a polo shirt, a pair of off-white linen pants, and leather sandals. The polo belt around his waist made him look nice and neat, and his buff body belied the fact that he was a forty-one-year-old man. Latrel looked a lot like his father but was much, much taller. Reggie was bald, but he kept his head clean shaven. They both sported goatees, but Latrel had a head full of dark brown waves. And the only things that Latrel had inherited from me were my light-colored skin and almond-shaped eyes, the corners of which were upswept.

"Hello to you too, Reggie," I said, washing my hands. "I didn't know you were coming with them."

"I wanted to call and tell you, but you know how our conversations can get at times. I'm not going there with you today, and for the last time, somebody may be in need of an apology."

I put my hand on my hip and pursed my lips. "And if not, what's going to happen?"

"Nothing." He walked away from me. "Nothing at all."

Reggie yelled for Latrel and Tracie to come upstairs. They did, and he suggested that they all leave.

Latrel stared at me, waiting for a response. "I don't know what to say about you," he said. "What was all of that for?"

"You heard your father, Latrel. He's ready to go. I suggest you don't get left behind."

Latrel turned to Reggie and shook his head. "I told you about her, didn't I?"

"Told him what? How I'd react to your girlfriend? If you knew, then why would you bring her here?" I said.

Latrel stepped into the kitchen and stood tall over me. There was little breathing room between us. Hurt was locked in his eyes, and I had never seen him appear so serious. "When are you going to back off and let me make my own decisions? I'm a grown-ass man, Mama. You disrespecting me like I'm some fool on the street that you know nothing about."

I backed away in the face of my son's aggressiveness. "Go do you, Latrel. You have my blessings, along with my sympathy."

He shot me a mean mug and flipped the pizza tray off the marble-topped island. The pizza hit the floor and splattered on the hardwood floor. "I don't need your blessings or your sympathy," he yelled. "To hell with it!"

Reggie stepped forward and put his hand on Latrel's heaving chest. Reggie then ordered him and Blue Eyes to go to the car, and they left. I swallowed the huge lump in my throat and squatted to clean up Latrel's mess. My head stayed lowered, as I didn't want Reggie to see the pain in my eyes from the hurt I'd just endured, compliments of *his* son.

Reggie held out his hand for mine. "Get up," he said.

I waved him off, and like always, I ignored him. He placed his hands in his pockets and jiggled his change.

"You know you brought this on yourself, don't you? For God's sake, Dee, why must you always make everything about you? Our son was so damn happy about coming here to see you, and since when did you start making comments like a racist?" His voice rose. "I'm speaking to you as his father. Don't you ever treat my son like that again! If your beef remains with us, take your shit out on me." He pounded his chest. "I can take it. Latrel can't. Now, he'll be at my place until Monday. Get yourself together and figure out how you're going to make this right."

As quickly as they came, they went. I had a headache that was out of this world, and after I cleaned up my kitchen, I took some Advil and went to my bedroom to lie down. My thoughts of Latrel were killing me, and my body felt as if somebody was sticking me with the tip of a sharp knife. I had always been the kind of person who reacted to matters too quickly. No, I wasn't enthused about Latrel being with a white girl, but maybe it was just me. Lately, I'd had hang-ups about everything, but something inside me told me he was dating outside of his race because of me. He didn't want a woman who looked like his mother, nor did he appreciate all that I had done for him. He was moving in another direction, and as long as a woman didn't look like me, he was all good. I hated that about my son, and for him not to consider my feelings was gut-wrenching.

I was passed out, until the loud ringing of the phone awakened me. My tired eyes were barely open, but I managed to reach over and grab the phone.

"Hello," I said in a raspy tone.

"Girl, get your butt up," Monica yelled. I could hear her fingers snapping. "Have you made up your mind yet?"

I sat up in bed, rubbing my eyes. "Made up my mind about what?"

"About doing the Stanky Leg."

"Uh, no. No, I'm not going to no nightclub."

"Why not?"

"Because I'm still tired and I want to go back to sleep."

"It is eight o'clock on a Saturday night. Who in their right mind is at home, in bed?"

"Me."

"Well, not for long. I'm on my way to pick you up. You'd better be ready."

Monica hung up, and I dropped the phone on the floor. I buried my face in the pillow, screaming loudly. I wasn't up to doing anything, but I knew how persistent Monica could be. She was definitely going to show up; therefore, it was in my best interest to be ready.

I showered and searched my walk-in closet for something to wear. It had been years since I'd been out to a nightclub. I couldn't decide on a black, strapless mini-dress or my pantsuit. I sorted through my accessories, and when I came across my black and silver dangling necklace and silver bangles, I decided on the mini. I slid it down over my hips and turned in the mirror to observe myself. My backside looked perfect, but my tiny love handles made my waistline look pudgy. I had a quick solution for that and found my corset, which gave my waistline a slim appearance. *Awesome,* I thought, reaching for my Nine West strapped heels with rhinestones. My feathery, long hair was never a problem, and the bouncing body that it had made me look and feel like a million dollars. I touched up my lip gloss and makeup and then stroked my already long lashes with thick mascara. After that, I was ready for whatever the night had in store for me.

The club scene had definitely changed since the last time I'd tried it out. There were wall-to-wall people inside the club, some younger, but many who looked to be my age as well. It was a nice setting, though, and the music was a mixture of jazz, hip-hop, R & B, and even a bit of the blues. Monica and I lucked out on two bar stools that surrounded the huge square dance floor, which was filled to capacity. Disco balls turned from up above, and red, yellow, and blue lights spun on everyone. Monica sat next to me, snapping her fingers while moving her hips. As usual, she looked nice. She was Vivica Fox all the way, and just as it was for me, age for her was just a number. From being on the scene for so long, she definitely had rhythm. Already she had turned away several men who had asked her to dance.

"If you're not going to dance," I whispered, "then why sit there in your seat, shaking yourself, leading these men on?"

"Just because I get funky in my seat doesn't mean I want to get jiggy on the floor. I'll dance, just not right now." She pushed my shoulder. "What about you? Are you going to dance? You've been the rejection queen all night, and I can't believe that margarita hasn't loosened you up."

"I already told you I can't dance. I'm not about to make a fool of myself. I will, however, have another drink, because this one seems kind of weak."

Monica signaled for the bartender and ordered both of us another drink. This time, she ordered me a cranberry cocktail and insisted on doubling up on the vodka.

"I bet that'll get your butt up and going," she said.

I wanted to enjoy myself, but my mind kept wandering back to Latrel and Reggie. I wondered what they were up to and if they were sitting around, discussing me. I sat daydreaming for a minute, until my eyes came across someone intriguing. *It can't be,* I thought. I squinted to be sure. *Nah, he looks much too clean to be him.*

"Who are you looking at?" Monica asked, interrupting my thoughts.

"Nobody. I thought I saw someone I knew."

Monica's eyes turned to where mine were looking. She homed in on the three young men sitting at a table. "That is one fine hunk of dark, sexy-ass chocolate right there! He's too young, but that brotha looks good."

"Which one?" I asked, pretending as if I hadn't noticed.

"The one with the gray tailor-made suit on and the black silk shirt underneath."

"How in the heck do you know that man's suit is tailor-made?"

"Look at how it clings to his broad shoulders and arms. A man can't just go in the store and find something that fits him like that, trust me."

I kept my eyes on the man, trying to see if he was actually Roc from the car wash. When he got up from the table, he smiled at the men he was speaking to and slapped his hand against theirs. That was all the confirmation I needed. I knew what seeing those pearly whites and dimples had done to me at the car wash. That same feeling came over me again. Monica kept her eyes on him too.

I cleared my throat. "I don't care too much for that skinny-leg suit he's wearing. Latrel has one of those, but that's because Reggie bought it."

"It's the style, Desa Rae, and that brotha is wearing it well. Look at all the women checking him out. I'm sure he likes the attention too. When he comes this way, ignore him. I don't want him to think he's all that, even though he definitely is."

I watched as Roc made his way through the crowd. The bartender came just in time with our drinks, and with him standing in front of me, it was easier to pretend as if I didn't see Roc. Right after the bartender sat our drinks in front of us, Roc stepped forward and approached the bartender.

"Are you takin' good care of these two ladies?" he asked. I was floored. It was as if his entire demeanor had changed. His voice appeared more mature, and the suit looked even better close up.

"I'm doing my best," the bartender replied.

"Good. Their drinks are on the house. Make sure they're well taken care of."

Monica was grinning from ear to ear. Roc had to have a twin.

"Thanks, but do we know you?" Monica asked.

"I don't think I've ever met you before," he said, then turned to me. "But I've definitely met her."

"Roc?" I questioned, still a bit unsure.

He winked. "In the flesh." He looked at the dance floor. "Do you want to dance?"

Monica quickly reached for my glass, taking it from my hand. "Yes, she would love to dance."

"Uh, no thank—"

I could barely get the word *no* out of my mouth before Roc took my hand and escorted me to the dance floor. Jay-Z's latest hit was playing, and some of the female dancers were trying to drop it like Beyoncé. There wasn't a bone in my body that allowed me to move like her, so I did the norm—snapped my fingers while moving from side to side. Roc, however, was all into it. He had his arms in the air, snapping his fingers. His suit jacket was open, and his silk shirt tightened on every single muscle in his chest. The lower part of his body was in motion, and the women couldn't stop looking in our direction. I was so embarrassed that I didn't know how to work it like he was. All I kept thinking was how handsome and well put together he was.

Roc displayed his award-winning smile and turned around so I could check out his backside. When I looked over at Monica, she encouraged me to move closer to him.

"What?" I mouthed from the dance floor.

She rolled her eyes to the back of her head, gritting her teeth. "Move closer," she mouthed back.

I ignored her, and as soon as the song was over, I informed Roc that I was done.

"So soon?" he asked. "I can't believe you got me kickin' up a sweat again and gon' leave me hangin'."

I pointed to my shoes. "My feet are killing me," I lied, sparing myself the embarrassment of dancing through another song.

"Au'ight," he said, taking my hand. I was shocked by the hand gesture, especially when he rubbed the inside of my hand with his finger. I pulled my hand away.

"Thanks for the dance," I said, taking my seat next to Monica.

"Promise me another dance before you leave, au'ight?"

"Sure."

Roc walked away, and Monica looked at me with wide eyes. "You really can't dance, can you? You had all of that man in front of you and didn't have a clue what to do with him."

We laughed, and I sipped from my glass. "I told you I couldn't dance. And if you expect for me to do all those dance moves the women up there are doing, you're crazy."

"I didn't expect you to do all that, but damn! Girl, you need to take some dance lessons. Forgive me for shoving your butt up there like that, but I had hoped you would at least take advantage of him and get your feel on."

"I didn't want to come off as desperate. Besides, was my dancing really that bad?" I slumped my shoulders and snapped my fingers. "I was kind of, you know, getting down a little bit, wasn't I?"

Monica held up her thumb and forefinger and brought them close together, as if measuring. "Just a tiny bit. Unfortunately, not enough to make that brotha remember a darn thing about you."

"I don't want him to remember me. A few days ago I saw him at a car wash, and he was trying to push up on me then. He's twenty-four, works at a car wash, and his slang is bothersome. There's not much a man like that can do for me."

"I beg to differ. There are plenty of things he can do for you."

I crossed my arms and pursed my lips. "Like what?"

Monica placed her hand on her chest. "You're my best friend, and even I can't muster up enough courage in my heart to tell you what *I* would do with a man that fine, sexy, energized, and interested." She placed her finger on the side of my temple and lightly pushed my head. "Use your brain, Desa Rae. Live a little and don't let life pass you by."

I knew Monica was right. Truthfully, she had no idea how quickly my brain had been working. In my mind, I had already visualized many heated encounters with Roc, but I wasn't sure if I was ready to make them a reality. The thought of him being so young was a struggle for me.

What could being with a man like him do for a woman like me? The only thing he would be good for was sex, but since I was so horny, maybe that wasn't a bad thing at all.

One o'clock in the morning came too quickly. Monica and I were having a wonderful time, and neither of us could stay off the dance floor. The alcohol I'd consumed had my whole body feeling as if heat was running through my blood. My neck had beads of sweat on it, and my vision was starting to blur. Neither of us was capable of driving home, and we knew it. Therefore, when Roc came over and offered us a ride home, I couldn't decline his offer.

"What about my car?" Monica slurred while slowly getting into the backseat of Roc's SUV.

"You can come back for it in the mornin'," Roc suggested.

I wasn't as wasted as Monica, but at our age we knew better.

"Where do you live?" Roc asked as he got in the car. "And will it be okay if I drop off both of y'all at the same place? I have somewhere else I need to be."

I was grateful that Roc was taking us home, so I gave him the directions. His comment about having somewhere else to be didn't bother me. With all the women in his face tonight, I was sure he had plenty of choices.

"Did you have a nice time?" he asked while driving.

"Wonderful time," I said, staring out the window.

"I could tell. I mean, you were out there shakin' your ass and everythang. I saw you, and I noticed that you picked up some numbers too. Too bad you can't dance, though, but you were damn good to look at."

I turned toward Roc and smiled. "You weren't all that, either, you know. Until you can dance like Michael Jackson, don't go criticizing the way I dance."

"No offense, but I ain't tryin' to dance like Michael. I'm me, and I wouldn't trade me for the world."

"Strangers in the night . . . ," Monica sang out from the backseat. She deepened her voice and made it baritone like Frank Sinatra's.

Roc and I laughed. "What the fuck?" he said. "She really needs to get home and sleep off that madness."

I looked at the backseat and saw that just that fast, Monica was out. When I turned, I noticed Roc's sneaky eyes checking out my thighs, which were clearly visible, thanks to the minidress I wore. I didn't say a word, but he knew he was busted. He reached for the knob on his stereo, turning up the music. As he rapped lyrics to the song, he nodded and tapped his fingertips on the steering wheel.

"That's the shit right there," he said.

No doubt, the loud music annoyed me. "Who is that?"

"You don't know who that is?"

"No."

"Kanye."

"Oh, okay. But do you mind turning that down just a little bit?"

He lowered the volume and continued to look at me intermittently while nodding his head.

"You know what?" he said. "You ain't gon' believe me when I tell you this, but this is, like . . . like, crazy, Ma."

"What's that?"

"I've been thinkin' about you. Just last night I said, 'Damn, I hope I see that Halle Berry look-alike again.' I mean, with the long hair and those curves, you look better than she does, but y'all do resemble. I could've kicked myself in the ass for lettin' you get away without givin' me yo' sevens."

"I appreciate the compliment, but you didn't *let* me do anything. I chose not to give you my number, because you're too young. I prefer not to date men who work at car washes, and I do not give my *sevens* to men I'm not interested in."

Roc stopped at the red light and gave me a stern stare. "I don't work at the car wash. I was just helping out my uncle, who owns the place. Same goes for the club you were just at. He owns that place too. So, if you don't mind, let me give you a li'l advice. I suggest you not judge a book by its cover, and lighten up a li'l bit. If you weren't interested before, my question is, are you interested now?"

"Are you still twenty-four?"

"Yes."

"Then, no, I'm not interested."

Roc shrugged, pressed hard on the accelerator, and sped off. It was obvious that he wasn't used to rejection. When we got to my house, he carried Monica inside and laid her on the couch. I immediately rushed in the bathroom to use it, and when I came out, Roc was waiting for me by the front door.

"You don't know how much I appreciate this," I said, rubbing my forehead to soothe my headache.

"No problem. But if you appreciate me as much as you say you do, then you'd give me yo' sevens so I can call you."

My head was banging. I really didn't have time to stand at the door with Roc and deny him. In an effort to get him out of my hair, I reached for my purse so I could give him my business card. I wrote my *sevens* on the back and gave the card to him.

"Here. And please don't overuse my number. Don't be surprised if you start feeling as if you're wasting your time. I've told you once already that I'm too old for you."

Roc pulled his suit jacket back and leaned against the door. He slid his hands into his pockets, along with my card. "Prove it," he said. "Show me right now that you're forty years old. If you are, I'll give yo' card back and you'll never see me again."

I reached in my purse for my driver's license and gave it to him. He looked it over, then gave it back to me. "Bullshit. That's a fake ID."

I smiled and shook my head at how cute and persistent he was. "Unfortunately, I don't have time to go get my birth certificate for you, but I do want my card back, because we had an agreement."

He winked and reached in his pocket for my card. "My word, my bond," he said, giving the card back to me.

I unlocked the door so that he could leave, but Roc eased his arm around my waist and pulled me close to him. He put my body right between his legs and moved his hips around, making sure I felt how excited he was down below. Our eyes lowered to each other's lips, and his tongue went for the kill. His lips were soft like butter against mine, and our tongues danced for at least a full minute. Like in my previous thoughts, I rubbed his neatly lined waves and allowed his hands to roam up my minidress to massage my ass.

You know better, I kept telling myself. *Shame on you, girl. What are you thinking?* But then again, I told myself, *Shut the hell up! Live a little, Desa Rae. Take this brotha to your bedroom and let him fuck away your misery. He's capable of doing it, and to hell with Reggie. Reggie who? Don't you feel how hard his dick is? Reggie's dick never felt that big. Get it, girl. Go get that dick in you right now!*

Roc backed away from our intense kiss, causing me to open my eyes. Our eyes stayed deeply connected. Thing is, neither of us knew where to turn next. *Fuck it,* I thought, reaching for his belt buckle. He touched my hand to stop me.

"My condoms are in my truck. Let me go get *some*. I'll be right back."

I nodded and opened the door for Roc. Since he had gone to get more than one condom, I predicted it was going to be a long, unforgettable night. I bit my nails as I watched him open the glove compartment to retrieve the condoms. He removed his jacket and laid it on the front seat. No doubt, he was hyped and had already started to pull his shirt out from inside his pants. I stood on my porch, fidgeting, and was as fearful as ever. *Darn it*, I thought. *Where are my chocolates?* I needed a bite of something, but then again, my chocolate was right there in front of me. No . . . he was only twenty-four years old! What if Latrel was dating a woman my age? Wouldn't I be upset? This young man had a mother, who, I was sure, wouldn't approve.

"Roc," I said, halting his tracks as he stepped onto the porch. "I'm sorry, but I can't. I apologize for misleading you, but this isn't a good time for me. My head isn't on straight, and I'm not sure if this is something I want to do."

Roc sighed and wiped down his face with his hand. "Damn, Ma. You got me all worked up for nothin'. I ain't gon' force you into nothin' you don't want to do, but why you makin' this so difficult? Age is a number, and a number don't mean jack."

"I say that myself, but in this case it may very well apply."

"Because you think I can't please you, is that it? I promise you that I'm not yo' average twenty-four-year-old brotha out here tryin' to get in and out. Let me show you what's up."

"I have a good feeling that you're able to show me what's up, but not tonight." I gave him my card again so he wouldn't feel as if I'd completely dissed him. "Keep in touch, okay?"

He looked at me with his hooded eyes, almost pleading for me to change my mind. "This shit ain't right," he said, tucking his shirt back in his pants.

He stepped forward and left a sliver of breathing room between us. My nostrils took in his panty-dropping cologne, and my thumping pussy sent off signals that told me I was being a fool. His lips touched my ear, and the words he then whispered stuck in my head like superglue.

"Tip one . . . I want to fuck you badder than a mutha, Ma, and I always get what I want. Two . . . you can be sure of that, so sleep tight on what I just said. Three . . ." He took my hand, putting it down inside of his pants so I could feel his thickness. "They don't call me Roc for nothin'. I earned my name, and you shouldn't be so worried about this twenty-four-year-old handlin' his business. I will, and I intend to do so very soon."

Roc kissed my cheek and backed away. I watched as he got in his SUV and left. It was such a disappointment to see him go, but I knew that his words had much validity to them.

Chapter Three

For the past week and a half, things had been awfully quiet. I assumed Latrel had gone back to school, because I hadn't heard from him or Reggie. I was bothered that Latrel hadn't called me, but I had no intention of picking up the phone to kiss his butt. That day, his tone had rubbed me the wrong way. To toss the pizza on the floor, as he had done, was disrespectful. As far as I was concerned, he owed me an apology, not the other way around.

Reggie too. I was sure he was boasting about the whole incident. It gave him and Latrel a great opportunity to sit around and talk about what a terrible mother and wife I'd been. Realistically, both of them had had the best of me. I had put everything into my marriage to make it work, and I had often given my son too much. Everything had backfired in my face, but I couldn't deny that I had seen all of this coming. Reggie had had the best wife ever, and how he had ever found a way to fall out of love with me, I'd never understand. Deep down, I knew there was someone else. He had never said there was, but that was just something a wife knew.

It was a sunny day outside, and the September heat was still going strong. I wanted to relax and clear my head, so I chilled in the backyard while resting on my cushioned patio swing. A book was in my hand, and a pitcher of iced tea was beside me. A strong breeze blew every now and then, and even though I didn't have the money to take a vacation, the perimeter of my backyard would do. I laid the book on my chest, thinking about the backyard parties Reggie and I used to have. He'd be firing up the gas grill right about now, and Latrel would be running around in the backyard, playing with his friends. The house would be packed with family and friends. When things started to take a turn for the worst, those kinds of days ended. Now the backyard had become my place to pray, read, and think about where my life was headed from here.

The wind picked up again, this time blowing my yellow and white flower-print sundress up like a balloon. I tucked the dress between my legs and got back to reading. Just as I started to get into it, the cordless phone rang. I looked to see who it was, but I didn't recognize the number. Those kinds of numbers meant bill collectors were calling, and since Reggie was often late on his alimony payments, some of my bills had to be put off. I ignored the call, but when the phone rang again, I hit the TALK button.

"Hello," I said.

"Can someone connect me to the prettiest woman in the house?"

I hung up and got back to my book. I didn't know who that was, and I wasn't interested in playing love games over the phone with a stranger.

The phone rang again. The storyline was too good to keep putting the book aside, and because of the interruptions, the caller was going to get an earful.

"You have the wrong number," I yelled out.

"Dez, it's Roc. What's up?"

"Why didn't you just say so?" I said, laying the book on my chest again. I wasn't sure how I felt about Roc calling me, but thoughts of our last moments together had often played in my head.

"I thought you'd recognize my voice, but I guess I didn't leave that much of an impression on you."

"That was almost two weeks ago. I'd forgotten about you since then."

He laughed, and I visualized his dimples in full effect. "Well, let me stop by and refresh yo' memory. I was close by and wanted to call before makin' a move that way."

"I'm glad you did call first. I'm kind of busy. Maybe some other time."

He laughed again. "I knew you were gon' say that shit. I must be psychic or somethin'. And while I'm on a roll, I'm gon' make another prediction."

"Feel free," I said, tuned in.

"I predict that I'll be pullin' in yo' driveway in ten minutes. I just want to drop in to see how you doin', but if you don't want to be bothered, let me know."

"Look, Roc. I was in the middle of reading a very good book. I've worked all week, and I'm truly exhausted. If—"

"I like to read too. Check that out . . . we already got somethin' in common. Who would have thought that?"

I took a deep breath and sat up on the swing. It was obvious that he wasn't giving up. "Fifteen minutes, Roc. You can stay for fifteen minutes, and then you'll have to go. I have plans for this evening, okay?"

Without replying, he ended the call. I had no time to go inside and put on something I felt was more appropriate than the sundress. No doubt, it made me look fat, but at least my breasts were held up by thick straps that rested on my shoulders. My hair had blown all over my head, so I quickly straightened it with my fingers. I slid into my yellow flip-flops and made my way around to the front of my house.

Minutes later, I could hear loud rap music from another block over. Roc pulled in my driveway, and he could tell by the look on my face that I wasn't pleased by the loudness of his music. He turned down the volume and looked at me standing on the sidewalk, in my dress. When he got out of the car, he looked more like the Roc I'd seen at the car wash. His clothes weren't dirty, but he was casually dressed in jeans, a T-shirt, and a cap. Clean white tennis shoes were on his feet, a silver cross dangled from his neck, and he sported a silver watch with a face filled with diamonds. He looked more like one of Latrel's friends than anything, and I was a little concerned about how he got the money to have such an expensive car, the watch, and the diamonds in his earlobes. With that said, he was still as gorgeous as ever, and the smile that he'd brought to my face hadn't been there all week.

He left his cap on the front seat of his truck and placed his hands in his pockets. "What's shakin, Ma? You lookin' good, as usual."

"Stop lying, Roc. You know I look as if I've been in the house, flipping pancakes all day, with this dress on."

We both laughed.

"So you got jokes today, I see. Remember, though, I see way more than you realize," he said.

"Dressed like this, I hope so." I walked off, and Roc followed me to the backyard. I offered him some iced tea, and he accepted. We both took a seat at the table, which was covered by an umbrella.

"You got a nice-ass yard," he said, drinking from the glass. "From what I saw, the inside of yo' crib looks sick too."

"I guess that means it looks nice. Thanks. I do my best to keep up the place." I looked at the high grass, which Reggie hadn't made his way over to cut. Even though we didn't live together, there were still some things he had agreed to help out with, including the upkeep of the property.

"The grass is kind of high. Do you pay somebody to cut it for you?"

I really didn't want to get into a conversation with Roc about Reggie, so I lied. "Yes, but he hasn't stopped by lately."

"You want me to cut it for you? I don't mind. Besides, I think you like watchin' me sweat."

No doubt about that, I thought. "How much are you going to charge me?" I asked.

"Nothin'."

"Usually, when a man does something for free, he wants something in return."

"I got a li'l somethin' in mind, but I don't think I'm gon' get lucky today. So after I finish cuttin' your grass, I'll settle for a kiss and be happy about that."

My grass did need to be cut, and there wasn't no telling when Reggie would show up to do it. I removed the lawn mower from the garage and happily turned it over to Roc. If a kiss was all I had to give up, that was well worth it.

Roc took off his shirt and displayed his washboard abs. His baggy jeans hung low, and I could see his blue and gray boxers.

"Are you sure you want to do this?" I asked. "I hate for you to mess up your jeans, and your tennis shoes look as if you just purchased them."

"I'm good," he said, neatly folding his shirt, then placing it on the table. He removed his chain with the cross and his watch, dropping them on top of his shirt. His eyes traveled around the huge yard, and then, before I knew it, he cranked up the lawn mower and got started.

I went into the house and got him some more tea, bottled water, and a cold, wet towel. It was awfully nice of him to do this for me, and I appreciated it more than he knew.

I put the tea, the bottled water, and the towel on the table, then returned to my spot on the swing. I started to read again, only to find myself taking peeks at Roc as

he cut the grass in a diagonal pattern. His body was to
die for. My erotic thoughts were back again. I had to get
myself under control before I did something I figured I'd
regret. I was so horny, though, and the last time I'd had
sex was almost eight months ago. It was with Reggie, of
course, and before that time, I could barely remember.
Reggie was the one I'd lost my virginity to, and that
was when I was seventeen years old. I had had sex with
one other person after that, and when Reggie and I got
married, I had been faithful to him. My attraction to Roc,
however, was a new experience for me. I didn't know how
I'd handle it.

For the next thirty minutes, I managed to get back into
my book. That was until Monica called and interrupted
me. I couldn't help but mention that Roc was cutting my
grass for me.

"I bet that is one Kodak moment to see," she said. "I'm
on my way!"

"He'll be finished by the time you get here and probably
gone. Don't waste your time."

"Are you telling me you're going to let that man leave
without showing him some, uh, love?"

"Monica, you know me. I can't go throwing myself at
him like that. I barely know him, and he has yet to ask
anything about me."

"The less you know, the better."

"What if he's some type of drug dealer or something?
I mean, he be wearing all these expensive clothes, and
from what he told me, his only job seems to be helping
out his uncle. I don't know where this young man lives,
who he lives with, where he works—nothing."

"Does all of that really matter? Stop talking like some
high-school chick worried about her reputation. You're a
grown, unmarried woman, and just . . . just get you some,
all right? I want details, and do not let him turn you out.

Represent for the forty-year-old woman. I remember you telling me how you and Reggie used to get down. Work your magic on Roc and send him home with a smile on his face."

I couldn't help but laugh. I took another peek at Roc and tucked my hand between my thighs. "Girl, this is a shame. I can't believe what my eyes are witnessing. I wish you were here to see this."

"I wish I were too. I can only imagine. You are one lucky woman. Tell me, did Reggie ever look like that while cutting the yard?"

"Reggie isn't a bad-looking man, Monica. You know that."

"No, he's not. But he ain't no Roc, either. Besides, forget about Reggie. Go do you, and do it for me too. I gotta go, but be sure to call me later with the scoop."

"Bye, girl. I'll call you later. Don't get your hopes up, though."

Monica laughed and hung up. When Roc turned off the lawn mower, I looked up. He was finished. The grass looked spectacular. He pushed the lawn mower up to the patio and reached for the bottled water. As he poured water on his face to cool off, it rushed down his chest. He used a cold, wet towel to cool off. Afterward, he guzzled down the glass of iced tea. I was in a trance while watching his abs move in and out.

"Ahhh," he said, placing the glass on the table. "That was damn sure satisfyin'."

I commented on the grass. "It looks nice. Thank you so much for cutting it for me."

"No problem. It ain't like you had me out here plantin' flowers. I would've done it for you, but first, I would've planted that dress you got on or buried it."

I smiled at Roc's comment and walked closer to him. "Insulting my dress will get you nowhere, and that comment caused you a major deduction." I got on the tips of my toes and pecked his cheek. "There," I said, backing away from him.

He held out his hands, but before he could say anything, his cell phone blasted with music. He looked to see who the caller was, then excused himself to take the call. He stepped a few feet away, near a willow tree. All I heard was, "What's up, nigga?"

Instead of listening to his conversation, I went back to the swing and took a seat. Moments later, Roc ended the call; I watched as he turned his phone on vibrate. He wiped his chest again with the towel, then came over and sat next to me on the swing.

"That really is a dope-ass dress you wearin'," he said, touching his chest. "And I truly mean that from the bottom of my heart."

We both laughed.

"Are you tired?" I asked. "If so, you may want to go home and get some rest."

"You ain't gettin' rid of me that easy."

He laid sideways on the swing and encouraged me to lie beside him. "Come on," he ordered. "Let's read this book you've been givin' more attention to than me."

"You know darn well you don't read books. Face it, you're just saying that to get close to me and impress me."

Roc took a glance at the cover and eased his arm around my waist. "I don't read those kinds of books, but I do read. I like self-help books—nonfiction, books like that. Now, lie down in front of me and get comfortable. Read the book to me, and let me get into your head to see what kind of things you like."

I lay sideways on the swing set with my back facing Roc and his arms comforting my waistline. He intertwined his legs with mine, and I felt quite at ease. I started to read my book, and twenty minutes into it, I could hear Roc's loud snores. He was tired, so I didn't want to wake him. I watched as his muscular chest slowly heaved in and out. When I turned my head slightly to the side, I saw that he looked so peaceful. I focused on finishing my book, but before I knew it, my eyes started to fade as well.

Roc's vibrating phone awakened me, but he remained in a deep sleep. I'd felt his phone vibrating several times, but I'd been too tired to move. The sun had gone down, and the night was definitely upon us. We'd been asleep for hours. I couldn't remember the last time I'd felt this good being cradled in someone's arms. I almost hated to wake up Roc, but it was getting late, and the caller seemed anxious to reach him. I moved around a bit, causing the swing to sway back and forth. Roc stretched before opening his eyes to see where he was.

"Damn," he said, looking at the dark sky. "What time is it?"

"Late, but I'm not exactly sure about the time. You might want to check your phone to see."

He reached for his phone to see who had called. I saw his lips purse a bit, and when he dropped the phone by his side, it was obvious that he wasn't pleased about who the callers were.

"I can't believe time flew by like that," he said. "Why didn't you wake me? I thought you had somewhere to be."

I lay on my back, and Roc kept his hand on my midsection. Our faces were extremely close, and he looked down at me as I spoke. "I did have somewhere to be, but I changed my mind about going."

"Are you sure your man ain't gon' be mad at you for bein' a no-show?"

"Is that your way of asking me if I'm involved with someone?"

"Nope. I was just askin'. I didn't see no ring on your finger, and I don't care if you have a boyfriend."

"FYI, no, I don't. What about you? You have any girlfriends?"

"I shake, rattle, and roll sometimes, but you can believe that don't nobody excite me like you."

I didn't know what to say. It really didn't bother me that Roc had admitted to having girlfriends, and at his age, what did I expect?

"You know what?" he said, looking at my lips. "That sure is a sick dress you're rockin'. I mean that mug—"

"Save it, Roc." I smiled. "You're only saying that because I backtracked on what I had planned for you. Sorry. You ruined it when you criticized my dress. That should be a warning for you to keep your mouth closed while you're ahead."

"Ha!" he shouted, then lightly squeezed my stomach. "Tell me, though. What did you have planned for me?"

I shrugged. "I don't know. Whatever it was, I guess we'll have to miss out."

"See, you playin' now. It's all good. I see how you gon' do me."

Roc's lips were already close. He seemed surprised when I lifted my head and initiated a lengthy kiss.

"Mmm," he mumbled while indulging himself and circling his hand around on my hip. His hand went under my flimsy dress, and when he moved his body between my legs, I bent my knees. My legs fell farther apart. His hardness was right where I wanted it to be. My pussy was doing a happy dance, and I felt juices trickling between my coochie lips. Roc's hand kept touching my hip, in search of my panties. When he didn't feel them, he halted our kiss.

"I knew there was a reason why I loved this dress so much. You ain't got on no panties, do you?"

I moved my head from side to side, gesturing no. Roc quickly jumped up, dug in his pocket for a condom, and removed his jeans. I lay there in doubt, considering whether I should allow this to happen. He was too young, but maybe I could get an orgasm and call it quits. I needed some kind of action in my life. If Roc was willing to give it to me, what the hell? He returned to his position on top of me and slightly raised my dress for easy access. He lifted himself a bit, just to get a glance at my shaved pussy.

"Damn," he whispered while wetting his lips. "I want to taste it, Ma. Can we go inside? I need way more room than this."

I shook my head no and reached down for Roc's hard meat, which was poking me. Going inside the house would waste time. It was not an option. "Work with what space you have," I suggested. "Be creative and don't keep me waiting."

Roc took heed and put things in motion. As soon as he separated my walls, my mouth grew wide. My walls stretched farther apart when he maneuvered all the way in, filling me to capacity. I inhaled a heap of fresh air. With every thrust, I sucked in more air and released soft, pleasing moans. I kept telling myself that he was not a twenty-four-year-old man. His big dick was doing its best to prove it to me too. *Reggie is nowhere near this big,* I thought.

"This shit feelin' so good," he whined. "I need to get at it, though. Why won't you let me go inside and dip into this pussy like I want to?"

I ignored Roc's request. His package was delivering too much satisfaction for me to pack up and go inside. At this point, releasing my grip on him would've been a crime. Instead, I massaged his dark chocolate, muscular ass, and just as I'd imagined from the moment I met him, he put my legs on his shoulders, making every bit of my day-dreams come true. I worked my body to the rhythm he'd chosen, and my insides tingled all over. When Roc pulled my dress over my head and started in on my wobbling breasts, my body trembled even more. His lengthy steel dipping into my cream-filled pussy made me as crazy as ever. No, I didn't want to come yet, but I had to. The rush was there, and I let it be known.

"Damn you!" I yelled with tightened fists. "I'm coming, baby. My pussy feels so good, but help it give you all it's got. Please help iiit!"

Roc picked up the pace and used two fingers to make circles around my swollen clit. It was rock hard, and he loved it.

"Shit!" he said, taking deep breaths. "I love this feelin', Ma. You . . . you workin' with somethin' that this nigga loves to feel."

Enough said, enough done. Roc got tense, his ass felt like I was gripping stone, and he tightened up all over. He kept toying with my clit, forcing my juices to ooze out quickly. I felt relieved, and my body went limp. Following suit, so did his body. He lay on top of me while the swing squeaked and swayed back and forth. I gazed at the twinkling stars, thinking about how I couldn't wait to tell Monica about the new man in my life, who had rescued me from loneliness and boredom.

Chapter Four

I was known for holding grudges, but I never thought I could go almost a month without talking to my son. It was the first time this had happened, and though I had picked up the phone to call him many times, I always wound up hanging it right back up. No doubt, I missed talking to Latrel, but I couldn't get over the way he had treated me, especially in front of his girlfriend and Reggie.

As for Mr. Wright, he had finally taken his vacation. I spent the entire week getting his office together. I cleared the papers from his desk, organized his files, and cleaned his office until it was spotless. Having him out of the office for the entire week was great. It was also peaceful. I made progress, even though I spent many of my days taking personal calls. On Tuesday and Wednesday Monica and I talked on the phone for hours. I took an extended lunch with her, and we spent some extra time at the mall. I purchased two new outfits and some books, and therefore, I needed Reggie to be on time with my alimony payment.

He was late again. Since the man owned his own real-estate company, I didn't understand the holdup with my checks. I tried to work with him on my payments, but the delays caused me to get behind on bills. Since our divorce, I had had to make many cutbacks. I had gotten used to purchasing things when I wanted them, and this was such a change for me. When I'd spoken to him earlier this week, he'd promised to throw in something extra. It was already Friday. I hadn't heard anything from him yet.

Since my enjoyable evening with Roc three weeks ago, I'd spoken to him only twice. We'd talked for hours. I liked that he was a good listener and that he didn't pry into my personal life. He continuously made me laugh. He'd expressed a desire to see me again, and I'd told him it would have to wait until this Friday. He'd been cool with that, especially since I'd agreed to make him dinner. I was just okay about seeing him again, and I didn't want our friendship to turn into a relationship. He didn't seem to want a relationship, either. He'd proved that by calling me only in his spare time.

I viewed us as nothing but sex partners, and it was still difficult for me to accept that I'd had sex with a twenty-four-year-old man. That was why our meeting place could only be my house and my house only. I didn't want to know where he lived, I never asked for a phone number to call him, and we could never, ever be seen in public together. Everyone would think I was out of my mind for being with him. For now, this was a secret that I intended to keep. Monica was the only one who knew what was going on behind closed doors.

I had thought about having a romantic dinner with Roc but had decided against it. I didn't want him to get the wrong idea, so I put the candles away and placed the china back in the cabinets. It was already 6:45 p.m.; he was expected to be here by seven. I had also changed my mind about cooking dinner. Instead, I'd called a Chinese restaurant to order some food. I wasn't sure what kind of food Roc liked, but nobody could refuse the special fried rice that came from the Chinese restaurant in my neighborhood. The lady at the restaurant informed me that the order would arrive within the hour.

I had just enough time to get comfortable in my canary lace boy shorts and tank top combination. I covered up with a knee-length robe and slid on my cotton house shoes, which matched.

It was five minutes to seven, and I was getting my MSNBC political fix on. When I heard the front door open, my heart jumped to my stomach. I rushed toward the front door to see who it was. Reggie met me while I was coming down the hallway.

"What are you doing here?" I asked, tightening my robe.

"I came to drop off your check."

"You could have called, Reggie. I don't like you popping up like this."

"Since when?" he said, following me into the kitchen. "It's not like you were doing anything, anyway."

If only he knew, I thought. And according to my clock on the wall, he had to go, because Roc would soon be here. There was no way in hell I wanted Reggie to know about what I'd been into. He would use this as another excuse to degrade me. Since our divorce, he'd kept his social life a secret, and it was only fair that mine was kept secret as well. That thought was short-lived. When the doorbell rang, he glanced at me, already making his way to the door.

"Are you expecting someone?" he asked.

"Uh, no." I quickly followed behind him. Through the living room window I saw Roc's SUV in the driveway. *Oh, shit! How can I get out of this?*

Reggie swung the door open. Roc stood on the porch, looking every bit his age. I stood behind Reggie and saw a cold look in Roc's eyes that said I'd better come up with something fast. With a wrinkled forehead, he appeared pissed. But before he said a word, I quickly spoke up.

"Jeremy, my son, Latrel, is still away at school. He told me that if you stopped by, I should give you his address and phone number so you could reach him."

Reggie moved aside as I invited Roc to come in. At first he hesitated, but I gave him a look that indicated that cooperation was needed. "Come into the kitchen. I'll write his number and address down so you can reach him."

Reggie extended his hand. "Jeremy, I'm Latrel's father, Reggie. Nice to meet you."

"S-same here," Roc said.

We all went into the kitchen, and in a panic, I searched the kitchen drawer for a pad and pencil. I found them and scribbled a quick note to pass to Roc.

Please bear with me. My ex-husband stopped by to bring me some money. He's leaving soon. Make small talk with me and don't leave. Sorry.

I gave the note to Roc, and he read it. He put it in his pocket. "Thanks for the info. I'll call him tomorrow."

"You're welcome," I said, then smiled. "In the meantime, how are your parents doing? I haven't seen them in a while."

"My mom's doin' good. My father just got out of the hospital, but he doin' okay now."

Reggie was too busy looking through the refrigerator. Seconds later, he closed the refrigerator door with a beer in his hand. "Here," he said, putting the check on the island. "I have to run. I'll give you a call tomorrow so we can talk about this thing with you and Latrel, okay?"

"Sure."

Reggie looked at Roc. "Nice meeting you, Jeremy. Take care, and when you talk to that knucklehead son of mine, tell him to give his father a buzz."

Roc nodded. "Will do, sir. No doubt."

I walked Reggie to the door and was relieved to see him go. This time, I locked the door and connected the chain. As soon as I turned around, Roc stood behind me.

"Lying for you like that gon' cost you big-time. Why you ain't just tell that nigga what was up and be done with it?"

"Because I don't want him to know my business, that's why."

"Why should he care? If he yo' ex, I don't understand what the big deal is."

I got a little frustrated because I didn't want to talk about Reggie. "Look, Roc, I didn't know he was coming over, and that's all there is to it. I appreciate you not making a scene, but there was no way for me to prevent that from happening."

"Yes, there was. If y'all are divorced, tell that mutha-fucka he can't be comin' over here when he get good and ready to. That's how you shut that shit down."

Roc stepped into my dark living room and sat on my sectional. I couldn't see much of his face, but I knew he wasn't happy about the situation, and was possibly jealous.

I stood with my back against the wall and folded my arms. "So I guess you're upset with me, huh?" I asked.

He leaned back on the couch and laid his stretched arms on top of it. "Nope. I ain't mad. I don't get mad over no shit like this. Besides, all we gon' be good for is fuckin' each other. So why should I trip?"

"What makes you say that? Was there something I said?"

"No, it's just somethin' I know. You don't seem as excited about me as I am about you. That's on a for-real tip right there."

"I'm very excited about you, but I just ended a long marriage. I'm not looking to jump into a serious relation-ship with anyone."

Roc didn't say anything, so I walked farther into the living room and stood in front of him. I still didn't see those pearly whites. All I witnessed was coldness in his eyes and attitude.

"If this is going to be a problem for you, let me know," I said.

"Where my food at? I don't smell no dinner cookin', no nothin'. I guess you lied about that too."

His attitude was working me, but since I felt bad about my situation with Reggie, I remained calm. "I didn't have time to cook, but don't think that I forgot about feeding you. I ordered Chinese. It should be here shortly."

"I don't eat Chinese food, so you might as well have forgotten about me."

Roc wasn't letting up with his attitude. I knew how to change things around, so I made a move to do just that, starting with turning on the lights. I opened my robe and tossed it on the couch next to him. I then straddled his lap, placing my arms on his shoulders. The cheeks of my butt were poking out of my boy shorts, and one strap of the tank top hung off my shoulder, revealing my hard nipple. Roc's eyes searched me, but he continued to sit like a bump on a log.

"I promise that I didn't forget about you," I said. "As a matter of fact, I can't stop thinking about what happened between us. I was glad that you called, and now I'm glad you're here."

"That's right. Clean yo' shit up," he said. The ringtone on his phone interrupted him. Dressed in casual shorts, he reached into his pocket for the phone. "Get up," he ordered. "I need to see who this is."

I got off his lap, and he looked at his phone. He put it back in his pocket and stood up. "I'm gettin' ready to bounce."

"So soon?" I said, totally upset that he was leaving. I sighed and combed my hair back with my fingers. "What about your Chinese food?"

"I told you I don't eat Chinese food."

He walked smoothly toward the door, showing no sympathy when he glimpsed the sad look on my face. I didn't want him to leave, so I had to think of something fast.

"Before you leave," I quickly said, "I bought something for you. Wait right here."

Roc put his hands in his pockets and stood by the door. I walked away, moving my curvaceous hips and leaving my boy shorts high above my cheeks. I didn't even have to turn around, because I knew he was looking. Moments later, I returned with a white plastic bag that had a book inside.

"I was at the mall this week and thought about you when I saw this. Here."

He removed the book from the bag and held it in his hand. His smile, which I hadn't seen yet that evening, finally arrived. *"The Ultimate Guide to Cunnilingus: How to Go Down on a Woman and Give Her Exquisite Pleasure,"* he read. "Are you sayin' you think I need help with that?"

"All I'm sayin' is you admitted to reading self-help books, and I thought you might enjoy it."

Roc snickered while keeping a tiny smile on his face. I took this opportunity to speak up and persuade him to stay.

"Please stay," I said. "I apologize about dinner. It was wrong for me to assume you like Chinese."

He looked as if he was mulling over my apology and kept his eyes on the book. "Come here, and for the record, I love Chinese food," he said. I stepped forward, and he eased his arm around my waist. "I'll stay, but you gotta promise me somethin'."

"What?"

"That tonight I can explore all your body parts and do so in any room of this house that I want to. No denyin' me anything I want to do, and stop tryin' to run this show from here on out. What happens, happens. What's gon' be is gon' be. Let the chips fall where they may, and stop playin' this tough role with me, au'ight?"

"Yes," I replied, looking into his serious eyes.

Roc sucked my lips with his and backed me into the living room. I sat back on the couch, and he kneeled between my legs. He placed the book next to me and reached for my boy shorts to remove them.

"Sexy, sexy, sexy," he said, massaging my thighs. "Thick and sexy, just how I like my women to be. I'm gon' make you mine. I can promise you that shit."

He pulled his shirt over his head and stood to remove his pants. His dick was so ready to enter me, but he dropped to his knees again, positioning my legs on his shoulders. His arms wrapped around my thighs, and his face navigated between my legs. As soon as his tongue separated my tingling slit, he licked the furrows alongside my clit, while holding my labia open with his fingers. He then licked me from front to back, as if he were enjoying an ice cream cone. A major shock, almost a convulsion, went through my body. I trembled all over but kept telling myself to relax. Needless to say, Roc was tearing it up. My shaking legs couldn't stay in place on his shoulders.

"Ohh, baby!" I screamed while squeezing the pillows on the couch. "I wasted my . . . my money on that book! I'm taking it back tomorrow. I promise you that muthafucka is going back tomorrow!"

Roc slid his tongue out of my pussy, leaving it overly pleased. He licked around his wet lips, tasting the flavored juices I'd provided. "You damn right you takin' it back tomorrow. I already read it before, and in case you ain't noticed, I'm very skillful at what I do, when I'm allowed a chance to do it."

Roc got back to business. Calling him skillful was putting it mildly. He was . . . the bomb!

***

I wasn't sure, but I thought I heard the house alarm go off. One of Jill Scott's favorite hits echoed loudly in the background as Roc and I lay sprawled out on my king-sized bed. I was in between his legs, with no clothes on, and nothing but a dark blue sheet covered our naked bodies. We were so exhausted from last night's events. Reggie's loving couldn't compare, and I had got a taste of what I'd been missing all those years.

I stretched my arms, and when I tried to back away from Roc, I realized my body was too sore to move. I lay back on top of him, causing him to wake up. He pinched my butt, then smacked it.

"You put it on a nigga last night," he confirmed in a whisper. "I almost hate to ask, but what time is it?"

"Time for you to get your shit and get the fuck out of here!"

Roc lifted his head to look over my shoulder, and my head snapped as I looked behind me. Reggie stood in the doorway to the bedroom with fury in his eyes. I was at a loss for words and hurried to cover my entire body with the sheet. Roc moved to the side of the bed and stood up.

"What in the hell is going on here?" Reggie shouted.

"Hey, man, I was just leavin', but you comin' at me like she your wife or somethin'."

"And I'm not," I added. "Last time I checked, I lived here—alone. Now, what are *you* doing here?"

Reggie gazed at me with pure disgust locked in his eyes. "Are you that damn desperate to be fucking Latrel's friend? Or was that a lie too?"

I didn't owe Reggie an explanation, but I knew he wasn't leaving until he got one. I didn't want to have this conversation in front of Roc, and it appeared that he wasn't too anxious to hang around, either. He already had on his shorts, and his shirt was thrown over his shoulder.

He grabbed his keys from the dresser and walked over to me as I stood by the bed. He lifted my chin and kissed my cheek.

"Handle your business, baby. The next time I come, I want that dinner you promised me. Don't be afraid to tell ole boy what's up, and I'll call to check on you later."

I nodded and watched as Roc made his way past Reggie. They mean mugged each other, and Reggie had a hard time keeping his mouth shut.

"Is this shit some kind of joke? Are you kidding me, Dee? Is this the kind of nigga you want?"

Roc's face twisted from anger. "Nigga, you don't know me. For the record, I ain't yo' son's muthafuckin' friend. Obviously, your time with Dez is up, and she breakin' new ground. Stop sweatin' her and stop showin' your ass up without callin'. There's a new sheriff in town, and you can address me as Roc."

I saw Reggie tighten his fist, and as soon as he swung, Roc ducked. I rushed over to both of them, but not in time to prevent Roc from pinning Reggie against the wall, with his arm pressed into his throat. Reggie's hands gripped Roc's throat, and they looked as if they were about to kill each other.

"Please stop!" I yelled while struggling to separate their arms.

In no way had I intended for this to happen. I pleaded with them to step away from each other. Roc looked at me, and seeing the hurt in my eyes, he backed away from Reggie. Roc gave him one last evil stare before walking away. Moments later I heard the front door slam. Reggie lifted his hand so that it was in a backhanded position, causing me to back away from him. He caught himself and gritted his teeth.

"I have never come this close to wanting to hurt you, Dee. I can understand you wanting to be with someone, but him? How old is that fool? You can't be serious."

I stepped farther away from Reggie and put on my robe to cover up. This was one awkward moment, but what Roc had said quickly came to mind. *Handle your business.*

"Reggie, who I see is my business, not yours. You have no business showing up at this house like you do. I've been allowing you to get away with it for too long. In the future, you need to call before you come. There's a possibility that I may have company, and I do not want something like this to happen again."

Reggie's eyes grew wide, as if he'd seen a ghost. My words must have stunned him. It was as if he couldn't find the right words to say. That was rare.

"I . . . I came over this morning to cut your grass. When I saw that punk's car still in the driveway, I knew something was up. No, it's not my business, Dee, but I can tell you this. You are making one big mistake. That gangbanger can't offer you a damn thing. How dare you fuck him in the bed I used to make love to you in!" His voice rose. "What in the hell is wrong with you?"

"In case you haven't noticed, my grass has already been cut." I pointed to my chest. "And if I'm making a mistake, I'll have to live with it, not you! For now, though, that gangbanger is doing all the right things. You saw for yourself, didn't you? The way he's made me feel in such a short period of time is better than the way your sorry ass made me feel during the last several years of our marriage." I pointed to *my* bed. "That bed belongs to *me.* I damn well will fuck anybody in it that I want to. Now, if you don't mind, I have plans for this afternoon. Lock the door behind you and throw away your keys, because you'll never be able to use them again. I'm having all the locks changed, something I should have done when you walked out on me and started your new life of freedom. I've adopted your theme. Now it's time for you to adjust, as I have."

Reggie dug in his pockets for his set of keys and threw them at me like he was a pitcher throwing a baseball. I ducked, but the keys slammed into the window behind me, cracking it. He stormed out of my bedroom, rushed through the house, and slammed the front door behind him. I dropped to the bed, shaking my head.

Damn it, I thought. How did I ever let something like this happen?

Chapter Five

Being with Roc on Friday nights and having him stay the night was becoming a weekend ritual. I was starting to enjoy his company more, and before long I agreed to let him take me out for the day one Saturday. We were hyped and ready to go that Saturday morning. It was kind of chilly outside, so I wore a waist-length blue jean jacket and wide-legged jeans that matched. A soft pink top was underneath the jacket, and three-inch stilettos covered my feet. I had put my hair in a neat ponytail and had left a fringe of bangs on my forehead. I locked the front door, and the second I got in Roc's truck, I handed a CD to him.

"Here, baby," I said. "Put this in your CD player."

He laughed, realizing that his kind of music wasn't going to do. "What you got on here?" he asked.

"Crank it up and you'll see."

Roc snickered and put the CD in. He turned up the volume, only to be hit with Patti LaBelle's "Somebody Loves You Baby."

"Hell no," he said and laughed, switching to the next song, Aretha Franklin's "Respect." "Next," he said, then switched to the next song, which was Marvin Gaye's "Let's Get It On." "Okay, we gettin' there. I can do Marvin, and I don't mind gettin' it on, especially with you." Roc leaned in for a kiss, then backed out of my driveway.

"So, where'd you say we were going?" I asked.

"I didn't say. And don't be tryin' to squeeze it out of me, either. I told you it was a surprise."

"I really don't like surprises, but I'm going to trust you on this, okay?"

Roc nodded. Marvin had become too much for him, so he ejected the CD. The truck vibrated as rap music blasted through the speakers.

"Please, please turn that down. How are we supposed to talk if we've got to yell at each other to do it?"

Roc turned down the volume and leaned closer to me. "I turned the music down, so what do you want to holla about?"

"For starters, did you enjoy dinner as much as you claimed you did?"

"Dinner was off the chain. I love steak and shrimp. You did the damn thing. Shit was seasoned to perfection, just how I like it."

"Good," I said, with much more on my mind.

I was starting to make a real connection with Roc, and at this point, I wanted to know more about him. We'd talked about some things, but there was still so much about him I didn't know. Before I could open my mouth again, he hit me with a surprising question.

"Now that you ain't married no more, are you just rollin' with me?"

I playfully rubbed the side of Roc's handsome face. "You and only you, snookums. As long as you keep satisfying me the way you do, I'd say there's a rare chance of me rolling with anyone else."

"Snookums? You are so full of shit, Ma," he said, laughing. "You be tryin' to play with my mind and make a nigga feel good, don't you?"

"I hope you do feel good about us. I'm serious when I tell you how happy I am that I met you at the car wash that day."

"You wasn't singing that tune back then. That day you looked at me like I was some kind of fool or somethin'."

"No, I didn't. If you only knew what I was thinking that day."

Roc displayed a big smile. "Tell me about your thoughts. I seriously want to know."

I cleared my throat. "I'm too ashamed to tell you. Just know that I had a feelin' about us."

"So you knew I was gon' be hittin' that pussy like I wanted too, huh?"

"Is that what you call it? Why do you have to be so blunt about everything?"

Roc looked himself over. "Because what you see is what you get. I am who I say I am. I say what I feel and feel what I want." He touched my thigh and squeezed it.

"I don't have a problem with that, but I'm surprised that your parents didn't teach you how to pull back on your choice of words sometimes."

"FYI, my mother died when I was three, and my old dude been behind bars for years. My uncle is the one who raised me, but the only thing he taught me was how to survive."

Our conversation was getting interesting. I was starting to step in unknown territory, as I wanted to, hopefully without upsetting him. "How do you make money? I hope you're not telling me what I think you are, and if so, you can do better."

Roc rubbed the neatly shaven hair on his chin and kept his eyes on the road. He leaned away from me, signaling that he didn't want to discuss this. "All I can say is it's not what you think it is. I'm just a mover and shaker in the family, but my hands are clean."

"Mover and shaker? Simplify that for me please. I don't understand."

He stopped at a red light and looked over at me. "I move, and I shake. It don't get no simpler than that. If you can't figure out what that means, then I can't help you."

I could tell he was irritated, but I pushed. "So how much money do you make moving and shaking? And what kinds of risks are involved?"

"There are risks involved in almost everything you do. As for the money, it's good, but it can always be better."

I raised my brows and folded my arms. "Look, Roc. We're cool and everything, but you make this moving-and-shaking thing sound kind of scary. Should I be concerned about riding with you and being in your presence?"

"No," he said, picking up his vibrating phone to avoid the conversation. "Roc," he answered. "Yeah, you know I'll be at the club tonight. Why wouldn't I? Right now I'm chillin' with this fine-ass woman, but she's startin' to work a nigga's nerves. You feel me?" He looked over at me to see if I had got the hint. I didn't want to ruin our first day out together, so I chilled on the questions and saved them for later.

To avoid any more questions, Roc talked on the phone with his friend until we got to our destination.

"Come on," he said, opening the door for me. I took his hand, gripping it tightly to get his attention.

"Listen, before we go inside, I need to say something," I said. He stared at me without blinking. "Please don't be rude and talk to your friends on my time. I know you did it just now to avoid any more questions from me, but if you want to continue this friendship, there are some things that I need to know about you."

"I just told you about my mother, old dude, and about what I do. Don't blame me if you're the one who can't put two and two together. And if you want to continue this friendship, I suggest you chill out with that tone you bringin' and enjoy this day that I got planned for you."

He kept holding my hand tightly and moved forward, as if our conversation was over. Obviously, Roc was used to having his way with women. Yet there were times when a man needed to be put in his place. I squeezed his hand again, halting his steps. He looked stunned that I was challenging him.

"Let me make a suggestion to you too. I'm not the one, Roc. If you continue with your controlling attitude, this will be the last time you'll ever see me. Got it?"

Roc let go of my hand and didn't respond. I followed behind him as we walked into the spa. He confirmed my appointment with the receptionist and ignored me.

"She's here for the ultimate private package," he said. "How long will it take? And tell us what it includes."

The friendly receptionist laid a brochure on the counter and opened it. "It takes about six hours and includes a custom blended facial, a Swedish massage, a pedicure, a manicure, a mineral body wrap, a haircut and style, a facial makeover using our makeup, and lunch with fresh flowers. How does that sound?"

Roc looked at me. "Are you down or what?"

"Are you going to stay with me?"

"I hadn't planned to."

"If you're not going to stay, then—"

"This is a place for women, not men—"

"No, sir," the woman interrupted. "You can stay too. We encourage men to stay. They can assist with pampering their women."

I wanted to ease the tension between us. This was a good opportunity. "Is he allowed to rub my back and feet too?"

"Yes," the woman said, massaging the air with her hands. "We'll show him how to massage you in all the right places to ease your tension."

"Now, you know I have plenty of tension. How can you resist that?" I asked Roc.

He cut his eyes but agreed to stay with me.

I kissed his cheek and thanked him. "You're so sweet, snookums," I said. "When you want to be."

"Get yo' butt back in that room and change clothes. Just so you know, I'll massage your back, but I'm leavin' those ugly feet up to the professionals."

We laughed, and things got back to normal, especially after I asked him to turn off his phone, which had continued to interrupt us. Thankfully, he didn't put up a fight. We both changed into robes. This day would be remembered as one of the best days of my life. You learned a lot about a man when you spent time with him. Thus far, Roc had impressed me more than I ever would've expected.

Just when I thought the day couldn't get any more interesting, it did. Roc and I finished up at the spa around 4:00 p.m. He took me to a clothing store at Plaza Frontenac. After the spa treatment, my body felt amazing and my makeup was flawless. I believed in a man taking care of his woman, but even so, I was somewhat uncomfortable with Roc spending money on me. He dropped almost a grand for our spa treatments, and we were now standing in a clothing store where the cheapest thing was a belt for three hundred dollars. The sales clerk had an off-white dress in her hand and twirled it around in front of us.

"Is this the one?" she asked Roc.

"Yes." He ignored the sales clerk and looked at me. "Now, go try it on so I can see how you look in it," he told me.

Only the Lord knew how uncomfortable I was with this, but in an effort not to disappoint Roc, I took the dress and went to try it on. When I got into the fitting room, I looked in the mirror and asked myself, *Girl, what are you doing?* If Roc was shaking and moving drug money, then how could I allow him to pay for the spa treatment and for this dress? I looked at the hefty price tag of $1060.00 and shook my head. I swallowed the huge lump in my throat and did my best to go with the flow.

The size fourteen dress looked amazing on me and was high enough to show my thighs, which Roc had admired so much. It left one shoulder bare and had long, swinging bell sleeves. It stretched around my curves, giving my body a silhouette look. It was very classy and made me feel as sexy as ever. I put on the sexy off-white and gold heels the saleslady had given me and was ready to walk the red carpet. Seeing myself looking so glamorous in the mirror helped ease the uncomfortable feeling I had inside.

I left the fitting room and stood close to Roc as he sat slumped down in one of the soft black leather chairs. Due to the blank expression on his face, I couldn't tell if he was pleased or not. He rubbed his chin and asked me to turn around.

"So, what do you think?" I asked, modeling the dress for him.

"I think you got it goin' on. That's what I think. How do you feel about the dress?"

I shrugged. "I think it looks nice, but the price is ridiculous."

He quickly shot me down. "Don't go there, au'ight? You look damn good, and this is what I want you in tonight."

I shifted my eyes away from the oval mirror that was nearby. "Tonight? What's going on tonight?"

"Fun," he said. "Now, go take off the dress and let's go. We're already runnin' behind schedule."

Since I'd given Roc the opportunity to plan our day, I kept quiet. I started to make my way back to the dressing room, only to hear Roc call my name. I turned without a smile on my face. He walked up to me and lifted my chin. He pecked my lips and looked into my eyes.

"I feel like the luckiest man in the world," he said. "But you gotta trust me, au'ight?"

I nodded.

"Then put a smile on your face. Show me how happy you are to be with me. I need love and compassion too. If that consists only of a smile, don't make it so hard to do."

"I am happy with you, Roc. It's just that all of this is new to me. I have concerns, and you make me uneasy when you don't want to talk about them."

"There's a time and a place for everything. Now ain't neither. We'll talk, but like I said earlier, just enjoy yourself now. Don't knock me for tryin' to do the right thing."

I placed my fingers on his lips and smiled. "Let me go change so we can go wherever you want to and have fun. And before I forget, thank you for everything. I've had an interesting and unforgettable day."

I kissed Roc, and for now, nothing else needed to be said. Before long, the dress was in a shopping bag, and then he dropped me off at home, insisting that I be ready at nine.

Like before, the club was packed. Roc had had a Hummer limousine pick me up, and the driver had escorted me inside the club and had found Roc. Dressed in off-white from head to toe, he could be spotted a mile away. His suit jacket was open, and the silk shirt underneath was unbuttoned, showing off his nicely cut chest and abs. A silver necklace with a diamond cross rested against his shiny black skin, and the waves in his hair flowed well. His lining was cut to perfection, and so was his mustache. I honestly had never witnessed any man like him, and given all the women hanging around him, they obviously hadn't, either.

Roc sat with his arms stretched out and resting on top of a circular booth that seated at least ten people. Bottles of champagne were in buckets on the table, and white and black balloons were all over. A huge cake sat on another table, which was filled with a bunch of women and men. One man sat to Roc's left, and a female sat to his right. She whispered something in his ear, but since the music was loud, I couldn't make out much of what she said. I stepped up to the table, watching Roc's dimples form. Before I could say anything, a man walked up behind me and eased his arm around my waist. His aggressive touch caught me off guard.

"Baby, you wanna dance?" he asked with an alcoholic's breath.

"No, not right now," I said, trying to remove his arm.

He tugged at my waist, pulling me in his direction. "Come on, girl. Let's go set this shit off!"

Roc told the female next to him to move and rushed up to intervene. Even the man who was sitting next to him got up. They both approached the man.

"Get yo' muthafuckin' hands from around my woman's waist. Nigga, are you crazy?" Roc growled.

The man took one look at Roc's furious eyes and then glanced at Roc's friend, who stood with his hands behind his back. He quickly let go of my waist and held his hands in the air. "Damn, all I was tryin' to do was dance. Is that gon' cost me my life or somethin'?"

I put my hand on Roc's chest to calm him down. "He's right. All he wanted to do was dance. Is all of this even necessary?" I asked.

The man shook his head and walked away.

Roc evil eyed him, then turned his attention to me. "He shouldn't have been touchin' and pullin' on you like that. Muthafuckas up in here know when somethin' belongs to me. A nigga like that should've known better."

"For the record, there's no ownership between us. Now, I'm here to have a good time. It would be nice of you to tell me the occasion," I said.

He pecked my cheek and looked as if my comment bothered him. "It's my birthday," he said before moving back to the booth. "Are you gon' stand there or sit down and join me?"

My mouth hung open. Why didn't he tell me it was his birthday? We'd been together all day, and he hadn't said one word. I slid into the booth and sat next to him. "I can't believe you didn't tell me about your birthday. I could've gotten you something, and I feel so bad for allowing you to splurge as you did on your special day."

"Thus far I've had a good day. And I plan on havin' an even better night, as long as you chillin' with me."

"I'm with you all the way, but what happens tonight depends on you. From what I can see, it looks as if you have an array of choices up in here tonight. Who's going to be the lucky lady?"

"Her pretty self sittin' right next to me. She's the only woman I can see bein' worthy enough of my time. Besides, I like her ass, for real. Ain't nobody up in here I'm feelin' more than I'm feelin' her." Roc picked up a glass of champagne and handed me one. He turned sideways and focused on me and me only. "I'm drinkin' to more excitin' days to come."

"I'll drink to that, as well as wish you the happiest and best birthday ever. May God bless you with many more."

We clinked glasses together and followed up with a lengthy kiss. No doubt, all eyes were on us, and the atmosphere became a bit uncomfortable. Roc knew nearly everybody in the club, and they knew him. The booth we sat at and the ones nearby were crammed with people there for his birthday celebration. He was "Nigga this" and "Nigga that." He'd say everything from "What's up, muthafucka?"

to "I'll kick that muthafucka's ass." This was the immature side of him, which I didn't like, but Roc was being himself. There was no way that a woman like me could change him. I wasn't even sure if I wanted to.

A few hours later, Roc was tipsy, and so was I. His attention had been on me all night, and when he excused himself to go to the restroom, I was able to stretch out a bit. Before he made it to the restroom, I watched him being stopped a million and one times. Either it was to get hugs from females hanging all over him, or it was to slap hands with some of his friends. There were two moments, however, that caused me to focus in. The club already had a dark setting, but I was so sure that I'd seen a female kiss Roc on his lips. She wiped her lipstick off his mouth and walked away. Another time was very noticeable. That was when another chick slapped the living daylights out of him. His head jerked to the side, but before he could make a move, a man dressed in a black suit grabbed the woman by her arm. He dragged her through the club, and she shouted words to Roc that I couldn't hear. The music was too loud to hear anything, but the action I had witnessed said enough. Roc avoided the restroom and opened another door, disappearing for a while.

After witnessing the incidents with the two women, I was ready to go. It wasn't like I hadn't expected Roc to be seeing other women, but this setting wasn't the one for me. I couldn't wait for him to return so I could tell him I was ready to go. As soon as that thought crossed my mind, I looked up and saw a man who resembled Roc in many ways. He was just as dark, had a shiny bald head, wore diamond earrings in his ears, and was dressed to impress in white. Two females were connected to his sides, and everybody treated him as if Denzel Washington had just walked into the club. Taking a guess, I assumed he was the uncle who owned the club and who was responsible for raising Roc when he was a child. He stepped over to the booths, slamming handshakes with everyone in sight, including the young lady I'd been sitting next to and conversing with all night.

"Where baby boy at?" he asked the young lady.

"He went to the restroom."

The man's eyes shifted to me. His head tilted slightly, and he cleared his throat. "I don't know you, do I?"

Before I could say a word, the woman next to me spoke up. "That's Roc's woman. She's here with him."

"Say it ain't so," he said.

He motioned with his hand for the other two women to back off, and they did. I couldn't believe how controlled some of these women were, and how this man and Roc seemed to have women in control. It was obvious where Roc had gotten his personality from.

Roc's uncle plucked the collar on his suit jacket and slid into the booth, next to me. He held out his hand for me to shake it. "I'm Roc's uncle, Ronnie. He ain't tell me he was doin' it like this, and I would be ungrateful if I didn't tell you what a fine-ass young woman you are."

"Thanks for the compliment," I said, returning the handshake. I swiped my feathery bangs away from my forehead, feeling uneasy about Ronnie's closeness and stares. The whole time he didn't take one eye off me.

When Roc came back to the booth, he looked as high as ever. His eyes were narrowed and redder than a cardinal. He smiled at his uncle, and I could see just how much he admired him. They slapped hands, gripping them tightly together.

"Baby boy," his uncle said. "Happy Birthday, my nigga."

Roc nodded and couldn't stop displaying his pearly white teeth.

"You enjoying yourself?" his uncle asked.

"You better know it." He looked over at me. "So, I see you met the love of my life, right?"

His uncle took another opportunity to look me over. "I'm impressed. You must've handpicked this one from Hollywood or somethin'. Red bone . . . thick and fine as ever. Is she from here?"

"Ask her," Roc said, making the woman next to me move. I sat between him and his uncle. His uncle put his hand on top of mine and squeezed it.

"You from here?" he asked.

"Born and raised," I said, immediately turning to Roc. "If you don't mind, I'm ready to go."

Roc sucked his teeth and appeared to be taken aback by my statement. "We'll leave in another hour or two."

My voice went up to a higher pitch. "I'd like to leave now. I'm getting tired, and . . . and have you been smoking something?"

His uncle slid out of the booth. He looked Roc directly in the eye, giving him an order. "Take care of that. Pretty women always mean trouble. She doesn't seem to be the exception." He looked at me and winked. "Nice meetin' you. Take care."

Roc downed another glass of champagne and ignored me. He laughed and joked with more of his friends, talked to more females, and even suggested that he cut his cake.

Cake or not, I was leaving. I scooted over to get out of the booth, but Roc grabbed my wrist. He scrunched up his face, and his forehead was lined with wrinkles.

"Where in the hell are you going?"

I snatched my wrist away, hating like hell to rain on his parade. I had definitely seen and heard enough, and all of it had completely turned me off.

"I'm going home."

Roc released my wrist and tossed his hand back. I wasn't sure how I was going to get home, but then I saw the limo driver who had brought me to the club earlier. I asked him if he would take me home, and as soon as we made it to the limo, Roc came after me.

"Why you gotta ruin my birthday like this? I asked you to give me one more hour, and you couldn't even chill and do that."

I pointed my finger at him. "You didn't ask me. You told me. I've been trying to go along with this, but my patience is running thin. You're high as hell, you have females in there kissing all over you, and what about the one who slapped you? Who the hell was she? I must thank her, because she did exactly what I felt like doing tonight."

No sooner had I opened the door to the limo than loud gunshots rang out in the background. Roc covered me with his body, and we both fell hard into the limo. I scrambled backward, and Roc hurried inside the limo and closed the door. I could hear people screaming, and I heard cars skidding out of the parking lot. Roc covered me again with his body, and when one of the limo's glass windows shattered, he pulled his body closer to mine, protecting me.

"Shit!" he hollered at the driver. "Hurry up and drive the fuck off!"

The limo's tires screeched, and it sped off. I was trembling all over. Roc looked down, as I was still underneath him, and shielded my ears from the constant sound of gunfire.

"Are you okay?" he asked.

I couldn't utter one word, as I had never, ever experienced anything like this. I had seen scenes like this only in the movies and had never thought I'd witness a real-life situation like this one. I was so done with this mess. Those who chose to live this kind of life—they could have it! Roc kissed my cheek and rubbed his hand through my hair. He rose up and reached for my hand so I could sit on the seat with him. I didn't reciprocate. All I wanted was to be left alone.

He dialed his cell phone. "Ronnie," he said. "You au'ight?" He paused, listening. "Yeah, I'm good. I'm in the limo, taking Desa Rae home." He paused for a longer time. I could hear his uncle's loud voice coming through the phone. "So, you know who it was?" He paused again. "Aw, just some drunk fools with a beef shootin' at each other. Niggas know they be trippin'." He continued to talk to his uncle.

As I said before, you never really got to know a man until you spent quality time with him. I had a whole new impression of Roc. It really didn't matter if he knew how I truly felt. As far as I was concerned, this little thing between us was over.

Chapter Six

Monica had been out of town for almost two weeks. I hadn't had a chance to talk to her about what had happened at the club that night with Roc. I was back to cooling out at home, watching movies and reading books. I didn't mind doing so one bit. After what had happened, I appreciated my boring life even more. I expressed my feelings to Monica over the phone when we finally spoke, and she couldn't believe it.

"Girl, I can't believe those fools were clowning like that. I've been to that club before, and nothing like that went down," Monica said.

"Well, it did, and it was so scary. I saw my life flash before me, and I was worried about Roc getting shot. I can tell he's used to that kind of mess, and he calmed down like nothing really happened. After he dropped me off, I ran my butt into this house, tore that dress off me, and thanked God for sparing my life."

"Now, you overreacted. I never would've torn that dress, but I can honestly say that Roc would be history. The way you told me he carried on, I don't know what to say about him now."

"I don't, either. He's a nice young man, but we don't have much in common. I suspected that being with a twenty-four . . . twenty-five-year-old would be difficult, and that was quite the experience."

"Have you heard from him at all?"

"Nope. And I don't intend to, either. He was more than upset with me, and for a man who's used to telling women when, where, and how, I think he got the picture that I'm not the one. People treated him like he was black Jesus or something, and his bodyguards jumped at the sight of anybody looking at him too hard. I saw this one chick slap him, and she was the same woman I'd seen at the car wash that day. I can smell the drama a mile away with that chick. The whole night was crazy. I couldn't believe I was sitting in the middle of all that mess."

"That's a shame. Some women know they be acting a fool over a man who could care less about them. But what goes up must come down. He was such a fine and sexy young man. I had hoped you and him would kick it for a while. It seemed as if you started to live a little, and I was starting to feel very happy for you."

"I thought so too, but things didn't work out in my favor. I'm okay, though. No need to worry about me. When the time comes for me to meet the man of my dreams, trust me, I will."

A call interrupted us, so I asked Monica to hold on. I was surprised to hear Latrel's voice on the other end of the line. I told Monica to call me back.

"Hey, Mama," he said softly. A mother knew her child, so I could definitely tell something was wrong. My stomach got tied in knots.

"Hello, Latrel. How are you?"

"I'm okay. I just wanted to talk to you and apologize for my behavior."

"I needed to hear that, and I'm sorry for the way I acted too. I know that you feel that I'm too overprotective, but that's because I love you. I only want the best for you. I meant no harm in speaking that way about your girlfriend, but things about the past make me feel the way I do. I don't expect for you to understand, and I can't promise you that I won't—"

"We broke up," he said.

The knots loosened in my stomach, and I looked up and mouthed, "Thank you." I could tell Latrel was upset, but I wanted to stand up and do the Stanky Leg. Needless to say, the news put a smile on my face. His career was my only concern, and I hoped that it was his priority.

I held my stomach with relief and hated to lie to my son. "I'm sorry to hear about your breakup. What happened?"

Latrel told me about his girlfriend cheating with one of his friends. I told him how sorry I was to hear that, and it wasn't long before we reconciled our differences. Before we ended the call, I asked if he'd spoken to Reggie.

"Yeah, I talked to him the other day. What's this I hear about you shacking up with a younger man? You had Daddy hot. He couldn't stop talking about what happened."

I was so embarrassed. I knew Reggie hadn't given Latrel the details, or had he? "Latrel, I was alone, and I met someone who seemed like a really nice person. We're not seeing each other anymore, but your father shouldn't be out there spreading my business."

"Sorry it didn't work out. I don't care how old he was, and as long as he made you happy, I'm cool with it. I told Dad the same thing, and he kind of got upset with me. But you can't control who you're attracted to or who you love. Who says people have to be the same color or a different sex to love? I can't promise you that I won't fall in love with another white woman again, but whenever I meet somebody else, my concern is to make sure they love me back."

I smiled, realizing that Reggie and I had done a phenomenal job raising our son. Any woman would be lucky to have him, but I still had my preference. "You're right, sweetheart, and cheer up. When are you coming home again to see me? I miss you, and we need to go somewhere and hang out together, okay?"

"Sounds good. I'll probably shoot that way in a couple of weeks. If you rekindle your relationship with your man, I want to meet him."

I told Latrel that wasn't going to happen. And after we ended the call, I danced around in my kitchen, pleased that I wasn't getting a daughter-in-law anytime soon.

Mr. Wright had me running around the office like crazy. But the busier I was, the quicker time moved by. It was already 3:00 p.m. In two more hours, I was going home. I was working on Mr. Wright's calendar for next week and was interrupted by a call from the receptionist, telling me a package was waiting for me up front.

I was expecting a FedEx or a UPS delivery, but it was a Sweetheart Bouquet from Edible Arrangements. The keepsake container was filled with fresh strawberries dipped in gourmet chocolate. A small teddy bear was attached to it with a card.

"This looks delicious," the receptionist said, handing it over to me. "You're so lucky to have a husband who cares."

Lucky was not how I felt, but surprised I was. I carried the package back to my desk and immediately read the card.

I'm really sorry about what happened, but some things are beyond my control. When you want to holla, hit me up. Roc (aka Snookums)

I couldn't help but smile. It had been a little over three weeks since I'd heard from Roc. And for the first time, I had his phone number to call him. I held the card in my hand for a few minutes, contemplating what I should do. I couldn't deny how much I'd been thinking about him, and how did he ever know that chocolate was the way to my heart? But the controlling man I'd gotten to know so well, the one who seemed to love living on the edge, wasn't the one for me. I tossed the card in the trash and inhaled the sweet chocolate covering the strawberries. I put one in my mouth and closed my eyes as I thought about having sex with Roc.

No matter what had gone down, I couldn't shake those memories of him being inside of me. His sexual performance was the best. I thought about the creative things he'd done while exploring my body. While delving into the strawberries, I could almost feel his curled tongue circling my clit, his lips plucking my nipples, and his long fingers fucking me like a dick. Too bad things had turned out as they had. I suspected it would be a long time before I received pure satisfaction like that again. I backed out of my thoughts, and when I opened my eyes, Mr. Wright was standing in front of my desk. I was so embarrassed. It was a good thing that he couldn't read my mind.

"That's a good-looking arrangement, Desa Rae. But you really should be eating those strawberries in the lunchroom."

I swallowed the strawberry and wiped my mouth with a napkin. "You're right, but I couldn't resist. They look so good, don't they?"

Mr. Wright nodded and couldn't keep his eyes off my strawberries.

"Would you like one?" I asked, giving him a napkin.

He smiled, then reached for two. "Why don't you get out of here for the day? It's Halloween. I know you're going to a party tonight, aren't you?"

"No, I'm not. I'm dressing up as a witch and giving out candy to the kids."

"A witch? You should be a princess or something. Witches are mean, and even though you may sometimes fit that classification, you'd still make a beautiful princess in my book."

I laughed at Mr. Wright's comment. I knew I'd been a force to be reckoned with lately. Calling me mean was putting it mildly.

"Just for you, Mr. Wright, I'll be a good witch, okay? I promise to be nice to all the children who come to my house. And I expect to see a lot of tricks."

My Wright tossed his hand back. "Don't count on it. Back in the day, I had to do flips or show some talent just to get one lousy piece of candy. These days, kids don't want to do anything. All they do is show you their candy buckets and grab handfuls of whatever you have to offer."

"I have to agree with you on that one. It'll be fun, though. I'm looking forward to seeing all the creative costumes."

Mr. Wright downed his strawberries and reached for two more before going into his office and closing the door. I gathered my things and left with the bouquet of strawberries in my hand.

Thus far, my witch costume hadn't scared away any of the kids. I had taken Mr. Wright's advice and had turned myself into a beautiful witch with MAC lip gloss and shimmering makeup. My pointed black hat allowed my long hair to show, and the black fitted dress I wore made me look like a character from the sixties TV series *Bewitched*. I had been treating kids all night, and during my downtime, I sat in the kitchen, watching reruns of *American Idol*. The singers were pretty good. When the doorbell rang in the middle of one performance, I rushed to get the door.

"Trick or treat!" the kids yelled while bravely standing in the drizzling rain, which was about to pick up.

"Take as much as you want," I offered, trying to get rid of the candy. It was getting late, and after this bunch left, my porch light was going off.

Some older kids came on my porch and grabbed candy, leaving my bowl empty. I encouraged them to be safe in the rain and turned off the light once they walked away. *American Idol* was still on, so I removed my witch hat and made my way back into the kitchen. No sooner had I pulled back my chair than the doorbell rang again. I knew I'd turned off the porch light, but some kids ignored it. I pulled the door open.

"Sorry, but I don't have any more candy."

Roc was leaning against my railing with his arms folded in front of him. He wore a black leather jacket and baggy denim jeans. A cap was on his head, and his diamond earrings sparkled in the dark.

"Don't think I'm stalkin' you or anything, but I feel bad about what happened. I can't get that shit off my mind, Ma, and I don't blame you for being upset with me."

"Look, there are no hard feelings, okay? Thanks for the arrangement today. The thought was awfully nice. Truth be told, though, if that incident at the club had never happened, I still don't think this would have worked out between—"

He quickly cut me off. "I disagree. It's like you already had your mind made up that we couldn't do this, so I was fightin' a battle that, through your eyes, couldn't be won. Give me another chance, au'ight?"

Another chance wasn't what Roc needed. Everything about this didn't feel right to me. I did my best not to come at him the wrong way.

"Before you say anything," he said, "can I come in, or you gon' make me stand out here in the rain and darkness?"

I sighed, knowing that Roc wasn't going to like what I had to say. "You don't have to stand outside, and you can always leave. I prefer that you let this go and accept it for what it is."

He turned his head, looking away. I saw him take a hard swallow. It was so obvious that my rejection wasn't working for him. "Are you back with your ex?" he asked.

I was somewhat taken aback by his question. "No, but this has nothing to do with Reggie, and you know it."

"No, I don't know," he said, raising his voice. "I know he the reason why you being so uptight and shit. I know he why you bitter than a muthafucka, and I know he the reason why you won't let another man come in and do what he failed to do."

Mentioning Reggie's name always brought out the worst in me. For Roc to stand there and throw this mess in my face . . . It angered me. I wanted to slam the door in his face. Instead, I gave him a big piece of my mind.

"You know what? Some of that may be true, but you're the one who messed this up. I don't like men who shake and move. I can't accept a man who gets high, and any man who thinks he can control women will never find a way to my heart. Maybe your other girlfriends accept that crap, but I'm not that kind of woman. You are wasting your time if you think I'm going to fit in. I guarantee you that will never happen."

The wind was picking up, and from the blowing tree limbs and scattering debris outside, I could tell the weather was about to get ugly. Roc stepped forward to shield himself from the drizzling rain.

"So, in other words, your ex is standin' in my way, right?"

"You're not listening to anything I'm saying."

He cut his eyes and snapped, "I hear you, damn it! And I ain't even want to do this to you, Ma, but sometimes women be so fuckin' blind and don't recognize a good thing when it's starin' them right in the face. Yo' ex ain't shit, Dez. He ain't thinkin' about you. I'm the type of nigga who watches his back, and when that fool stepped to me at your house that day, I had to see what was up."

I was confused about what Roc had said. This had nothing to do with Reggie. "What are you talking about? Why are you putting the blame on Reggie?"

Roc asked me not to shut the door, and then he ran in the rain to his truck. He retrieved an envelope, ran back with it, then handed it to me as I stood in the doorway.

"What is this?" I asked.

"Just open it."

I opened the envelope. Almost immediately, my hands trembled while holding the pictures. I looked through them. They were of Reggie in a lip-lock with a *skinny* Asian woman. It broke my heart. Tears rushed to my eyes. Yes, I'd known he'd been seeing someone else, but at that moment, reality kicked in. I dropped the pictures, allowing them to scatter on the porch. My tears kept falling, but I covered my face to hide the pain. I felt Roc's arms wrap around me. He insisted over and over that the last thing he came over to do was hurt me.

"I'm sorry. I wasn't gon' show those to you, but I knew that he had a hold on you and that you needed to let him go. Let that nigga go, Dez, and let's see what's up."

I sobbed even more, thinking about the hurt Reggie had caused me. This wasn't supposed to be how my life turned out. He wasn't supposed to be with another woman, and I wasn't supposed to be left with an empty house to come back to every night. I had bills that I couldn't even take care of, and my credit score had sunk to an all-time low. I had been living paycheck to paycheck, and I had Reggie to thank for the ongoing turmoil that wouldn't go away. My tears turned into anger, then into passion for Roc as he embraced me in the doorway. I pulled away from him, hurrying to wipe my tears. Lord knows I hated for him to see me like this, but I couldn't help it. My chest heaved in and out as I stared at him without blinking. He hesitated to speak, looking very uneasy.

"Are . . . are you okay?" he finally asked.

I didn't respond, but my flowing salty tears, which rolled over my lips, showed that I wasn't.

Roc backed me up inside the house, but before he could close the door, I unzipped his jacket, yanked it off, and let it drop behind him. I then pulled his T-shirt over his head, and my hands touched his chest, which I admired so much.

"Fuck me," I told him. "Please help me make it through this."

Roc took my hand, kissing the back of it. "I'm gon' help you, but not like this. Let's go lie down and chill."

I was in no mood to go lie down and chill. My aggressiveness showed just that. I ignored Roc's comment and reached for his belt buckle. His pants dropped to his ankles, and I got on my knees in front of him. I didn't care that the door was still wide open, and when my hungry mouth went to work, neither did he.

"Dezzz, damn," he said, with his fist full of my hair. "Baby, stop. Come here . . . I gotta tell you somethin'."

The way Roc pumped in and out of my mouth, I knew he didn't want me to stop. It required both of my hands to stroke him, and they were in a fast up-and-down rhythm with my soaking wet mouth and tightened jaw. I felt the need to give Roc all of me. Reggie had had me for many years and hadn't deserved all that I'd given to him. How dare I hold back on a man who seemed willing to be there for me when I needed him? From this moment on, I had no intention of depriving myself. The concerns that I had had about Roc had to be put off for another day. All I needed was for him to help ease my pain. For the moment, he was working out just fine.

Roc didn't want to come, so he backed out of my mouth, holding his ten hard inches in his hand. I removed every single stitch of my clothing at the door and lay back in the darkened foyer, offering him my throbbing pussy. Roc did what he knew best, and as my legs fell apart, he went right between them. His peace sign separated my pussy lips, giving full exposure to my stimulated clit. While his fierce tongue worked me over, he used his other fingers to bring down my juices. Over the thunder and rain, which had picked up even more outside, I still heard my juices flowing. I squirmed against the hardwood floor as Roc demanded and received my undivided attention.

"I love suckin' this pussy," he confessed. "I missed this shit, and I don't want you to give up on me."

I wasn't up to hearing Roc speak. His words took time away from his immaculate performance. I rolled my body over, my thighs straddling his face, which was underneath me. Just as he'd entertained my mouth, I entertained his. I rolled my pussy around on his lips, making sure that he tasted the depths of my tunnel.

"Damn!" Roc shouted. "Work that muthafucka, baby! Do that shit, girl. I like how you puttin' that pussy in motion."

I tightened my thighs around his face, and as I neared coming, I backed away. I inched my body down to his hardness and prepared myself to give him the ride of his life. I kept a strong arch in my back, allowing my ass to do most of the work. It bounced up and down on him, but the tight grip of my insides caused him to yell out even more.

He squeezed my hips, pumping himself into my waiting wetness. "I knew yo' ass was holdin' back on me. G-give me all you got! That's right. I want all of it! Turn around and work that ass in my direction."

I turned, giving Roc a clear view of his hard meat sinking into my pussy. His hands separated my ass cheeks, giving him the best view in the house.

"Umph, umph, umph," was all he could say. With each pleasurable stroke on top of him, he lifted my butt to the tip of his head, making sure that I felt every inch when I dropped back down. No doubt, I was in pain, but it was pain that I didn't mind being on the receiving end of.

"Ohhh, Roc," I whined. "Why does this have to feel so good? My pussy hurts, but you make it feel so good."

"I don't want to hurt you," he said, halting his actions and moving me over to his side. Right then, the thunder crashed, bringing light through the doorway. Roc kicked the door closed with his foot and resumed his position behind me. Doggy style made me feel him even more. Each time I moved forward, he pulled my hips back to him. I spewed nothing but dirty talk at him, and he fired back. I gripped my hair tight, weathered the pleasurable pain, and dropped my head low.

"That's right. Fuck it, baby," I said, breathing heavily as a result of my raging heartbeat. "Fuck this pussy however you want to. With a dick like this, you . . . you have my permission to do whatever you want."

Roc let out a snicker and took our sex session to a higher level. He went from one position to the next, touching my body in all the right places and causing me to come six times that night. I put on an impressive show myself, and if he had never experienced sex with another woman of my size before, then he now knew what some healthier women were capable of bringing to the party. A skinny and frail woman didn't have anything on me, and this was one time when I felt as if I had something to prove.

The lights had gone out because of the heavy rain. I lit one candle, and we lay sprawled out on my bed, with many silk pillows surrounding us.

"I don't think I've ever had a woman shake, rattle, and roll on me like that. That shit was off the chain, Ma. I hope like hell I don't have to upset you again in order for you to put it in motion like that."

I chuckled a bit while rubbing Roc's chest. "I don't know what got into me. Seeing those pictures hurt like hell. It was the first time I'd seen Reggie with someone else."

"Again, I'm sorry for the pictures, but I was just tryin' to do my homework. I can't take no chances with people I don't know, and that's why I had one of my boys check him out for me. He gave those to me, but I didn't want you to see them. I was gon' tell you about that nigga, but I definitely didn't want to bring that kind of hurt to you."

I thought about the pictures, and in an effort to move on, I looked up at Roc. "Nobody could ever bring as much hurt to me as Reggie did. I don't want to talk about him, and promise me that you will never bring up his name again."

Roc zipped his lips. "Case closed. But it wouldn't be wise for me not to recognize the reason I'm here. I know the hurt from that nigga is swingin' you in my direction, but you ain't the only one dealin' with some crazy shit. I told myself that if you took me back I would lay *some* of my shit on the line. I'm diggin' you like a muthafucka, Dez. If I could make some of my fucked-up situations disappear, I would. Thing is, though, I got people dependin' on me. I just can't slam the door in their faces."

He went on. "There are times that I want to walk away, but I can't. It ain't like I'm on no street corners or nothin', but from time to time, I do move *things* around for my uncle. Like always, he takes damn good care of me, and if I have to return a li'l favor, then I do it. That's why I work at his car wash and at the club. Some of his shit legit, but then again, some people's opinion about what he do may differ."

I wasn't sure how to confront Roc about what he'd just, admitted. The last thing I wanted was to be judgmental. I hadn't walked in his shoes, and I understood how a young man like him could get so caught up with the money.

"I'm not going to judge you, but you've got to consider other options. You are a handsome young man, and I know you can get a modeling gig anywhere. There are so many things I'm sure you're capable of doing, and you can't sit back and accept things as they may be. I know what it's like for people to depend on you, but you've got to look out for yourself. You are living a dangerous life, and unless you do something about it, your situation will end like all the others. I don't want that for you, and the people around you shouldn't, either. All I'm saying is, challenge yourself to do better. Don't travel down the same road as your father and his father, or the rest of your family members. Break the cycle and start a generation that your family can be proud of. Remember, money isn't everything. How you make it is what defines us."

Roc kissed my forehead and was silent for a while. Finally, he spoke up. "I hear what you're sayin', and I wish it were that easy. Unfortunately, society requires you to have all these degrees to make money. I dropped out of school in the twelfth grade. I have money to buy whatever I want, so changin' course don't make sense to me right now."

"It might not make sense to you now, but one day it will." I touched the hair on Roc's chin and lifted my head to kiss him. "If there's anything I can do to help you turn your life in another direction, please let me know."

He nodded and cuddled me in his arms. I had a feeling that, going forward, he would impact my life in a positive way. I would try my best to do the same for his life.

***

The lights were back on, and after I took my morning shower, I headed downstairs to find something to cook for breakfast. My fridge didn't have much in it, so I reached for the milk, opting for a bowl of Frosted Flakes. Roc was still asleep, so I sat at the table and made a long grocery list. He hadn't mentioned any of his favorite foods, but with a body like his, I was sure his fat intake was minimal. I wrote down fruits, vegetables, and even turkey burgers, which I was sure he'd like. I then thought about baking him a cake, only because of the one he didn't get to cut on his birthday that night at the club. I searched through my cabinets and came across ingredients for red velvet cake, which I'd promised to make Latrel. I had wound up making him a German chocolate cake that day and had never got around to the red velvet one. I wasn't sure when Roc would wake up or how long he'd stay, so I hurried to whip the batter and get the cake in the oven.

Thirty minutes had gone by when I headed to my bedroom to check on Roc. He was still resting peacefully. Nothing covered his naked body, and sexiness was written all over him. I wanted to jump on him, but I figured I'd wait until his cake was finished. As I made my way down the hallway, I heard a vibrating sound coming from my living room. I noticed Roc's phone on the floor, and when I picked it up, it showed that he had nine text messages waiting. I thought about not looking at the messages, but that was just a thought. I clicked the VIEW button and began to read text messages from someone named Vanessa. She seemed pissed.

Where in the fuck are u? Yo' ass just up and disappeared, and I'm gettin' tired of the BS! I know u wit' some bitch. When she don't fuck u like I do, don't come running back 2 me! The clothes u left here are on fire, nigga! I don't need u anymore, and neither does your son.

I heard Roc cough, so I quickly laid the phone back on the floor. This was definitely not the kind of drama I wanted or needed in my life, and as a black woman, I felt as if we had to do better. I wondered why Roc hadn't mentioned anything about his son to me. The text messages frustrated me, but given his age, what in the hell did I expect? His baby's mama seemed very immature. If she had to leave nine messages and refer to the father of her child as a nigga, then she didn't need him, nor did he need her. Roc had been spending a lot of weekends with me. I wondered how much time he'd been spending with Vanessa and their son.

Just as I was putting icing on the cake, I heard my hardwood floors squeak. I quickly turned around, and Roc was standing by the island. He stretched, and before he asked what time it was, I told him.

"It's almost noon," I said, standing in front of the cake to hide it.

"How you know I was gon' ask you that?"

"Because you always ask, like you have somewhere to be."

Unclothed, he made his way up to me. "What you tryin' to hide?" he said, wrapping his arms around me. "I smell somethin'."

I turned around to face the cake while Roc kept his arms around me. "Ta-da! It's your birthday cake. I didn't have much to cook for breakfast, so I thought a cake would be nice."

Roc pecked his way down the side of my neck with his lips, repeatedly thanking me. "You so sweet. And I mean that literally."

I smiled as I carried the cake over to the table. He sat in a chair, while I stuck twenty-five candles in the cake and then lit them. I started to sing "Happy Birthday," but he interrupted me.

"If we gon' have a for real birthday celebration, then you gotta put on your birthday suit like me. I ain't feelin' the silk robe, and if you want to make this more excitin', you should get comfortable."

I had no problem getting naked with Roc, so I allowed my silk robe to drop behind me. I straddled his lap on the chair, while resting my arms on his shoulders. I looked into his eyes and seductively sang "Happy Birthday" to him. I ended with a lengthy kiss and asked him to make a wish and blow out the candles.

"I wish that you and me could kind of hook up and do the significant other thing. But since you goin' through my phone and shit, maybe you think I'm taken by somebody else. Everything ain't what it appears to be, and if you ever want to know anything about me, all you gotta do is ask. Some things are open for discussion. Then again, understand that some things ain't."

Roc turned his head and blew out the melting candles. How in the hell did he know I'd checked his phone? I wanted to ask about Vanessa and his son, but I knew my answers would come later. For now, his significant other wish went in one ear and out the other. There was more that needed to be revealed. I wasn't about to set myself up for another broken heart. Instead of ruining the moment, I cut a huge chunk of the cake and told Roc to open his mouth. He did, and I put half of the piece inside his mouth, saving the other half for myself. He chewed, nodding his head.

"Damn, that's good. So far, yo' ass can cook."

"My ass doesn't cook. I do. I'm glad you like it."

Roc gripped my ass and shook it. "My bad. Yo' ass good for many other things I get so excited about, like bending over."

He swiped his finger across the top of the cake, removing a healthy portion of the white cream icing. "Do you know what I could do with this?" he asked. "I can make this taste so much better."

"My imagination is starting to run wild, and while we're in our birthdays suits, let's not let any more time go to waste."

"You're a hot-ass somethin', for real. What the fuck I'm gon' do with yo' pretty ass? You got my young mind all twisted and shit. Why you tryin' to mess with a nigga's mind?"

I took Roc's hand and spread the icing from his fingers onto my nipples. I knew he'd find other places to put it, but my breasts were a good start.

"You're a very smart man, Roc. And diploma or not, you've gained an enormous amount of knowledge from the streets. In no way do I have your mind twisted, and the streets have taught you how to play your game and play it well. For the record, I'm digging the hell out of you too. But we're going to approach this one day at a time. Like last night the ball fell in your court. Today it's in your court again. Right now you're playing your hand correctly, but don't be afraid to face a new dealer. She's a force to be reckoned with, and unlike your baby's mama, who is bringing you drama, my mind can't be twisted, neither."

I knew Roc wanted to fire back at me, but my tongue went into his mouth to shush him. I then lifted his hand to my breasts, and once he started licking the icing on my nipples, I was defeated. His intimate belated birthday celebration went out with a bang, and I was sure there were many more days like this to come.

Chapter Seven

Latrel called, and instead of him coming home, he wanted me to come to his school for an awards ceremony. Due to his excellent grades, he'd been offered another scholarship to further his engineering education. He had already received a scholarship for basketball, but since college was so expensive, every little bit helped. I told him I would definitely be there. That was when he told me not to come alone. I asked him why I shouldn't, and he revealed that Reggie was bringing someone with him.

I pretended as if the news didn't bother me, but it did. I wasn't sure if I'd be able to hold my peace after seeing him with another woman, but I had to be there for my son. As usual, I expressed my concerns to Monica. She always had a solution. This time it was to take Roc along and not go alone. She even offered to go, and since she was Latrel's godmother, that made sense. I wasn't sure if Roc would be willing to go or if I was comfortable with introducing him to Latrel. When I talked to Roc about it, he was all for it. According to him, we needed to get out and have some fun. I figured a car ride to Mizzou wouldn't do much harm, so the three of us rode together.

We arrived at Mizzou three hours before the ceremony. I was nervous about Latrel meeting Roc, and on our way to Latrel's dorm room, I pulled Roc aside.

"I am really nervous about this," I said, facing him. I brushed the fine hair off his shoulders from his fresh haircut, then touched the side of his smooth face. "Can you do me a favor?"

"What's that?" he asked.

"I know how blunt you like to be, but please don't mention anything about us having sex. Eliminate the *P* word and don't be so vulgar, okay?"

Roc stared at me without saying a word.

Monica pulled my arm and told Roc to ignore me. "Please forgive her. She got issues."

"Obviously," he said, reaching for my arm. He turned me so that I faced him and spoke sternly. "I need to get this off my chest. I am who I am, and I don't put on no front for nobody. If you didn't want me to come here, then you shouldn't have asked. Your son is a grown-ass man, and I'm sure he's come across people more blunt than me. So chill the hell out, au'ight?"

"He told you," Monica mumbled.

I rolled my eyes at Monica and turned my attention back to Roc. "I'm sorry. I didn't mean for my words to come out like that, and my intention wasn't to offend you. It's just that my son has never seen me with another man. I don't know how he's going to react."

Roc shrugged and winked. "All we can do is see. Either way, I promise to be on good behavior."

We made our way to Latrel's room, and after one knock, he opened the door. His face lit up, and we embraced each other.

"Hey, Mama," he said, kissing my cheek and inviting me inside. He hugged and kissed Monica too. Afterward, I introduced him to Roc.

"What's up, man?" Latrel said, gripping Roc's hand.

"Nothin' much. It's good to meet you. I've heard a lot about you. Congrats on your achievements."

"Thanks," Latrel said, patting Roc's back.

We all stepped into the tiny room, which had two bunk beds, two computer desks, and one closet stuffed with clothes. Posters of Beyoncé, Ciara, and Kim Kardashian were plastered on the walls, but the two posters of half-naked models were the ones that bothered me. If that wasn't enough to disturb me, Latrel had come to the door with no shirt on and a female was sitting on his bed. Didn't he know I was coming? I thought.

"Mama, Monica, and Roc, this is Jeanne," he said.

She stood and gave us a quick wave. "I'm going back to my dorm," she said. "I'll see you at the ceremony." Jeanne left the room, but not before taking a double look at Roc.

Hell, who wouldn't look? I thought.

"Who's Jeanne?" I asked while giving Latrel's room a once-over. It was junky, as usual. I hadn't raised my son not to take care of his things.

"She's just some trick I'm trying to lay."

Monica laughed, and Roc smiled.

I didn't hear anything funny, so I folded my arms and addressed Latrel. "So that's what you're here for, huh? And when did you start referring to young ladies as tricks?"

Latrel put his shirt on and walked up to me. He shook my shoulders and smiled. "Would you please take a load off and relax? I'm just playing, Mama. Can't you take a joke? Jeanne is just a friend of mine, okay? And check this out. Did you notice that she was black?"

I smiled and rolled my eyes. "Yes, I noticed, but there is still something about her I don't like."

Latrel shrugged. "Why doesn't that surprise me?"

Monica chimed in. "Face it, Latrel. No woman is ever going to be good enough for your mama. And when she sees all these condoms over here in this trash can, you'd better have a good explanation."

I quickly made my way over to the trash can. There was one used condom inside it. Latrel hurried to defend himself.

"That does not belong to me. It's my roommate's. You can ask him when he gets here."

I frowned. "You know I don't believe that for one minute. If you're up here having all this sex, I don't understand how you're capable of getting good grades."

Latrel defensively held out his hand, with a huge grin on his face. I could always tell when my son was lying. "I, uh, don't . . ." He looked at Roc. "Man, help a brotha out, would you? They ganging up on me," he said, laughing.

"Hey, I got checked on the way in here. If I could help, I would. You know your mama be trippin' sometimes. But do like me and ignore her," Roc told him.

I playfully cut my eyes at Roc, then at Latrel. "Clean this room, and we'll meet you in the auditorium. We still haven't checked into the hotel."

I kissed Latrel's cheek. As we were leaving his room, he pulled me back inside, closing the door behind me.

"It's good to see you smiling again. You look nice. And just so you know . . . I love you, and I appreciate you for coming," he said.

I hugged Latrel, telling him I loved him too. I knew he hadn't seen this side of me in a long time. I was starting to feel better about life in general.

We checked into the hotel, then rushed to make our way to the university auditorium before the ceremony started. It took me longer than expected to get dressed, and I would be lying if I said seeing Reggie and his woman wasn't on my mind. It was. I did my best to look flawless. I wore a strapless, silk peach dress with hand-beaded crystal detailing above my healthy breasts. The dress hugged my curvy hips and butt, and it secured my tummy to make it flat as ever. T-strap silver sandals with three-inch heels covered my feet, and my pedicure was in full effect. Not one strand of my straightened, long hair was out of place, and bangs swooped across my forehead.

Roc was on point too. He wasn't as dressed up as I was, but the ribbed cashmere sweater he wore clung to his muscular frame. His dark denim jeans were highly starched and had a crease that could cut. His square-toed leather shoes looked expensive, but not as much as the diamond watch he sported or the diamonds he had in his ears. We made a very attractive couple, and several people checked us out as Roc remained close by my side.

When we reached the auditorium, Monica took a seat to my left, and Roc sat to my right.

"Girl, he is one good-looking mofo," Monica whispered, low enough so that Roc couldn't hear her. "You look nice too, and I can't wait for Reggie to get here. That sucker's face is going to get cracked."

All I did was smile and pay her a compliment as well. Right after I saw Latrel sit down up front with some of the other students, I turned and saw Reggie walk in with his woman. It wasn't the woman in the picture. The woman by his side was black. Honestly, the sight of them didn't bother me as much as I thought it would. The woman was a shade darker than I was, and her body looked as if she worked out. She had on a simple gray dress, and a silver purse hung from her shoulder. Reggie was suited up in a brown pin-striped suit, with a white shirt underneath. Admittedly, he looked nice too, but he had nothing on my Roc. I smiled about that, and when I turned back around, Roc was staring right at me.

"What is it?" I asked.

"Did I tell you how much I'm diggin' you in that dress?"

"Yes, you told me at the hotel, but you also told me you were digging me in flowered dress I had on a while back. I don't know if I can trust your word, because we both know that dress looked awful."

"On a for real tip," he said, "that dress was even better than this one. The only difference is this one got that plump ass sittin' up just right. I can't get my mind out the gutter while sittin' next to you." He looked down at his lap and slumped down a bit. "Look at my steel. It's tryin' to jump out of my jeans and get at you right now."

I couldn't help but laugh, and so did Roc. "I swear, you are so nasty," I whispered. "Why are we having this conversation right now? Sit up straight, and I promise to take care of *that* when we get back to the hotel."

Roc cleared his throat and sat up. He moved closer to me and whispered in my ear. "I'm not in the market for no mother, and just so you know, I can't sit up straight with a hard-on like this. If you keep talkin' that madness, I'm gon' spank that ass hard when we get back to the hotel and make it hurt."

Again, my words didn't come out the right way, but I was learning how to lighten up. "I guess I'm in trouble, huh?"

"Big, big trouble."

I pecked his lips, which was something I wasn't always willing to do in public. "I love being in trouble. Just make sure you have what it takes to discipline me."

Roc snickered and moved away from me. He slumped down even more and rubbed the trimmed hair on his chin.

The ceremony got started, and I couldn't keep my eyes off Latrel. I was so proud of him. When they called his name so that he could accept his award, I got emotional. He thanked his father and me, gave thanks to the organization that gave him the scholarship, and spoke so eloquently. I knew my son would grow up and make something out of himself. Knowing this had put me at ease. Monica touched my hand and squeezed it.

"You did good," she whispered. "Keep up the good work."

I nodded, and when Latrel was done speaking, we all stood and clapped our hands. At that moment, I didn't give a care about Reggie or his woman, who sat a few rows behind us. I was thankful he'd given me a son whom I could love, support, and appreciate for the rest of my life.

The ceremony lasted for at least three hours. When it was over, we waited for Latrel in the lobby. Roc's hand comforted the small of my back, and he occasionally let his palm roam around my butt. I didn't mind, especially since I could see Reggie from afar, his eyes glued to us. Monica had warned me that he was coming our way, but I had already seen him heading toward us.

Roc was next to me, talking to a young man he knew from his neighborhood. And when Reggie got closer, Roc lowered his hand to my butt again. This time, I moved his hand up to my back. Roc smiled, and with his hand remaining where it was, he continued his conversation with his friend.

"Hello, Monica," Reggie said, ignoring me. "How are you doing?"

Monica was as fake as ever. She displayed a wide grin, like she was so happy to see him. "I'm fine, Reggie. How are you?"

"Couldn't be better." He turned to the woman behind him. "This is my fiancée, Yvette."

Yvette extended her hand to Monica, and they shook hands.

"It's so nice to meet you," Monica said.

I couldn't help but turn away from the fakeness, and when Roc squeezed my butt, I looked at him. His dimples were coming through for me. Plus, the compliment his friend had just laid on me was right on time.

"Yeah, this my baby right here," Roc had told the other guy. "I wouldn't trade her for nothin' in the world."

"I wouldn't, either," the guy had responded while looking me over. He had slapped hands with Roc and then had walked away. No sooner than he had, Reggie tapped my shoulder.

"Do you mind if I talk to you outside for a minute?" he asked.

Before I could say anything, Roc spoke up. "She might not mind, but I do. Whatever you got to say to her, you can say it right here, 'cause she ain't goin' nowhere."

Monica cleared her throat and coughed.

This was the wrong time and place, so I had to speak up quickly. "Reggie, I'm waiting for Latrel. You and I haven't talked in quite some time now, and I'm not sure why you wish to speak to me now."

Reggie stared Roc down and ignored me. "You are really starting to bug the hell out of me," Reggie said. "I was talking to my wife . . . ex-wife, and you just can't keep that big mouth of yours shut. Why don't you go somewhere and play, young buck? You got all these young girls in here sniffing after your ass, and I'm sure your dope money can excite them better than it does Desa Rae. Then again, maybe not."

I placed my hand on Reggie's chest and stood face-to-face with him. "Stop with the insults. We're here for Latrel. I'm not about to let you ruin his day."

Roc pulled me away from Reggie. "Baby, don't waste your breath. That muthafucka just jealous. I would be too if I had an ugly bitch like his by my side. Let's go find Latrel so I can take Reggie's advice . . . and go home and play. I got a fine-ass woman to play with, and I ain't got no beef with a foul nigga for rewardin' me with what used to be his." Roc laughed while looking at Reggie. "You fucked up, playa. Get over it."

Roc shook his head and walked away. Monica followed behind him, and when I turned around, Reggie reached for my arm.

"Aside from the dumb shit he's talking, I need to talk to you about some things. Once you get your bodyguard out of the way, call me," he said.

I didn't say whether I would or I wouldn't. I walked away to see what was taking Latrel so long to leave the auditorium.

Latrel and six of his friends finally came into the lobby. I walked up Latrel to give him a hug, and again, I expressed how proud I was of him.

"I know," he said, looking embarrassed as I rubbed his hair. Monica was teasing him too, and Roc had jumped in to congratulate him as well. Latrel introduced us to his friends, who he was going out with later that night.

"Y'all be careful," I said. "And please don't be drinking and driving."

"Are you going out with us too?" one of his friends asked. "You can be my date. My friends would envy me."

Latrel playfully grabbed his friend by the back of his neck and squeezed. He looked at Roc. "Man, you want me to hurt him? I got your back, if you want me to."

Roc smiled and spoke with confidence. "Nah, I'm good. He ain't got nothin' comin'. Only in his imagination."

The young man pointed at Roc, then at me. "That's you, dog? Dang you lucky."

Roc eased his arm around my waist. "I keep tellin' myself the same thing every day."

Latrel smiled, and before he and his friends got ready to go to the pool hall, he asked Roc if he wanted to go along.

Roc shook his head. "Nah, I'm gon' chill tonight. Y'all have fun, and don't do nothin' that I wouldn't do."

Since I wanted to cool out with Monica for a while, and I also wanted Latrel to get to know Roc a little better, I turned to Roc and made a suggestion. "Why don't you get the address of the place where they'll be and meet them there?"

"Yeah, man, come on," Latrel said, encouraging Roc.

Roc took down the address and agreed to meet up with them later. We then left the auditorium and headed back to the hotel.

Later that evening, Monica and I sat in the hotel's dining room, eating a late dinner. Roc had several phone calls to return, so he had stayed in the room to make them. He was planning to meet up with Latrel and his friends, and when he entered the dining room, he told me he was getting ready to go.

"Okay. I'll see you later," I said.

He leaned in for a kiss. "Wait up for me. Leave the clothes in the closet and make sure that pus—"

I covered Roc's mouth. "I know, okay? You don't have to tell all my business to my friend, do you?"

"She already knows what's up." Roc looked at Monica and smiled. "Don't you, Monica?"

Monica bit into a piece of bread, playing clueless. "Wha . . . what?" she said.

Roc laughed and put a hundred-dollar bill on the table. "Ya'll full of it. I'm out of here, and that should take care of dinner."

I was just about ready to give the money back to Roc, but Monica wasn't having it. "Thank you," she said, picking up the money and placing it inside her bra.

Roc winked at me and walked away.

Monica shook her head. "I have to be honest with you about something, Dez. Roc is a mess, but I love, love, love the way he handles you. I knew you were about to give that money back to him, weren't you?"

"Yes, and you know why. And since you're loving him so much, I guess you love how disrespectful he can be. Roc is too blunt. He says whatever he wants, and to me, he should watch what he says around people."

"Disrespectful? Reggie was the one who was disrespectful. Roc put a check mark on his tail, and I was so glad he put that fool in his place."

"How? By telling Reggie that he was going home to play with my you know what? You know that was too much. Reggie was out of line, but Roc should have ignored him."

Monica disagreed. We went back and forth, debating the issue. Personally, I didn't like what either of them had said to the other. It was the wrong place and time.

Dinner was delicious. We sat for hours, talking about Latrel's accomplishments, her kids, Roc, and Reggie. I had so much fun with my best friend. We definitely had to do this more often. We headed back to our rooms around midnight. I told Monica I'd see her at eight in the morning for breakfast. I headed to my room, and just as I put the key card in the door, I heard Reggie call my name. He was standing at the other end of the hallway. My head quickly turned.

"Wait a minute before you go inside," he said as he approached.

I sighed and rested my back against the door. "What is it, Reggie?"

"Look, I'm sorry about what happened earlier, but I'm not going to apologize for saying those things to your boyfriend. All I wanted to do was thank you for being such a great mother to Latrel and tell you how proud I was of him today. I know you've dealt with a lot lately. And I'm happy to see you up and lively again."

"Thank you. I have to give you credit for being there for Latrel too. I applaud your relationship with him, even though at times, I do feel a little jealous of it."

Reggie laughed, and we stood silently for a moment.

"Are . . . are you staying at this hotel too?" I asked.

"Yes. Yvette and I are on the second floor. I saw you and Monica having dinner, so I waited around so I could talk to you."

I bit my nail and looked down at the floor. I had never been uncomfortable when talking to Reggie, but for whatever reason, I was now. "So, are you and Yvette really engaged? I heard you tell Monica that the two of you were."

"No," he said. "I said that to upset you. Yeah, it was stupid, but you know what? I couldn't help it." He took my hands, held them in his, and laughed. "I hate to tell you this, but I am so damn jealous of your relationship with that Roc character. It's like the shit is driving me crazy or something. Ever since that day I saw you in bed with him, I can't get it off my mind. Something about the way he touches you makes me cringe. And the sad thing is, I can tell how much you like him. Do you really like him as much as I think you do?"

After all that Reggie had put me through, I told him exactly what he needed to hear. "Yes, I do like him a lot. To me, age is just a number, and being with Roc isn't any different than being with you."

His voice rose slightly when he said, "How can you say that, Dee? He's still wet behind the ears, and what does he have to offer you? I know the sex can't be all that great, and if it is, I know damn well he isn't better than me."

Reggie waited for a response. I hated to be the bearer of bad news, but why not? "Don't let his age fool you, Reggie. I'm not going to stand out here and discuss my sex life with you, but I will say that I think we were married for too long. There was another world out there waiting for me. The new, ongoing experiences have been more than I could have ever imagined."

He shook his head. "That's messed up. When we were married, you would go weeks . . . months without making love to me."

I placed my finger on Reggie's lips to quiet him. "I guess it's obvious why we're not married anymore. No need to look back, right?"

Reggie couldn't say a word. He took a deep breath and attempted to lean in for a kiss. I quickly turned my head.

"No," I said. "Never again. We're done."

"The thrill is gone," I heard Roc sing. He walked smoothly down the hallway, and when he was a short distance away from me, I could tell he was drunk. "It's gone away." He walked up to us, looking directly at Reggie. I could smell the alcohol, and I knew he was high.

Reggie smirked and shrugged. "Go do you, baby. If this is what makes you happy, hey, what can I do?" Reggie walked away.

"You can't do a damn thing," Roc said.

I hurried inside the room, and Roc followed behind me. He started taking off his clothes, but I sat on the bed and then lay back on my hands. I wasn't smiling, so Roc knew something was up.

"Awww, shit." He laughed while standing naked in front of me. "My ass in trouble, ain't it?"

"Big trouble. Why would you go out with my son and get blasted like this? I thought you'd contain yourself, Roc. How could you embarrass me like that?"

"Hey, I did my best to hold it down, but yo' son and them had some shit that was fire! What was I s'pposed to do?"

"Stop your lying. Latrel might drink, but he does not smoke weed. I know that for a fact."

"Okay, Mommy, if you say so." Roc crawled on the bed and started kissing my neck. "Mmm," he moaned. "Take your clothes off. Why you still got on yo' clothes?"

"Because I don't want to have sex. I don't like it when you're high like this. Why can't you stop messing with that stuff?"

He held himself up over me and gazed into my eyes. "Okay, so you don't like me when I'm high, you don't like when I speak bluntly, you don't like when my phone rings, you don't like the way I wash cars, you don't like me kickin' game at the club with my crew, and you don't like me to slump in chairs. Damn, Dez, what do you like about me? My dick? Is that all you like? I don't hear you complaining about that muthafucka. Let's just stop hangin' out with each other, and whenever you want to wet that pussy, holla."

Roc got up and went into the bathroom. He closed the door, and I heard the shower come on. I knew he was tired of my gripes, but I couldn't help that some of the things he said and did bothered me. Was I supposed to keep my mouth shut about him getting high? Drugs were no good, and if Latrel was smoking weed, I was going to kill him. There was no excuse, and I couldn't wait to see him at breakfast in the morning.

For now, I had Roc to deal with. I removed my clothes and entered the bathroom. Roc was lathering his chocolate body with soap. He looked surprised that I wanted to join him. I removed the washcloth from his hand, then gave him a thorough wash. Minutes later, he returned the favor but promised that he hadn't forgiven me for my bad attitude.

"I ain't playin', Dez. You ain't got nothin' comin'. You can't come in here, tryin' to seduce me, and think I'm gon' make love to ya."

I pressed my soapy, wet body against Roc's and put my arms on his shoulders. I pouted and then spoke with sincerity. "I don't want you to make love to me. I want . . ."

Roc nodded. "I know what you want. You want me to fuck you, don't you?"

"Yeah, that's what I want," I whispered.

"Yeah?"

I nodded and rubbed my nose against his. "Yes, Snookums."

"No. Can't do it."

"Why not? Am *I* the one in trouble?"

He backed me into the wall, leaving no breathing room between us. "Big, big ten and a half inches of trouble."

"That much, huh?"

"Unfortunately so."

"So are you going to punish me right here or out there?"

"Oh, right here, Ma. Definitely right here."

Roc punished me, all right, by leaving me hanging high and dry. I couldn't get anything out of him, and when he laid his head on my lap and went to sleep, it was almost three in the morning.

When it was time to get up and go to breakfast, he opted not to go. "I'm too tired," he grunted. "Tell Latrel I'll holla later."

I got dressed and left to have breakfast with Latrel and Monica. They were already in the dining room, and I couldn't wait to ask Latrel about last night. He looked hung over too. I knew he would've given anything to be in bed right now.

"Good morning," I said, pulling my chair up to the table.

"Hey," Monica said. "If you don't mind, Latrel, pass me the salt."

"Hi," Latrel mumbled, then passed the salt to Monica. He gulped down his orange juice and rubbed his temples.

"You look just as bad as Roc did when he came in last night," I said. "Did you have fun?"

"Lots. Roc's a pretty cool dude. Good choice."

"Somehow I knew you were going to say that, especially since y'all seem to have a lot in common."

"Do we?" Latrel said, cutting into his pancakes.

"Well, not a lot, but enough to be concerned about."

"What is it that you're concerned about?" He sighed and shot me a look, as if he was irritated.

"Your drinking, your drugs, and your numerous lady friends. Where do I start first?"

He shrugged and had the nerve to blow me off. "So what? I drink. And so what? I have sex. Do you think I'm stuck up or something?"

"Latrel, did you get high last night?"

"I smoked *a* joint, Mama. I didn't get high, but I did have *a* joint. So there. What's the big damn deal? Dad said you and him tried weed before."

"Your father is a liar, and you'd better calm your tone. You are never too old for me to jump over this table and slap some sense into you. You are here on a scholarship program, and with you playing basketball, you could be tested for drugs. If that mess is in your system, your career goes straight down the drain. Don't ruin your life over stupid mistakes. I've heard of young black men going to jail for years after being caught with one single joint in their possession. Consider this a warning, and it's coming from someone who loves you. Don't be a fool. And remember this. You're the one who will write your life story, not me. Therefore, make it good."

Monica added her two cents, but she seemed to be on Latrel's side. "It's too early for this, Dez. I get what you're saying, but the truth is, it was only a joint."

She sounded just as foolish as he did. I was so disgusted that I pulled my chair away from the table and headed back upstairs to my room.

How dare Reggie tell Latrel that I tried marijuana before? So what? A long time ago maybe I did. I didn't like it, and therefore, I never tried it again. I knew Monica was calling me a hypocrite. I could hear her saying, "How soon do we forget."

Chapter Eight

Unlike the last time, Latrel and I quickly settled our differences. That evening I left the hotel with Roc and Monica, but I received a phone call from Latrel, apologizing for his stupidity. He realized that doing drugs wasn't in his best interest, and he promised me that he wouldn't pick up another joint. I wasn't sure if I believed him or not, but he was the one who had to live with his choices.

I felt the same way about Reggie. After seeing him with Yvette, I knew it was time for me to get over my hurt and forget about what could have been. Yes, it was a true disappointment that our marriage had ended as it had, but what could I do if my husband didn't love me anymore? That was what he'd said, but I could see in his eyes that he was now starting to realize his mistakes. I was not sure if my being with Roc had Reggie looking at things a little differently now, but I sensed that he regretted his decision. For me, it was too late. I had no intention of ever looking back again.

I sat at the St. Louis Public Library for a few hours, reading books and surfing the Internet on my laptop. I had asked Roc to meet me there, but he was already about an hour late. When he finally showed, he seemed to be in a rush. We sat at the round table together and did our best to whisper.

"Do you have somewhere you need to be?" I asked.

"Kind of, sort of. Why? What's up?"

"I won't keep you, but I bought something for you."

I reached in my leather bag, which was full of books, and gave Roc two books that I'd purchased for him. One was titled *A Complete Guide to Preparing for Your GED*, and the other was *Secrets to Becoming a Professional Model*.

"Listen," I said. "You don't have to jump into these right away, but consider looking through them, okay?"

Roc flipped through the modeling book first, then lifted the other book. "You really tryin', ain't you?"

"Yes. I think you have major potential, and I'd love to see you living your life to the fullest. Ever since that incident at the club happened, I've been worried about you. When the news comes on, I'm so afraid they're going to mention your name. You go days and days without calling me, and there are times when I fear I'll never hear from you again. Please don't take my gifts as an insult. Consider them given to you by someone who cares."

Roc sat back in his chair and folded his arms. "I know you care, but like I said before, I'm doin' me. I'm not interested in becomin' a model, and a GED can't do much for me. I mean, I was inspired by Latrel's success, but we come from two different backgrounds. He has you and yo' silly-ass ex-husband for support, and I'm sure that makes all the difference for him. You don't even want to know where I come from, but whether you recognize it or not, I do view my life as being successful. I got money, I take care of my kid, and I keep a roof over my head. What more do you think a nigga wants?"

"Legitimacy and peace. Stop living in a fantasy world, thinking you can live as you do forever. All I'm saying is that getting your GED can start to open some doors for you that may otherwise be closed. You've got to start somewhere, Roc. I can't think of a better time than now."

I reached in my bag and retrieved some black-and-white professional photos of myself that I'd had taken almost twenty years ago. Some of the pictures were very provocative, and many were not. In one of my favorite pictures, I was shirtless and my breasts were covered by my crossed arms. My lower half was covered with bikini bottoms, and I wore high heels. I gave the pictures to Roc, and he looked through them.

"Those were taken back in the day, but I gave up on pursuing my modeling career. I had plenty of offers from major modeling agencies, but Reggie insisted that he didn't want me to go that route. He promised to take care of me and insisted that I kept working to a minimum. I gave up everything and became content with my marriage. Years later, here I am. I'm heavier. I barely get by as an administrative assistant, and in no way did I envision the life that I now have. I will always wonder where my modeling career could have taken me. All I'm asking you to do is to take care of Roc and love yourself enough to want better."

Roc kept looking at my pictures. He put my favorite one inside his jacket and zipped it. I knew this conversation was too deep for him. He didn't seem to have much else to say. "Look, I gotta go take care of some business," he said, standing up. "If I don't talk to you before Thanksgiving this Thursday, have a good one."

He leaned down to kiss me, but I moved my head back. "You can't kiss me in the library."

"Shit," he said, loud enough for the people at another table to hear him. "Don't you know by now that I can do whatever the hell I want to do, where I want to do it, and when I want to do it?"

He tucked the books I'd given him underneath his arm and reached for my hand. "Come here," he said. I stood and took his hand, and he directed me down one of the empty aisles. He turned me to face him and moved my bangs away from my forehead. He then reached in his pocket, took out five hundred dollars, and tried to give it to me.

"Here. Take this money and put it to good use. I don't want you strugglin', and to hear that kind of shit just makes me mad."

"No," I said, refusing to take his money. "I'll be fine, even though it may take some time for me to get on my feet. I'm a survivor, Roc. That's what my mother always taught me to be."

He touched my bangs again, getting a clear view of my makeup-free face. "You are such a beautiful woman, Dez, and your body is sexier than ever. I know you're not insecure about it, and if you are, I sure as hell can't tell. The woman in those pictures looks nice, but I like what I got in front of me. I don't deserve you, but I'm glad you stickin' with me. Nothin' means more to me than a woman who has my back. Remember, I got yours too."

He leaned in again for a kiss. This time, I didn't stop him. The kiss went on for quite some time. It was good to hear that Roc was just as comfortable with my weight as I was.

"Mmm," he moaned with approval. "I love the shit out of those lips. After I get finished with my business, can I come over tonight?"

"Why are you asking? Like you said, you do whatever you want, when you want to do it, and wherever. I guess if I see you tonight, that depends on you."

Right then, his phone vibrated. After he looked to see who it was, he quickly kissed my cheek. "See you later," he said, then rushed off.

Roc never showed up that night, and since he'd told me to have a Happy Thanksgiving, I didn't expect to hear from him until it was over. For years, I had looked forward to Thanksgiving Day. Now it was just another day to give thanks and a day to be by myself. Latrel was spending Thanksgiving with one of his friends, and since my mother had died almost four years ago, I had no place to go. Monica had gone to visit her kids, and I was sure that Reggie had made arrangements with his family and his woman. It was times like this that being an only child really hurt. I had always had Reggie and Latrel to spend the holidays with, and this year alone would be a first.

When Latrel asked what I was doing, I lied, telling him that Monica and I had plans. I didn't want to cause him to change his plans because he worrying about me. And when Monica asked what I was doing, I told her I was spending some time with Latrel. I didn't know why I was being dishonest, but I decided to attend my pity party all by myself. I did, however, cook a small Rock Cornish hen and some dressing and gravy to go with it. I laid a comfortable blanket on the floor in my family room, in front of the fireplace, and got some wine. I turned down all the lights and clicked on the television. Nothing that I wanted to watch was on, so I turned on the stereo and listened to one slow jam after the next. Patti LaBelle's "Love, Need and Want You" was playing when the phone rang, so I turned down the stereo.

"Hello," I answered.

"Happy Thanksgiving," Reggie said loudly. I could hear all the noise in the background and suspected that he was with his family.

"Same to you."

"Are you busy?"

"No."

"Are you alone?" I didn't answer, so Reggie cleared his throat. "I wasn't trying to disturb you, but I just wanted to call. My mother asked about you. She thought you'd stop by to see her."

"I thought about it, but I changed my mind. Be sure to tell her I said, 'Happy Thanksgiving.' Tell the rest of your family I said so too."

"I will. Take care and we'll talk soon."

I hung up and sipped from my wine. All of Reggie's family knew he'd been cheating on me, including his mother. I couldn't stand to be around any of them. I would've been embarrassed to show my face. I hoped he was having fun, and, at least he'd called to wish me a Happy Thanksgiving. I guess I should be grateful, because he didn't have to do that.

The Lifetime Channel had a good movie on, so I lay on my stomach while checking it out. I continuously sipped from my wine and left the volume on the stereo slightly up so I could hear it. All my lights were out, but the fire still burning in the fireplace provided a comfortable and peaceful setting. A commercial came on, and that was when I got up to refill my glass of wine. I was in the kitchen when the phone rang again. This time it was Roc.

"What you doin'?" he asked. I could hear noise in the background where he was as well.

"Watching television."

"Have you been at home all day, or did you spend time with your peeps?"

"I've been here," I said dryly.

"Did you cook?"

"A little."

"Is there enough for me?"

"No. I ate it all."

"So, you mean to tell me you didn't save me nothin'?"

"Unfortunately not."

"Why? Are you mad at me about somethin'?"

"Do I have a reason to be mad?"

"No. I'm just askin'. You sound as if somethin' is wrong. Do you have company?"

"Is this Twenty Questions?"

"No, it's To Tell the Truth. Again, do you have company? If so, I can always check back with you some other time."

"Happy Thanksgiving, Roc. Good-bye."

I hung up. Yes, I was a little perturbed that Roc hadn't shown up or called the other night, like he'd said he would. I had been tuned into the news, and like always, I had expected to hear that something bad had happened to him. That was the first time he had said he was coming over, and never did, so I tried to cut him some slack. As for today, it was almost 9:00 p.m. Hearing from him this late left a bad taste in my mouth.

I carried my wine bottle into the family room, refilled my glass, and resumed watching TV. The movie had gotten even better. As it neared the end, my doorbell rang. I kind of knew who it was, but I could never be too sure. I tightened the belt on my silk robe and teased my messy hair. I took one last sip from my glass of wine and went to the door. It was Roc, and he was leaning against the doorway. He had a plate in his hand, which was covered with aluminum foil.

"Can I come in, or is that other nigga still over here?"

I opened the door wide, allowing him to enter. He looked spectacular in his casual dark brown leather jacket with fur around the collar and denim baggy jeans. A V-neck T-shirt was underneath his jacket, and an arrowhead necklace that looked like it came straight from Africa gripped his neck. There was a fresh pair of leather Timberlands on his feet, and he wasted no time in taking them off, along with his jacket. Like always, the T-shirt hugged his muscles and showed off the numerous tattoos on his arms.

"How did you get rid of him that fast?" he questioned.

"Did I tell you there was someone here when you called?"

"No, but you sounded like there was."

I threw my hand back and went back into the family room. Roc followed, putting the plate that was in his hand on a table as he went.

"You got it awfully damn cozy in here. House all dark, fireplace burning, music playin', wineglasses on the floor." He reached his hand underneath my robe, feeling my bare ass. "Panties off and shit. What the hell been goin' on with you?"

I ignored Roc and got back on the floor. I turned on my stomach, picked up my glass of wine, and focused on the television. He immediately lay on my backside and held himself over me in a push-up position.

"Are you gon' talk to me or not?" he asked.

"Only when you start talking what I want to hear. Thus far, you're throwing false accusations at me, and I'm not interested."

Roc dropped his heavy body on mine, pressing down so I couldn't breathe. "Can you talk now?" he joked.

I tried to push him back but couldn't. "Get up," I said, straining to get out the words. "You're too heavy."

"What's that? I can't hear you. What you say?"

I was defeated, and when I told him I seriously couldn't breathe, he moved over next to me. "That's what yo' bad ass get. Don't be tryin' to ignore me."

I turned on my back and looked over at Roc. "For your information, I've been here all day by myself. I've been watching television, and I ate a little something before you came."

"Why didn't you go visit your family?"

"Because the family I did have was Reggie's family. My mother died a few years back, and my father died when I was nineteen. I told you before that I was an only child."

"You should have told me you was gon' be by yourself. I would've come over earlier."

"It's okay. If you haven't noticed, I don't mind being by myself."

"I noticed. You stay in the house too much. I don't think I ever met nobody as secluded as you."

"I haven't always been like this. Things changed, and this is how it is."

Roc rubbed my stomach while looking down at me. "Are you depressed? Maybe you should see somebody about how you've been feelin'."

"I don't know. I just think it takes time to heal, that's all." I touched the sexy trimmed hair on his chin. "Either way, I'm glad you're here. Thanks for coming."

"You knew damn well I was comin'. I seriously thought you was over here slappin' bodies with some nigga."

"And if I was, what would you have done?"

Roc smiled. "Yo' ass would've been in trouble."

"Big trouble?"

"Yeah, eleven-inch trouble."

"I thought it was ten-and-a-half-inch trouble?"

"You thought wrong. I'm still growin'. Would you like to see?"

"Nah," I teased. "Not today. Some other time."

Roc started tickling me. My stomach was killing me from laughing so hard. My robe had slid open, exposing my wobbly left breast and hard nipple. Roc wasted no time putting his tongue in action. His hand crept down between my legs, but when I heard Beyoncé crooning "At Last" on my *Cadillac Records* CD, I interrupted him and stood up.

"I love this song," I said. "Turn off the television and slow dance with me, okay?"

Roc stood up, laughing. "You know you can't dance."

"Whatever. Then just hold me."

I turned off the television, cranked up the volume on the stereo, and Roc had no problem holding me in his arms. My head rested against his chest, and we slowly moved from side to side. I took in every word that Beyoncé sang, feeling as if at last, my lonely nights were over. In my head, I thought back to the moment I met Roc at the car wash, to the first time I saw him at the club. The night of his birthday was still fresh in my memory, and so was the first night he entered me as we had sex on my swing. At this moment and time, I was falling for him. His age no longer mattered. All I wanted was to be with the man whose heart I could feel beating just as fast as mine. One song ended, and another one played. We remained in the same position, having very little to say. The fire had even stopped burning in the fireplace, and when the room turned pitch-black, I still wasn't ready to release him.

"What are you thinking?" I asked Roc.

"Let's see . . . Where do I start?"

"You can start wherever you want to."

Roc backed away from our embrace, holding my hands together with his. "I got a lot of shit goin' on, Dez. But make no mistake about it. Nothin' compares to bein' right here with you. It's like I'm in another world, tryin' hard to do somethin' different. When I get back to reality, sometimes my shit be so fucked up. I don't want to take you into that world, Ma, but it's almost impossible not to. There's no way for me to have it both ways, and I'm afraid of losin' this. How can I not lose this, travelin' down the road I am? The closer we get, the more you gon' make me choose. I don't know what the fuck to do. All I know is you ain't here for nothin'. And this ain't no fuck thing, either. I love that pussy, but it ain't just that anymore, trust me."

At first, I had no response to what Roc had said. I reached up to touch his face and felt the need to share how I felt in the moment. I wasn't sure if it was my loneliness making me feel this way or desperation over having any kind of man in my life. Roc had continued to ease much of my pain, causing my feelings for him to intensify.

"I . . . I feel myself falling in love with you," I admitted.

"And anything I can do to make your life simpler and peaceful, let me know. That's the only reason I'm here. In the meantime, all I ask is that if you tell me you're coming to see me, and you're unable to make it, just call to let me know. That way I won't worry so much about you, okay?"

"I promise. But I want you to do me a favor too. Let me take care of you. I know you don't approve of the way I make money, but no matter where it comes from, it spends the same way. Also, stop stayin' cooped up in this fuckin' house. Let's get out and do somethin'. Wherever you want to go, I'll take you. I don't give a fuck if it's to the gym or to Japan. Let's go. All you gotta do is say the word."

"I'll think about it, okay? But as far as the money is concerned, you're asking me to accept what you do. I don't say much about it, but I can't accept your contributions. I know you mean well, but this is something I have to stand my ground on."

Roc kissed my forehead, and our lips soon met up. Moments later, we returned to our position on the floor. I felt something good stirring between us, and even the sex between us felt different. I wasn't even disappointed that he hadn't said the *L* word to me, and I in no way wanted him to say it, unless he meant it. For Roc, that would take time. I didn't know yet if I would allow him that time, but I would continue to be patient. I was having fun; so was he. The empty void I had endured was being filled by a man who I had never thought could do it. For that alone, I was grateful.

Chapter Nine

When Christmas came, I spent the day with Monica. We cooked a bunch of food and took it to her family's house. Latrel stayed away again, and on this holiday, I didn't hear from Reggie at all. I didn't hear from Roc, either, leading up to Christmas, but on Christmas Eve he stopped by to bring me presents. One was a diamond curved journey pendant in white gold, and the other gift was several sexy negligees. I thanked him for the gifts, and instead of telling him that I would never wear them, I planned to tuck the necklace and the negligees far away in the back of my closet. In return, I gave him a shirt and a tie, a personalized fourteen-karat gold dog tag pendant, and a "key to my heart" message in a bottle. I addressed the personal note to Snookums, and like always, I encouraged him to strive for the best. He told me he had plans to spend Christmas with his son, and he also mentioned working at the club. Working at the club was his plan for the New Year's as well, and he did his best to get me to come. I refused, spending my New Year's Day at home, where I wanted to be.

I couldn't complain, because Roc had stuck to his word about getting me out of the house. We started going out to dinner a lot, checking out the latest movies together, and working out, and we even had a road trip to Las Vegas planned. Everywhere we'd gone, Roc was known. He had to be the most popular person in St. Louis. We could barely eat dinner without being interrupted by someone he knew. That included females, but as long as Roc didn't disrespect me when we were together, I was fine. I had some concerns about his son's mother, Vanessa, but thus far, she hadn't said anything to me. She continuously rang Roc's phone, she stressed the hell out of him about their son, and she left some of her personal belongings in his truck so I could see them. As a woman, I knew what her intentions were. Just as I knew about her, I was sure she knew about me.

I wasn't sure if she and Roc lived together or not, until he invited me to his penthouse apartment in downtown St. Louis. He said it was one of the many places he called home, and I must admit that his place was laid out. Disapproving of his lifestyle, I definitely didn't stay long, but I was there long enough to realize that whatever he was into, the shit was deep. I could smell the money in his rooms, and the whole place was decorated with some of the finest contemporary furniture, which only a rich man's money could buy. His penthouse was spacious and had not one, but three floors.

Everything was neat and in place, and if it hadn't been for the walk-in closet I'd seen that was filled with Roc's clothes and tennis shoes, I wouldn't have believed he lived there. Further proof was the books I'd given him, which were on the floor next to his bed, and I was happy to see that he'd delved into them. I was pleased not to see anything belonging to a woman, but I did notice several pictures of his son and, I assumed, his baby's mama. The black-and-white photo he had taken from me at the library that day was on the stainless-steel refrigerator. He claimed that he had to see my pretty face every morning, and he said that seeing the picture motivated him.

The day of our road trip to Vegas, Roc came to get me in a rented RV. Needless to say, it was laid out as well. It had everything from a compact kitchen to a spacious bedroom in the far back. Flat-screen TVs were in both spaces. The bed was dressed with a blue and gold paisley-print bedding ensemble. Plush pillows were on the bed for comfort, and two reclining chairs were included in the room for extra relaxation.

After showing me around the RV, Roc jumped on the bed, lay back, and put his hands behind his head. "We about to have some fun up in this muthafucka. My man up there got the wheel, and we ain't got nothin' but hours and hours of time on our hands."

I lay on the bed next to Roc, resting my head on his chest. "Yes, hours to catch up on some sleep and read some of my books."

"*Shit*. I hope you ain't bring none of those books with you, because you damn sure ain't gon' be readin' them. As for sleep, you'll sleep when I do, and that won't be no time soon."

I poked at his chest. "So, let me get this straight. You got everything planned out already, and all I have to do is follow you?"

"Yep. Been thinkin' about this vacation all week. You may as well get naked right now, because it's about to go down in here."

"What's the rush? Like you said, we have hours and hours and—"

Roc reached for a pillow, then hit me with it.

"Oh, no, you didn't," I said, picking up one to hit him back. I got up and we went back and forth, hitting each other with pillows. Unfortunately, one of them busted, spreading feathers everywhere.

"Awww," he said, grabbing my waist and luring me back on the bed. "Look what you did."

"Damn. Am I in trouble again?"

"Big trouble. Eleven-and-a-half-inch trouble."

"Growing again, huh?"

Roc reached for his belt to remove it. "Yes. You want to see?"

"Nah, I want to feel it. Let me judge how big it's getting."

"You ain't said nothin' but a word."

Roc wasted no time *showing* me how big he'd gotten. I had never fucked so much in my life, but I could never get enough of him. He couldn't get enough of me, either, and I was always required to step up my game. After one lengthy ride on top of him, he turned my sweaty body to the side, then plunged into me from behind. My right leg was being held high, separated from my left one, which remained straight and relaxed on the bed. Roc entered my dripping wet hole while stroking my swollen clit like a violin to bring more pleasure. He plucked my heavy nipples, and I sucked in major air, unable to keep my mouth closed.

"Wha . . . what is it with this pussy?" he inquired. "Why yo' shit gotta be so good like this?"

I turned my head sideways to suck in his thick lips. "It's your dick, baby. Your good dick tends to bring out the best in me."

"Well let me keep on bringin' it."

He let go of my leg, turning me flat on my stomach. My legs were squeezed tightly together, and Roc slid into my tightened butt cheeks. He dropped his head on my back, letting out a deep sigh of pure, satisfactory relief.

"Ahhh. Don't move yet, okay?" he said.

I wouldn't dare move. With my legs closely together, his growing, hard inches were killing me. I requested that he proceed with ease, and he honored my request. I then hiked my butt in the air just a little and gripped the sheets as he navigated in and out of me from different angles. My eyes were closed, and all I could think about was how

Roc was delivering all the right moves to make me his. He lowered his head and pulled my hair aside to place continuous wet kisses on my shoulders and upper back. His rhythm stayed on point, until he stopped and called out my name.

"Yeah, baby?" I said, raining cum on him.

He nibbled on my ear and whispered, "I love you, au'ight? I don't say that too often, but when I do, you'd better know that shit is real."

I kept my eyes closed and nodded. I knew we were dealing with something special, but I was in no way sure about trusting his words. It was so easy to say something like that when caught up in the moment, and it was important for me to hear those words when we weren't. He lived in another world, one that I really didn't care to know much about. I did, however, know about the other women revolving around him in that world, and the possibility of him truly loving any woman was slim. My thing was, show me love. Don't tell me. And until he was willing to let go of his other life, the only thing he was showing me was that he enjoyed having his cake and eating it too.

For now, things were okay. I felt no need to turn up the pressure. I wasn't really sure how I felt about my growing feelings for him, but I was optimistic that we could somehow manage this relationship.

According to Roc, we had almost eight more hours to go until we reached Vegas. I was tired from my ongoing workout with him, so I took a moment to catch a nap while lying across his lap. He sat up and watched television, and when his phone rang, it woke me from my sleep. I kept my eyes closed and continued to fake snore. I figured Roc could see me in the many glass mirrors in the room.

"Speak," he said. He paused for a moment, but I couldn't make out a word that the other person was saying. "Just tell them muthafuckas to be patient. I'm on my way. When I get to the hotel room, I'll call you." He paused again. "Ronnie, you know better than I do that them niggas anxious. I got this shit under control, and it's gon' bring great rewards."

Ronnie kept talking; then Roc spoke again. "Nah, I ain't with her. I'm with Desa Rae. I almost had to cut that bitch before I left, and I'll talk to you about that shit when I get back." He paused. "Yeah, I'm good. My dick hurt." He laughed. "But I'm good. Baby girl been workin' this muthafucka out." It was Ronnie's turn to speak again, and I heard laughter. "All I can say is she got yo' nephew wide open. Yo playbook failin' a nigga bad over here." He laughed again. "Yeah, I know. That's what I'm afraid of. Like I said, though, I'll get at you when I arrive in Vegas."

Roc ended his call, and I still pretended to be asleep. I knew damn well this Vegas trip wasn't planned so he could make one of his runs. If so, our trip was about to get ugly. I continued to rest on his lap, and after a few more minutes, a familiar smell hit my nose.

I lifted my head, just to be sure. Roc was inhaling smoke from a joint.

As I gazed at him, he could barely get the word *what* to come out of his mouth, and when he finally talked, it was like he had gunpowder clogging his throat. "Why you lookin' at me like that?" He swallowed and held the joint with the tips of his fingers.

"I'm stunned," I said, shaking my head. "I can't believe you would do that in front of me, knowing how I feel about it."

He laid the joint in the ashtray beside him. "Damn, Dez, I wasn't doin' it in front of you. Yo' ass was sleepin'. After all that sex, I needed somethin' to relax me."

I sat up straight, no smile on my face. "There are certain things that I'm not going to tolerate. Your weed habit is one of them. If you don't put that mess out, then we're going to have a serious problem on our hands. Your baby's mama won't be the only *bitch* you'll have to cut, and if there is one ounce of cocaine or any kinds of drugs in this RV, I'm turning you in to the police." I tossed the covers aside and got off the bed.

Roc responded, "Fuck you," and then took another hit from his joint.

No lie. He caught me off guard. My face scrunched up big-time. "What did you say to me?"

He got off the bed and stood over me. His fiery eyes stared deeply into mine, and he clarified what he'd said, gritting his teeth. "I said, 'Fuck you!' You ain't my muthafuckin' mama. I told you about that shit, and rule number one . . . don't you ever threaten to call the police on me. Two, if you start actin' like that bitch Vanessa, you will be treated like her. Three, you just ruined my fuckin' day. Don't say shit else to me, and when we get to Vegas, feel free to take the first flight back home."

So much for optimism. Roc went into the bathroom and slammed the door. I got dressed and spent the remainder of our drive to Vegas sitting at the circular booth in the kitchen. As soon as we got to Vegas, I took his advice. I called a cab, which took me to the airport, and left on the next flight. Roc went on to handle his business, feeling, as I did, that there was nothing left to say.

There was a delay at the airport, but I got home early Sunday morning. I had already taken a vacation day for Monday, and I truly needed the extra day to clear my head. I could have kicked myself for putting my guard down. Deep down, I knew what kind of man Roc was. Had I been in denial? I thought. And what had made me think that a man like him would change because I wanted him to? I was hurt by what had happened, and I couldn't stop thinking about his angry face as he stared at me with disrespect.

After I showered, I sat on my bed to check my messages. Latrel and Monica had called, trying to find out how my vacation was going. I didn't feel like talking about it, so I waited to call them back. I had three other messages, one from a bill collector and two from Roc's baby's mama, Vanessa. She had left a number for me to call her back, insisting that it was *now* time for us to talk. I wasn't sure how she had gotten my number and figured that she had probably found it while searching through his phone. I had no desire to speak to her, so I deleted her messages. Besides, her tone was shitty, and I wasn't going to listen to a woman whom I thought was very childish. She'd have to get her answers from Roc, but I was sure his response would be full of lies.

Due to the short workweek ahead of me, I got in bed early that Monday night. My eyes were tired from reading, and I put the book on my nightstand so I could go to sleep. Almost simultaneously, the phone rang and there was heavy knocking on my door. I carried the cordless phone in my hand, but before answering the call, I went to the door to see who it was. I opened the door, and it was Roc. I immediately answered the phone, and the first words I heard were, "Ancient-ass bitch, what's up with you and Roc?"

"Hello?" I said while observing the pissed expression on Roc's face.

"You heard me. I got his son, and you ain't never gon' take my man from me."

"Good luck with that," I said, handing the phone over to Roc.

He looked at it curiously, then put it up to his ear. "Hello," he snapped.

I could hear Vanessa blasting him through the phone. He pressed hard on the END button, disconnecting the call. And when the phone rang again, he looked at the caller

ID. He showed it to me. Why was Reggie's name and number flashing across it? Roc threw the phone at the wall, shattering it into pieces.

"What the fuck is up with you?" he yelled with a pit-bull mug on his face. I could see how irate he was, and I did my best not to go there with him.

"We're not going out like this, Roc. I swear, I'm not going to do this with you. Why don't you leave and come back when you've calmed down?"

"Why? Because that nigga called to tell you he was on his way?"

"No. I don't know why he's calling. Maybe—"

"Maybe my ass! You ain't stopped fuckin' with him, so quit yo' lyin'."

I couldn't bear to see him so angry; it was such a turnoff. He wasn't going to stay another minute in my house like this. I spoke as politely as I could. "You're not welcome here under these conditions. Please don't do this to us. You're going to ruin what we have."

He pointed to his chest. "*I'm* gon' ruin it? Nah, yo' ass ruined this shit when you talked about callin' the police on me and accused me of some shit that wasn't even happenin'! I thought you had my muthafuckin' back? How you gon' say some shit like that to me?"

I pressed my lips together, trying to muffle my words. I could see that any wrong move would set him off. This was a dangerous position to be in.

He was persistent about getting me to respond, and obviously, he was used to the back and forth "fight me, then fuck me" drama.

"Answer me, Dez!"

I remained stone-faced, until Roc pulled the back of my hair and shoved me into the living room. I stumbled to the couch, where I fell face forward. I hurried to turn around and used my kicking feet to keep him at a distance.

"You're a real man, Roc. Is this the kind of shit in your uncle's playbook?" I yelled.

"And then some," he said, trying to grab my swinging legs. I did my best to disable him by kicking between his legs, but to no avail. Roc's strength was too much for me to handle. He gripped the back of my neck while holding my face down on the couch. He used his other hand to tear at my panties, promising to give Reggie his sloppy leftovers. I wanted to cry so badly, but I didn't want to give him the satisfaction. How could this man, who had just told me he loved me the other day, treat me so badly?

Without a condom on, he plunged deep into me, pounding my insides hard. So hard that when I felt the wetness between my legs, I didn't know if it was my juices flowing or blood. Like a thief in the night, he busted me wide open, taking what did not belong to him. Did I consider it rape? Possibly. But as he questioned me about stopping, I pleaded for him not to.

"No, but please slow down," I suggested. "We don't have to go out like this, do we?"

At the sound of my soft tone, Roc slowed his pace. I had to be out of my mind to feel anything for him, but there was something about the way he made me feel that I couldn't control. I squeezed my eyes, taking deep breaths to soothe my pain. *This can't be happening,* I thought. *Why would he treat me like this?* Roc was about to come, so he sped up the pace again and continued to tear into me like a hammer slamming against a piece of meat. He finally let go of my neck, and as he slowly pulled out of me, a gush of his juices ran down my inner thighs. He breathed heavily and tightened his eyes.

I eased myself away from him and rushed to the bathroom to clean up. While in the shower, I wet my face so Roc wouldn't see the many tears that had fallen. I then scrubbed between my legs, and there was some blood on the washcloth. I knew Roc would come into the bathroom, and when he did, it was filled with steam. I couldn't even look at him, so all I did was stare at the wall in front of me without saying a word. He slid the glass door aside, then stepped into the shower, facing me, with his clothes still on. He rubbed my wet hair back and wrapped his arms around my trembling body.

"I am so, so sorry," he said in a whisper. "I know you ain't tryin' to hear this, but I've been goin' through so much shit lately. I never meant to take my problems out on you, and this is what I was afraid of. My uncle, Ronnie, has been on my back, the cops been snoopin' around, and I don't need to tell you what's been goin' down with me and Vanessa. I wasn't goin' to Vegas to deliver no product. I had plans to meet with some of Ronnie's partners about some possible future connections, but that's it. Other than that, the trip was about you and me. You my peace of mind, Ma. I need that shit. When you said you'd call the cops on me, I didn't know how to handle it. I do my best to avoid jail, Dez, and I'm fearful of any woman who starts talkin' about having me locked up. How I know you ain't Five-O? I trusted you, and I felt like you would betray me."

I still hadn't said a word. At this point, I didn't have to. My psychotic look said it all. Roc knew that it was time to leave me alone.

"Dezzz," he pleaded while touching my chin. I snatched my face away from his touch. "Don't do this. I know you, Ma. You gon' stop messin' with me, ain't you? Don't. I . . . I promise I'll never hurt you again. My word, my bond."

I looked up at Roc, blinking as water dripped from my eyelids. "Please leave," I whispered and moved my head from side to side. "I ca-can't do this with you. It's too much."

"Please don't say that. I'll go, but not for long. Anything you want me to do, I'll do it. I give you my word that nothin' like this will happen again. I'll stop smokin' that shit, and if you want me to stop movin' and shakin', I'll consider doin' that too. I'll stay right here with you, just so you can keep your eyes on me. I ain't lyin' to you. I need this shit between you and me, more than you know. I fucked up, but I'm willin' to make things right."

Roc wasn't listening to me. He was so determined to have things his way. I honestly didn't know what to do or where to turn. I wanted him out of my house, but he was so on edge. I thought about calling the police, but that would make matters worse. Instead, I stepped out of the shower and wrapped myself with a towel. I lay across my bed, thinking about all that had happened. I suspected that I would never forgive Roc for what he'd done, and it broke my heart that this had come to an end. I cuddled the pillow next to me, and several tears fell onto it. Roc removed his wet clothes, and after he dried himself, he wrapped the towel around his waist. He got in bed behind me and pulled me close to him.

"I'm leavin' in the mornin'. I want to spend what may be my last night with you, holdin' you in my arms. You've grown on me so much, and I did my best not to bring my drama to you. I'm gon' make some changes, only because I got mad love for you. You'll see. Yeah, you definitely gon' see."

I closed my eyes so I wouldn't see and gathered up enough courage to remain in bed with a man who had broken my heart. Morning couldn't come soon enough. I hoped that it would the last time I ever saw Roc's face.

Chapter Ten

After all the flowers, the apologetic cards, the ongoing phone calls to tell me how sorry he was, the unexpected visits to my job and to my house, and even the water in his eyes that I'd seen the other night, as he pleaded for forgiveness on my porch . . . I still wasn't moved. This had been going on for at least a month, and Roc was driving me crazy. Finally, after not hearing from him for a couple more weeks, I decided he'd backed off. I was okay with that. My life had started to feel normal again. I got my phone number changed, not because of the phone calls from Roc, but because of the calls from his woman. She and her girlfriends were playing on my phone. It frustrated me even more that I'd gotten myself caught up in some foolishness like this.

I stopped at the bank on Friday, then headed to Target to pick up a few items. The March weather was playing tricks on us in St. Louis: one day it was chilly, and the next day the sun was shining bright. Today was kind of in between. The sun was coming through for us, but it was a chilly forty-eight degrees outside.

We'd had a casual day at work, so I had on an off-the-shoulder fuchsia sweater, a pair of fitted jeans, and black leather, high-heeled boots. Pantene had my hair on point, and it was full of everlasting body. While at Target, I reached for a cart and rolled it around to find some of the items I needed. I stopped in the lingerie section and looked for a new bra, then picked out a few simple cotton nightgowns to bum around the house in. Just as I was going to look at the pots and pans, someone caught my eye. I saw him in the concession stand, his back turned and his arms folded across his chest. He was talking to two young women, who were standing in front of him, grinning. Why wouldn't they be happy? After all, as dark and smooth as his skin was, he looked dynamite in his white jeans and black-and-white, fitted Nike shirt. His tennis shoes looked brand new, and a Nike gym bag was on the floor next to him. It appeared that he'd just come from the gym.

The chicks must have said something funny, and when he turned his head sideways and blushed, he also laughed, showing those addictive pearly whites. For sure, it was Roc. When he put the gym bag on his shoulder and covered his eyes with dark shades, that was my cue to get back to shopping. I did watch him walk away from the concession stand and noticed that his fineness demanded attention. It was as if he was moving in slow motion in a rap video. The two women at the concession stand kept their eyes on him, several of the cashiers had turned their heads, and the women at customer service were nudging each other too. I took one last look, and when his head turned in my direction, I rolled my cart into the aisle.

I picked out a new set of pots and pans, got towels for Latrel, and couldn't leave without my toiletries. I wanted to look for another book to read, but I changed my mind. The cashier bagged my items, and once the transaction was finished, I headed out the door. I stepped outside and saw Roc leaning against the trunk of my car. His arms were folded, and his legs were spread apart. I rolled my cart right up to him and politely asked him to move so I could put my items in the trunk. He lifted the shades from his eyes and rested them on top of his head. A book was on my trunk, and when I looked at it, I saw it was the GED study guide.

"Check this out," he said, picking up the book and turning to a particular page. "I've been doin' some studyin', but I'm confused about somethin'. Do you think you can help me with this problem? You seem like a pretty smart lady."

I popped my trunk, then put my bags inside. When I closed it, Roc pointed to the book.

"Are you gon' help me? I just need to know how to do this, that's all."

I knew what he was up to, but I took the book and held it in my hand, anyway. He stood behind me while looking over my shoulder.

"That one right there," he said, pointing to a mathematical equation. Honestly, I tried to figure it out but couldn't. And the longer I stood, the closer Roc got to me. "You look nice," he whispered in my ear. "Can I get yo' sevens again?"

I quickly turned around, closing the book. "You'll have to check into this on the Internet or hire a tutor. I've been out of school for too long, and I've forgotten how to do a lot of that stuff."

"Why can't you tutor me? I'll pay you for your time."

"I just told you I don't know how to do it. You'll be wasting your money." I walked away, heading for my car door.

"Wait . . . wait a minute," Roc said, coming up to me. He handed me a large envelope.

"I hope this isn't some more stuff about Reggie. I really don't care, Roc, and—"

"No, trust me, it's not. It's somethin' I want you to look at. I need your help with that too."

I shrugged and opened my car door. "Sure."

Roc held the door so I wouldn't close it. "Can I come over tonight?"

"For what?"

"'Cause I miss you, Ma. I want to hold you, and truthfully, my dick ain't been right since you've givin' up on it."

"You got all these women out here throwing themselves at you, so I doubt that your dick has been deprived. It never has been, nor will it ever be. My only problem is, how dare you *take* sex from me and not use a condom? I don't know who Vanessa has been with, and I have not a clue how many women you've had sex with since you met me. In case you haven't been paying attention, our city is ranked high when it comes to STDs. I've been thinking a lot about that night you hurt me, Roc. Have you?"

"I think about it every single day. I wish like hell I could take it back, and you ain't got to worry about me givin' you no disease. I stay strapped up."

"So, are you honestly telling me I shouldn't be worried? Are you saying that you're one hundred percent safe? Was I the only one giving you head without a condom? I doubt it, and damn you for putting me at risk."

"Why you bringin' up all this shit? Did I give you somethin'?"

"Not sure. But I got one hell of a discharge. I'm going to the doctor next week, and when I find out what's going on with my body, you don't want to be anywhere near me. Just leave me alone, okay?"

Roc didn't have much else to say. I left the parking lot and pulled into a nearby gas station to look inside the envelope he'd given me. There were several pictures of him inside, all taken by a professional photographer. I smiled, looking through them one by one. Roc was absolutely gorgeous. He had definitely missed his calling to become a model. I truly hoped it wasn't too late for him, and I was pleased that he'd had the photos taken. There was a note included, and it read:

Do me a favor and pass these on to some of your connections. Let's see what's up and thanks for trying to encourage me. I need you, Ma, now more than ever. I thought a Christian woman like yourself was taught to forgive. Please, forgive me.
Love, Snookums

I laid the pictures on the seat next to me and let out a deep sigh. Why did Roc have to take us there that day? I thought. I wanted him erased from my memory, but that was so hard to do. I had to forget about him, and maybe my doctor's appointment would be the jump start I needed. I hoped there was nothing wrong with me, but with Roc being approached by so many women, I doubted that he was able to turn many of them away. I was sure his young mind encouraged him to have at it. I could only imagine what he'd been doing. I was so angry with myself for thinking that I and maybe Vanessa were his only sex partners. Still, I felt protected, because we had almost always used condoms. I silently prayed that everything would be okay, but until my appointment came, I knew I'd be on pins and needles.

Monday had come too fast. My doctor's appointment wasn't until Wednesday, and now I couldn't stop going to the bathroom to urinate. I wasn't sure what was going on. More than anything, I hoped my condition wasn't brought on by a sexually transmitted disease. I was so mad at Roc, and I couldn't get focused on doing my work while sitting at my desk.

Around noon Mr. Wright called me into his office. He asked me to close the door, and after I did, I took a seat in front of his desk. Closing the door meant there was something serious to discuss, so I listened in.

"You've been here for almost fourteen years Desa Rae, and I've been here for almost thirty. I received a call today from my boss, and unfortunately, they're eliminating my job. As you know, the economy is weak, and it's definitely had an effect on us all. If they're eliminating my job, I guess you know they'll be eliminating yours too. I was told that we'll have no more than three months to find another job. After that, we're out."

I sat in disbelief. I had too many bills to pay. Why did this have to happen to me now? I knew a lot of people had lost their jobs because of the economy, but it had never dawned on me that I would be affected. Thank God my house was paid for, but I had to fork over a pretty penny each month for my car and other bills. I had already made numerous cutbacks, and I couldn't figure out how I could possibly make ends meet without a paycheck.

"I don't know what to say, Mr. Wright. I mean, what can I do? I have bills to pay, and ever since my divorce, I've relied on my paychecks from here. Is this final, or did your boss say it was up for discussion?"

"Unfortunately, Desa Rae, it's final. You can start applying for some of the other positions around here, but many of those are being cut too. I'm sorry. I know how difficult things have been for you. You'll get some money from the college, but not much. Also, you can always draw your unemployment."

I was more than disappointed. I didn't have what one would call a plan B. I hadn't had one with Reggie, I didn't have one with Roc, and now this. Feeling sad, I looked down at my lap while fumbling with my fingernails. Mr. Wright explained that he had intended to retire soon, anyway, so this definitely wasn't a setback for him. I thanked him for sharing the news, then left his office. And as soon as I got back to my desk, I went online to check out some of the other positions available at the college. After almost fourteen years of not needing to find a job, I had to update my résumé. I sat at my desk and did just that. I also checked out other job opportunities online and jotted down a few that I was interested in.

My head started to hurt, so I downed two aspirins and headed for the bathroom. My urine just kept on flowing, but the discharge had lightened up a bit. Under enormous pressure, I splashed water on my face and rubbed my temples. My life sure was getting shitty, and as a forty-year-old, I had expected it to be so much better. If push came to shove, I'd have to ask Reggie for a job at his business and pretty much go from there. It was the last thing I wanted to do, but it was an option.

When I got home that evening, I sat in the family room, searching for more job opportunities on the Internet. I occasionally sipped from my glass of wine and nibbled the cheese and crackers that were next to me. Because of my situation, I got up enough nerve to call Reggie, just in case I needed him.

"Something has to be wrong. You haven't called me since Lord knows when," he said.

"I know. I've been busy, and I haven't had time to reply to any of your messages."

"That's why I stopped leaving them. I was calling about your alimony payments. I hope you've been getting them in the mail."

"Yes, I have. And thank you for being on time. It really helps."

"No problem. So, what's been up with you? You still hanging out with you know who?"

I wasn't about to tell Reggie the truth. "Sort of. We've been cooling out for a while because I've been so busy with work. My job is coming to an end, and Mr. Wright has had me very busy."

"What? You're losing your job?"

"I'm afraid so."

"Dee, I'm sorry to hear that. You know I'll do what I can to help you, but the housing market hasn't been doing well, either. I had to lay off some folks, but I just sold one of my rental properties. Years ago it was worth one hundred forty-five thousand dollars. I had to sell it for almost half of that. You know you got some money coming from that, and when the deal is finalized, I'll make sure you get it."

"Thank you. I can use all I can get."

"Well, look at it this way. The house is paid for, and you'll always have a roof over your head. If there's one good thing we did during our marriage, it's that we had sense enough to pay off our mortgage. Don't get me wrong. There were a lot of good things about our marriage, but that was one of the smarter moves."

I nodded, even though Reggie couldn't see me. Since Reggie was making cutbacks at work, I changed the subject. We talked for at least another ten minutes. During that time, he mentioned that he was thinking about getting married again. All I said was, "Congrats" before ending the call.

The day of reckoning had finally come. Thus far, my week had delivered major setbacks. The news about Reggie getting married had me on edge. I was so angry, and when I thought about all the years I'd put into my job, I was upset about that too. I was definitely on a roll, but I did my best to prepare for this moment.

During the examination, my gynecologist talked about STDs and wanted me to get an HPV test. After the exam, she stepped out of the room to handle some of my paperwork. I sat on the examination table, fidgeting. She had me nervous as hell, and I started to bite my nails one by one. I envisioned Roc having sex with many women and wanted to kill him for what he'd done. No doubt, my insides hadn't felt right since then, and I had to face the fact that something was up.

Finally, my doctor came back into the room, a smile on her face.

She pulled a chair up beside me, then crossed her legs. "I'm sorry it took me so long, Desa Rae, but the office is pretty crowded. I've sent your specimens out for lab work to be done, but in the meantime, sweetie, you're going to have yourself a baby."

Now, I knew I didn't hear what this woman had said. My face scrunched up, and I shook my head from side to side. "A what? No, I'm not pregnant. There's no way. I just got off my period, and I haven't been sick or anything."

"The tests revealed that you are. You said yourself that you've been having headaches, and you're discharging and urinating a lot. Women have many different symptoms, and all of those apply. It's possible for you to have your period and still be pregnant. Eventually, that should stop or begin to get lighter."

"But, Dr. Gray, I'm forty years old. How could I . . ."

"It is very realistic for a woman in her early forties to have babies. Some women wait until then. I recommend that you increase your exercise a bit and give up on eating so much chocolate," she said in a joking manner. "At this point, I don't see this pregnancy being a huge risk for you. You have to keep your stress levels down, and like any woman, I know how much the changes in your body will concern you."

I dropped my head into my hands and closed my eyes. "Trust me, my body is the least of my worries." *God, why are you doing this to me?* I thought. *Are you punishing me for something I did? What?*

I stayed for a while and talked to my doctor about my options. I had always been against abortion, but being faced with a situation like this, I wasn't sure what I'd do. I left her office more worried than ever. With me losing my job, how could I even provide for this baby? Besides that, I didn't want to do this alone. Maybe it was best for me to restore my relationship with Roc. I couldn't believe how lonely I'd felt without him around. I missed having fun, and my boring life made me feel as if I was getting older. No, he was in no way perfect, but our baby needed a father. I wondered what kind of father he would be, and the more I thought about it, the more he was so on my shit list for putting me in this predicament. I should have taken my butt back to the office that day, instead of going inside that car wash and complaining. Or I could thank Monica for dragging me out to the club that night. The moment I saw him again, I knew he would serve some kind of purpose in my life. I wasn't sure yet if it was good or bad.

It was Friday. I had to motivate myself to get up and go to work. Since Mr. Wright had hit me with the news about losing my job, I really didn't want to be there. Basically, I had no choice. Each time I touched my belly, I knew I had to keep it moving. The incident with Roc had taken place in late January, so I figured I was almost two months along or a little more. I had an appointment set up with my doctor for an ultrasound. That would give me an idea about when to expect my baby.

Ever since the doctor had hit me with the news, I hadn't been getting much sleep at all. I hadn't told anyone yet, and I wasn't even sure how Latrel would feel about having a sibling. I wasn't sure about telling Roc anything, and the last time I'd heard from him was when we were at Target that day. I guess our discussion about STDs had scared him away.

As the end of the day neared, I learned that my assumption about Roc was wrong. The receptionist transferred a call to me, and it was him.

"Is the verdict in yet? Am I in trouble or not?" he asked.

"Big . . . gigantic, massive, gargantuan, colossal trouble."

"Aww, shit. That bad, huh?"

"I'm afraid so. Tell me this. How many women did you have unprotected sex with when you were with me? I really need to know the truth, because you may have to contact a lot of people."

He was silent for a moment, and then he spoke up. "I . . . I, uh, . . . Shit, I ain't have unprotected sex with nobody. I had sex with a few chicks, but nothin' was on the regular. Those were stick-and-move situations, and I was always strapped up. Why you puttin' me on the spot, though? We ain't never make no commitments, did we? I don't see how you got somethin' and I don't. You might want to call up ole boy."

"No need to call Reggie, because I haven't gone there at all. I've only been with you, and for the record, if all of those women gave you head, you could still have something, you know?"

Roc's response was delayed again. "Au'ight, stop with the lecture. Did I give you somethin'? Man, you got me over here feelin' like shit. I don't know what to say."

"Yeah, I got something. And it's something I can't get rid of."

"Herpes?" he shouted.

"Nope. Why don't you do me a favor and start asking around? Maybe one of your multiple sex partners can tell you what it is."

"Dez, don't play with me. I'm coming over tonight. I don't care what you say, and you gon' tell me what the fuck is up."

"Good. I look forward to seeing you. When I leave here, I'm stopping at Schnucks. I should be home by six."

Roc hung up, and I couldn't help but laugh. I was so sure numerous phone calls were being made.

Traffic was crammed, and by the time I made it to Schnucks, it was already five o'clock. Because of the baby, I had to be even more health conscious than ever. I had already made my grocery list, which started with the fruit and vegetables section. I picked up two bags of mixed fruits, then made my way over to the packages of lettuce so I could make a salad. As I sorted through them, I felt someone rub my butt. The touch caused me to quickly swing around. There stood Roc.

"Are you stalking me? Every time I turn around, you're there."

"Nice ass, and hell no, I ain't stalkin' you. Didn't you tell me you were comin' here?"

"Yes, but I also told you to meet me at my place, not at the grocery store."

"I was already in yo' hood, so why wait?"

I rolled my eyes and got back to shopping. Roc followed me around, throwing things in my cart. He even tossed in several boxes of condoms.

"Can't forget those," he said.

"Yeah, right. I'm not convinced."

He laughed. "You should be. Now, what you gon' cook for me tonight? How about some of those steaks and shrimps you cooked that day?"

I stood in the frozen food section, looking over the Hungry-Man dinners. "I'm not cookin' at all tonight." I put one of the dinners in the cart. "You can eat this."

"No thanks," he said, putting it back in the freezer. He went right to the meat and seafood sections to get steak and shrimp. "I'll cook these for me, and you ain't gettin' nothin'."

I threw my hand back at him and went into the cereal aisle. I contemplated getting Special K or Froot Loops. "Which one?" I said, folding my arms in thought.

Roc grabbed both boxes and a box of Apple Jacks for himself. The same thing went down in the ice cream section. I couldn't decide on chocolate or strawberry. I knew my doctor told me to cut back, but if she thought I was going to give up my chocolate, she was crazy.

Roc put both containers of ice cream in the cart and added a gallon of black walnut ice cream. I looked at the full cart and snapped my fingers as I turned to him.

"Say, I forgot to ask you something. Did you get a chance to find out about what we discussed earlier?"

"No. And we ain't gon' talk about that up in here. Keep swishin' that ass up and down these aisles so my dick can keep smilin'. It damn sure ain't contaminated, and like I said before, you might want to start diggin' those skeletons out of your closet."

I had one more aisle to go to, and I was sure Roc would be able to assist me with this one. I stood with my hand on my hip, scanning the numerous rows of baby food, formula, and Pampers.

"Let's see," I said as if I were in deep thought. "What kind of formula do I—"

"What? You drinkin' baby formula or somethin'? Or you tryin' to hook up one of your friends?"

"No, nothing like that." I picked up a can of formula, then turned it to read the label on the back. "Yep, this would be for newborns," I said, putting the can into the cart. I looked at Roc and smiled, but he seemed clueless. "What?" he said. "What's wrong?"

I smirked. "Nothing."

I picked up a bag of newborn Pampers and whistled as I tossed them into the cart. "Do you think those will work? If anything, I just hope they're affordable."

Roc shrugged his shoulders. "Shit, I guess they'll work. And affordable for who? You?"

"No, not me. You."

I looked into Roc's eyes again, and this time he stared back. His hands went up to the back of his head, and he swung around. "Ohhh, shit! How could I be so stupid!" He turned around to face me. "Earlier, you said that you got somethin' you can't get rid of. You fuckin' with me in this baby aisle and shit. Dez, Ma, please tell me. Are you pregnant?"

Roc was so loud. I now figured this was a pretty bad idea. It was too late to change my mind, so I slowly nodded.

He tightened his fists and turned back around. "Hell, yes!" he shouted and raised his fist as if he were Tiger Woods and had just put the ball in the eighteenth hole for the win. "That's what's up!" He swung back around to face me. "Why . . . ? When . . . ? Why you fuck with me like that? I've been goin' through some shit all day, and this the kind of shit that brings happiness to a nigga for real!"

I hadn't gotten a chance to say anything, and it was interesting to watch Roc express himself. He picked up several bags of Pampers, throwing them into the cart. "Hell, yeah, I can afford this shit. And then some. I ain't gon' argue with you about this, either, and my li'l nigga will have nothin' but the best."

Problem numbers one and two had already arisen. I was sure there were more to come, but I wasn't going to accept Roc's money to take care of our baby, and our child was not going to be referred to, especially by his father, as a nigga. For now, he was so happy. I wasn't going to steal his joy.

"What's wrong?" he said, easing his arm around my waist. "Are you okay?"

"I'm fine. I'm just glad to see you so happy, that's all."

"I'm ecstatic," he assured me, then licked his lips. "Ca-can I kiss you right now? I know you still got some issues with me, but I promise you that things will get better."

I wasn't up to hearing broken promises, so I leaned in to kiss Roc. Admittedly, I enjoyed our kiss. We were known for having lengthy kisses, and this particular one was not cut short. My eyes were closed, and when Roc held the sides of my face, that was when I opened my eyes.

"You changin' my life for the best. I love you for that shit, and I know my baby gon' have the best mother in the world. Its gon' have a good daddy too. I'm workin' on getting my life in order, but give me some time, au'ight?"

"I plan to. But please don't disappoint me, okay?"

Roc nodded. We headed to the cashier, along with all the things he'd put in the cart for our baby.

"Say, man," he said to a white man standing in line with us. "She's havin' my baby. I just found out. That's what's up, ain't it?"

The man gave Roc a pat on his back and smiled at me. "Congratulations. That's great news."

I cut my eyes at Roc.

As the cashier waited on us, he announced the news to her as well. "Yeah, she just told me. I got a li'l shorty on the way," he said, pulling out a wad of money to pay for the items. His hand could barely keep a grip on the stash.

The lady smiled at both of us. "I'm sure the two of you will have a beautiful baby. Do you know what you're having?"

"No," I said. "Not yet."

Roc intervened and spoke with confidence. "Trust me, it's a boy."

"Well, whatever you have, congratulations. He seems like he's going to be a great father."

I hurried to leave the store, and as we were putting the groceries in my trunk, Roc stopped another person. "Say, man," he said. "Let me holla at you for a minute."

"Roc, please stop it," I said. "You're embarrassing me."

This time he cut his eyes at me and went on to tell the man about his "baby on the way." Once again, the man congratulated us, smiling and offering us his blessings before he walked away.

"I mean, why don't you just get a marker and write it on your forehead so everyone can see it?" I suggested.

"And why don't you just shut the hell up, get your fine self in the car, and go home to cook my food? I got some other things in mind too, but that'll be discussed in more detail later."

When we got back to my place, Roc helped me put up the groceries. He insisted that I cook his food.

"Please," he begged. "I can't cook like you."

"I said no, Roc. I'm tired. If you'd like me to throw something in the microwave for you, I'd be happy to do it."

He shrugged and stepped up to me. He then lifted my chin and pecked my lips. "When you become my wife, I'ma need for you to do as I wish and cook my meals for me. As for now, who needs food when I can eat you? It's been a few months since I last tasted you. I'm ready for my full-course meal."

I held up two fingers, then eased up one more. "Two . . . maybe three months. It's taken too long for you to get it together. How could you stay away from me for so long?"

"I've been comin' at you with everything I got. You the one been dissin' the hell out of me."

"Sorry, and I hope I'm not in trouble. Am I?"

"Yeah, Ma, I'm afraid so. Big, massive, gargantuan . . .
'my dick want to sink into you right now' trouble. It can't
go another day without you, and you gots to let me put
things in motion."

"And if I don't, will you take what you want?"

He rubbed his finger along the side of my face. "Never
again. That shit will never happen again. My word, my
bond."

"What about all this stickin' and movin' you've been
doing? What's up with that?"

"I'm done. I ain't about to lose you again, and that shit
gon' cease."

I pushed. "What about Vanessa?"

Roc swallowed hard, thinking about what to say. "What
about her?"

"I mean, she made it clear that I could never have you.
What do you think?"

"Fuck her. You don't need to worry yourself about her.
My shit with her is under control."

"It better be. And if she gets my number again, I'm
dealing with you, not her."

Roc nodded, but I could see straight through him.
There was more left to this story, but when it all came
to a head, he'd have to deal with it. He unzipped the
back of my fitted skirt. It fell to the floor, along with my
panties. He lifted me up onto the kitchen island and stood
between my separated thighs. My legs fell in place on his
shoulders, and when his tongue divided my slit, I sucked
in my stomach.

"S-so, we're back in action, huh?" I moaned.

Roc was too busy making me his again by using his fierce
tongue to turn circles inside my pussy. An electrifying
shock transmitted through my body caused me to spew
dirty but stimulating words at him. I rubbed his waves
while injecting my juices into his mouth. His hooded, sexy

eyes made contact with mine, and his dimples went on display.

"You damn right we back in action. And we gon' be in action for a long while too," he murmured.

Roc had spoken the truth. For the next few days it was all about me and him. He turned off his phone. I ignored mine, and there were no interruptions. It was funny how I had never thought I could feel so connected to him again. But there I was, enjoying every moment, every stroke, and every compliment that he gave me. Basically, I had my man back. I was certainly elated about that.

Chapter Eleven

I had plenty of vacation time left, so I took two weeks off from my job. Reggie was right on time with the money he'd gotten from selling his property, and so Monica and I shopped our butts off. Monica had taken some vacation time too. Just so we could relax from all the walking we'd done while shopping, we stopped at Houlihan's to get a bite to eat. I plopped down in the booth, laying all my bags next to me.

"My feet are killing me," I said, removing my strappy sandals.

"Mine are too," Monica said, following suit. "I hope my feet don't stink. If they do, too bad."

I laughed. "Now, the last thing I need is to be smelling your funky feet while I'm eating. If you have any concerns about them stinking, please keep your shoes on."

We laughed and got comfortable at the booth. Monica kept her shoes off, but I didn't smell a thing. The waiter was right on time with our menus, and after we ordered, I called home to see if anyone had called. There were no messages, but I was expecting to hear from Roc about our getaway at Monica's parents' cabin in Branson, Missouri. He viewed it as a boring camping trip and had joked about "a nigga from the hood" being in such a place. According to him, he hated insects. If he was bitten by one, or if he saw a snake, he was going to kill me. He still hadn't gotten back to me yet, but when I reminded him about the intimate and romantic time we could have, he said he'd let me know. I closed my phone, seeing that Monica was eyeballing me.

"Roc, right?"

"Yes. I was trying to see if he called. Remember, you're the one who told me to let down my hair, have fun, girl, and don't break your back trying to ride him."

Monica laughed. "I did, didn't I? But I didn't tell your butt to go get knocked up by him. Now, that I didn't say."

I rubbed my hand on my belly, which wasn't showing much yet. "No, you didn't, but I feel good about this. I never wanted Latrel to be an only child like me, and I know this baby will bring me so much joy."

"I know it will too. I'm so happy for you, and I'm jealous that Roc didn't have his eyes on me first. I don't know what to say about him, Dez, but I can tell you one thing. He's an original. I have honestly never witnessed any man like him. Girl, I would be going crazy with a man like that in my life. He'd have to screw me every day. I wouldn't let him out of my sight."

All I could do was laugh. Monica inquired about Vanessa and her friends calling my house, and our conversation turned to her.

"If she's the one I saw at the car wash that day, she's a really pretty girl. But her mouth is foul, which makes her ugly in my book. The chick I saw looked very materialistic, and I'm sure Roc is taking good care of her shopping needs. I could see her breaking a nail, then screaming Roc's name like she done lost her mind."

We laughed.

"So he got a gangsta bitch, huh?" Monica asked.

"I'm not sure what a gangsta bitch is."

"A ride-or-die chick. She gon' ride it out with that Negro until she die or he die. One or the other. And a woman like you don't mean anything to her. You will not take anything that belongs to her, so watch your back. I'm sure she's protective of him, and you need to find out more about her, because the more I think about it, the more I believe anything could happen, especially with you being pregnant."

"I've been keeping my eyes and ears open. I'm definitely not going to allow someone like her to upset me, and her dealings are with Roc, not me. I told him to handle his business with her. It's up to him to make sure she doesn't overstep her boundaries."

"Roc may not have any control over her. Then again, I take back what I said. He got control and then some. I don't believe there's a woman in this world who can tame him. Unfortunately, that includes you."

"I won't disagree, but taming him is not what I want to do. I got other things in mind, and you'll soon see what they are."

Monica tried to get me to tell her what I meant, but there really wasn't any secret. I wanted the best for Roc. Now that I was pregnant with his child, my mission to get him to change his life around had picked up steam.

I had one more week of my vacation left, and Roc and I were on our way to the cabin in Branson, Missouri. He'd been complaining about insects since we left, and when we stopped at Waffle House to grab a bite to eat, I assured him that we would be safe.

"I can't believe you're making such a big deal about insects. Enlighten me. What's up with that? Or are you aiming to ruin another one of our vacations together?"

"I ain't aimin' to do nothin'. I don't do this kind of shit, and settin' up tents and all that mess for these white folks. If you ever lived in the projects, then you'd know what the big deal is about insects. When you got roaches runnin' all around the place, in your food, crawlin' on yo' ass, then you'd know what I'm talkin' about. You must have had that silver spoon hangin' from your mouth and don't know what's up."

"We're not going to be setting up any tents, and the cabin is really nice. You'll like it. If any insects or Freddy or Jason come out to get us, I'll protect you, okay?"

"If Freddy or Jason come fuck with me, they gon' get shot." Roc pointed to his truck. "I got that nine millimeter in there, and after I fire those eighteen rounds in that ass, game over. I bet people won't be going to the movies to see them no more."

"Is it necessary for you to carry a gun around?"

Roc chewed his waffle and stared at me like I had asked a stupid question. I returned the stare, waiting for a response. When his cell phone rang, he broke our trance and answered. I wasn't sure what was up with him, and if the insects had caused him to have such an attitude, maybe it was in our best interest to head back home. I thought about making that suggestion, but for now, I kept my mouth shut.

Roc had been talking to Ronnie all morning. He was on his way to meet us at Waffle House. When he got to the restaurant, he seemed upset that Roc was leaving.

"All I'm sayin' is I need for you to handle somethin' as soon as you get back. Are you sure you'll be back by Friday?" Ronnie asked.

"I got you," Roc said, looking across the table at Ronnie, who had taken a seat next to me.

"Nigga, I know you got me, but I want to make sure this gets taken care of. If you too busy rollin' with yo' bitch, hangin' out in the wilderness, then I'll get somebody else to handle it."

I pulled my head back and looked at Ronnie. "Excuse me? I'm sorry, mister, but you don't know me well enough to call me a bitch. And even if you did, that still gives you no right."

Roc touched my hand and squeezed it. He could see the fire in my eyes.

"Hey, Ronnie. Cool out with that shit, man. I told you I'm gon' handle it, and no need to disrespect my lady. I ain't ever let you down before, so there ain't no need for you to be concerned, right?"

Ronnie sucked his bottom lip. "Talk to me, baby boy. I hear you. I'm just a li'l paranoid about some thangs, that's all. I need you focused right now, especially since you know what's been goin' down." He nudged his head in my direction. "Is she the one carryin' *our* li'l nigga?"

Roc squeezed my hand again, as a cue not to say anything. He knew me all too well.

"Yep," Roc said. "And I can't wait till he get here."

Ronnie turned to me again. His eyes cut me like a sharpened knife. I returned the gaze and did not break it.

"Congrats, li'l mama. You've made yo' way up to the winner's circle. I hope you survive, especially when many others have failed." Ronnie got up and slammed his hand against Roc's. "Have fun, my nigga, and leave your phone on in case I need to get at you." He pounded his chest, and Roc did the same thing back. "Much love, but handle that for me, au'ight?" I noticed his eyes cut in my direction. I was steaming inside. Roc could tell that I was, and as soon as Ronnie left, he had the nerve to ask if I was okay.

"No, I'm not. But I have a feeling that what I say or how I feel doesn't matter. Just do me a favor, all right? Don't ever refer to your child as a nigga, and please see to it that I'm never around your uncle again. As you can see, we don't click."

"Ronnie was just being Ronnie. I can't change no grown-ass man, Dez, and it ain't my job. We talk that way all the time. He meant no harm referrin' to our baby as a nigga. It's just somethin' we say."

I had had enough and couldn't stop myself from raising my voice. "Well, stop saying it! I don't like it, especially when you're referring to our child."

I scooted out of the booth and made my way to his truck so we could leave. A few minutes later, Roc came outside and stood in front of me.

"Why you gettin' all hype about this? I thought we was supposed to be havin' some fun this week? You need to calm down and stop lettin' tedious shit upset you."

He kissed my cheek and opened the door so I could get in. I in no way felt as if I had overreacted. For Ronnie to call me a bitch was one of the most disrespectful things I'd ever witnessed. I had waited for Roc to correct him, and even though he had somewhat, I felt as if it wasn't enough. I told him just that when we were on our way to Branson.

"What did you want a nigga to do? Jump up and knock the muthafucka upside his head? Would that have made you feel better? I asked him to cool out, and he did."

"If you say so, Roc. I don't expect you to fight with your uncle, and the last thing I want is to come between the two of you."

"That ain't gon' happen," he assured me. "Ronnie my nigga. I owe that man my life."

Enough said, enough done. This thing between them was even deeper than I had thought. I'd be a fool to keep pouncing on something that was beyond my control.

When we arrived at the cabin, Roc got out of the car and looked around as if something was going to jump out at him. He wasn't lying about his gun. He pulled it out from underneath the seat and tucked it into the back of his pants.

I shook my head and made my way to the door. When we got inside, Roc was completely shocked. Then again, so was I. The 3,350-square-foot cabin had high log walls, giving it much support. There were three fireplaces—one in the kitchen, one in the bedroom, and another in the family room—and they were all made of stone. The country kitchen was spacious as ever, and the arched glass windows offered a view of the hundreds of trees in the forest. A custom-made balcony surrounded the entire back of the cabin, and it had two levels. In order to get to the upper level, we had to climb the handmade log spiral staircase that looked down onto the sunken living room on one side and the great room on the other. The cabin was lit up with handcrafted wooden lights, and some were made from deer antlers. The cherry-colored hardwood floors creaked as we walked on them, but some of the floors were covered with round tweed rugs, which matched the decor in every room.

Simply put, this place was fabulous. It was not only cozy, but also quiet. I had been there on only one other occasion, with Monica, and that was a long time ago. She'd said that her parents had redone the cabin, but I hadn't expected to walk into something like this. No doubt, Roc's penthouse was banging, but even he was impressed.

"I told you this was nice," I said, slightly pushing his shoulder.

He nodded and continued to look around. "Yeah, it's off the chain. I may have to hook up somethin' like this down the road."

I didn't want to give him any ideas about spending his money, so I asked him to unpack our suitcases. The bedroom was decked out with wrought-iron furniture and had a comfortable-looking king-size bed. The tub in the bathroom was an old-fashioned white claw-foot tub and was more than big enough for me and Roc. I couldn't wait to sink my body into it, and before I could get the words out of my mouth, Roc had already suggested it. He wrapped his arms around me as we stood in the doorway to the bathroom.

"We gon' have a good time here," he said.

"With no interruptions?" I asked.

"No interruptions." He reached for his phone to turn it off. He then tossed it on the bed, already luring me back to it.

"Wait a minute," I said. "I gotta pee."

"Nah, that's just that pussy tinglin' because it knows I'm tryin' to get in it."

"Soon enough, you will."

We kissed, and after I used the bathroom, I went downstairs to make us some sandwiches. Roc stayed in the bedroom, and when I got back upstairs, I discovered that he had made himself comfortable. He was lying across the bed in his boxers while paging through his GED study guide. The pages were ruffled, so I could tell he'd been using the book. I was impressed.

"So I see you've been making use of that, huh?"

"Yep," he said, not taking his eyes off the book. "I told you I would."

I laid the tray of food on the bed, and after we ate and drank some wine, I turned on some soft music. We talked for a while, but then Roc got back to his book. I left him alone and lay next to him, reading mine.

It had gotten dark outside, but the cabin was lit up like it was Christmas. Roc had fallen asleep, and so had I. When I got up, I went downstairs to turn down some of the lights, and then I went back upstairs to start my bubble bath. I wanted Roc to join me, so I put on the sheer hipster panties I'd bought, with a matching embroidered, cleavage-boosting, sheer bra. It had pink silk ribbon straps, and a tiny pink bow sat in the middle of my chest. I stood at the side of the bed, calling out Roc's name. He lifted his head and squinted. When he saw me, his eyes opened wide.

"Damn," he said, rubbing his eyes. "You look good in that shit, Ma. Where the negligees that I bought you, though? I ain't seen you in it yet."

"It's at home. I'm going to wear them, but I wanted to wear this today."

"Good choice," he said.

I turned and sauntered my way to the bathroom, swaying my hips from side to side. I could feel air on my butt cheeks, and I suspected that Roc's eyes were all into it. I stopped at the doorway and stood with my back against the door. I put my index finger in my mouth and sucked the tip of it.

"Are you going to take off your shorts, or shall I?"

Roc removed his shorts and placed a condom on his manhood, which had flopped out, long and hard. He stood in front of me and aimed his goodness right between my legs. I widened them, and he pulled the crotch section of my panties over to the side. He found home, then lifted me higher to seek comfort. I held on to his neck, rubbing and soothing the back of his head. I expressed how much I wanted things to work out between us and reminded him that our hot bath was waiting.

We finished our quickie and then resumed in the tub. Water and bubbles were splashed everywhere. There was nothing sexier than Roc kneeling between my legs, with water and soap dripping down his jaw-dropping body. My hands roamed every inch of him, and I swear, at that moment I wanted to thank Reggie for divorcing me. If I could give him an award for doing so, I most certainly would.

For the next several days, Roc and I got along well. Basically, I had one of the most enjoyable times of my life. He admitted to the same. I knew he had to get back home before Friday, and as soon as he turned his phone back on, which was early Thursday morning, it rang like crazy. One call after the next interrupted our time together. By early afternoon, I had to say something. Besides, he had been all into studying from his GED guide, and I was in the middle of quizzing him.

I sighed, then dropped the pencil on the table. "Come on now, Roc. Let's get finished with this. Can't you ignore your phone? I don't know why you turned that thing back on."

He held his hand up near my face. "Cut it off," he said to me and then answered his phone. "What up?" he yelled to the caller. "Yeah, man, I'll be back sometime tomorrow. Why you niggas keep callin' me?" He paused for a long time. "So it's goin' down like that, huh? Y'all should have taken care of that shit. I recommend payin' them fools off. Check with Ronnie to be sure, but I'm sure he'll be down with it." He paused again. "Au'ight, hit me back later."

Roc ended his call. All this talk about "handlin' business" was making me ill. I graded the test quiz Roc had taken and laid the error-free paper in front of him. "Excellent," I said. "You've been doing your thing. I'm proud of you. I hope we're not wasting our time and—"

Oh my God! His phone rang again! I got up to walk away. He grabbed my arm but still answered his phone. After a few minutes of griping to Ronnie, he told him he was on his way back. After he hung up, he looked at me while still keeping a grip on my arm.

"Look, you haven't been wastin' your time, and neither have I. I asked you to be patient, and I need you to do that shit for me. Now, we gotta go. Unfortunately, somethin' requires my immediate attention, so we gotta cut this short."

This week had been too good to be true. I swallowed the lump in my throat and did my best to face reality.

"Is this what I signed up for? Tell me, Roc. Will it always be like this? I need to know, because I think I'm fooling myself, hoping and wishing for something better."

Roc stood and delivered a clear message, not with his mouth, but with his eyes. "If you're hopin' and wishin' for somethin' better than me, then go find it. I am who I say I am, and if you don't like it, bounce. You're startin' to work a nigga nerves, Dez, and I've been dealin' with that shit for too long. Silence yourself sometimes. If it's the baby that's got you all worked up, I can deal with that. But I got a feelin' that you like fuckin' with me, and that shit seriously needs to stop."

Roc walked off to gather his belongings. It wasn't long before we were back on the road, heading back so he could resume his life.

Chapter Twelve

Finally, I told Latrel about the baby, and he was ecstatic. I wasn't sure how he'd take the news, but he really was pleased that I had moved on with my life. Of course, he broke the news to Reggie, and when he came over that day, I thought the police were banging on the door, since he hit it so hard. Like always, we argued up a storm. Reggie told me that he never wanted to see me again. He called me a disgrace, and before he left, he had the nerve to suggest that I would pay for what I'd done.

Now, what in the hell did I do to him? He was the one who had happily ended our marriage and had moved on with his other women. He had told me he was getting married, so why was it any of his business that I was having a baby with Roc? I couldn't understand some men for nothing in the world. They were crazy.

I had been going through hell with Roc too. He claimed that working at the club had been keeping him real busy, but I didn't know what to believe. He always tried to make things right by showering me with gifts or taking me somewhere so I could get out of the house. I did appreciate his efforts, but just last night, his silly little girlfriend got my number again. This time, she was calling to tell me how many times Roc had made her come the other night. She kept emphasizing the child they had together, and she wanted me to know how much Roc loved her dirty drawers. I listened to her message on my voice mail, thinking that if he loved her so much, then why in the heck had he been spending so much time with me? Why was he constantly underneath me, showing me and telling me how much I meant to him?

Now, I wasn't no fool, and I was well aware of what was transpiring behind my back. I knew the deal with Roc, and based on what he had shared with me about his past, it was clear that the word *love* didn't belong in his vocabulary. It seemed to me that he didn't even love himself. If he did, he would focus more on getting himself together. I was doing my best to be there for him, simply because I had hopes that he would change for the better. Lord knows I was pulling for him, but I couldn't deny that his behind-the-scenes situation was starting to work me.

I had warned Roc about Vanessa calling my house. I had enough to worry about with the baby and my job, and I definitely didn't need the extra pressure. Last week, when Roc took me to the park for a picnic, I noticed her makeup bag full of M•A•C cosmetics, which she'd purposely left in his truck. When Roc stopped at the gas station, I dumped her belongings right in the trash. Another time she left a pair of her panties tucked nice and neat right by the passenger's side door. I was sure they were for my eyes only, so I kicked those on the ground. She wanted me to know about her so badly, but I already knew. Roc didn't have to say a word, and his lies about the whole situation angered me. From day one, Vanessa had been in the picture. She wasn't going anywhere, because he didn't want her to.

Like clockwork, Roc called to say he was on his way. It was a late Friday evening, and I couldn't wait to discuss my concerns about the ongoing stupid phone calls. I had been on edge since the calls started up again, and while in the kitchen, I splashed water on my face so I'd calm down. Being pregnant had me feeling as if I was angry at the world. I knew this kind of feeling wasn't healthy for the baby. I took deep breaths and brushed my hair back into a ponytail. I still had on my workout clothes from earlier—a navy blue stretch shirt that showed my midriff and stretch pants that matched. I looked in the mirror and couldn't believe the gap that had grown between my legs. No doubt, I had Roc to thank for that. My belly was just starting to poke out some, but if I sucked in my tummy, it wasn't that noticeable yet. I turned sideways to be sure and was glad to see that my body wasn't out of whack.

Several hours went by, and Roc still hadn't made it here. I gazed at my watch; it was almost midnight. I had made him promise always to call if he was going to be late, and so this situation seemed kind of odd. He knew how much I worried about him, and I figured the last thing he wanted to do was worry me at a time like this. I called his phone, but I got his voice mail. I dialed again, and the same thing happened.

When one o'clock came around, I tried to find the late news in St. Louis on TV, but I didn't have much success. I then got on the Internet to see if Fox 2 News had any late-night updates. They didn't. I was about to go crazy, and that was when my phone rang. I rushed to it, hit the ANSWER button, and heard Roc's voice on the other end.

"Say," he said in a scratchy voice, "somethin' happened. I'm at the hospital."

My heart sank right into my stomach, and the knot in my stomach felt as if it had tightened. All I could say was, "Where are you?"

"Barnes-Jewish . . ."

I hung up, got in my car, and headed to the hospital. When I got there, the parking lot was packed with cars, and the emergency room entrance was filled with people. I was a nervous wreck. When the double doors opened, I rushed straight to the check-in station.

"I'm looking for Rocky Dawson. Can you tell me where to find him?" I said, nearly breathless.

The woman behind the counter pointed to the huge gathering of people in the waiting room. "Have a seat over there. The doctor will be out in a minute."

There were too many people in the waiting room and too much confusion. All I wanted to know was where I could find Roc. I asked the woman if I could see him right away.

"Have a seat over there," she repeated. "I promise you the doctor will be out to talk to everyone soon. FYI, he'll be okay."

I released a sigh of relief and walked over to the waiting room. I saw some familiar faces from the club, but the most noticeable person in the room was Ronnie. He was cussing at somebody over the phone, acting a fool. Several men stood by the soda machines, some were by the television, and some hung out by the bathrooms. As for the women, I noticed the woman whom I'd sat by at Roc's birthday party, some women I had never seen before, and the woman who had slapped Roc at the club. Of course, she was there with his son on her lap. She was also the woman in the pictures at his penthouse, and all I could do was take a deep breath to prepare myself.

I headed for the bathroom just so I could check myself. One of the men whistled at me, but I ignored him. I looked in the mirror and raked my fingers through the bangs covering my forehead. All I could do with my ponytail was redo it. I refreshed my makeup just a little, but I had no intention of overdoing it. My workout ensemble was hugging the thick curves of my body, and I was glad about that. I left the bathroom with my purse tucked underneath my arm. As soon as I stepped out, the same man who had whistled at me grabbed my hand.

"You don't remember me," he said.

I looked again and realized that it was Bud from the car wash. There was nothing like seeing someone I knew, or knew of, to get me to relax. Bud had my attention.

"Yes, I do remember you. Are you still at the car wash?" I joked. "I hope not."

He laughed, and I did my best to be nice, just to get some answers. He told me Roc had been shot in the upper shoulder by two men who had tried to rob him. When I asked if anyone knew who they were, he nodded and confessed that they'd already been taken care of. I pretty much had come to that conclusion, especially given the hard-looking brothers I'd seen in the waiting room. Bud didn't have to convince me.

I looked over at Ronnie, who was now sitting in one of the chairs, and noticed that everyone was sucking up to him. Roc's son was on his lap, and I had to admit, he was one of the cutest kids I'd ever seen. Vanessa was representing too. She looked even prettier close up. I noticed that she had a heart with Roc's name in the middle tattooed on her leg. And just as I had expected, she had a Coach bag by her side, a diamond necklace was blinging from her neck, and her manicure was in full effect. "I'm Roc's woman" was written all over her, but was she prettier than me? Nah, not at all.

I wasn't sure if she knew who I was, so I decided to let my presence be known. I excused myself from Bud and walked between the two rows of chairs that faced each other. Ronnie was only two seats away from Vanessa, and there just happened to be an empty chair directly across from them. I plopped down in the chair, crossed my legs, and looked over at Ronnie.

"Hey, Ronnie," I said, letting Vanessa know that I knew *some* of the family. "How are you?"

He tossed his head back without saying a word. He kept punching Roc's son in his chest, knocking him down. Roc's son was laughing and punching him right back.

"Don't hit him hard like that, Ronnie," Vanessa said with attitude. "Y'all be playin' too much."

"Be quiet. He ain't no punk," Ronnie muttered.

Ridiculous, I thought. *If it were my child, I'd get up and knock the hell out of him.* I picked up a magazine from the table next to me and opened it up. I pretended to be occupied, but I could see Vanessa checking me out from head to toe. A few minutes later I closed the magazine, then looked at my watch, as if I had somewhere to be. I then pulled out my cell phone and dialed out to no one.

"Hey, Monica," I said, with the phone pushed up to my ear. "I'm at the hospital now. Bud says that Roc will be just fine. I haven't had a chance to talk to Ronnie yet, but I'm still waiting to see Roc. When I got his call earlier, I rushed right up here. He sounded as if he needed me. He was supposed to come over, and I knew something was wrong when he didn't show up." I paused, as if I were listening to someone on the other end.

Vanessa was taking in every word I said. I rubbed my stomach and moved around in the chair like I was uncomfortable. "No, the baby is fine, and I'm going to hurt Roc for causing me to worry about him. In the meantime, I'll tell him what you said." I chuckled a bit, then paused. "Okay, Monica. Gotta go. I'll call you when we leave. Hopefully, he'll be able to leave the hospital soon."

I ended the call and watched Vanessa put on her show. She stood just so I could see her shapely backside and breasts, flaunting it all in my face. She was right in front of me, stretching her leg so I could see the tattoo on it, and to complete her show, she held out her hand, loudly calling her son.

"Come on, Li'l Roc," she said. "Let's go get a soda. You should be able to go see yo' daddy in a minute."

She cut her eyes at me and walked off. It was so funny how a woman had so much crap to talk over the phone, but when you got face-to-face with her, she always had very little to say. I left my seat and waited for someone to buzz the emergency room doors open so I could sneak into the room where Roc was. The atmosphere was not my cup of tea, and my only purpose was to see Roc.

I peeked into many of the closed curtained rooms. When I found the one Roc was in, there were two doctors in there with him. One of them left, and when I peeked into the room again, Roc saw me. He winked and gave me a slight smile. I slowly walked into the room, and the doctor looked at me.

"I'll be another minute or two," he said. "Are you his wife?"

"Maybe," I replied.

"Yeah," Roc softly fired back.

We smiled at each other. He looked so tired and was forcing his fluttering eyes to stay open. His entire left shoulder and part of his arm were wrapped in bandages. It looked uncomfortable. The doctor told me they removed the bullet during surgery. He said that with a bunch of rest and pain medication, Roc would be fine.

After the doctor left, I got closer to the bed. I held Roc's hand in mine.

"Are you okay? Why do you worry me like this?" I asked.

"It wasn't my fault those fools tried to rob me. I was sittin' in my truck at the light, thinkin' about yo' ass. Those niggas came out of nowhere."

"What were they hoping to get? Money?"

"Yeah. They tried to take my stash, but they ain't even notice my boy drivin' in the car next to me. Shit happened so fast, and next thing I knew, I was shot. The bullet caught me in the shoulder, and I was, like, 'Damn.' At first, I didn't know where that muthafucka had hit me. I saw all that blood and started prayin' my ass off. I thought about you and my baby, my son, and . . . It was fucked up, Ma."

I placed tender kisses inside the palm of Roc's hand and closed my eyes. I knew this could have been a lot worse. "I'm just glad you're okay. If something ever happened to you, I'd probably go crazy."

"Nah, don't do that. I'll be cool. I'm thankful that it wasn't my time to go yet."

"Me too," I said, leaning down to kiss his very dry lips. Our tongues added a little something extra, and I felt so relieved that he'd be okay. "Listen, I'm not going to stay, because you have many people waiting out there to see you. Let's just say it's *crowded,* and I want to prevent any more confrontations. I'll call to check on you, but please call to let me know when you're going home. I want to help you get better any way I can."

"You gon' take care of me? Is that what you're sayin'?"

"I always do, don't I?"

Roc snickered. "Hell, yeah. I can't complain."

I turned slightly to make my exit. "Bye, Snookums," I said.

He kissed his hand, then blew his kiss in my direction.

I barely made it to the curtain before he called my name. "Yes?" I said, making my way over to him.

"Come here. Let me whisper somethin' in your ear." I leaned down and put my ear close to Roc's lips. "That ass lookin' real good, and I hate like hell that I missed out tonight. I had a surprise for you too."

I turned my head and was now face-to-face with him. "You want to tell me now or save it for later?" I asked.

"Now," he whispered. "I took my GED test today. I'm positive that I did real good, but the results won't come back for a few weeks."

Honestly, I wanted to cry. Maybe a GED wasn't a big deal to some people, but the fact that Roc had even put forth the effort to get it truly meant the world to me. If anything, it proved to me that he wanted to make some changes in his life. That was all that mattered.

"I'm so happy for you," was all I could say while continuously pecking his lips. "Things are going to get so much better. Just wait and see."

As soon as Roc spilled the words "All because of you, thing will get better," his son came into the room. So did Vanessa. I couldn't help but give him an extra peck on his lips. Afterward, Roc turned his attention to his son.

"What's up, man?" Roc said, smiling. He reached out his hand to give his son a high five. I said good-bye to Roc again, and he winked. I ignored Vanessa on my way out, walking right past her.

Just as I was getting ready to leave the hospital, she called after me.

"Excuse me," she said, repeating herself at least three times. I kept on walking, as if I didn't hear her. I didn't turn around until I reached my car.

"May I help you?" I asked.

She folded her arms, rolled her eyes, and pursed her lips. Much attitude was on display, and thanks to that, she wasn't getting much of anything out of me.

"Are you supposed to be pregnant by Roc?"

"Are you supposed to be Roc's woman?" I retorted.

"Twenty-four hours a day, seven days a week. You can bet that."

"Well, if you're his woman, then I suggest you go inside and discuss your issues with him. And if you've committed yourself to him twenty-four hours a day, seven days a week, then you have a serious problem on your hand. He's not with you for that many hours in a day and that many days in a week. I know that for a fact, because he's with me. Stop calling my house, little girl, and grow the hell up."

I got in my car to leave, but not before she called me every name she possibly could. One of the ladies from inside the hospital had to come outside to calm her down. She attempted to kick my car, but since I drove off so fast, all I was able to do was smile and wave at her.

No doubt, things were looking up. I'd gotten a new job as an executive administrative assistant, working for the VP at another college. But I wasn't going to make the transition until my current position ended. I wanted to send the message that I appreciated the fourteen years they'd given me and that I wished to leave on a good note. Mr. Wright agreed that it was the right thing to do. The only thing I was sad about was not being able to work for him much longer. Recently, I had confessed that I hated my job. The truth of the matter was, it was my responsibility to make things better, and doing so enabled me to appreciate my blessings even more.

Roc had been out of the hospital for a while now. He'd spent numerous days at my house, and some days at his. He'd even started going to church with me on some Sundays, and I was so grateful for the change I was starting to see in him. Not once did he mention anything about what had gone on between me and Vanessa, but I was positive that he'd gotten an earful from her, especially about the baby. But, as usual, he kept quiet. He was just that kind of man, and he knew how to play his hand. Bringing up Vanessa's name would require him to discuss his relationship with her. And even after all this time, he still wasn't willing to do that. If he did, I knew he'd lie his butt off, so why waste the time? In my heart, I knew Roc cared for her. Their son kept him tied to her. I felt as if he cared for me too, but caring for me just didn't seem like enough.

I turned my focus on getting him to see that there was a more prosperous, legitimate life out there waiting for him. Maybe then, he'd view his future as I did. He had gotten the news that he passed his GED test, and we celebrated that day like none other. I cooked dinner for him, had balloons all over the place, and gave him a keepsake personalized frame that he could put his certificate in. Sex was on the agenda that night, and Roc continuously expressed how grateful he was for me. It was my goal for him to start seeing the light, and that had been my intention for as long as I could remember.

Summer was back in action. The weather in St. Louis was doing its thing. The sun was shining as bright as ever, and it was a sizzling ninety-six degrees outside. People in my neighborhood were outside washing cars, taking walks, swimming in their pools, or jogging. I was standing on my front porch, waiting for Roc to come and take me to the park.

My belly was sticking out enough that anyone could tell there was a baby inside. I continued to work out. Exercise and cutting back on the chocolate were the best things I could do for my body. My hair had grown even longer, and for the day, I took the easy way out and put it in a ponytail. My white maternity shorts were knee length, and the turquoise shirt I wore crisscrossed over my healthy breasts. My turquoise sandals, which I wore for comfort, allowed my pedicure to show.

I could hear the music coming, but the loud zooming sound was what confused me. When the yellow Lamborghini with tinted windows pulled in my driveway, I wasn't sure who it was. I didn't find out until the side door flipped up and Roc got out. He was dressed down in some baggy cargo shorts, a black wife beater, and leather tennis shoes. It looked as if he'd gotten more tattoos on his arms, so I moved closer to take a look.

"What you think?" he asked.

I searched his arms, but there wasn't anything new. "I think you look nice," I said with a smile.

"Nah, I mean about the car. Do you like my new ride?"

"It's nice. I can't wait to see how fast this thing goes," I said sarcastically. "I'm sure you're going to show me."

Roc laughed, flipping the door so I could get in. He got in and covered his eyes with dark shades.

"How are you supposed to see with those dark shades on and with tinted windows?"

"Trust me, I can see. Just make sure your seat belt is on."

I made sure it was fastened. Then Roc took off. The Lamborghini was moving fast, leaving nothing but dust behind it. I hung on for dear life, and as Roc swerved in and out of traffic, I asked him to chill out.

"You can't drive slow in a car like this. It kind of takes over. Do you want to drive so you can see what I'm talkin' about?"

"No, but your foot is the one controlling the accelerator. Lighten up, okay?"

Roc cooled out a little, but when we hit the highway, it was all over with. He took it to the limit, zooming past other cars like a NASCAR driver. I just kept my mouth shut, as the last thing I needed was for him to turn his head toward me and start fussing. It was best that he kept his eyes on the road.

I was relieved when we got off the highway, but I was nervous again when we had to drive through the city. Everybody was looking into the car, trying to see who it was. Several cars kept pace alongside us, making me feel as though I was on pins and needles. Each time, Roc sped away from the cars. When he finally parked the car at Forest Park, I dropped my head back on the headrest, thanking God for my safe arrival.

We got out and started to walk the trail. My arm was tucked under Roc's as we moved at a slow pace.

"It's hot as hell out here," he said. "I'm walkin' for only an hour today. After that, I'm out of here."

"Fine with me. As long as you stop on the way home and get me some frozen yogurt."

"It's your time to buy me some. I paid last time."

"I got you. You know I do."

We walked silently for a moment. I could tell Roc had something on his mind. So did I.

"Since you got your GED, what's next?" I asked.

"I've been thinkin' about takin' up a trade or goin' to a community college. Ain't nothin' in stone yet," Roc said, moving his shades to the top of his head. He squinted from the sun shining in his face. "But listen. I need to tell you somethin', Dez."

Whenever Roc was willing to tell me something, I got worried. My stomach had already tightened. "What's up?" I asked.

"A few weeks ago Ronnie got arrested. He was released on bail, but he gotta go back for his trial."

I wanted to jump for joy, but I played down how happy I was that this man would possibly be away from Roc and out of his life for good.

"I'll be called to testify on Ronnie's behalf, but things may get a li'l tricky."

"What do you mean by that? I mean, if Ronnie has done something wrong, you can't perjure yourself and lie for him. That would put you at risk and possibly come back to haunt you."

Roc stopped in his tracks and turned me so that I faced him. "There's a plan, and all I gotta do is follow through with it. I hate comin' at you like this, but I don't really have a choice."

I had a frown on my face. I didn't like where this conversation was going. "What are you talking about? Please stop beating around the bush."

"What I'm sayin' is, I gotta do some shit you may not like. It'll all be worth it in the end, and I'll be free from this shit once it's done."

I stood stone-faced, looking into Roc's eyes, with tears welling in mine. I felt the bullshit about to go down.

"Don't look at me like that, Ma. You breakin' my heart. I . . . I gotta do this. I owe Ronnie my life, and you have no idea what that man has done for me."

"What do you have to do? Tell me and stop talking in riddles."

"I gotta take the fall. The only way he gon' get out of this is if I do it. Ten years, Ma. That's all I gotta do."

My mouth dropped wide open. I almost fell to my knees. "Are you kidding me!" I yelled. "Ten years! You are willing to do ten years behind bars? I can't believe this shit!" I turned and abruptly walked back to the car. I smacked away the tears that were falling from my eyes and kept shaking my head. Roc rushed after me.

"Dez," he said, grabbing my arm to halt my steps. "Ten years ain't much. I can get out on good behavior, and I may be lookin' at even less than that."

I swear . . . if I had a gun, I would have killed him. "Can you stand there and say to me that ten fucking years in prison is not that much? How can you say that, Roc, when by the time you get out, I'll be fifty? Your baby . . . oh God!" I cried harder and was unable to control my tears. "Your baby will grow up without you."

I gasped and held my stomach. This was too much. Roc pulled me close to his chest and did his best to soothe my pain. Nothing in life had prepared me for this moment. How in the hell had I managed to let him get close to me? How had I allowed something like this happen?

"Don't do it!" I cried more with every deep breath I took. "Please don't do it."

Roc didn't say anything else. He knew, as I did, that he wasn't going to change his mind. On the way to my house, we didn't stop for frozen yogurt, because I didn't want to. And when we got to my house, I got out of the car without inviting him inside. There was nothing left to say. In my eyes, Roc had chosen Ronnie over me and his child.

I went to the bathroom to wipe my teardrop-stained face clean. My eyes were red, and I wished like hell that what he'd told me was in a dream. It wasn't. It was time to face reality. I had fooled myself by believing that Roc could be better than what he was. He was walking away from all the progress he'd made, and what a waste of time it had been. He knocked on the bathroom door.

"Do you want me to stay or go?" he asked.

"Do what you want," I said.

"I want to stay, but you act like you don't want me around. I'm dealin' with this shit too, Dez. The last several weeks of my life ain't been no picnic. I had to tell you what was up. If I didn't say nothin', you would have been mad at my ass for not tellin' you."

I wiped my runny nose with a tissue. "Is there anything I can say or do to get you to change your mind? Please, Roc, tell me. If you won't do it for me, do it for your baby. What about your baby? He or she will need you, and I can't do this by myself. Don't do this to us. Think about the baby, okay?"

"Open the door. I can't talk to you like this."

I opened the door and fell into Roc's waiting arms.

"I already thought about all that you're sayin', Dez, and you know how much I want to be there for my baby. The police are willin' to let some of this shit slide only if they get me or Ronnie to do the time. If not, he'll be looking at twenty or thirty years. I can't let that shit happen.

That nigga took care of me when I was abandoned by my parents. If I didn't have him, I would've been dead. You gotta understand why it's important for me to do this. I hate like hell that I'm bringin' this kind of hurt to you, but my hands are tied."

"When is his trial?"

"It starts in a couple of weeks. Until then, I'm gon' spend as much time with you as I can. But I gotta get busy tying up some loose ends too. Let's take this one day at a time. The last thing I want to do is spend these days arguin' with you or with you bein' upset."

Roc was right. His mind was made up. What good did my being upset do me? It did nothing but add to my hurt.

Roc had been busy "tying up some loose ends." As the days and nights ticked away, I was getting more scared by the minute. I couldn't stop crying and was on an emotional roller coaster. Whenever Roc came over, I put on my game face for him. I knew he was worried as hell about going to jail, but he played it down, as if it didn't bother him. That was until we talked about it one night. He came clean about some of the things he and Ronnie had done, and a tear fell from his eye. I was crushed. It made me fight even more to try to turn this mess around.

I wrote letters to Ronnie's attorney, the prosecutors, and even to the assigned judge, in an attempt to clear Roc's name. No one replied, but when I got an interesting letter that was unrelated to the legal case, I dropped back on the couch in my living room and started to read it. Months ago, right after Roc gave his professional photos to me, I sent his pictures to some of the connections I had made when pursuing my modeling career. One of the modeling agencies had inquired about Roc's pictures and had forwarded them to a well-known beverage maker and an up-and-coming clothing line establishment in New York City. They wanted Roc to call right away. This could be the opportunity he needed.

Excited, I rushed over to the phone to call him. His voice mail came on, so I left a message for him to call me back. An hour went by, and I still hadn't heard from him. I was so eager to talk to him that I snatched up my purse and left. Other than that one time, I had never gone to his penthouse. However, I was going there today. I had to prove to him that there was a way out of this, and that the doors were opening for him to come in.

It took me forty-five minutes to get to Roc's penthouse in downtown St. Louis, and when I got there, I rushed through the lobby and took the elevator to the seventh floor. I could hear the loud music coming through the door, and I paused before knocking. I wasn't sure what I was about to get myself into, but Roc had to change his mind about going to jail, and he had to do it fast.

I knocked, but no one answered, so I knocked again. My knocks got faster and harder, and that was when Roc pulled the door open. The look on his face said it all—I wasn't supposed to be there. He was shirtless, high as hell, and his jean shorts hung low on his waist, showing his boxers. The loud rap music continued to thump in the background, and marijuana smoke filled the air. I could hear people talking and laughing a lot.

Roc appeared to have seen a ghost, and my presence wasn't enough to put a smile on his face. "What are you doin' here?" he asked.

He stepped into the hallway and attempted to close the door behind him but somebody pulled on it, opening it wide. I figured it was Vanessa, but instead, it was another young woman. I hadn't seen her before, but just like me and Vanessa, she was very pretty.

"Who is this?" she said, sipping from the straw that had sunk into her tall glass of Long Island Iced Tea.

"Go on back inside. And don't be walkin' up to my door unless I ask you to."

The chick rolled her eyes at me and walked away. Before Roc could shut the door, I saw his uncle Ronnie in the background, a few more fellas, and even more women.

Roc folded his arms and moved his neck from side to side to stretch it. "What's up, Ma?"

I wasn't about to shed one tear about this. It took everything I had to hold back all that I felt inside. I swallowed hard, then blinked my eyes. "So this is how you do it, huh?" I asked.

He shrugged. "Sometimes. Even more so lately, considerin' what's about to happen. Now, why are you here?"

I gave him the envelope and placed the contact letter on top. "They want you to call them. I hope like hell that you do, but the ball is in your court. You may not get another opportunity like this, Roc, and it would mean the world to me if you would take it."

Roc read the letter and nodded his head. I thought he would smile, but he didn't. All he said was, "I'll call them."

"When?"

"Soon."

The door opened, and Ronnie walked out, then closed it behind him. He gripped Roc's shoulder. "I'm gon' run to my car and get some blow. You au'ight? This bitch ain't out here causin' no trouble, is she?"

My hands trembled, and before I knew it, I swung my hand and landed a hard slap across Ronnie's face. "You low-life son of a bitch," I yelled through gritted teeth.

Roc grabbed my waist to hold me back. Ronnie grabbed my neck and squeezed my jawline with his fingers. He reached for his gun, which he had tucked behind him, then placed it on my temple. I was beyond nervous and could feel beads of sweat dotting my forehead.

"Man, don't you do that shit!" Roc yelled. "Put that muthafucka down and cool the fuck out!"

Ronnie maintained his grip on me and the gun. "Nigga, I told you to get this bitch under control, didn't I?" He shoved my temple with the gun. "The only reason you gon' live is because of that nigga you got growin' in yo' belly. If you wasn't pregnant, I would blow yo' fuckin' brains out for touchin' me."

Roc reached for the handle of the gun, then moved it away from my head. He kept his arm around my waist and backed me away from Ronnie, who turned to walk away.

"By the time I get back up here, her ass better be gone. If not, I may change my mind about killin' her. Do the right thing, baby boy. You already know how I am about bitches who don't respect me."

Roc let go of my waist, then punched the door with his fist. "Why in the fuck did you just do that? I can't believe this shit!"

My eyelids fluttered, and I jumped from the sound of his loud voice. Without saying anything else, I silently thanked God for sparing my life again. I walked past Roc and made my way to the elevator.

"Dez," Roc yelled repeatedly. I kept on walking. "Come back here!"

I got on the elevator and looked out at him as he stood by his door with his hands pressed against it. He could keep his double life. After finally seeing what was going on with my own eyes, I couldn't continue to be a part of this. This chapter in my life was now coming to a tragic halt. Roc turned his head toward me, and our eyes connected once again. The elevator doors slowly closed, symbolizing the near end to what we had shared.

Chapter Thirteen

It was three days into Ronnie's trial, and the only reason I knew that was that I'd been keeping up with the news. He and his posse, including Roc, had some heavy things going on, including money laundering, racketeering, the possession of illegal drugs with the intent to sell, and even murder charges against Ronnie, which, apparently, weren't going to stick. The prosecutors were determined to get Ronnie on anything they had, but just by keeping up with everything that was going on, I could tell their case was sloppy. Numerous people had already been arrested, and every day the news mentioned other individuals who had just been arrested for their connection to the crimes. I just knew I'd see Roc's face on TV, but I never did.

The night before Roc was expected to testify, I couldn't sleep at all. I was upset, and the baby kept moving too, and I turned from side to side, trying to get comfortable. Around midnight, I got out of bed and went into the kitchen to get some orange juice. I stood there drinking it, with thoughts of Roc heavy on my mind. I hadn't talked to him or heard from him since that day at his penthouse, and I wasn't even sure if I was going to Ronnie's trial. A huge part of me still wanted Roc to change his mind about taking the fall for his uncle, and I knew that if he saw me, maybe, just maybe, he would come to his senses. I had no idea if he had called the modeling agency or not, but I hoped that tomorrow would bring more good news than bad.

As I was about to turn off the kitchen light, I heard a squeaking sound coming from my backyard. I cautiously walked to the back door, and when I pulled it open, I saw Roc outside, on the patio, sitting on my swing. He was smoking a cigar, but he put it out with his foot before I walked up to him. I sat next to him, gathering my robe to close it. Yes, I wanted to slap him, curse him, and order him to go home, but my heart went out to the man I had fallen in love with. I could tell he was going through something deep. I felt no need to argue about things that didn't matter right now. Tonight I would be there for Roc, but tomorrow he needed to be there for me. I took his hand and held it in mine.

"Are you worried?" I asked. "I know that's a dumb question, but I have to ask."

"Yeah, I'm worried. That's why I'm here. I need peace. I've always known I could get that with you."

"Then why didn't you knock to let me know you were here?"

"I was goin' to, but I wanted to chill out here first."

I stood, then tried to pull him up from the swing. "Come on. Let's go inside."

"Nope," he said, not making a move.

"Why? Because I'm in trouble?"

Finally, he smiled. The whites came out, and so did the dimples. "Hell, yeah, you in trouble. Big . . . twelve-inch trouble. Can I make love to you?"

As much as I wanted to, I couldn't. It was now time for Roc to stop making me promises and show me that he was serious about changing his life around.

"No. I don't want to go there tonight. We have some things that need to be resolved, and you know exactly what they are. The last thing I want to do is bring more stress upon you, so let's just go inside and enjoy our night together." I took Roc's hand, but he still didn't budge.

"Nah, let's stay right here," he said. "We can play back the day when it all got started. Maybe I can persuade you to change your mind."

"But you complained about not having enough room. Remember?"

"Yeah, but I've gotten much more creative since then too."

Roc remained on the swing, and I stood in front of him. I cradled his face with my hands, and he laid the side of his head against my stomach.

"So, this may be it, huh?" I asked. "It doesn't have to be, and remember, the choice is yours. Tell them about Ronnie, Roc. Free yourself and tell them everything you know. They want him, not you."

Roc directed me back onto the swing and lay behind me, like the first time he entered me. "I don't want to talk about tomorrow, okay? This night is for you and me, Ma. That's it. Now, lie on your back so I can kiss my baby."

Ever since I'd got pregnant, Roc had been making me open my legs so he could "kiss his baby." This night was no different. He placed tender, loving kisses on the outside crotch of my panties, because I wouldn't remove them. Normally, he'd kiss my coochie lips, telling the baby how much he loved *him*. And even though things hadn't gone as he planned tonight, I did offer him my kisses. I lifted my head and gave him juicy, unforgettable kisses throughout the night. I also told him how much I loved him. The way I felt now, there was no more denying my feelings.

"Who you wit', Roc? Tell me, who exactly are you with?" I asked as we lay there on the swing.

"Wit' you," he assured me. "I love you too, and I'm stickin' wit' you."

Tomorrow would surely tell if there was any validity to his words.

***

The courtroom was packed with people. I had gotten there just in time to find a place to sit. The normal crew was in full effect, and there was no question in my mind that Vanessa was there too. She was, but thank God she had sense enough to leave their son at home. She kept turning her head to look at me. I was glad that my belly was now showing. I wore a beautiful white linen maternity dress, and my hair was thick and full. Several long black beads hung from my neck, and my Nine West Jamil open-toed sandals really set me off.

Roc had left my house early in the morning. I hadn't seen him or talked to him since then. He told me he had to meet with Ronnie's lawyers, and I prayed that everything went well. Before he left, I begged and pleaded with him again to do the right thing, but he never gave me confirmation that he would. His embraces and continuous kisses to my forehead worried me. And before he left, he told me everything would be okay.

I sat there, biting my nails and waiting for things to get started. Every time Vanessa turned to look at me, I looked in another direction. I wasn't there to confront her; I was there for Roc. Before long, Ronnie made his way into the courtroom, and so did his lawyers. The prosecutors had been working their case for the past three days, and now it was Ronnie's lawyers' turn.

When the judge came in, everybody stood. My legs started to shake a bit, but I calmed down once I sat. Roc hadn't come in yet, but as soon as things got settled, Ronnie's lawyers didn't waste any time calling for their first witness. The first person they called was Roc. He came through the double wooden doors, dressed in a navy blue suit. A lighter blue shirt was underneath, closed tightly by a silk tie. His hair was flowing in waves, and his lining was done to perfection. He had toned down the diamonds, but he did have one in his left ear. Everyone in the courtroom turned to take a look, and as he passed by me, he turned his head slightly to the side and winked. I watched as he made his way up to the front, and even though I couldn't see if he made eye contact with Vanessa on his way by, her smile at him implied that he did.

Roc was sworn in, and then he took a seat on the witness stand. From the beginning, and for question after question, Roc defended Ronnie. He almost made him seem like an angel, but everyone knew that was a bunch of bullshit. I was kind of happy about the way things were going until the prosecutor got his chance to cross-examine. That was when things took a turn for the worse. The prosecutor yelled at Roc to "man up" and encouraged him not to perjure himself any more than he already had.

"I want the truth," he yelled and pointed his finger at Roc. "The whole truth and nothing but the truth!" he said, turning and pointing to Ronnie. "With that, that son of a bitch goes to jail!"

I eased forward in my seat and uncrossed my sweating legs, which had started to tremble. My eyes were glued on Roc. He glanced at me; then his eyes shifted to Vanessa for a second. He then looked at his lap and cleared his throat.

"I, uh . . ." He paused to take a hard swallow. He looked up, then cocked his head to the side. His eyes shifted to Ronnie, who slowly nodded. "Ronnie's not the one who's been behind all of this."

I moved my head from side to side and tightened my lips to muffle my words. Roc took another glance at me, and I mouthed, "No."

The lawyer opened his jacket, and with pure arrogance, he placed his hands in his pockets. "Then who is responsible, Mr. Dawson? You? Somebody's got to pay for these crimes, so tell me. Will it be him or someone else?"

Roc didn't hesitate. "It's gon' be me. I've been the mastermind behind all of this. It should be me who goes to jail, not Ronnie."

The courtroom erupted with noises, but none were louder than the judge slamming down his gavel. With each loud thud, it felt as if he was slamming the gavel into my heart. I took a deep breath and sucked in the air around me, trying not to faint. *How could he?* I kept thinking. I stared at Roc, hoping that he would make eye contact with me again. He did, and I immediately had flashbacks of meeting him at the car wash, the club . . . of our intimate moments on the swing, at the cabin. Of our talks and the movies we watched together . . . our lengthy walks in the park, the day I told him I was pregnant, the late-night dinners we shared. I hoped he was thinking what I was, and through the look in my eyes, I wanted to transmit our times together.

Out of all those times together, though, last night stuck in my head like glue. I had asked Roc who he was with, and he'd said he was with me. Today revealed what I'd known all along. Roc wasn't with me, nor was he in love with me. Fortunately, the same applied to Vanessa. He was with Ronnie. The love Roc had for Ronnie was worth giving up everything.

Following the plan, Roc proceeded to confess to the prosecutors all that he'd done. The entire courtroom took in every word he said, and so did the judge. When Roc was finished, the judge called for the bailiff to arrest him, and the courtroom turned into chaos. Vanessa wailed loudly and dropped to her knees in tears. Some other people were crying, but many were left shaking their heads. Ronnie leaned back in his chair, with his hands resting on the back of his head. Roc stood tall, and without a blink, his eyes stayed on Ronnie. He put his hands behind his back, and for the last time, his eyes shifted to me. He winked again, and I got up, then left my seat. I shed not one tear and didn't dare to look back.

Damn him, I thought. How and why did I ever allow somebody like him to come into my life?

The answer to my question came only a few months later. I gave birth to a five-pound, six-ounce baby girl. While going through my divorce with Reggie, I had asked God to take away my lonely nights and remove my pain. There were many mountains to climb and much pain to endure, but when my daughter was born, He gave me everything I had asked for and more. Latrel started coming home from school more often, just to spend time with his little sister and me. Nothing in the world meant more to me than being with my children. I was overwhelmed by happiness, especially when I saw the two of them together.

Roc had been writing me for a little over a year, and getting no response. I kept all his letters, but I was rarely moved by anything he said. He begged me to come see him and wanted me to send pictures of myself and his child. I did neither. Yet I struggled with the thought of going to see him, because I still had feelings for him. I didn't seriously consider going to see him until he or someone else sent me his framed GED. In the attached note he told me it belonged to me, and he wanted to make sure that his daughter knew all about him. I hadn't a clue how Roc knew we'd had a daughter, but I was sure someone had been paying attention.

The following week, I made arrangements to go see Roc. Latrel was home, so his sister, Chassidy, stayed with him. I put some of her pictures in my purse and took the long drive to see Roc. All that I had to do to be in his presence at the prison was ridiculous. I sat on a cold bench, waiting for Roc to come out. I was a year older, and my full figure was still going strong. I sported a button-down dress that cut right above my knees. It seemed just right for the occasion—I definitely wasn't trying to look sexy.

When the door opened, I quickly looked up, and there stood Roc. A guard was behind him, but he stood at the door. Dressed in an oversize blue shirt and baggy jeans that were cuffed at the bottom, Roc made his way over to me with a smile.

"It's about damn time," he said, sitting across from me. "I thought you'd never get here."

I spoke softly, as seeing him always did something to me. It hurt like hell that all I could do was hug him. "How have you been? In your letters you seem fine, but I'm not so sure."

"I'm good, but I can always be better. I miss doin' me. This place don't allow any of that."

"I'm sure it has its limitations. You are definitely not the kind of man who plays by the rules."

Roc laughed. "That's puttin' it mildly. Ronnie makes sure that I get some special privileges in here, so I work with what I can."

The thought of Ronnie made me cringe. I instantly got quiet.

"So where my pictures at? I know you brought me some."

I had to be thoroughly checked before coming in, and the pictures of his daughter had been placed in a ziplock bag.

"This is Chassidy," I said, handing the pictures over to him. "As you can see, she is a baby model and has a really bright future ahead of her."

Roc grinned from ear to ear while looking at the pictures. I was so sure that he saw much of himself in her. "Damn, she's beautiful," he said. "I had no doubt she'd be this pretty, and we did good, didn't we?"

"Yes, we did. Latrel told me to tell you hi too, and the two of them spend a lot of time together."

"Tell him I said, 'What's up?' Reggie ain't been snoopin' around, has he? Or are you gon' hang in there and wait for me?" Roc put his hands behind his head, waiting for an answer. The guard reminded him to keep his hands on the table, where he could see them.

"No, Reggie hasn't been coming around. I've been pretty content by myself."

"But you ain't answer the second part to my question. Are you gon' be there for me when I get out of here? I've been readin' a lot, even been reading some of those damn books you read. It be some freaky shit goin' on in them books, and no wonder your ass stay horny. I also been talkin' to a brotha in here about how I can earn myself another degree. I already started to sharpin' my skills, and you'd be surprised by all the positive things I've been doin'."

"Are you willing to do those things when you get out? That's the question. I can't make you any promises, Roc, and unfortunately, I can't keep coming back here to see you like this. I am still so angry about what you cost us, and I don't know when I'll be able to completely forgive you."

Roc looked down at Chassidy's pictures. "Sounds like I'm in trouble," he said, then smiled.

I laughed. "Big-ass trouble!"

"Well, it's a good thing that trouble don't always last too long. I'm gon' get out of here, Ma, and I comin' for you. I ain't gon' make you no promises about what I'm gon' do. I just have to show you what's up."

"Whatever you do, do it for yourself. And I hate to cut this short, but I have to get back home. Latrel is heading back to school tonight. I told him I wouldn't be long."

Roc nodded and reached out to touch my hand. "Take care of my baby and keep sending me pictures. I still got that one of you that was on my fridge, but I want more. These niggas in here goin' crazy over that picture of you, and I still kiss that muthafucka every mornin' that I wake up. I miss rockin' that pussy to sleep, and sometimes I feel as though I'm going crazy because I can't touch you. I appreciate everything you done for me, Dez, and no matter what you think, I have a special kind of love for you in my heart. This shit was destined. It couldn't have turned out any other way. It was time for me to pay the piper, learn from my mistakes, and so be it."

I saw things much differently than Roc did, but I didn't say what I felt—betrayed. To me, he had had a choice. Many doors had opened for him, but he had chosen to close them. Opportunity after opportunity had presented itself, but Roc had a mind-set that the world he lived in was set in stone by those who came before him. According to him, his mother, father, and Ronnie had set it all up for him, leaving him very few options. He had had options, and he'd settled for what he thought was best. This last time, his best wasn't good enough for him, for me, or for his children. His latest decision affected many lives, and there was no way for me to accept that this was destined.

The guard allowed Roc and me to embrace. He even threw in a lengthy kiss, implying that it was one of his privileges. We stood forehead to forehead, searching each other's eyes.

"Take care, Snookums. I'll write you back and keep in touch."

"No doubt. When you get home, do me a favor. Look in your garage, by the lawn mower, okay? I got a surprise for you, and I want you to keep it."

I nodded, and after one final kiss, Roc left the room.

I was so happy on my way back home. I was glad that I'd gone to see him. It had given me closure, and that was truly something I'd needed.

When I got back home, Latrel was in the yard, playing with Chassidy. I kissed both of them and then went to the garage to see what Roc had left. While searching, I found a black leather briefcase tucked away in the corner. I flipped the locks, and it came open. Inside was a lot of money. There were stacks and stacks of one-hundred-dollar bills. I couldn't even imagine how much money it was. I knew it was enough money to allow me to quit my job and to live off for the rest of my life. I could travel the world and pay for Chassidy's education. Roc had put a note inside the briefcase, telling me that he had saved this money for a rainy day.

I knew this day would come, and I want you and my child to have everything y'all need.
Love, Snookums

I kept the note but closed the briefcase tight. Didn't he get to know me at all? I thought. I rushed outside and told Latrel that I would be right back. I knew he had to drive back to school tonight, but I had to do this. I drove like a bat out of hell to Roc's penthouse, and just my luck, Ronnie was standing outside, talking to several men. Some kids were nearby, playing on a playground, and many young men were outside playing basketball. I parked and made my way up to Ronnie with the briefcase in my hand.

"Don't start none, won't be none," he said.

"Go to hell, Ronnie. And I want you to know that this shit ain't over just yet. I'm going to do everything in my power to make sure you pay for what you've done to Roc. Your downfall is definitely coming." I flipped open the briefcase. Several guns were aimed at me.

"Hold it down," Ronnie ordered the men around him.

"This belongs to you." I tossed the briefcase high up in the air, causing all the money to tumble down like rain. The young men playing basketball chased after the money, and so did the kids from the playground.

I headed back to my car, not knowing if a bullet would catch me from behind or not. I heard Ronnie mumble, "Stupid bitch," and then he yelled for his partners to get as much of the money as they could. I sped off, closing one long chapter in my life, happily waiting for the next.

Latrel was home for the summer and would start his junior year at college in the fall. He was doing well in school, and I couldn't be more proud. Reggie was glad that his son was doing well too, and even though we both felt the same way, unfortunately, we never rekindled our friendship. He was so upset with me for getting pregnant by Roc, and according to Reggie, each time he saw Chassidy, it broke his heart. I was sorry to hear that, because my heart was fulfilled. He was the one who was already planning a second divorce. It was so funny how things had managed to turn out.

The day of my visit, I told Roc that I would keep in touch, but our conversations were here, there, and far between. I had received at least a hundred letters from him, but he'd gotten just a few from me. I wanted so badly to forgive him for taking the fall for Ronnie, but as I watched Chassidy grow without having him in her life, I couldn't get over what he'd done. It wasn't like Roc would've been the "perfect" role model or anything, but to me, he could have changed his life around and tried to be there for his daughter. He was starting to prove that he wanted to do it, but the grip that Ronnie had on him was hard to break. Knowing so, I washed my hands clean and did my best never to look back.

I could hear Latrel outside, playing with Chassidy in the rubber-ducky blow-up swimming pool he'd gotten her. He had the music up loud, but I could hear the water splashing, along with her laughter. I was in the kitchen, preparing dinner, and had bent over to remove the croissants from the oven. I burnt my hand and immediately snatched it away from the hot pan.

"Ouch," I yelled, then placed the tip of my tongue on my finger to cool it. I opened the pantry closet and looked for my oven mitt. The back door came open, and I heard Chassidy calling for me.

"Here I come, sweetie," I said, still looking for my mitt. "Latrel, turn that music down a little. Did you turn off the water outside?"

He didn't answer. When I stepped away from the closet to see why, I got the shock of my life. My heart picked up speed. I blinked several times just to be sure. I saw those dimples, which I'd figured I'd never see again. Those pearly whites were still going strong, and the man whom I craved was still as clean cut as ever. Roc balanced Chassidy on his shoulders, while she bent down and pecked the top of his head.

"Daddy's home," he said. "I told you I was gon' do this, didn't I? Question is . . . who you wit', Dez? You still wit' me, or you wit' some other nigga? Tell me what's up."

I swallowed, as speechless as ever. I hadn't a clue how I would answer his question, because a huge part of me had thought this day would never come.

Chapter Fourteen

I stood there in shock. The verdict wasn't in yet about Roc being the man I needed him to be. He didn't understand that things had changed. I had required very little room for error in my relationships. The drama he had previously brought my way—that he could do no more.

According to him, somehow or someway, he had managed to get out of the ten-year bid he'd been sentenced to and had been released from Bonne Terre Correctional Facility after completing only a year and a half. He mentioned that his lawyer had gotten the sentence reduced, but there had to be more to it. Either way, I was very glad about that. The thought of him being able to be a father to Chassidy pleased my heart.

"Now that you know all of that," he said, "let me ask you again. Who ya wit', Dez?"

"I'm not sure who I'm down with. There is a lot at stake, and I don't know if I can trust you again. I suspect that Vanessa is still in the picture, and what about Ronnie? I don't know if I can deal with some of the mess I put up with before. I'm sure you understand my concerns."

"I do, but let's face it. You've never trusted me. Vanessa won't be no problem for us, and neither will Ronnie."

I could have laughed at his response, only because he knew that was a lie. "It would be so wrong of me to go there with you, so I won't. Just . . . just give me a hug and allow me to say, 'Welcome home.'"

I moved closer to Roc, and as soon as his arms eased around my waist, the feelings for him that I had been unable to release came back to life. I wasn't sure if this connection I had with him would be everlasting or if a part of me wanted to keep this going for the sake of our child. That answer would come soon, but there was no doubt that I was happy to see him.

It was scorching hot outside, but Roc spent much of the afternoon trying to get to know Chassidy. He played with her in the swimming pool, chased her around the spacious backyard, watched TV with her, and even cut the grass. It was good seeing the two of them together, and she took to him very well. Later that day, we left and followed Latrel back to college. After staying with him for a couple of hours, we returned home.

Chassidy was exhausted by the time we walked back into the house, so I laid her down for a nap, and then went into the kitchen, where Roc was sitting shirtless at the kitchen table, sipping from a Coke can and eating some barbecue-flavored potato chips. The calories would do him no harm, as the muscular frame that he'd had before did not compare to the one he now had. His biceps looked bigger, his chest was carved to perfection, and more tattoos covered his arms. His daily workout regime in prison had definitely paid off. I couldn't ignore the fact that seeing him always made my panties moist and my palms sweat. Today was no exception.

With Roc having been in prison, certain things came to my mind about what kind of person he was now. Was he still the young man who lived in the fast lane, selling drugs and having sex with many different women? Was he still willing to do whatever his Uncle Ronnie wanted him to do? Was movin' and shakin' still his occupation? And what could he offer me? Basically, had he matured at all, and had being in prison redeemed him? I sat across the table from him, eager to continue our conversation from earlier.

"Now that we have a little more time to talk, are you telling me that you're a changed man?"

Roc squinted and then stared deeply into my eyes. "I'll let you decide. As far as I know, I'm done with all that mess. Give me a chance to show you what's up, and you won't regret it. I've had time to reflect on some things, and my goal is to live a better life. I tried my way before, so let's roll with your way."

I wasn't sure if Roc could handle doing things my way. My way consisted of him getting a job, helping me take care of our daughter, leaving the drug game behind him, making sure there was no drama from Vanessa, and distancing himself from the people around him who had helped to bring him down, particularly Ronnie.

"Then let's. As for now, it's late and I'm going to bed. Will you be joining me?"

"I thought you'd never ask."

Surprisingly, all I allowed Roc to do that night was hold me in his arms. As we lay in bed, I questioned his early release and his future plans. He insisted that with lots of money and a damn good lawyer, anything was possible. As for his future, he wasn't sure. Lord knows I wanted to have sex with him, but opening my legs to him just didn't seem right. My life had changed in so many different ways while he'd been gone. Furthermore, I hadn't forgiven him yet for choosing to take the fall for Ronnie, and more than anything, I couldn't afford any setbacks.

My new career with Florissant Community College was going strong. Things were finally looking up. I couldn't, however, say the same for Reggie. According to Latrel, Reggie was in the midst of finalizing his divorce, which was turning out to be more costly for him than ours had been. I had asked only for what was due me, but his new wife, who he'd been married to for only four months, she wanted it all! The house, the cars, part ownership of his real estate business, and ten thousand dollars a month in spousal support. I couldn't believe all that she was asking for, and to my recollection, Reggie didn't have that much money to dish out. I truly wished him the best with his situation, but that was what he got for marrying a woman he had known for less than a year.

Thinking about Reggie's situation made me think about how Roc would impact my life going forward. I had spoken to him briefly yesterday, but he'd seemed busy. He'd been trying to move his things from the penthouse he once had to the condo he was now living in on the south side of St. Louis.

While at work, I wiggled my fingers on the side of my face and eyeballed the phone on my desk. I contemplated calling him. Why? Because he'd said he was busy, and since he hadn't called me back, maybe that meant he was *still* busy. I wanted to allow him all the time he needed to get settled, so I quickly dropped my thought about calling him and got back to work.

Minutes later, the ringing phone interrupted me.

"Mr. Anderson's office. How may I help you?"

"Desa Rae, this is Sherri. Is my dad around?"

Sherri was my boss's daughter. He would never tell his kids when he was going out of town. And it wasn't my place to tell them, either. "No, he isn't, Sherri. He's out of the office today, but you may want to try his cell phone."

"Okay. Thanks. I'll do that, but in the meantime, how's Latrel doing?"

"He's fine. I had hoped the two of you would go out on another date, but he told me how busy both of you are."

"Unfortunately, we are. But I have every intention of calling him soon. You know I'm in med school, and I never have time to do much of anything."

"Oh, I understand, sweetie. You definitely don't have to explain anything to me. I'm sure Latrel understands too. Call him when you can. He did mention you the other day, and I'm sure he would be happy to hear from you."

"I sure will. Let me call my dad now, and be sure to tell Latrel I'll call him soon."

I told Sherri that I would, but shame on me for lying. Latrel hadn't mentioned her at all. He'd told me that the two of them didn't click. Personally, I thought Sherri was perfect for Latrel, especially since she was in med school, and from what Latrel had said, she was a virgin. She seemed better than those hoochie mamas he'd been seeing, for sure.

Mr. Anderson was out for the entire week. I was caught up on most of my work, but just to keep busy, I started merging a letter that wasn't supposed to go out to the students until next week. Next to me was a pretty red basket filled with chocolate chip cookies. I had already eaten three of them. I couldn't believe how much my appetite had increased since Roc had come home. I'd probably picked up five pounds in two days, and I couldn't stop snacking. It was probably my nerves, and even though I hated to go there, I wondered if he was still okay with the *weight* thing. He did compliment me on how beautiful I was, but it was hard to hide the ten pounds I had packed on over the past few months. My hips were more curvaceous, and my thighs had gotten thicker. I guessed the weight was going to the right places, and for that reason, I couldn't complain.

Getting back to my letters, I scooted my chair up to my desk. My cubicle was so spacious that I had access to everything, including a four-in-one HP printer, fax, copier, and scanner. I also had access to my Hershey's Kisses, so I reached over to grab one. After that, I reached for the phone to call Roc. He answered right away.

"Dez," he said immediately. "I'ma hit you up in about ten minutes. I'm in the middle of doin' somethin'."

Well, crack my face, why don't you? "Uh, okay. I'm at work, so call me here."

"Will do."

He hung up, leaving me to wonder what was up. Seemed like that spark he had once had for me wasn't there anymore. I could be wrong, but time would tell.

Less than five minutes later, the phone rang. I knew it was Roc by looking at the flashing number.

"Desa Rae Jenkins," I said.

"Dez, it's me. I was just callin' you back. What's up?"

"I didn't want anything. Just checking to see if you got settled in your new place. Did you?"

"Just about. I still have a few things to do, but it's gon' take a lot to make my condo feel like home. It's a li'l cramped for my taste, but a nigga gotta do what he must do to stay out of jail."

"I agree, and leaving the past behind, especially the drug game, is a good start."

Roc was silent. All I heard was a deep sigh on the other end.

"Roc, are you there?"

"Yeah, I'm here. But before we get off on the wrong foot, let me say somethin' to you, au'ight? I know I've made some mistakes, but there are no guarantees that more mistakes won't happen. All you need to know is that I'm gon' do my best to stay on the right track, but even my best may not be good enough for you. If we hook up again, and I truly hope we do, please don't nag me about my decisions in life. They are mine to make, and mine only. If you can't handle that, then don't waste your time."

Oh, no, he didn't just try to tell me off, did he? I thought. I knew he was busy trying to get everything in order, and I figured coming home to something new was frustrating. Knowing so, I remained calm. "I just want the best for you, that's all. If my comment offended you, I apologize."

"Yes, some of your comments offend me. Especially when I wanted to get at you the other night, and all you wanted to do was tell me what you expected me to do. That shit is a turnoff, Ma. I'm not down with nobody tryin' to give me orders. I've been takin' orders for the past year and a half. Had enough of that shit, so time-out."

I hadn't looked at it from his point of view, but now I realized that he was right. I had been nagging him. "Forgive me, as it's the motherly thing in me that always kicks in. With that being said, does this mean I'm in trouble? I hope so."

Roc laughed out loud. It put a smile on my face as I visualized his deep dimples.

"Big, eleven and a half, maybe twelve inches of trouble."

"Wow. I'm impressed, but is that all you got? I didn't know a penis could grow that fast, but I'm willing to take whatever you have. The question is, when can I get it?"

"It's all yours. All you have to do is say the word. My place or yours? Today or tomorrow? Morning or night? A bed, table, shower, or the floor?"

"I'll let you decide. Just let me know so I can make some arrangements for our beautiful daughter."

"Yeah, you may have to do that, because I don't want her around to witness all the hollerin' and screamin' I may cause you to do. Come to my place tonight. I will make sure all the floors are clean."

"Can't wait," I said with excitement, picking up a pen. "Address, please."

Roc gave me his address and the directions to his place near Tower Grove Park. Afterward, I called Monica to see if she would watch Chassidy for me. She told me to bring her over for the weekend. I thanked her and told her I would drop off Chassidy around 6:00 p.m.

I couldn't wait to see Roc, and unfortunately for me, yes, I was in trouble. The only person I'd had sex with in Roc's absence was a man I'd met at work named Greg. We went out a few times, but I wasn't feeling him at all. He was boring to be with. I had to pretend as if I was enjoying our dates. I thought that having sex with him would help to break the ice, but that did nothing but turn me off more. He was the same age as me and was very nice, but he was not for me. He continued to pursue me for a while and just recently backed off. Thank God. I guessed Roc had spoiled me. I knew it would be difficult to find a man who was capable of making my body do what he made it do, and for the record, it was time for me to have some fun, which seemed long overdue.

A few hours later, I stood at Roc's door, wearing the sundress he had always liked to see me in. Flip-flops were on my feet, and my straight hair was parted down the middle. It hung along each side of my face and fell way past my shoulders. Needless to say, I was comfortable. I was sure that Roc would appreciate my look.

I knocked on the door, knowing that I was late. I was also feeling a bit nervous. My eyes scanned the address that I had written on the paper, and I compared it to the numbers on the newly built two-family flat with stairs going up on one side and down on the other side. The landscaping was beautiful, and the huge picture windows on the front gave the property a luxurious look. I couldn't understand why I was uncomfortable with this, especially since I had gotten to know Roc so well. I took several deep breaths before ringing the doorbell. I could hear Roc's hard footsteps coming down the stairs.

"Who out there ringin' my bell?" he asked playfully.

"Desa Rae."

"Who?"

"You heard me, Roc. Stop playing."

"You're late."

"And?"

"And if it were me, you would be all in my shit. So I'm gettin' in yours."

"Well, that's why I'm here. I was hoping that you would get into, well, something."

He opened the door with a heart-melting smile on his face. He wore a pair of dark denim jeans, which hung very low, showing his light blue boxers and rock-hard abs. His eyes scanned my dress, and his smile got even wider. So did the door. "Damn, Ma. You out there lookin' all sexy and shit. Please come in."

I stepped inside, blushing. "I thought you would like my dress, and just so you know, I have no complaints, either."

Roc shut the door and then turned to face me. His eyes dropped to my lips, and even though we had kissed the other day, this time felt different. My nervousness subsided, and when his hands went underneath my dress to touch my bare ass, I felt relieved. He backed away from our intense kiss.

"Did I tell you how much I love this dress? Seein' you in it always makes my dick ready to aim and shoot."

I rested my arms on his shoulders, already feeling his hardness. "I think you appreciate what's underneath my dress more, but that's just my opinion."

He winked and continued to feel my ass. "Both. And to be honest, I appreciate all of it. Every single bit of it."

My hands roamed his rock-hard body, and I could feel my temperature rising. As we both indulged ourselves, Roc leaned back on the steps leading upstairs and pulled me on top of him. I could feel cool air on my ass—every bit of it was now exposed.

I paused from the intense kiss, just to look him in the eyes. "Aren't you going to show me around first? We could talk about how your day went or how mine went before we start screwing each other's brains out, right?"

"As hard as my dick is right now, we gon' have to save the chitchat for later. And trust me when I say you will get the tour you've been waitin' for in just a few minutes."

Roc attempted to raise my dress over my head, but I backed up. I stood, looking at him as he leaned back on the stairs, resting on his elbows.

"Can we at least get up the stairs? I need way more room than this. It's not like I weigh a buck o' five."

"You are the one who always told me to be creative and work with what space I have. You do remember tellin' me that, don't you?"

I couldn't deny my own words, but the stairs were not my cup of tea. I started up the stairs, ignoring Roc as I passed by him. When I reached the top, he stood close behind me. I could see into the small living room, which was to my right, and into his bedroom, which was down the hallway to my left. Roc wasted no time removing his jeans and tossing them down the stairs. He pulled the top of my sundress apart, ripping it straight down the middle. Wondering if I cared? Hell no, I didn't. My thick breasts were now exposed, and so was my shaved pussy. Roc peeled the sundress away from my body, tossing it down the stairs as well.

In no way could I make it to the living room or to his bedroom, so I lay back on what I assumed was a very clean carpeted floor. Within seconds, Roc rested his body between my trembling legs, allowing me to feel a big piece of hard meat. I couldn't wait for him to enter me. He started in on my wobbly breasts, squeezing them in his hands and sucking them at the same time. I was on fire. All I could do was rub my hands all over his sexy, dark body, which had me hooked! I could already feel my juices boiling over, and when Roc slipped his finger inside of me, I gasped out loud. He made many rotations, causing my groans to increase. I couldn't take the foreplay much longer and was in a rush to receive the satisfaction I had waited on for so long. I reached down, touching his monstrous dick, which made my mouth water.

"Baby, *please* put on a condom. Hurry, okay?" I begged.

Roc removed his fingers from inside of me, unleashing a small flood of my juices. He sucked his wet fingers and kneeled between my legs. Putting me in position, he placed my legs around his back. He lightly rubbed his hardness against my slit, causing my eyelids to flutter. As he toyed with my insides and circled his mushroom head around my clit, I felt so weak for him.

"Do I have to use a condom?" he asked. "I really don't want to, and I'm dyin' to feel the real deal."

The foreplay he delivered was feeling so good to me, and stopping the action would have been a crime. But I guessed I was about to commit one, because there was no way in hell he was entering me again without a condom. I reached down and moved his hardness away from me.

"Please. Let's do this the right way. I know you understand my concerns."

He shrugged. "I don't, but when we're finished, I'm sure you'll tell me."

I kept quiet. I didn't want to ruin the moment. Roc stood up, then made his way down the long hallway and into his bedroom. I sat up on my elbows, observing him open a drawer and break open a condom package. I was in awe as I looked at his side profile. The sight of his bulging muscles made me hungry. I got off the floor and made my way into his bedroom. He had barely put the condom on before I moved him back to the bed and kneeled on the floor in front of him. I held his hardness in my hands, preparing myself to please him in every way possible.

"Nice room," I said, not paying much attention to the room, and instead focusing more on my grip on his stick.

"I knew you would like it," he replied, looking at his goods with a wicked grin.

I covered his package with my mouth, making sure it hit the back of my deep throat. Due to his size, that wasn't an easy task. Roc dropped back on the bed and allowed me to have my way with him. Almost immediately, I brought him to an eruption.

"Dezzz," he whined. "Damn, you're good at that shit."

I gave him little time to regroup and expected him to return the favor. I eased my way onto the bed and then positioned myself so my thighs straddled his face. My pussy sank to his thick lips, and he already knew what to do with it. As his tongue dipped into my overheated pocket, all I could shout was, "Welcome home, baby. I'm so glad you're home!"

Hopefully, I would feel the same way tomorrow.

Chapter Fifteen

I slowly opened my eyes, slightly remembering parts of a dream I'd had about my mother. All I remembered was her sitting at a table, telling me to be very careful about my choices. She was holding Chassidy in her arms, and for some reason, Reggie stood beside her, laughing. It was a very weird dream, and I was so glad to come out of it. I yawned and sat up to observe my surroundings. I was still at Roc's place, but he was nowhere in sight. His room was lit up by a picture window that had no curtains, and the sun shone so bright. In front of me was a flat-screen television, which sat on an entertainment center. A wavy black microfiber chaise was next to the queen-size bed I was in, and a dresser with a mirror was to the left of the bed. A ceiling fan in the shape of a palm tree hung from above, and the beige-colored walls looked freshly painted. The whole room was quite simple. It was nice, but not as lavish as his penthouse.

Feeling a bit woozy, I pulled the soft blue sheets away from my body and sat up on the edge of the bed. Yes, Roc had sexed me all night; my coochie was real tender. More than anything, I needed a shower. I also needed to find something to put on, since my flowered dress was now history. There were two doors in Roc's bedroom besides the door that led out to the hallway. I didn't know what was behind the other two doors, but when I opened one, I found a very long closet filled with clothes and shoes. I could tell Roc still had some unpacking to do. I reached for the first thing I saw, and that was a long purple and yellow Lakers T-shirt. After I put it on, I opened the other door. That one led to a bathroom. I walked in, looked at myself in the long mirror, and teased my wild hair. Once my hair was in place, I splashed cold water on my face, then patted it dry with my hands. I wanted to brush my teeth, but my toothbrush was in my purse. I couldn't remember where I had left that, but I assumed it was somewhere near the stairs.

I left the bathroom and started down the hallway to find Roc. Almost immediately, I could hear voices. The floor squeaked a little, so I halted my steps just to listen in on the conversation.

"I'm tellin' y'all, them fools had me fucked up," Roc said. "I was one nigga they didn't want to pull them gates open for, and I wanted to spit on that white son of a bitch who opened it. But all I did was smile at his ass and salute! Adios, muthafucka. I'm out!"

I heard hand slapping; then another voice chimed in. "That's how you gotta do 'em. And the fact that you never showed fear, nor did yo' ass get in any trouble—it fucked them up. I told you Watts was gon' make a way out of no way, but I had to pay that fat sucker a bundle of cash. It was worth it, though, baby boy. You know I will always have yo' back."

I heard the sound of hand slapping again, and unfortunately for me, I knew that voice all too well. It was Ronnie. Why Roc would want us underneath the same roof at the same time, I didn't know. I continued to listen and heard another voice.

"I do think it's a good idea for you to lay low for a while. Ronnie, me, and BJ got this. You know we gon' hold it down for you."

"Just like you held down Vanessa while I was away, right? Sippi, you know I'm still bitter about that shit, but it takes a ho to show her true colors when a nigga get locked up."

"I hit that bitch twice. If you got a beef about it, take it up with her. She the one who came at me. I'm not gon' turn down no available pussy. Besides, you told me she was just your baby's mama. Nothin' more, nothin' less. Correct?"

I inched forward, waiting to hear Roc's response.

"She ain't shit to me no more, but a long time ago I would have given her ass the shirt off my back. She couldn't get a damn gummy bear from me now."

I heard laughter, and that was when I decided to make my presence known before I got busted. I also wanted to make Ronnie aware that I feared him in no way. Since Roc had no intention of keeping him away from me, why not show my face?

I took a deep breath. As I made my way to the living room, the floor squeaked loudly. Everyone turned, looking in my direction. Seeing Ronnie made my flesh crawl, and the other young man, whom Roc had referred to as Sippi . . . Oh my God! I wanted to run! If Vanessa had slept with him, she was out of her mind. He was tall, too muscular, and he had long dreads and a rugged goatee. His hazel eyes were frightening and damn near matched his gold grill. I didn't mean to stare, but I sure wouldn't want to see him in a dark alley.

Roc stood and tugged at his cargo shorts to pull them up. "Dez," he said, sucking on a toothpick. "You already know Ronnie, but this is my boy Mississippi. Sippi, this is Dez. Chassidy's mama."

Normally, I would have extended my hand, but this time I didn't. Then I thought, *Okay. What the hell?* I reached out my hand, but Sippi barely touched it.

He tossed his head back. "Sup? Glad to meet you."

Ronnie hadn't said a word. I ignored him and turned my attention to Roc.

"Honey, I was looking for some towels so I could take a shower."

"Damn, you wasn't gon' wait for me?"

"No. Besides, you're busy."

Ronnie stood there with a twisted face. He cut his eyes at me, then reached in his pocket and pulled out a wad of money that was too thick for his ashy hands to hold. Diamond rings were on each finger, and a platinum and gold watch glistened on his wrist. He cut the wad in half, then dropped money on the table. "My move," he said, looking at Roc. "You already know what I told you, and I won't say it again. The next move is yours."

Dressed in an all-linen, cream-colored suit and sporting diamonds in both ears, Ronnie walked toward me. He put his hands back in his pockets and jiggled his keys.

"Desa Rae 'Risk-Takin' Jenkins. I see you back in business, but I wonder for how long. This time, I suggest that you don't overstay your welcome." He winked, looking identical to Roc. "As that would please me more than you know."

Ronnie going to hell would have pleased me, and it was obvious that he still had a beef with me for taking up too much of Roc's time. Particularly, for trying to keep Roc away from the drug game. Before I could say anything, Roc intervened. I was sure he remembered what happened the last time the three of us were together, and I knew he was in no mood to see another gun upside my head. Trying not to go there again, I kept quiet, giving Roc an opportunity to address his out-of-control uncle.

"Man, lighten up and chill," Roc said, moving next to Ronnie. He kept staring at me, and I stared back. Roc swung his hand in front of Ronnie's eyes, and Ronnie smacked Roc's hand away.

"Don't put your goddamned hands near my face, nigga! I don't give a fuck who you are. You out of line," Ronnie growled.

I was surprised, as Roc in no way backed down. Now his face was twisted, and his forehead showed thick wrinkles. "Muthafucka, yo' ass the one out of line. If I didn't touch you, nigga, don't touch me. Show a man some respect in front of his woman, and don't be treatin' me like no punk."

Sippi got between Roc and Ronnie, but from the way he gazed at Roc, I could tell he had Ronnie's back. Lord knows I didn't want to get in the middle of this, and so I had to put forth some effort to calm the situation down.

"Look, Ronnie. I apologize if my presence makes you uneasy. I will do my best to stay out of your way, and I don't want you and Roc arguing—"

"Shut the fuck up. No talkin' to me, bitch," Ronnie spat, keeping his eyes on Roc. "I see you done got some extra balls in prison, but you'd better cut them suckers off and get back to just havin' two. Watch yo' tone with me, youngblood. And the next time you slip up at the mouth, I will bust you in it."

Roc tapped his lip with his finger. "Are you threatenin' me? Right here, old school. Go ahead and put it right there."

I witnessed the mean mug on Ronnie's face and saw his fist tighten. My stomach dropped when he slammed his fist into Roc's mouth, causing him to stagger backward. In no way did he fall. When Roc quickly charged forward, Mississippi stopped him dead in his tracks. He placed his gun on Roc's heaving chest.

"Don't touch him, Roc!" Sippi yelled. "Back the fuck up!"

There was no way I could just stand there, and when my eyes wandered over to the phone, Sippi turned the gun toward me. All I could think was, *Not again.*

"If you move, you die," Sippi snarled.

"Y'all muthafuckas trippin'," Roc said, wiping a dab of blood from his lip. He seemed as calm as ever, but I wasn't. My stomach tightened, and my hands had a slight tremble. All kinds of things were roaming in my head, and all I could think of was my dream.

"Put that gun down," Ronnie said, giving Sippi an order. "You need not act unless I ask you to. As long as that fool got my blood running through his veins, don't you ever pull a gun on him! You got that shit?"

Sippi had already lowered his gun when he nodded.

Ronnie turned to Roc again, poking at his chest. "You and me gon' holla later. We don't do this, Roc, especially because you ain't bigger than me yet. A wise man can go a long way in this world, and he also knows to never put pussy before partna. I hope you understand what I'm sayin', and don't you ever bite the hand that feeds you, and feeds you well."

Roc cocked his head from side to side, saying not a word. Ronnie and his goon headed down the stairs, and I was relieved when I heard the door shut. Roc stormed by me, making his way down the hallway and into his bedroom. When I got to his room, he was lying back on the bed, looking up at the ceiling, with his arm across his forehead. I figured it was time for me to go.

"I'll be out of your way in a minute. I had a nice time last night, but I'm discouraged by what just happened. You know how much Ronnie despises me, so why didn't you just wake me up and ask me to leave?"

"Good-bye, Dez. I'm not up for a bunch of your irrita-tin'-ass questions."

Roc was as stubborn as stubborn could get, but so was I. I was also a person who had to have answers when I wanted them. I walked over to the bed and lay sideways next to him. To put him at ease, I dabbed the blood on his lips with a tissue; then I pecked his lips.

"Listen, can we please not get off on the wrong foot? You just made that suggestion yesterday, and I don't want my feelings for Ronnie to get in the way of what I feel for you. I hope you don't, either," I told him. "For the sake of our child, let's do our best to get along. It would really mean a lot to me. I promise that I will not pressure you about our relationship, or about what you decide to do with your life. I just want to be happy and have fun. I can't think of a better person I could enjoy myself with more than you."

Roc turned his head, then used his finger to touch the side of my face. "You're right. I'm sorry that happened in front of you, but shit like that happens all the time. We'll be drinkin', smoking herbs, and laughin' about that shit tomorrow, so no big deal. I apologize for how Ronnie is, and I really need to make sure the two of y'all keep your distance."

"Please." I laughed. "And how can you laugh, drink, and smoke blunts with someone who treats you like that?"

Roc placed his finger on my lips. "Let it go, Dez. Puttin' my hands on Ronnie would be like fightin' with my own father. He's dead now, and you know Ronnie's been like a replacement. So sometimes I gotta chalk that shit up and take it. You would never understand, and I'm not gon' waste my time explainin' it to you. Now, if you're leavin', good-bye. If you prefer to stay, I have some other suggestions."

I smiled, wondering what his *other* suggestions were. "You're right. I don't understand, but tell me about your other suggestions. I have some idea, but I just want to be sure."

We kissed, but instead of having sex again, I got up to take a shower. Roc left me in peace and started unpacking more boxes. After my shower, I helped. Around four o'clock, we took a break to eat. I also called Monica for the third time to check on Chassidy. She didn't answer, so I left a message on voice mail, telling her to call me soon.

Roc went from room to room, making sure everything was to his liking. He had no organization skills at all, and since he kept stopping the process to answer his phone calls, I gave up on helping him. The loud hip-hop music was working me too, and I could feel a headache coming on. I plopped down on his bed and turned on the TV to watch the news. I could hear Roc talking to someone on the phone, cursing and laughing some more. I closed my eyes, trying to soothe my headache, and that was when he came into the room.

"Uh, what are you doin'? I thought you were supposed to be helpin' me."

I yawned. "I was, but I got a headache. Plus, I'm tired. You've been slacking, anyway, and you've talked on that phone more than you've done anything else around here."

"Nigga, let me get at you later," he said to the caller, then hit the button on his Bluetooth to end the call. "I ain't talked to some of my boys in a while, so they were just callin' to see what was up. Sippi out runnin' his mouth about me and Ronnie too, so everybody wanted to make sure everything good."

"Is it?"

"Yeah, I already talked to that fool. We good."

I had no comment, but I did ask Roc to turn down the music. He did as I asked, and then sat on the bed next to me.

"If you don't mind, I want to take Chassidy and Li'l Roc with me to a picnic," he said. "They need to get to know each other. I hope you don't have a problem with that."

The thought of Chassidy being anywhere near Roc's crew in no way sat right with me. I didn't know how to say it without offending him, but Chassidy wasn't going anywhere with him, without me. "I don't mind Chassidy getting to know her brother or relatives, but where is this picnic supposed to be? Am I invited?"

"It's next weekend at Fairground Park. One of my boys havin' a barbecue bash, and I want to bring my kids to show them off. I don't care if you come or not, but you don't really click with my crew. You know how we get down, and I don't need you there watchin' my back and rollin' those pretty eyes."

"Yes, I witnessed today how you get down, and unfortunately, Roc, I don't want Chassidy exposed to that kind of foolishness. Have all the fun you want, please, but I'm not comfortable with her being surrounded by a bunch of people getting high, drinking, pulling guns on each other . . . you know what I mean. I would love for us to have a picnic, and the kids can join us. How about that?"

Roc got off the bed, seeming a bit irritated. "Chassidy is my daughter too, Dez. Whether you like it or not, she will get to know her family. All of them ain't ghettofied Negros, and plenty of them are down-to-earth, normal people. I have a serious problem with people who look down on others, so correct yourself on that. I'ma do this picnic thing with you, but there will come a time when you gon' have to ease up on our daughter."

There were times when I knew it made sense for me not to comment. This was one of them, but Roc was so wrong about me easing up on Chassidy. No way, no how would I subject her to anything like what had happened today. Roc would have to come to grips with that.

After I took two aspirins and talked to Monica and Chassidy, I lay back on the plush pillow to take a nap. Roc said he would rest later, and what seemed like hours later, I was awakened by a loud boom. I jumped from my sleep, then noticed that Roc was lying next to me, asleep. His arm was around my waist, and the room was partially dark. I looked at the alarm clock on the dresser. It showed 9:45 p.m. Since Roc was still sleeping, I figured I was just hearing things. My eyes searched the room for a while; then I lay back to watch TV. A few seconds later, the booming sound happened again. This time it was constant and sounded like someone banging hard on the door. I shook Roc's shoulder to wake him.

"Roc, wake up. I think someone is knocking at your door."

Roc forced his tired eyes open, listening for a knock. He heard several, and that was when he threw the covers aside.

"Wait right here," he said, slowly getting out of bed. He turned on the lights, causing me to squint. Wearing nothing at all, he grabbed his robe, put it on, and then opened a dresser drawer. I noticed him put a gun in his pocket, and then he made his way down the hallway.

"Who is it?" he yelled. "And why in the fuck you bangin' on my damn door like the police?"

I had already started to bite my nails. Being with Roc at his place was starting to become a problem. I had never spent the night with him in his territory. In the past, we had always stayed at my house. There was a possibility that going forward, I would resort to staying at my house only. I was trying to give him the benefit of the doubt, but this was getting ridiculous.

As I sat there in thought, I could hear a female's voice yelling and screaming. Yes, Roc had told me to stay where I was, but I was never one to listen to his orders. I got out of bed, wearing his long white T-shirt that I'd changed into before taking my nap. His white socks were on my feet, and I raked my fingers through my hair to straighten it. I made my way to the top of the stairs, then looked down to see what was up. The front door was wide open. Roc stood on one side of the door, and Vanessa was on the porch. She looked up at me, causing Roc to turn his head in my direction as well.

"Good-bye, Vanessa. If you don't stop all this clownin' and shit, you gon' regret it."

She tried to come inside, but Roc held up his arm to block her from entering. "Nigga, move your damn arm! Let me in!" she shouted. "I see why yo' ass ain't been answerin' your stupid-ass phone."

Roc shoved her back slightly, but she kept charging forward, trying to get inside. "I haven't answered my phone, because I told you I don't fuck with you no more. What's so hard for you to understand about that?"

Vanessa ignored Roc. She ducked underneath his arm and made it to the second step. He grabbed her waist and tossed her back out the door like a paper doll. I felt bad for her, and in no way was I going to stand by and let him go overboard with her.

"Roc," I said. He turned his head toward me. "Just come inside and close the door."

When his attention was on me, Vanessa lifted her foot like a punter in the NFL and kicked him right between his legs. When he doubled over and grabbed himself, she slapped the shit out of him. He was caught off guard, and she ran inside again. This time, she almost made it up the stairs. She lunged at me but immediately went tumbling back down the steps. Roc grabbed her ankles, pulling her. She hit the steps so hard, I knew she had to have broken something. Roc reached for her hair, squeezing it tight and jerking her head.

"Bitch, didn't I tell you to exit? I can't be nice to yo' ass for nothin'! You just ain't satisfied unless I got my foot up yo' ass."

"Let me go, muthafucka! I hate yo' ass, Roc! I hate your fuckin' guts!"

Roc slammed her face into the wall, and I swear that every breath in my body left me. I could in no way watch things go down like this, so I hurried down the steps to pull him away from her.

"Is this what you want?" he said, turning her around and holding her in a headlock. She couldn't say a word, as his grip was too tight. "What's that?" he said, seething with anger. "I can't hear you. You was just talkin' all that shit, but yo' ass ain't sayin' nothin' now."

Tears poured down Vanessa's face. She couldn't open her mouth if she tried. I reached out, trying to remove Roc's arm from her neck.

"Don't touch me, Dez! Go back upstairs and stay the fuck out of this!"

Still trying to loosen his grip, I ignored Roc. Finally, he let Vanessa go, and her body was so weak that she dropped to the floor. I was so angry that I turned around and headed upstairs, planning to gather my things and leave. With my back turned, Vanessa rushed up and grabbed the back of my hair, pulling me backward. Thank God for the banister. She moved so quickly that I would've been knocked on my ass without it. Roc grabbed her again, this time twisting her arm hard behind her back.

"I will break this muthafucka off! Let her fuckin' hair go," he yelled.

The pain had to be too much for Vanessa to bear. She let go of my hair in an instant.

I pointed my finger in her face, fuming. "Touch me again, and Roc won't be the only problem that you have. And trust me, he's not nothing compared to me."

I kept it moving up the stairs and didn't even turn around to see what would happen next. If Vanessa thought that I was her problem, she was sadly mistaken. Her problem was with Roc; then again, so was mine. I went into the bedroom and closed the door behind me so I wouldn't have to listen to what was happening. I wondered why Vanessa wouldn't just leave. If a man said that he didn't want to be bothered, then why force the situation?

About ten minutes later, the bedroom door flew open. Roc came inside. I was sitting against the headboard with my knees pressed close to my chest. Roc looked at me and then went over to the dresser to put the gun back inside.

"Before your mouth starts goin', Dez, I don't want to hear it. You know nothin' about my situation with her, so keep your comments to yourself."

I got off the bed and reached for my keys and purse on the nightstand. My flip-flops were already next to me, so I slid into them. I made my way toward the door but stopped before exiting the bedroom.

"Enjoy your evening, Roc. No, I don't know many details about your relationship with Vanessa, but I do know this. A man should never hit a woman, but I guess you felt as if you had to do what was necessary. That's your decision to make, but in my eyes it makes you look really bad. I can't help the way I feel, even though that bitch works the hell out of me."

His mouth dropped open. "You saw for yourself what she did. And I'm gon' always defend myself. That bitch has tried to shoot and stab me before. She gangsta like that, and some women you have to handle in a different way. She'll be all right. When you keep gettin' your head bumped enough, you eventually learn somethin'."

I couldn't help but shake my head. "If you've continued in a relationship with a woman who has tried to shoot or stab you, then you're getting what you deserve. The wake-up call obviously came a while back, but too bad you missed it. Trying to cut her off now may not work in your favor, and head bumping will get you nowhere but back in jail. I hope you know that."

Roc didn't respond, so I walked out the door. He shouted my name as I made my way down the hallway.

I turned with an attitude. "Yes?"

"Being with me will not be easy," he said, now standing in the doorway to his bedroom. "What you see is what you get. I'm not gon' sugarcoat nothin', and you need to decide if you're wit' me or not. I can't have no woman who thinks she can walk in and out of my life when she gets ready. I need one who knows my situation and accepts it. As you can see, much of this shit is beyond my control. I'm tryin' to get rid of the bad seeds, but they won't disappear as quickly as you want them to. Think about what I'm sayin', and get at me when you've come to grips with the way I do things."

I didn't respond and left with a sour taste in my mouth. After I closed the front door behind me and made my way to my car, I noticed my passenger-side window was cracked. B.I.T. was spray painted on my door. I let out a deep sigh, as the truth was now staring me in the face. Roc was home, and it wasn't such a great thing, after all.

Chapter Sixteen

I had talked to Roc every day for almost two weeks straight but had not been back to his place. He hadn't come to mine, either, but since we had planned to have a picnic, he was now on his way over with his son. He was upset about what had happened to my car, but not as much as I was. He'd promised to give me the money to pay for the damages, but I knew where his money was coming from. According to Roc, he was no longer "hands on," but his condo and any money that he had was given to him by Ronnie. This concerned me. I had plans to see what I could do to help him earn his own money.

I had already contacted my insurance company to have my car taken care of. The window was fixed right away, but I had to wait another week for the paint job to get done. Until then, I would drive around in a rental and keep my car in the garage. What a stupid thing for a woman to do. At this point, I had very little sympathy for Vanessa. A fool she was. Not only had she damaged my car, but she had also pulled my hair, and I considered this strike number two for her. There was only so much one could tolerate. My patience with her had worn thin.

It was a Saturday afternoon, and I stood in the kitchen, making sure I had everything packed and ready to go for our picnic. All I was missing was the insect repellant, so I hurried to the closet to get it. Chassidy followed me, trying to keep up. She was such a happy child, and she giggled as she chased me.

"Girl, you can't keep up with me," I teased.

When the doorbell rang, she rushed to the door, and I could barely keep up with her. Roc had a new steel-gray Lincoln Navigator, and I could see it parked in the driveway. I opened the door and invited him and his son inside. The first thing he did was ease his arm around my waist and peck my lips.

"What's up, sexy? You know, anytime a woman can dress down and still look good, she one bad mamma jamma."

His compliments always made me blush, and seeing him, period, genuinely excited me. He reached for Chassidy and picked her up, kissing her cheeks.

"Muah," he said. "Hey, beautiful. Girl, you know you lookin' more and more like your daddy every day."

I cut my eyes, as sometimes the truth was hard to admit. Li'l Roc was still standing by the door, so I reached out my hand.

"Hi," I said politely. He wouldn't smile at all, but he did reach out to shake my hand. "You are so adorable. How old are you?"

"Five," he responded but pouted right after.

"Are you okay?" I asked.

"Leave his knucklehead ass alone," Roc said. "I had to get in his shit in the car. Now he got an attitude."

I closed the front door. "Well, I'm just about finished getting everything together. We can leave in about ten minutes."

As I gathered our things to go, I listened to Roc speak to his son.

"You know who that is right there?" he asked Li'l Roc.

The boy shrugged.

"That's your sister, Chassidy. She got it goin' on like you and me, don't she?"

Li'l Roc nodded.

"Always have her back. That's blood right there. The same blood runnin' through your veins runnin' through hers." Roc crossed his fingers with his son. "We tight like this, okay?"

Li'l Roc repeated what Roc had said. "Yep. Tight like this."

Roc rubbed the top of his son's head. "Now, that's what's up."

It appeared that everyone was back on the same page, so I gave Roc the picnic basket, blankets, and pillows to put in his truck. As we stood outside, loading up, he looked at me like I was crazy as I had fishing poles in my hands.

"Where in the hell are you goin' with those?"

"We're going fishing. Have you never been fishing before?"

"If I have, I can't remember. But I thought we were supposed to be havin' a picnic."

"We're doing that, but we can also catch fish."

"Are you cookin' the fish later on tonight?"

"Nope."

"Then what's the purpose?"

"The purpose is to have fun with the kids and with you."

Roc just cut his eyes at me.

After the kids were strapped into their safety seats, we left. When we arrived at Forest Park, I could see a cozy spot for our picnic from the distance. It was underneath a shaded tree on a slight hill. A few feet away was a pond where several people were already fishing. The kids would have plenty of room to run around and play there.

Roc carried most of our things to the designated spot, and I held the kids' hands. He laid the blankets on the green grass and dropped the pillows on top. I blew up two huge balls for the kids, using an air pump. They couldn't wait to play with them, and when I suggested eating first, they refused. I sat on the blanket next to Roc, who was already lying back on one of the pillows. A cool breeze was blowing, making it so relaxing.

"Aren't you going to eat something?" I asked Roc. I pulled out the ham and cheese sandwiches, showing them to him.

"What is that? Ham and cheese? No, thank you. Had enough of that shit in jail. What else you got in there?"

I pulled out the chips, fruit cups, and cupcakes. "Okay, which one?"

Roc turned on his side, resting on his elbow. He reached for a fruit cup and a small bag of Doritos.

"Thanks," he said with a smile.

He looked so sexy in a plain T-shirt and cargo shorts, with Jordans on his feet. All day I had wanted to kiss him, just to let him know that I wasn't bitter about what had happened at his place. I took the opportunity and leaned in to give him a lengthy, juicy kiss. He reached up and grasped the back of my head, holding it steady and softly rubbing my hair. My eyes closed. Kissing him always seemed so perfect. Chassidy interrupted our kiss when she came over and reached for a cupcake. I opened the package for her and then gave Li'l Roc the bag of chips he was reaching for. When I asked them if they wanted a Popsicle, both of them said no.

"Why doesn't anyone want a Popsicle? It's hot, and I thought they would help to cool us down."

"Shit, then give me one," Roc said, looking down at his goods. "I definitely need somethin' to calm me down right about now."

He wasn't the only one, so I gave him one of the Popsicles and kept one for myself. The kids ran off to play again, and Roc and I slurped on each other's Popsicles.

"Remind me to thank you later," he said. "This pic-nooky was an excellent idea, and who would have thought I'd be havin' this much fun?"

The Popsicle juices were dripping from his lips, and you better believe I was there to suck them. He was working my lips and my Popsicle too. We couldn't help but laugh.

"You know, if the kids weren't with us, I would lay you back on this blanket and fuck somethin' up. Feel how hard my dick is right now."

"I don't have to feel it. I can already see it through your shorts. Calm down, baby. You know I'm going to take care of that real soon."

"Soon? Shit. I was hopin' you'd take care of it for me now. Let me play with those titties, touch your pussy or somethin'. That will calm me down real quick."

I watched Chassidy and Li'l Roc as they continued to play with their balls and chase each other. They seemed to be having a good time, so I responded to Roc's suggestion. "Not out here, okay? There will be so much time left for that later."

Roc moved behind me and straddled me as we both sat up. He wrapped his arms around my waist and nibbled on my ear.

"Be creative, Roc," he said, mocking my own words. "Work with what space and . . ."

I turned my head to the side. "You are not going to let me forget what I said to you about being creative, are you?"

"Nope. And I'm goin' to live by those words, especially when we're together."

His hands eased up my shirt, touching my lace bra. My nipples had already become erect, and when he softly ran his hands across them, I could feel my breasts tighten.

"See," Roc whispered in my ear. "This looks totally innocent but brings great pleasure. Keep smilin' and lookin' at the kids playin'. They will pay us no mind."

I couldn't believe I was letting Roc massage my breasts and get me so aroused in public. There weren't too many people around, but it did feel pretty awkward. His touch felt good, so I couldn't complain.

Roc placed his lips on my earlobe and whispered in my ear, "Damn, these titties soft as hell. I want to suck them, though. Can I?"

My body tingled all over, but sucking my breasts would be going too far. "No, Roc. This is as far as we go."

"Aww, you ain't no fun. All you gotta do is throw these covers over your head for a minute or two. We can pretend that we're wrestlin' or playin' around."

My eyes were still focused on the kids, but my mind was elsewhere. "No." I laughed. "Absolutely not. And is this your idea of a pic-nooky?"

Roc lowered his hands from my breasts, causing the tingling to go away. "Exactly. Now answer this question for me. Are you wet yet?"

I turned my head to the side as he rested his chin on my shoulder. "What? What's it to you?"

"I know you are just by how hard those nipples were. Keep on grinnin' and watchin' the kids. Sit Indian style, and I'm gon' bend my knees. Pull up the blanket and lay it across your lap."

"You got this all figured out, don't you?"

Roc didn't answer. He bent his knees and remained straddled me, straddling me. I reached for the blanket and covered myself from the waist down. Roc touched my hips and then eased his hands underneath the blanket. He popped the buttons on my capris, and his fingers dipped into my wetness. His touch always made me gasp, and now was no different.

"I knew you would like it," he whispered in my ear. "Chill. And . . . and how in the hell did you get this wet so fast? Damn, Ma, this shit feels too good."

My eyes fluttered from the depths of his rotations. All I could do was suck in my bottom lip. "Please don't talk anymore. You will make me jump on top of you sooo quick and fuck your brains out."

"That's what I want you to do."

"But I can't," I whined.

"Then chill and just let me finish."

I took a few deep breaths as Roc's thick fingers turned circles inside of me. His thumb rolled around my clit, and we could hear what his actions were doing to my insides.

"I love the sound of that," Roc whispered again. "Don't you hear it?"

I nodded, squeezing my stomach tightly and tightening my legs. I looked at the kids, who were coming our way, and dropped my head. "Hurry, baby. They're coming."

"So are you."

Roc halted my orgasm when he pulled his fingers out of me. With the kids only a few feet away, I was left high and dry—well, actually, wet as ever.

Chassidy jumped into my lap, and Roc stood up. "I'ma go over there to this restroom," he said, smiling. "I'll be right back." He looked at Li'l Roc. "Man, do you need to go take a leak?"

Li'l Roc said no and stayed with me and Chassidy. They reached for the cupcakes, allowing me time to get up and button my capris. I felt very sticky between my legs, and when I got Roc home, I intended to make him pay for what he'd done.

Roc was in the restroom for several minutes. When he came back, I didn't have to ask what had taken him so long. "That was a good one," he whispered to me as I was trying to untangle the line on one of the fishing rods. "I let go of some mad-ass sperm. You should have seen it."

"Uh, thanks for sharing, with your nasty self. You are so nasty. I can't believe I let you do that to me."

"That's because you nasty too. Now, what's up with these fishin' rods?"

We spent the next few hours fishing and having a ball with the kids. The drive home was noisy as ever. The kids were talking to each other, and so were Roc and I. I had really enjoyed my day with him and looked forward to many more days like this to come.

When we got back to my house, I cooked dinner, we watched a movie, the kids took showers, and then we called it a night. Chassidy had fallen asleep on Roc's lap. He carried her to her room, and I got the guest room prepared for Li'l Roc. Latrel had many action figures, video games, puzzles, and other toys in his room in the basement, so I took Li'l Roc down there so he could gather some things to take to the upstairs guest room with him. He picked up Latrel's Xbox and also got some games. He liked the big puzzle pieces of *Iron Man,* so I picked those up too. All kinds of books lined Latrel's bookshelves, so I picked up two that I figured Li'l Roc would like.

"Do you like to read?" I asked.

"No. I hate books."

"Why?"

"Because my teacher makes me read them at school."

"Then you must have a very smart teacher. She just wants you to be smart too, and I do as well. Reading books is so good for you. It's an excellent way to feed your brain. Your brain has to eat, you know. And when you feed it . . . wow. So many wonderful things can happen to you. Remember that, okay?"

Li'l Roc nodded, and we carried the items upstairs to the guest room. I could hear Roc talking to someone on his phone, so I let him handle his business with whomever and got Li'l Roc situated for bed.

"You can watch the television and play with the puzzle tonight," I told him as he climbed into the bed. "Since it's late, your dad can hook up the game for you tomorrow. I hope you're comfortable. Do you like lights on or lights off?"

"Lights off!" he yelled, then pulled the covers over his head.

"Well, okay." I smiled and turned off the lights on my way out.

"Miss Dez," he said.

"Yes?"

"Thanks for being nice. My mama said you were a mean B."

I was stunned, but then again, no, I wasn't. "You're welcome. And I'm glad that you got a chance to see that I'm not mean. Good night, and don't forget to say your prayers."

"But I don't pray at night. Do you?"

I went back into the room and asked Li'l Roc to kneel beside the bed with me. We prayed, and then I tucked him back in. I walked down the hallway, having to shake my head. How dare Vanessa say something like that to her son, with her dysfunctional self. What a poor excuse for a mother she was, and some of this was on Roc too.

When I got to my bedroom, Roc was sitting in my chair, laughing at what someone was saying on the other end of the phone line. I went into my closet, stripped naked, and gathered my things for a shower. I tossed my nightgown over my shoulder and slipped into my house shoes. Leaving the closet, I eyeballed Roc, and his eyes got wider. He licked his lips and tried to cut his conversation short.

"Uh, say, man . . . hold that thought."

The person on the other end kept talking, and I watched Roc nod his head. I made my way to the bathroom and turned on the water in the shower. Wasting no more time, I got inside and started to lather myself. A few minutes later Roc joined me. I had the pleasure of lathering his body. To witness white, sudsy soap on his sexy body was priceless. I dropped the soap and pressed my body close to his. My arms rested on his shoulders, and before I said anything, I delivered a passionate kiss that locked our lips for minutes.

After the shower, we went to the bed, where I got on my hands and knees and let Roc have at it. I couldn't get enough of him. I threw myself back at him as he tightly squeezed my hips. I massaged my own breasts and was on cloud nine from feeling his hard, long meat slide in and out of me. His rhythm was perfect. The way he eased in from different angles was impressive. I felt defeated and pulled on my hair.

"You . . . you got me, Roc. I am hooked on the way you do this pussy. You treat it so well, and I love it!"

"Royalty, Ma. Ju-just so you know, you make my shit feel like royalty."

I cut loose on Roc, coating his shaft and leaving his balls dripping wet. He held on tightly to my hips, and we both fell forward, completely out of breath. He moved next to me, trying to gather himself.

My chest heaved in and out as I looked over at him. "Do you think the kids heard us? We were pretty loud, you know. Maybe you should go check on Li'l Roc. I'm surprised you didn't go tuck him in."

"With your door closed, I doubt that they heard us. As for tuckin' him in, please. He don't need to be treated like no baby. Those days are long gone. And if they did hear us, Li'l Roc knows what's up."

"What does that mean?"

"It means he knows what it sounds like when a woman and a man are havin' sex. It also means stay put, because it ain't your business."

I reached over and rubbed his chest. "You know, I often wonder how we're going to make this work. It's like we come from two different worlds and we're trying to pull it all together to create one that will make sense. Do you think it's possible for us to do it? I mean, the way you want to live your life is so different from the way I want to live mine. I'm getting older, Roc, and even though I sometimes think this is only about us having fun, there's so much more to it than that. I truly believe that I love you, but then I ask myself if I could be serious. This thing between us is complicated in many ways, but maybe I'm analyzing things too much. Do you ever think or feel the way I do?"

"All the time, but I'm hopin' that the love we have for each other keeps us together, no matter what. We gon' have to learn to compromise on some things, especially you. I'm usually down for whatever, but you're the one who set in your ways. Never will I make you feel hoodwinked, bamboozled, or led astray. My shit is out there for you to see, plain and simple."

"Let's be real here. You haven't been that open and honest with me about much. I'm left to assume a lot, and not once have you said where you would like our relationship to stand. I mean, what are we? Friends, companions, lovers . . . what? I need to know, only because I want to know what I can and cannot expect from you. Does that make sense?"

"We can be whatever you want us to be."

"No, that's bullshit, and you know it. I already told you that I would never pursue a relationship with a man who wasn't ready. Are you ready to give me all that I may require?"

Roc was silent for a while. I already knew that this was a conversation he didn't want to have. "I would love to give you everything you require, but I got some loose ends to tie up. I planned on doin' so, and I can assure you that it will be taken care of soon."

"*Loose ends* meaning who or what?"

"Loose ends that I can deal with, now that I'm out of prison."

I sat up in bed and pulled the covers over me. Roc followed suit.

"So, for the record, are you having sex only with me?" I asked.

Roc turned to me with a very serious look on his face. "No one but you."

"Are you sure?"

"Positive."

"Why only me?"

"Why not you? I'm one hundred percent satisfied with how we get down. I seek no one else to give me what only you can."

Unfortunately, I didn't believe him. If he was telling the truth, he was going to have to forgive me for giving him no credit. There was something about him that made me not want to trust a word that he'd said. Then again, he was so into this thing with us that maybe I was wrong for feeling as I did. At this point, I wanted to pull my hair out for not being able to put my finger on the feeling of doubt I had inside. I didn't know why I had such a feeling of skepticism, but I knew my gut didn't lie.

Chapter Seventeen

For the last month and a half, things had been pro-
gressing very well. Roc and I were spending an enormous
amount of time together, especially with the kids. Latrel
had been home twice, and he and Roc had got along well.
We went everywhere together. It was such a joy to see
all of us on the same page. I had not been back to Roc's
place to visit, but he had spent plenty of nights at my
house, maybe even more than he had spent at his. He
often brought Li'l Roc with him. Latrel was overly thrilled
about me and Roc getting back together. So thrilled that
when I asked if he'd call Sherri and take her out again, he
promised me that he would.

Another good thing that had happened was that I'd
gotten Roc a job in the mail room where I worked. I
wasn't worried about Greg working there, because our
so-called relationship was over. Roc didn't deliver the
mail on my floor, and that was a good thing. In no way
did I think it was a good idea to have him around 24-7,
because he seemed like the kind of person who needed
space. I did too. So whenever he didn't call for a couple
of days, I was okay with it. As long as we didn't go weeks
without speaking to each other, that was fine by me.

Mr. Anderson had been back from his business trip
for a while now, and as usual, he had me running around
the office like a chicken with its head cut off. On this
afternoon I was standing in another VP's office, waiting
on him to sign some papers that Mr. Anderson needed

right away. Dressed in my silk, purple, ruffled blouse and hip-hugging gray skirt, I waited for Mr. Blevins to end a call. He held up one finger and whispered that he'd be with me in a minute. Just to give him privacy, I exited his office and took a seat in the chair that was right outside his door. As soon as I looked up, I saw Greg coming my way. I did my best to avoid him by turning my head in the other direction, as if I didn't see him. That, of course, didn't work.

"Hello there, Miss Thickety Thick," he said, checking me out.

I hated to be called that, and it bothered me that he always referred to me as thick. Whether it was true or not, he didn't have to always say it. I stood to address him.

"Hi, Greg. How are you?"

"Sexy lady, I would be so much better if you would agree to go out on another date with me. I hope that's not asking too much."

I didn't want to hurt Greg's feelings, but he really wasn't my type. He wasn't a bad-looking man, but he was a bit too thin for my taste. He was kind of nerdy too, and he was very much the opposite of Roc.

"Let me think about it, Greg. I am seeing someone else right now, but it's nothing serious."

He swiped his forehead and smiled. "Whew. I'm glad to hear that. I hope you call soon. You know I'll be waiting."

I heard Mr. Blevins call for me, so I told Greg I would talk to him later. When I walked back into Mr. Blevins's office, he had the papers signed and ready to give back to me.

"Sorry for your wait," he said. "Tell John I'll see him around seven and don't be late."

"Will do." I smiled.

I returned to Mr. Anderson's office. He had his back turned to the door and was on the phone. He didn't hear me come in, but I could hear him whispering something into the phone. Now, as his administrative assistant, I knew what his phone calls were all about. I knew what his so-called extended business trips were all about too, but it wasn't my place to say one word. When he laughed at something the person on the line said, I cleared my throat. He quickly swung his chair around and abruptly ended his call. I handed the papers from Mr. Blevins to him.

"Mr. Blevins said he'll see you around seven and don't be late."

Mr. Anderson slapped his forehead. "Oops! I almost forgot about that. Thanks for reminding me." He looked at his watch. "Have you had lunch yet, or would you like to run across the street with me to get a bite to eat?"

"I'll pass. I'm trying to watch my weight a little, so I'm going to grab something quick from the cafeteria. Thanks, though. And if you don't mind, I'm leaving for lunch in about five minutes. Is there anything else you would like me to do before I go?"

"Nope. Just close my door on your way out. If I'm not back when you get here, I will see you tomorrow."

"Okay. Thanks again."

I removed ten dollars from my purse and headed to the cafeteria to get something to eat. A couple of times I had been to the gym with Roc. Since I had been cutting back on eating so much, I felt that I had lost a little weight. It wasn't much to brag about, and it wasn't like I had been trying.

The cafeteria was crowded with some of my coworkers, as well as students. I sat with several ladies who just so happened to be talking about the "new guy." I slowly turned around, just to look in the direction in which the ladies' eyes had roamed. Roc stood by a soda machine, debating what kind of drink he wanted. How he ever made a simple mailroom uniform look so enticing, I didn't know.

"Are you all talking about the young man at the soda machine?" I asked.

"Yes," Emma said. "What a piece of artistic work."

We all laughed. I couldn't help what I was about to do. I turned to the ladies. "He is too fine, and see, I'm the kind of woman who when I see a man I want, I will go after him." I looked at Val. "Give me a pen and a piece of paper."

Val's mouth hung wide open. "Nooo," she whispered. "Are you going to confront him?"

"Yes. I'm going to give him my number. Hurry, before he walks away."

The ladies sat there, almost speechless.

"Wha . . .Well, he's already moved to another vending machine," Bethany said. "If you want to catch him, you'd better hurry."

Val hurried to give me a piece of paper and a pen from her purse. "I can't believe you're doing this. That's being a bit aggressive, don't you think? A woman should never approach a man. I don't care how gorgeous he is."

I shook my head. "I beg to differ. My mother always told me to go after whatever it is in life that I wanted and to never let a good opportunity pass you by."

The ladies sat in disbelief as I got up from the table and made my way over to the vending machines. I crept up behind Roc and lightly tapped his shoulder. He turned and smiled.

"What's up?" he asked.

I held up the piece of paper and the pen. "Nothing. I just wondered if I could get your sevens or possibly get you to come to my house and lay me tonight?"

The eyes of the young woman standing next to him bugged, and she pursed her lips. When Roc replied, "You can have anything you want," she walked away. He eased his arm around my waist, and when I looked over at the table where the ladies sat, their eyes were popping out of their heads and their mouths were covered with their hands. I shrugged, as if I was shocked by Roc's actions too.

"Why you playin'?" Roc asked. He pecked my lips, and all I could do was laugh. I took his hand, asking him to follow me.

I didn't even notice Greg sitting close by until he spoke. "It looks pretty serious to me."

I ignored Greg, but Roc stopped in his tracks. "What you say?"

Greg repeated himself. "I said the relationship looks pretty serious to me. Only a few hours ago Desa Rae said she wasn't in a serious relationship. Obviously, that wasn't true."

Roc looked puzzled.

I couldn't believe Greg was trying to put me on blast. "Greg, please. It is what it is, okay?"

Greg shrugged. "Whatever. Hey, your loss, not mine."

I moved forward, but Roc stopped me again. Luckily, his voice wasn't that loud. "What in the hell was that all about? You fuckin' that nigga or what?"

"No. I'll tell you about it later. Right now I want you to meet some of my coworkers." I stepped up to the table and couldn't decide who looked the most shocked.

"Girlie, wow. Do you move fast!" Bethany said. "If I had known it was that easy, I would have taken the initiative."

I decided to enlighten the women. They'd heard me speak of Roc before, but no one knew he had been in prison. "Ladies, this is Chassidy's father, Roc. I know you all remember me mentioning him, right?"

The ladies' tongues were tied until Roc reached out and shook their hands one by one.

"Oh, Desa Rae, you made us all look like fools," Val said. "But nice to meet you, Roc. You are really a handsome young man."

"Appreciate the compliment," Roc said, blushing. "I do have to get back to the mail room, but you ladies enjoy your lunch."

I spent ten minutes with Roc before we both returned to our jobs. Normally, he got off at three o'clock, but I didn't get off until five. Sometimes we'd meet up to get a bite to eat, and other times he'd meet me at my house. As I was driving home, my cell phone rang. It was him.

"What's the play for today?" he asked.

"Not sure. I'm not really hungry, but after I pick up Chassidy, I'm stopping at Monica's house to see her. I won't be long. I should be home by eight. Are you coming over?"

"Nah, not tonight. I think I'm gon' just chill."

"Did you cash your check yet?"

"I dropped it in the bank. Never thought I'd see the day that I, Rocky Dawson, would be gettin' a paycheck. But anything for my Dez."

"I hope you're not working because of me. I hope you're working for yourself. You have to admit that it feels pretty good to make money the legit way, doesn't it?"

"Listen, I'm grateful, but I didn't mean it the way I said it. And if you think I'm supposed to be over here, jumpin' up and down over a check for nine hundred sixty dollars that I make every two weeks, I'm not that moved. Grateful, but not moved."

I had to slam on my brakes, almost hitting the car in front of me. I had jumped through hoops to get Roc that job in the mail room, and with a police record like his, it damn sure wasn't easy. He was being ungrateful. Twelve dollars an hour wasn't bad at all. With the economy as bad as it was, millions of people would kick ass to hold his position. I couldn't even respond, so I didn't. I hung up on him, and when he called back, I didn't answer.

I picked up Chassidy from day care and then headed to Monica's house in Maryland Heights. When I got there, I was shocked to see Reggie's car in her driveway. I wondered what the hell was going on, and I couldn't wait to get out of my car to see what was up. I rang the doorbell, with Chassidy on my hip. Monica opened the door and whispered that Reggie had just come over and needed someone to talk to.

I went inside, whispering back at her, "What in the hell does he want?"

She shrugged. "He called out of the blue, looking for you. I told him you were on your way over here. The next thing I knew, he just showed up."

To make a long story short, I sat across the table from Reggie, listening to a bunch of foolishness.

"I had this dying urge to see you," he said. "I stopped by your house a few times, but I could tell you had company. I want my life back, Desa Rae. The life that I once shared with you and Latrel, I want it back. We were so happy together, and even though I didn't understand what it was that I was going through at the time, I now know that leaving you was one of the biggest mistakes of my life. I'm not asking you to drop everything right now for me, but I want you to think about it. Have you been on stable ground since we divorced? Can you honestly say that you have been happy with the person you're with? Roc is not the one, baby, and you know that he's not. All I'm asking for is another chance. I've spent these past several months trying to figure out the best way to confront you about this. My life has been in shambles. I need a woman like you to help me piece it back together. You're the only woman capable of doing it and the only woman I have truly ever loved."

Reggie said a mouthful. I didn't even know where to start. But I did my best to spare his feelings.

"I have very few words for you right now, Reggie. Obviously, you are going through something because of your failed marriage. I definitely know how that is, but traveling backward is not the solution to your problem. Besides, I'm not in love with you anymore. I care deeply for you, and I wish that we could have a better relationship because of our son. You didn't seem to want that before. All I can say is, I've moved on. I may not be all complete yet, but one day I will be. I don't see you in my plans, not now, not ever."

Reggie lowered his head and rubbed his forehead. "I knew you were going to say that, but just think about it before you—"

"There's nothing to think about. I'm sorry."

This situation was sad, but I had to admit that a part of it felt good too. This time, I reached for my daughter and left Reggie at Monica's house to deal with his hurt. Quite frankly, I had nothing else to say.

When I pulled in the driveway, Roc was already at my house, waiting for me. When I got out of my car, he stepped up to me.

"Yo' battery on your phone went dead, right? Or did you hang up on me? Which one?"

Ironically, just as I was getting Chassidy out of her car seat, my cell phone rang. I was sure it was Monica, checking to make sure we'd made it home. I ignored Roc and the phone and made my way to the door with Chassidy asleep on my shoulder.

"Well, we damn sure know it wasn't the battery," he said.

I sighed, really not in the mood for an argument. "Would you mind unlocking the door for me, please? Chassidy is heavy, and so is my purse."

Roc unlocked the door, then tried to take Chassidy from my arms.

"I got her. I'm going to go lay her down, and then you can yell at me all you want to, okay?"

"Hurry up, then."

I carried Chassidy to her bedroom, and Roc headed to mine. I tucked her in bed, kissed her cheek, and turned on her night-light. When I got to my bedroom, Roc was sitting in his favorite chair with his hands behind his head.

"First things first," he said. "Who the fuck is Greg?"

I blew Roc off and threw my hand at him. "Greg is a nobody. That's exactly who he is."

"Really? A nobody who came out and said what he did today? Did you tell him you weren't in a serious relationship?"

I was stunned that Roc was even going there, and I could tell he was in the mood to argue. I stood and defended my one-month relationship with Greg. "I dated him while you were in prison. We went on three dates, I wasn't feeling him at all, and I stopped returning his phone calls. Anything else?"

"Okay, so you dated him a few times. Did you up the pussy?"

If I spoke the truth, I suspected it would cause a lot of problems tonight. It really wasn't his business, anyway, so I said what I felt I needed to say.

"No, I did not give up the goods, because, like I said before, Greg is not my cup of tea. I was bored, and being with him gave me a chance to get out of the house, hopefully to have some fun. Unfortunately, that didn't happen. Now what?"

I walked into the closet, attempting to avoid this conversation. But Roc didn't want to let go. He got up from the chair and stood in the doorway.

"Why did you hang up on me?"

"Because you were sounding ungrateful. I didn't like it."

"So when you don't like what I have to say, you hang up the fuckin' phone? Since when?"

I shrugged and made my way out of the closet. Roc moved aside to let me pass by him.

"So that's how you want to get down, huh?" he said, reaching for his keys in his pocket. "I'm good with that, and I'ma holla at you real soon, okay?"

Roc left the room. Moments later I heard the front door close. I was going to apologize for hanging up on him, but since he had left, I picked up the phone to call him. He answered right away.

"What?" he snapped.

"I'm sorry for hanging up on you, and maybe I should—"

He hung up on me. When I called back, he had turned off his phone. I was too tired to deal with any drama, so I called it a night, hoping and praying that my little white lie wouldn't catch up with me. Not only that, I hoped I wouldn't regret getting Roc a job, especially one in which he worked with someone I had dated. While I had made no promises to Roc that I'd be there for him when he was in prison, something told me all of this would come back to haunt me.

Chapter Eighteen

Roc was trying to play me shady. For the next week and a half, he didn't pick up the phone to call me. I called him, though, but he either cut me short or told me he was busy. While at work, he avoided me altogether. I tried to catch up with him a couple of times in the mail room, and when I did, he pretended to be occupied. I couldn't believe all of this was going down over a stupid phone call. There had to be more to it.

On Thursday, we had just come out of a meeting, and I was on my way to the restroom. I had to go real bad, but I was approached by Roc before I went inside.

"We need to talk," he said with a disturbing look on his face.

"I've been trying to for a week and a half now, but you've been avoiding me."

"Handle your business and meet me across the hall, in the stairwell."

"Give me a minute," I said, then went inside the restroom. I quickly used it, and as I washed my hands, I wondered what Roc wanted to talk about. Maybe it was something with his job. It was no secret that he didn't like it that much. After drying my hands, I headed across the hallway and into the stairwell where Roc had asked me to meet him. He was sitting back on the stairs, looking at me with a hard stare.

"What's going on?" I asked.

"You're a goddamned liar, that's what's up."

My brows scrunched inward from the sound of his tone. "What are you talking about?"

"You know damn well what I'm talkin' about. You fucked that nigga, and you still been fuckin' his ass. He told me what was up, Dez. Why did you lie about the shit?"

I swallowed, wondering exactly what Greg had told Roc, if anything. "He told you what? And you believed him?"

Roc stood, leaving no breathing room between us. "Are you callin' him a liar? I will go get that muthafucka right now and have him repeat what he told me. Ain't no way in hell he knows what your bedroom looks like if he ain't been in it. Ain't no fuckin' way he knows how your pussy feels if he ain't had it! Ain't no cock-suckin' way he knows that you have a mole on your right thigh if he ain't hiked up your damn dress and seen it for himself. So tell me, Ma. Who's the liar? You or him?"

I looked into Roc's fiery eyes, regretting what I had said the other day. I looked so guilty, and I really wasn't guilty of anything but a lie. There was no telling what Greg had told Roc, and in no way was I in a position to defend myself.

"Twice," I said in a soft tone. "I had sex with him two times, only when you were in prison. If he told you we have recently been intimate, that was a lie."

"Yeah, kind of like the one you told me." Roc sucked his teeth and put his hands in his pockets. "You know what? I thought you was about somethin', Dez. You ain't shit, Ma, and you just like these other fake-ass bitches out here. Then you always tryin' to judge me like yo' ass all that. You played the shit out of me, and you best believe there are consequences for that."

Deep down, yes, I was hurt, because I felt as if this was on me. "I apologize for not telling you the truth, but please don't talk to me like that or refer to me as one of your fake bitches. You're way out of line. The only reason I wasn't truthful with you about me and Greg is that I didn't want to argue with you that night. We had been getting along so well, and I didn't want to go there with you."

Roc looked me over and released a light snicker. "To hell with you, Ma. Now I know why you didn't have time for me while I was in prison. I don't believe shit you say, and whatever the hell was up with you and that nigga, you should have said that shit the other night. Regardless."

I crossed my arms in front of me and defended myself. "And you have always been so on the up and up with me, right? Please don't stand there and pretend that you have been honest with me about every single thing, knowing that you haven't."

Roc let go of the doorknob, which he had grabbed. "That's right. Play the blame game and throw that shit back at me. Blame me for your fuckups, but that's the oldest damn trick in the book. Find a new plan and another play toy too. To hell with this job. And do me a favor. Ditch my number, and if you need anything for Chassidy, have Latrel call me."

Roc opened the door, but I couldn't allow us to go our separate ways over something so ridiculous. I reached for his arm, but he snatched it away.

"Not now, not never. Touch my arm like that again and you will really see a side of me that you won't like."

I could see the anger in his eyes, so I let it be. Roc walked out the door, and even though I wanted to go after him, I didn't. I also wanted to go and confront Greg, but I didn't do that, either. I headed back to my desk and tried my best to get some work done.

When Friday rolled around, I went to the mail room to see if Roc had come to work. His boss said that Roc had called in sick. I figured that was good news, since at least

he had called in, and he hadn't told his boss that he was
quitting. In no way did I want this situation with Roc to
be permanent, so around noon, I asked Mr. Anderson if
I could leave early. I told him I had many errands to run,
but I was actually on my way to Roc's place so we could
quickly resolve this matter.

I arrived at his place around one, and when I rang the
doorbell, it took him a while to answer. Finally, I could
hear him coming down the stairs. When he opened the
door, he had no shirt on and was wearing only his gray
Jockey shorts.

"I'm busy," he said.

"Do you have company? If you do, I'll leave."

He stared at me, then turned to make his way up the
steps. I followed him up the steps and watched as he lay
down on the couch and propped his feet on the armrest.
He focused on the TV, as if he was all into it. The room had
a very smoky smell, and I couldn't tell if it was marijuana
or smoke from the cigar that was lying in an ashtray. I sat
on the love seat that was across from him and placed my
purse on the table.

"Can I please talk to you without you getting upset with
me over something so ridiculous?"

Roc continued to look at the TV, pretending to ignore
me. He had a toothpick in his mouth now and was
dangling it from his lips.

"I said I was sorry. How dare you not forgive me after
all the things you've done to me in the past? I'm not here
to play the blame game, but I did forgive you in the past
for some of the things you've done. If my lie was so bad
and you refuse to forgive me, fine. I made a mistake, and
I'll have to deal with it. But please don't quit your job, and
do not give up on your daughter. I'm not going to involve
Latrel in our mess, and you should always be there for
her, no matter what."

Roc removed the toothpick, then looked over at me. "Are you finished? Let me know when you're done so I can walk you out."

His eyes shifted back to the TV, and the toothpick went back into his mouth. This was becoming so irritating. I took a deep breath, then combed my feathery hair back with my fingers and gripped it in the back.

"I'm not going to kiss your ass, Roc. If that's what you want me to do, I'm not. You can pretend that you have been so on the up and up with me all you want, but I know better. I know you've been over here tying up your so-called loose ends, and what about Vanessa? After all those years together, now, all of a sudden, it's over? Please. Who do you think I am? I wasn't born just yesterday."

This time, Roc didn't even look at me when he spoke. "You finished yet?" He picked up his watch from the table and looked at it. "You don't have much time, so hurry up and say what else you need to say."

Okay, if drama was what he wanted, then drama was what he was going to get. I stood and snatched my purse from the table. "Yes, I'm finished. And to hell with you too. Don't call me, either, and as a matter of fact, I'm going to get my darn number changed."

"Sounds good to me," he said, sucking on the toothpick.

He sure as hell knew how to get under my skin. His nonchalant attitude was doing more than that. I picked up a pillow on his love seat and threw it at him. It bounced off his chest and knocked his ashtray and watch on the floor. That surely got his attention, and he jumped up from the couch. He held out his hands and stepped up to me.

"What you want, Dez? You want me to kick yo' ass? Is that it?"

"No," I said, blinking away the water that rushed to the rims of my eyes. "I want you to listen to me and understand that I have no desire for any man but you. We will always have some disagreements, but don't treat me like I mean nothing to you. I need for you to man up and stop acting so darn childish."

Roc sucked his teeth, and when his phone rang, he ignored it. "Good-bye, Dez. What you need is a grown man. Looks like you've found one in ole boy at your job."

"Fine. Forget it. You're not listening to me, and I'm wasting my time." I moved away from Roc, pushing him back slightly so I could clear my path. He reached for my wrist and squeezed it tightly.

"Watch where you're steppin'. If you think a li'l crocodile tears are enough to move me, then you got me all fucked up. I don't care nothin' about no tears or those fake cracks in your voice."

"Then what do you want from me, Roc? Do you want me to get on my knees and beg for your forgiveness? What? I'm confused." I stepped forward, this time stepping on his feet. He pushed me back on the love seat, and I lost my balance.

"You may not know what I want," he said, removing his boxers. "But I damn sure know what you want."

Roc used his foot to kick open a compartment in his coffee table. He reached for a condom package and put the condom on. He then pointed to his dick, which was as hard as ever.

"This is it, ain't it? Just like the others, this all you want from Roc, ain't it? When he ain't around to give it to you, you take your ass elsewhere, right?"

I knew Roc was trying to compare me to Vanessa, but that was in no way the case. He was so wrong about me, but I let him get whatever it was off his chest. I sat up, but he caged me in, so I couldn't move. All I could think about was the last time he forced himself on me.

"Please don't do this, Roc. Sex is not all I want from you, and you know it."

"Then what *do* you want? You still haven't told me, and fuck all that talkin' and listenin' shit. What's really up?"

"I want whatever it is that you want. Now, get off me. You're hurting me."

"So damn what? And since you won't keep it real with me, I'll tell you what I want. I want to know why you ain't told me that you love me. I've been home for four months, and you ain't said that shit to me but one time. I'm spendin' all my time with you, tryin' to do right by you, and all you've done is lie to me and complain. What's holdin' you back this time? Tell me so I can understand what the fuck is up. Is it Greg, Reggie, some other muthafucka, or what?"

I closed my eyes, taking a moment to think about Reggie. No, he wasn't holding me back. It was all about Roc. "None of the above. I'm just afraid, Roc, that's all."

"Afraid of what?" he said through gritted teeth.

"Afraid of being hurt again. I'm so afraid that you're going to hurt me and leave me and Chassidy without you. I can't let my guard down, only because I know how easy it is for you to choose Ronnie over us. Vanessa doesn't concern me as much, but your dedication to Ronnie scares me. I had fallen in love with you, and you just . . . just said to hell with me and your child and took the fall for him, choosing to go to prison. I was angry. It's so hard for me to believe that you will never play us like that again. I don't trust you, and it's difficult for me to tell you that I love you, even when deep in my heart I know I do."

There, I'd said it, and now he knew it. I had tried to fool myself into believing that this was just fun, but I knew it was more than that. Roc had ownership of my heart. All I could do was hope like hell that he wouldn't break it. He lifted himself off me, allowing me to sit up. He sat on the table in front of me and rubbed his hands up and down my thighs.

"Listen, I'm not goin' back to jail, so that decision will never have to be made again. You and Ronnie on different levels, and in no way can I compare my love for him to the love I have for you. I do love you too, Dez, but holdin' back on me like you've been doin' makes me uneasy. In a relationship, I need a woman who is willin' to give her all. She needs to accept me for who I am and not try to change some of the things about me that I will never change. I told you I'd meet you halfway, but I feel like I have to go all the way with you. Then lyin' to me about some dumb shit ain't even cool. If it had been me, you'd be all over me, talkin' shit. I'm not thrilled about you havin' sex with that fool while I was in prison, but you made no promises to me whatsoever. As far as I knew, you'd moved on with your life, but I damn sure wish you'd been there for me."

I bit my nail, already admitting to myself that he was right. "So, I guess this means I'm in trouble, huh?"

Roc cut his eyes and grinned slightly. "Hell, yeah, you in trouble. Big trouble, but I'm not gon' give you no dick. I told you that's what you wanted, and you tryin' to play it down like that ain't it."

I pouted. "Of course I want it. I always want it, but not today. We—"

His phone rang, and he quickly answered it. "BJ, make it quick. What's the address?" Roc wrote down an address on a piece of paper. "'Preciate it. Now, don't call me back for the next hour." He looked at my thighs. "Maybe two. Two or three hours. And tell Ronnie I'm busy."

After that, he dropped the phone and showed me how much he forgave me for my little white lie.

Chapter Nineteen

Roc had invited me to his cousin's wedding. We arrived at the church on Grand Boulevard around 3:45 p.m. The wedding hadn't even started yet, and since Roc was one of the groomsmen, that was a good thing. He'd driven like a bat out of hell to get there, only to be told that the minister hadn't shown up yet. I sat by myself in the crowded church, which was filled with many of Roc's relatives and friends, or so I assumed they were.

The church was beautifully decorated, and the dim lighting made the sanctuary look even more elegant. The color scheme for the wedding was turquoise, black, and white. I could tell that someone had put a lot of money into the wedding. Beautiful lilies were everywhere, and each pew had a bundle of carnations held together with pearls. A big picture of the bride and groom was propped up on an easel on the stage. The pianist started doing his thing, but he seemed merely to be tuning the piano.

I crossed my legs, looking down at my black silk and leather heels with pleats near my open toes. The half-shoulder mustard-colored dress I wore tightened at my waist and hugged my curvaceous hips. It was knee-length, but it inched up a bit when I sat down. My hair was pinned up, giving me a very classy look, which attracted stares from those seated around me in the sanctuary. Whenever someone smiled at me, I smiled back. One older lady in particular, she came over and stood next to me, holding onto her cane.

"Ooh, young lady, you're so very pretty," she said. "What gentleman in here do you belong to?"

I could only laugh. "Thank you for the compliment, and you are beautiful too. I'm here with Rocky Dawson. He's one of the groomsmen."

The lady smiled and whispered, "You mean Roc? Nobody calls him Rocky anymore, and he hates that name. I'm a longtime friend of the family. We all go way, way back."

The lady stood next to me, going on and on about the Dawson family. I asked if she wanted to take a seat next to me, but she insisted that she was sitting elsewhere. Almost fifteen minutes later the pianist asked everyone to take their seat. That was when the elderly woman finally walked away. By then, more people had crammed into the church, and there were no more empty places next to me to sit.

The wedding got started, and instead of the grooms-men coming down the aisle, they all walked in at once and stood at the front of the church. There were eight men in total, all of them very handsome men, with the exception of Ronnie. Well, he was nice-looking too, but I couldn't stand him. To me, Roc looked the best. The black tuxedo fit his body perfectly, and it, along with his fresh haircut and the trimmed hair on his chin, kept my eyes glued to him. I couldn't help that I was sitting in a church, thinking about what had transpired only a few hours ago. My mind was definitely in the gutter. God would have to forgive me.

My attention turned to the bridesmaids, who were now coming into the sanctuary, and then to the flower girl and the ring bearer. The bride was also pretty, but I wasn't going to say anything about her caked-on makeup. Whoever had done her makeup needed to rethink his or her career. Other than that, she was perfect.

While the ceremony was in progress, I occasionally looked at Roc and he looked at me. We smiled at each other, but I also noticed his attention was focused elsewhere. I followed the direction of his eyes, only to see Vanessa sitting in one of the pews, with another man next to her. I thought I'd seen the man before, and then I quickly realized it was that goon Mississippi, who was at Roc's place that day. His dreads had been cut off, and even though he looked a little better, he still wasn't all that great looking to me. I wondered for a moment if Vanessa was now seeing him. I took another look at them. As close as they sat, it was obvious they were together. I didn't know how well that had gone over with Roc, and I really wanted to know how he felt about it. I suspected the day would get interesting.

The "I do's" were exchanged, and so were the rings, and then the broom was jumped over. The wedding party was asked to stay so that photos could be taken, and instead of waiting around, I left the sanctuary and went to use the restroom and to call and check on Latrel and Chassidy. The hallways were so crowded that you could barely move. And when I got to the restroom, the line was outside the door. I dug in my purse to get my phone. I would be lying if I said I didn't hear someone say "Bitch" behind me. I turned and saw Vanessa standing only a few feet away with three other women. To be honest, she looked really nice in her lavender, sheer-like, strapless dress with a small slit on the thigh. Her long hair was pulled away from her face, bumped up a bit, and clipped in the back. All I did was cut my eyes at her, and then I moved in another direction. I was glad to see Roc exiting the sanctuary a moment later.

He saw me and motioned for me to come his way. I made my way over to him, and he eased his arm around my waist. "I want you to meet some people," he said. He introduced me to several of his cousins, aunts, uncles, and some friends. He was all smiles; he seemed really proud to have me with him. I was kind of shocked by his reaction, and more so by his arm, which he never removed from my waist. People were taking many photos, and I couldn't tell you how many times we had to stop and pose for the cameras. I even posed in two pictures with Ronnie. Thankfully, he was on one end, and I was on the other.

By the time the photo session was over, everyone was starting to leave the church to make their way to the reception. I still needed to use the restroom, so I interrupted Roc, who was talking to a couple of his friends.

"Say, honey," I said. "I'll be back, okay? I need to go to the restroom."

Roc held my hand and asked me to hold up a second. He exchanged a few more words with his friends, and then they walked away. He then turned to face me while wiggling his bow tie away from his neck.

"It's hot as fuck in here," he said. "So what did you think?"

"Think about what? The wedding?"

"Yes, the weddin' and my family. They ain't as bad as you thought they would be, are they?"

I smiled, thinking how surprised I was that he had some very nice, down-to-earth people in his family. I then reached out to help him remove the bow tie, which he seemed to be having trouble with. It came loose, and Roc placed it in his pocket. He wrapped his arms around me, and I wrapped mine around him.

"I think the wedding was beautiful. You looked very handsome, and your family is everything I imagined them to be. Wonderful people."

Roc laughed. I swear, his bright white teeth against his dark skin was a combination that set me on fire. "Quit lyin'. You are such a good liar, but you good."

He pecked my lips, encouraging me to go for more. As we kissed, an older man interrupted us and held up his camera. He took a picture with the flash on, making us laugh.

"Boy, you got yourself somethin' right there," he said, squeezing Roc's shoulder. "Good God almighty. If you can't handle all that goodness, be sure to let me know!"

"Will do, Cousin Freddy. But I'm positive I can handle it."

Freddy walked away with lust in his eyes. I couldn't help but blush from his compliment.

"I really need to get to the restroom," I said.

Roc let go of my hand. Thankfully, the restroom wasn't that crowded. After using it, I washed my hands while checking myself in the mirror. My lip gloss had gotten light, so I pulled out the tiny purse I had clutched underneath my arm and searched for my gloss. I couldn't find it—I must have forgotten it at home—so I snapped my purse closed and left the restroom. No sooner had I walked out than I saw Vanessa, who had already made her way up to Roc. She was close to his face, pointing her finger and gritting her teeth. Several other people were standing around. Didn't she know how much she was embarrassing herself? Roc slapped her finger away from his face. That was when he saw me coming. He looked over Vanessa's shoulder at me.

"Are you ready to jet so we can go to the reception?" he said over her shoulder, trying to ignore her.

She quickly turned around, with a mean mug on her face. I stepped around her and stood next to Roc. She couldn't stop herself from reaching up to hit him. This time, however, I grabbed her wrist, catching it in midair. Her eyes widened. She couldn't believe I was protecting Roc.

"That will land you on this floor," I growled. "I don't think you want to catch a beat down in this church. Take this up with Roc later. If you don't, you will regret it."

She snatched her wrist away from me, and before any words left her mouth, the man standing next to Roc pushed her backward. She almost fell, but a second later she charged again. This time, the man next to Roc squeezed her arm and ordered her to leave.

"Move out of my way, Steve!" Vanessa hissed. "That bitch don't put her hands on me. She don't know me, and I will kick her ass! I'm just tryin' to talk to Roc!"

"Wrong place," Roc said with a smirk. "Wrong time." He looked at Steve, who seemed to have some control with his grip. So many people there were shaking their head. The whole scene was quite embarrassing. "Please do somethin' with her," Roc said to Steve. "Throw her ass in the river, for all I care, but get her the fuck out of my face."

Vanessa called Roc all kinds of sons of bitches and "You muthafucka this" and "You muthafucka that." She was being pushed in one direction while we walked in the other. As soon as we walked out of the church doors, we found Mississippi standing outside, talking to a gathering of young men and several ladies. Roc was holding my hand, but I guessed he couldn't stop himself from saying something.

"Sippi, you need to go inside and calm your bitch down. She's clownin'. If you care about her, like your hatin' ass say you do, then go handle that."

Sippi pointed to his chest. "Nigga, you talkin' to me? I know you ain't talkin' to me."

Roc tried to let go of my hand, but I squeezed his fingers. He snatched his hand away and made his way up to Mississippi. I knew this day was too good to be true. Didn't somebody recognize that we were at a church? I

called out Roc's name, but he ignored me. A few people
had already started to move out. Many stayed to watch,
as Roc stood face-to-face with Mississippi with tightened
fists.

"You damn right I'm talkin' to you, you fake-ass muthafucka. Now what, nigga? Yo' move," Roc said.

Mississippi didn't have a move, especially since Ronnie
and three of his henchmen had walked up behind him.
Ronnie gripped Roc's shoulder, massaging it.

"Calm down, baby boy. There won't be no bloodshed
today. Go on and take your pretty young thang to the
reception and enjoy yourself. Sippi ain't mean no harm,
did you?"

Roc didn't move, didn't blink. He waited for Mississippi
to respond.

"Roc know he my boy, but he don't need to be comin' at
me about no dumb shit over no trick."

"One who ain't even worth it, so we gon' leave this shit
right here at the front door of the church," Ronnie said.
"Squash this and let's move out. We got a party to go to."

Mississippi held up his fist for Roc to pound and
squash, but Roc cut his eyes and walked away. He took
my hand, and at a speedy pace, he walked with me to his
truck. Honestly, I didn't feel like going to the reception.
This ongoing drama with Roc was working my nerves.
And then for Ronnie to suggest that they leave the drama
at the church door ? *Please.* God was probably shaking
His head at all of us. There was no denying that every
time I attempted to be a part of Roc's circle, something
tragic almost happened. I prayed for him, and definitely
for my safety.

Roc sped through the parking lot, only to be stopped
by Ronnie, who stood in front of the truck, holding up
his hand. He strutted around to the driver's side, and Roc
lowered his window.

"You good?" he asked Roc.

"I'm fine. That fool was the one trippin', not me."

"I don't give a shit about him. All I care about is you. I don't want no shake, rattlin', and rollin' goin' on, so calm down and sleep on it."

Roc nodded, and before he raised the window, Ronnie looked over at me.

"Sup, Desa Rae? You lookin' lovely as ever. Glad you decided to come. When you and my Roc gon' tie the knot?"

Roc smiled and put his hand on the switch to raise the window. "Man, stop talkin' shit. You high, drunk, on crack, or what?"

I leaned forward to address Ronnie. "You look awesome too, Ronnie, and as for me and Roc tying the knot, not a chance in hell. I use him only for sex."

Ronnie laughed and backed away from the truck. Roc looked disturbed by what I'd said, and I was bothered by what he'd said as well. That was why I responded the way I did. We couldn't get out of the parking lot before he tried to tear into me.

"Not a chance in hell, huh? And all I'm good for is sex? You shot me down like I wasn't shit."

"I knew you were going to say that, but it was no worse than you saying Ronnie was high, drunk, on crack, or whatever if he thought we'd ever get married," I retorted.

"I was just playin'. I told you that's how we talk."

"Well, I guess I'm learning from you, and at the time, I couldn't think of a better response."

I playfully shoved Roc's shoulder, and just to irritate me, he blasted the music. I turned it down, feeling a need to ask him a few questions.

"Snookums, I don't really want to bring this up right now, but please tell me what is up with Vanessa. Why does she always carry on like that? Has she always been that way?"

"She's a crazy and deranged bitch. She actin' like that because I don't fuck with her no more. She didn't always act like that, but she definitely ain't got it all upstairs."

"Well, it's been a while since you got out of jail. Almost six months, to be exact, and I don't understand why she doesn't accept the fact that you've moved on."

Roc stopped at the red light on Lindell Boulevard and looked over at me. "I don't know, either. But since you showed her how gangsta you can be, next time you see her, why don't you ask her? I can't tell you why she's a nutcase. Some people are just that way when they don't get what they want."

"Gangsta, no. I just don't have time for games, that's all." I touched the side of Roc's face. "Besides, I didn't want her messing up that handsome face. Not today, anyway."

"No worries here. But I don't believe for one minute that you ain't got a li'l hood in you. It's there, and ain't no way you'd be messin' with me if it wasn't."

I threw my hand back at Roc and ignored him. I had my suspicions about why Vanessa reacted the way she did. I couldn't believe any woman would constantly be carrying on the way she had been if she wasn't still someway or somehow involved with Roc. Maybe it was just me, but the next time I saw her, I intended to ask.

Roc and I were staying the night at the Renaissance Hotel where the reception was held. I decided to turn in early, so I gave him a kiss and headed up to our room. The doors to the elevator were about to close when someone put their hand between them to open them wide. It was Ronnie. He stepped onto the elevator with me.

"Going up?" he asked.

I nodded, feeling very uncomfortable about being alone with him. We pushed the sixth floor button at the same time.

"I had a damn good time today," he said, sucking his teeth. "How about you?"

"Great time," was all I said.

The elevator opened on the sixth floor, and he extended his hand, inviting me to exit first. I walked down the hallway, and Ronnie followed me. The key card had the number 612 written on it, so I followed the arrows and made my way to the room. When I found the room, I stopped and Ronnie stopped behind me. I quickly turned.

"Is there something I can help you with, Ronnie?"

"Just . . . just open the door. I need to go inside and holla at you about a few thangs."

I folded my arms. There was no way I was going inside the room with him. "Whatever you have to say, you can say it out here."

"It's private, Desa Rae. I'm not gon' hurt you. I just want to get at you about some things with Roc, particularly about him gettin' out of the game. I'm concerned about some things he's been bringin' on himself, as a permanent move like that can do more harm than good. I'm sure you understand."

I really didn't want to let Ronnie inside the room with me, but I also didn't want to stand in the hallway, discussing Roc. I told myself that if Ronnie tried anything stupid, I'd kick him hard in his nuts and run.

I opened the door with the key card and went inside. The suite was very nice, but I didn't have time to check it out like I wanted to, because of Ronnie. He removed his suit jacket, then took a seat in one of the chairs by a window. I stood close to the bed, with my arms folded.

He cleared his throat and rubbed his hands together. "Let's not pretend, Desa Rae. You don't like me, and I damn sure ain't got no love for you. You've managed to get at my li'l nigga's heart, and I'm not quite on board with that shit. I've thought about several schemes to get rid of you, and when anybody starts messin' around with my money, I gotta do what I gotta do. You know what I'm sayin'?"

"No, Ronnie, I don't know what you're saying. I don't understand how I'm messing with your money, and quite frankly, I haven't spent one dime of what belongs to you. As for your schemes to get rid of me, please let me know if that is a threat so I can get a restraining order against you and make the cops aware of this situation."

Ronnie chuckled and swiped his hand on top of his head. "Roc slippin', Desa Rae, and when you slip, eventually you fall. When you fall, you fall six feet under. He slippin' because he ain't focused on what needs to be done. I've lost a lot of money in the past several months, and while you got him out there at a two-bit-ass job, makin' twelve or thirteen lousy dollars an hour, I'm losin' more money. While he busy over there, playin' house with you and your goddamned family, my family ain't gettin' taken care of. Now, I'm bein' as nice as I can possibly be about this, but you and that baby girl need to quickly make your way out of St. Louis. Tell that nigga somethin' came up and that you gotta go. If you don't, well, see, I would hate for somethin' tragic to happen." Ronnie shrugged. "Can't say who it will happen to, because I don't know yet. But if you fall back, everything will be peaches and cream."

I stared at Ronnie and couldn't even respond. All kinds of hate for him were running through me. I had never felt like this about anyone in my life. I hadn't even known fools like him existed, but sadly enough, they did. I went to the door and opened it.

"Please get out," I said. "You will have to do what you wish, because I will never take orders from you."

Ronnie slowly stood up and stretched. With venom in his eyes, he walked to the door, looking me over as he went. He reached his hand up and touched the side of my face. Before he could say anything, I smacked his hand away. He chuckled out loud and left. I slammed the door behind him, unsure if I should tell Roc about this incident or not.

Chapter Twenty

For whatever reason, I kept what Ronnie had said to me a secret. And I didn't say one word to Roc about the letters I'd been getting in the mail, letters threatening my life. All they said was: *You die, bitch! Your days are numbered!*

The letters started coming after my confrontation with Ronnie. And someone was constantly calling my house and hanging up. When a man ran into the back of my car the other day, I was quite shaken up and paranoid. I wanted to go to the police about this, but without any evidence against Ronnie, what could they really do? I intended to watch my back, and I did tell Roc to be very careful about his surroundings. He assured me that he would. I did my best to make sure he spent plenty of days and nights with me, away from the drama that seemed to happen when he was on his turf. Roc seemed as if he had a new attitude about life, and he had not missed any more days of work. I was happy for him, and I was definitely happy about the way things were going between us.

Christmas was just around the corner, and for Thanksgiving, I had dinner at my house. Latrel finally brought his girlfriend home to meet me, and I held off on making any comments. All I could say was I liked her, she seemed nice, and she was African American. At this point, I realized that it didn't even matter, and as long as he was happy, I was. Until he intended to marry someone, I told Latrel, he would not hear my mouth again.

Things were going so well that I had even started talking sensibly to Reggie again. He was in counseling, and he told me how much it was helping him. We hadn't laughed together in quite some time, and when he came over one day and apologized again for what he'd done, I was okay. I was pleased that he'd realized his mistakes, but I made it clear that we could never turn back the hands of time. He understood.

On Christmas morning I got a call from Roc, telling me that he wasn't feeling well, so he was staying at home. I had been looking forward to our time together, and so had Chassidy. She wanted to give Li'l Roc his gift, and I wanted to give him the ones I had bought him too.

"Aw, I hope you feel better," I said over the phone to Roc. "And if you come over, I promise to take care of you."

He let out a hacking cough and asked me to hold while he spat. "I'm feelin' so miserable, I can't even move. I'll get at you on the weekend, promise. Now, let me talk to Chassidy so I can wish her a Merry Christmas."

I gave the phone to Chassidy, very disappointed that Roc wasn't coming over. While she talked to him, I turned to Latrel, who was coming up from the basement and was on his way over to Reggie's house.

"Where's Roc at?" Latrel asked.

"He's not feeling well today. Said he wasn't coming over until the weekend."

"I've been feeling a little under the weather too, but I took some Tylenol Cold and Flu last night. I feel much better."

I touched Latrel's forehead to see if he was running a fever. He wasn't. "Well, go ahead over to your father's house. Tell him I said hello, and don't forget to get his presents underneath the tree."

"I won't. But since Roc isn't coming over, why don't you and Chassidy go over to Dad's house with me? It's not like you're doing anything else."

"No, I don't think that's a good idea. Have fun and I'll see you later."

Chassidy gave the phone to me. Roc had already hung up.

"Can Chassidy go with me, then? I mean, it's Christmas, Mama. She doesn't want to be cooped up in the house."

"We aren't going to be cooped up. I plan on baking some Christmas cookies and chocolate cupcake bears."

"I don't want to leave you by yourself, but if you don't want to go with me, at least let her go."

Chassidy always loved to go with Latrel, so I put on her outdoor clothes and told the two of them to have fun. It wasn't the first time I was alone on Christmas. I suspected it wouldn't be the last.

My house had gotten kind of messy, so I decided to spend my day cleaning. Around noon, I took a break from vacuuming the floors and sat breathlessly at the kitchen table, listening to the news on the radio. I had a tall glass of ice-cold water in my hand and was guzzling it down pretty quickly. At the top of the hour there was breaking news. Apparently, there had been a murder in St. Louis, and a police officer had been shot at. The murder victim had been identified. He was a twenty-nine-year-old black man by the name of Craig M. Jackson. I kind of ignored the story, because it disturbed me that so many black men were getting killed. It always made me think of Roc. As the reporter wrapped up her story, she repeated the victim's name. This time, she said that Mr. Jackson also went by the street name Mississippi. She added that if anyone had any information, they should call the number on the screen.

Almost immediately, my heart dropped to my stomach. I couldn't believe Mississippi was dead. Just a little while ago, he and Roc had stood outside of that church, arguing. I wondered if there was any connection. My gut was sending off signals that there was. I rushed to my bedroom to put on some clothes. I wanted some answers. I didn't think Roc was capable of murder, but he damn sure knew something about this.

When I got to Roc's place, I started to use the key he had given me a while back, but then I stopped myself and knocked instead. I got no answer, so I knocked again. Finally, after knocking for about five minutes, Roc opened the door. I immediately noticed a small bruise underneath his left eye and a scratch on his neck. No, he didn't look happy to see me, and the cold stare in his eyes said so.

"May I come in?" I asked.

He covered his face with his hand, then wiped it in a downward motion. "Dez, I'm tired. I was upstairs sleepin', tryin' to work off this cold."

"I won't be long."

Roc turned and headed up the stairs. He went back into his bedroom and got underneath the covers. The room was partially lit by the sun's rays coming through the window, but I turned on the light.

"What happened to your eye?" I asked.

"I ran into somethin'."

"And the scratch on your neck?"

"Somethin' bit me, and I kept scratchin' it."

"Roc, stop lying. I thought we didn't go there with each other like that anymore."

He sat up in bed and put his hands behind his head. "Are you over here because I didn't come to your house for Christmas? I told you I wasn't feelin' well. Nothin' else needs to be said."

"What happened to Mississippi?"

He cocked his head back, as if he hadn't heard me. "Who?"

"Sippi. The one you got into it with at the wedding. The news reported that he was murdered. I thought you might know something about it."

Roc shrugged. "That's what that nigga get. No love lost here, and if I do know somethin' about it, so what? What you gon' do? Call the police on me or somethin'? You runnin' up in here like you tryin' to get info for a reward."

"I don't know what I would do with the truth, but I want to know if you had anything to do with it."

Roc didn't answer. He reached for the cigar on the nightstand next to him and lit it. "So you don't know what you would do, huh? Ain't that a bitch? I feel you, Ma, but just so you can sleep at night, no, you don't have a murderer lyin' in bed next to you and runnin' up in that pussy. I don't get down like that. Sippi had a whole lot of haters. Ain't no tellin' who put two in his head, but it damn sure wasn't me." Roc held out his hands defensively. "Could have been anybody. Now, please, please can I get some rest? If it makes you feel better, I will stop by tomorrow. Promise."

Roc took a few more puffs from the cigar and then put it out in the ashtray. I watched as he threw the covers back over his head, trying his best to ignore me. I wasn't in the mood for this on Christmas Day, so I left his bedroom and headed for the front door. As I walked down the hallway, though, I stopped dead in my tracks. The news hadn't mentioned anything about Mississippi being shot twice in the head. How would Roc know that? I turned and made my way back to his bedroom. I cleared my throat.

He snatched the covers off his head and sighed.

"I'm going to get out of your hair soon, but I wanted you to know that your cough is already sounding better.

Let me know what kind of medicine you've been using, as it seems to work magic. Pertaining to Mississippi, I don't really care what happened to him, as I firmly believe you reap what you sow. But the news didn't mention that he was shot twice in the head. The only person who would know that is the killer, or *the one* who gave the order to have it done. That's just something for you to think about while you're resting."

Roc held out his hands again and stared at me with a cold expression. "I said it wasn't me."

With nothing else to say, I left the room. I suspected that Roc had something to do with Mississippi's demise, but he would never tell. This secretive life he lived was killing me. There was so much about it that I didn't want to know; then again I did. I figured the truth behind all of it would hurt me and Chassidy. I never wanted to sit her down and tell her what kind of man I suspected her father was. *A killer?* I wasn't sure yet, but I prayed that it simply wasn't true.

I had gotten about two miles away from Roc's place when I saw a familiar face driving in the opposite direction on Grand Boulevard. It was Vanessa. I didn't think she saw me. When I got to the light, I quickly made a U-turn to see where she was going. She was driving a white convertible BMW. I wasn't about to let it get out of my sight. That thought was short-lived, because when the light turned yellow, she rushed through it. I had to stop at the light; it seemed to take forever to change. I tapped my fingers on the steering wheel, already feeling the knot in my stomach tighten. I tried to loosen the knot by taking deep breaths, but the deeper my breaths got, the more the knot seemed to tighten.

The light changed, but Vanessa's BMW was long gone. That in no way mattered, because when I got to Roc's place, her car was parked out front. She had to be inside, so I waited to see how long she'd stay. I couldn't believe that I was spying on Roc, but there were some things that I needed to know, and he wasn't telling. *Do I stay out here?* I kept asking myself. *Or do I go to the door?*

I sat in the car, debating with myself. I also thought about just going home. That was what I should do, but it didn't seem like much of an option. Before I knew it, I had been sitting in the car for about forty-five minutes. I had hoped that Vanessa would've come out by now, but she hadn't. I was so hurt inside, but my hurt wouldn't allow me to shed one tear, even though my throat felt as if it was burning and my hands were starting to tremble. I took another deep breath, then said, "Fuck it."

I made my way to Roc's front door and fumbled around with my keys, in search of the one Roc had given me. I knew he had plenty of guns inside, and there was a possibility that I could get hurt. I figured Vanessa was the kind of woman who would protect her man at any cost, but I didn't care. I was numb and wasn't thinking clearly. I turned the lock, then slowly pushed the door open. Immediately, I heard loud rap music playing, and it wasn't until I got midway up the stairs that I heard Vanessa moaning, as if she was in tremendous pain. My entire body felt weak, and my legs felt as if I had been running a marathon.

At that point, I knew I had all the answers I needed. I wanted to turn around and leave, but this was an out-of-body experience, which I had never felt before. I kept on moving up the stairs, and when I almost reached the top, I turned to my right. That was where all the action was taking place. Roc was sitting up on the couch with no clothes on, leaning back and looking helpless. Vanessa's near-perfect naked body was on top of him, straddling him. Her back was facing him, and she was giving him one hell of a ride. His head was dropped back, and his eyes were squeezed tight. So were hers. Seeing his dick plunge into her insides made me ill. His hands roamed her ass, and he had the nerve to smack it. Then he eased his hand around to her clitoris, teasing hers like he often teased mine. She was near tears. All she could do was tell him how much she loved him.

"Love you so much, and you know this dick was made for me," she cried. "Only meee!"

I'd be damned if he didn't respond, "Damn, I love how you do this shit! Keep on fuckin' me like this. *Nobody* makes me feel like you do! *Nobody*, Ma."

I had heard it all before and could have fallen down the stairs as I quickly made my way out. As weak as my legs were, I almost did fall. I didn't care that I probably had their attention, and by the time I reached the porch, it was obvious that I did. Roc called after me, but I kept it moving. I hurried to my car, and he chased after me with a towel wrapped around his waist. Dick was probably still dripping wet from the festivities. As he crossed the street, a car almost hit him but swerved out of the way. The driver blew his horn and yelled profanities out his window.

"Fuck you too," Roc said, running up to my car. He banged on the window, telling me to lower it. I looked in my side mirror, making sure it was safe to pull off. It was, so I did.

I was a nervous wreck while driving home. I kept smacking away my falling tears, fighting my pain. I didn't know what it was about me that had me always trying to play the tough role, but this time, Roc had broken me down. I didn't even think my divorce from Reggie had hurt this bad, and it was because at this age, I found myself in a very similar situation. The choices I had made had cost me dearly. Anyone could say what they wanted, but the fact was that I in no way deserved this. Obviously, bullshit came at any age, and some men would never stop bringing it. It had been up to me to do better, and I'd known it. Sadly, I had taken a risk, and in no way did it pay off.

As soon as I got home, I rushed inside and hurried to take off my clothes. I turned on my shower, got inside, and let the warm water pour down on me. I picked up a sponge and scrubbed my skin hard, attempting to wash away the touch of Roc's hands. I knew the scrubbing was doing me no good, but I felt like the water was cleansing my mind, body, and soul. I closed my eyes and thought of every single time he'd touched me, but I couldn't get thoughts of what I had just witnessed out of my mind.

Finally, the tears streamed down my face, and I cried harder than I had ever cried before. I asked myself over and over again, Where did I go wrong? I'd let my guard down, but how in the hell could I allow myself to trust a man like him? That was one big mistake. I should've seen this coming. He couldn't give up Vanessa if his life depended on it. And there was no telling who else was in the picture. He'd been running from one woman to the next, pretending as if I was the one who had changed his life around. I hadn't changed anything.

I showered until the water turned cold. By then, my body was quivering, and I was a complete mess. I sat on the seat in my shower, with my head hung low and my hair dripping wet. My hands covered my face. I felt like I couldn't even move.

"You . . . you left the front door open," Roc said. I heard the shower door slide open. He had no clue how upset I was—right now I could have killed him. I had often wondered what made Vanessa as angry as she was, and now a part of me understood her actions. Being screwed over and lied to by a man definitely wasn't any fun.

"Dez," Roc said, touching my hand and trying to move it away from my face. "I'm sorry. But can I tell you why I did what I did?"

I really didn't care, only because there was nothing he could say that would ever repair this kind of damage. I removed my hands from my face, then tried to wipe my face clean. Roc squatted down beside the shower and tried to explain his actions.

"Maybe I should've told you this, but I've been upset with you for a while. Only because you didn't tell me that Ronnie approached you at the hotel, basically threatenin' my life and yours. I couldn't understand why you didn't say nothin' to me, but it bothered me that you didn't. As a woman who is supposed to love me, you need to have my back. When somebody—anybody—get at you with some shit like that, it is imperative for you to say somethin'. You made me feel as if I couldn't trust you, so I was like, 'Fuck it.' I felt as if you wasn't givin' me your all, so I decided not to give you my all."

I still had nothing to say. Roc could sit next to me and explain his mess until he was blue in the face. It wouldn't even matter. He knew damn well that he had never stopped seeing Vanessa. Whether I had told him about Ronnie or not, what happened today would have happened, anyway.

"The truth about Vanessa . . . Here it is. Yes, I was dippin' and dabbin' in that every blue moon. Nowhere near as much as you think, only because I wanted to do right by you. When I found out that you neglected to tell me about your conversation with Ronnie, I went back to the woman I felt safe with. Vanessa would lay her life on the line for me, Dez, and anytime Ronnie has said some shit that affected me, she's told me. Even so, I didn't want to be with her. I wanted to be with the woman who was helpin' me grow into a better man and encouragin' me to live a better life. The one who captured my muthafuckin' heart like no one had ever done before. I'm so sorry for what your eyes witnessed today, but I did it because I was hurtin' inside too."

Roc waited for a response, but I still didn't have one. Obviously, he was with the right woman, if she was willing to lay her life on the line for him. I wasn't willing to do so. I closed my eyes again, rubbing my forehead and hoping that he would leave.

He stood and placed his hands in his pockets. "Lastly, I wasn't the one who killed Mississippi, but I do know who it was. He owed someone close to me a lot of money, and shit happens when you don't pay up. The bruise underneath my eye and the scratch on my neck are from Vanessa. She was upset because I told her I was spendin' Christmas with you and Chassidy. I didn't want to come over, because I knew you'd question me about my marks. When Vanessa came to my place, I was upset with you again, not knowin' what you would do with information about Mississippi. It's shit like that, Dez, where you leave me with too many unanswered questions about you. So, if this is a wrap, so be it."

Roc left the bathroom. I wasn't sure if he left the house, but when I heard the front door shut, I figured he had.

Chapter Twenty-one

I stood in the foyer, reading another letter that had been mailed to me. The words were a little different this time. *You's a dead bitch,* it said. A smiley face sticker had been stuck to it. I tore up the letter and threw it in the trash. A part of me felt as if the letters were coming from Ronnie, but could a man as old as he was act so darn childish? I wasn't sure. The thought that the letters were coming from Vanessa crossed my mind as well.

I went in the kitchen and gazed out at the backyard, watching Latrel and Chassidy make a snowman. I had to do whatever was necessary to protect them. In this case, calling the police to report the letters wasn't an option. I didn't want to involve them, because I'd have to mention Roc. I'd never had a gun in the house, but a few weeks ago I'd gone and got one. If I had to use it, I would do it in a heartbeat. Ronnie didn't seem like the kind of man whom I could take lightly, and I was starting to worry more about his threats. Maybe it was a good thing that Roc and I weren't seeing each other anymore, but the letter that came today proved that someone wasn't backing down.

As soon as I took a sip from the coffee I had made earlier, the phone rang. I picked up, but no one answered.

"Hello?" I said again.

No reply.

"You know, I could get my number changed, but I won't. Whoever this is, you don't scare me. Show your damn face, you coward. And when you do, you'd better believe I'll have something waiting for your ass."

I slammed down the phone. Even though I was afraid, I would never show it. I took a deep breath, hoping that this matter would quickly resolve itself.

Like in the past, Roc called to say he would give me time to get my thoughts together and would not pressure me about what I ultimately decided to do. Time was in no way what I needed. I already knew that our relationship was over. It was hard for me to swallow, especially since I still had to continue to deal with Roc because of Chassidy.

I also had to see him at work from time to time, though I had expected him to give up on his job by now. In no way did he need to be working, for it was obvious that there was still some moving and shaking going on behind the scenes. With him keeping his job, I figured he was only trying to prove something to me.

The New Year had swooped in so fast. If you blinked, you missed the month of January. My birthday was in March. I didn't quite feel my age nor did I look it, either. That was a good thing.

In August of this year, Latrel would finally be a senior. He wouldn't graduate until the following year, but time had definitely gotten away from me. He was still playing basketball, but he seemed to be focusing more on his engineering degree. His visits home had slacked up a bit, simply because he was starting to spend more time with his girlfriend. I was a little upset about that, but Latrel had a life to live, and I had to accept that. Reggie had been griping about how much time Latrel had been spending with his girlfriend too. When he told me Latrel had mentioned getting married, I was stunned.

"Married?" I said over the phone as I talked to Reggie. "Are you serious?"

"Very. I'm just warning you. I have a feeling about this one. There is something in our son's eyes that I'm seeing, and I know what that means. He's in love with Angelique. I would put some money on it."

"I think he's in love too, but I don't know about this marriage thing. It's too soon, and he hasn't even known her for a year yet, has he?"

"He's known her for a while, but they started dating a while ago. I didn't call to get you uptight, and like I said, I just wanted to warn you."

I thanked Reggie for the heads-up.

On the following Monday, it was back to work for me. I plopped down in my chair and saw a note on my computer. The note was from Roc, asking if he could stop by after work to see Chassidy. It had been a little over three weeks since I'd had a conversation with him about her, and even though I'd debated in my mind what to do, I didn't want to keep them apart. I immediately called Roc's cell phone, and he answered.

"Yes," I said. "That will be fine."

"I can come over?"

"Roc, you are welcome to see your daughter anytime you wish. She misses you too, and I would never prevent you from being a part of her life."

"'Preciate it. I'm leavin' work early today because I gotta go handle some business. I'll see y'all around six, and no later than seven."

"Sure."

Roc came over and spent the entire evening with Chassidy. I stayed in my bedroom, reading a book. Before he left, he stopped to ask if he could see her on Tuesdays and Thursdays. He also wanted to know what I was doing for my birthday.

"Tuesdays and Thursdays sounds fine. As for my birthday, I'm not doing anything."

"Can I take you to dinner or somethin'?"

"No, but thank you. I'll be right here on my birthday, and if it falls on a Tuesday or Thursday, maybe I'll see you then."

"It's on a Tuesday. Enjoy your book, and I'll see you tomorrow at work. Remember tomorrow is Tuesday, so I'm comin' back this way again."

Every single Tuesday and Thursday, Roc showed up to spend time with Chassidy. Sometimes, I would leave and go to the library or the Galleria, just to give them some time alone together. He kept his word about spending time with her and about keeping his job. Sometimes, he brought Li'l Roc with him to visit, and the farthest they would go was to some of the playgrounds in my neighborhood or to the grocery store to buy junk. I had become more relaxed with the situation and was pleased about the connection he had with his children.

Mr. Anderson had ordered a birthday cake for me, and on the day of my birthday, many of my coworkers came to my desk to get a piece. Monica had sent me some flowers, and so had Latrel and Reggie. Needless to say, my desk was full of love. I felt pretty darn special. I packed up everything around three o'clock and left for the day. I picked up Chassidy early from day care and headed home to cook dinner.

Since it was a Tuesday, I knew Roc was coming over. I suspected that he would bring Li'l Roc with him. We had spoken earlier, and I had mentioned that I had plenty of cake left. Roc got there around 6:30 p.m., his normal time of arrival. Li'l Roc was with him, and he couldn't wait to tear into the cake, which I had placed on the table. I told him and Chassidy to have at it, but what did I say that for? Cake was everywhere, leaving me with one big mess to clean up. As I walked over to the sink to get a rag, Roc asked me to follow him into the family room. I was still able to keep my eyes on the kids, so I went into the den to see what he wanted. He gave me two boxes and a card.

"Here," he said. "This is what Li'l Roc picked out for you. He would've given it to you, but as you can see, he's too busy with that cake."

I sat down and opened the card first, reading what Li'l Roc had written in his own handwriting.

Happy Birthday, Miss Dez. I love you very much and thank you for being like a second mama to me. Sometimes I wish you were my first mama, but I know you can't be. Thanks for my little sister too, and you are a wonderful family.

I closed the card and saw that he had written my name and Chassidy's on the images of the woman and the little girl on the card. My eyes watered, but I held back my tears. I swallowed the lump in my throat and opened the box from Li'l Roc, which contained a cross with diamonds. I was so touched, and I stood up to go give Li'l Roc a hug and a kiss.

"Wait a sec," Roc said. "Can you open my gift before you go back into the kitchen?"

"I told you not to do anything for me, Roc. And I don't want you spending your money on me."

"I didn't spend that much money on you, so just chill."

At his request, I opened the other box and couldn't help but smile when I found my favorite sundress inside. I knew he'd had to go to hell and back to find one exactly like the one he'd torn. His efforts impressed me.

"Thank you," I said, looking up at him.

"Are you goin' to wear it for me tonight? I hope so."

I didn't respond. I opened the envelope inside the box. There was a beautiful card, along with a cashier's check for twelve thousand dollars. I held it in my hand, wondering what it was for.

"I've been saving my checks for Chassidy's education. That's my hard-earned money, so I don't want you trippin' with me about it. Every dime that I make will be for her."

I was speechless. This was a very tough situation. I loved and appreciated so much about him, but then there was a side of him that I could in no way cope with. Roc stepped closer to me and reached into his pocket. My heart dropped, as I thought he was going to pull out a ring. Instead, he pulled out a folded piece of paper. He unfolded it, then let out a deep sigh.

"You'd better not laugh at me. If you do, I'm never doin' this shit again."

I didn't know what the note said, but in no way would I laugh at something he'd written. "Go ahead," I said, watching him look over the paper. "Read it."

He cleared his throat. "What is black love, and what does it really mean to me? For years, I thought that black love represented drama and disrespect. In order to get somewhere as a black couple, there had to be pain or no gain. My partner didn't have to show love, 'cause she didn't know love. And if we ever had to go to blows with each other, then that just meant we were angry because we couldn't bear to be without each other. Yeah, that's what I thought, but for all these years, I've been wrong about black love. Dead wrong.

"Now I know better, because true black love is alive in me. I feel love like I have never felt it before, and it's so energizing that it takes over my mind, body, and soul. It makes me laugh when I want to cry, it makes me strive harder when I want to give up, and it causes me to be real with myself, which is sometimes so difficult for me to do. Even in my darkest hours, when I feel hopeless or I don't want to go on, the feeling of black love picks me up and lets me know that I must move forward. Yeah, I finally get it, but I hope black love don't give up on me, because I will never give up on it." Roc folded the paper and seemed embarrassed to look at me.

"That was nice," I said with tears in my eyes. "I have to ask. Did you write that? I mean, you just don't seem like the type of person who—"

"Yeah, I wrote it. I know it was corny and everything, but I just wanted to share with you my thoughts, which I often write on paper. I did a lot of writin' when I was locked up, and these are my real thoughts, Ma. I wanted to take this opportunity on your B-day to share that with you, even though we got some serious problems in this relationship."

"Thanks for sharing. Your words were beautiful. I really don't know what else to say, but I will never give up on black love, either."

I reached out to give Roc a hug. He squeezed me tight and kissed my cheek. "You've had your back turned, but when you turn around, please do not be mad at me."

I quickly turned my head. Cake was everywhere. Li'l Roc's and Chassidy's mouths were full of cake, and their hands were covered with cake. Needless to say, they both got in trouble and were sent to bed.

Just as Roc walked into the kitchen, his phone rang.

"Speak," he said, with a smile on his face. Seconds later his smile vanished quickly. "What?" he yelled. "Nigga, I can't understand a word you're sayin'." Roc paused to listen, then responded, "All right. Calm the fuck down! I'm on my way."

He looked at me. "I need to go. I'll be back to get Li'l Roc later."

Roc rushed to the door, and I hurried after him.

"Wha . . . what happened?" I asked.

He yanked open the front door and stared at me for a few seconds with a confused look on his face. "Somebody shot Ronnie."

Roc ran outside, and it wasn't long before I saw his truck speeding down the street. I slowly closed the door, feeling bad for Roc but unsure about my feelings about Ronnie. Yes, I hated him with a passion, but did I really want the man to die? There had been times when I wanted to kill him myself, but those were just expressions of the anger I felt inside. Hopefully, he was in the hospital and the situation wasn't that serious. I said a quick prayer by the door, then went into the kitchen to clean up.

Hours later, I couldn't sleep. I called Roc's cell phone but got no answer. Finally, at 3:45 a.m., I heard the doorbell ring. I pulled the covers back and rushed out of bed. I could see Roc's truck in the driveway, so I immediately opened the door. He came in so fast that it scared me to death. So much blood was on his shirt, and he staggered inside, appearing to be in much pain. I touched his chest and tried to help him keep his balance.

"Have . . . have you been shot?" I yelled in a panic, still touching all over his bloodstained shirt. "Oh my God, Roc, what happened?"

He staggered into the living room, then fell back on the couch. His arm dropped on his forehead, and he squeezed his eyes tightly together. His entire face was wet from tears. His breathing was very fast. He cried out, but I wasn't sure what he said. Then it made sense.

"He died, Dez. Ronnie died on meee!"

I had never, ever seen Roc like this, nor had I ever witnessed any man crying so hard. My hands trembled as I reached out to touch his body, which wouldn't stop shaking.

"It'll be okay, honey. I'm so sorry. Really I am."

Roc wailed out loud, tightening his fist and slamming it into the couch. I didn't know what to say or do to help him. Putting my arms around him only caused him to push me away.

"Just leave me the fuck alone," he cried. "Back up and give me some goddamned breathin' room!"

I backed away from Roc, giving him the space he'd requested. Seconds later, Li'l Roc came into the living room after hearing Roc's loud voice.

"Why you crying, Daddy?" he asked tearfully.

Roc didn't respond. He just kept on sobbing and pounding his fist while screaming, "Damn."

I took Li'l Roc's hand, and he looked up at me. "What's wrong with my daddy, Miss Dez?"

"He lost someone very special to him," I said. I continued to hold Li'l Roc's hand and then walked him back to the guest room so he could get back in bed. "Give your dad time to cool off. He'll tell you about what happened soon."

Li'l Roc looked up at me again. "Did Uncle Ronnie get killed? Did my dad kill Uncle Ronnie?"

"No, sweetheart, no. Go back to sleep, and we'll talk in the morning."

I didn't know what to say to Li'l Roc. I wasn't sure about his relationship with Ronnie, and the last thing I wanted was to bring a child to more tears. I noticed him wipe a tear. He must have shed a few for his father. I had done so as well, and after I tucked Li'l Roc back in bed, I stood outside the door to gather myself. I took several deep breaths, then made my way back into the living room, where Roc was. He was sitting on the floor now with his knees bent and his back resting against the couch, shielding his face with one hand. I got on the floor and sat next to him. I put my arms around him and laid my head on his shoulder.

"Don't worry. You'll get through this. I will do whatever it takes to make sure you do. If you need me for anything, I'm here."

Roc leaned forward, removing my arms from around him and making sure my head left his shoulder. He squeezed his stomach and continued to break down on me.

"This shit hurts, Ma. Losing that muthafucka hurts. He's all I had, Dez. Now what the fuck I'm gon' do?"

Roc rocked back and forth while I rubbed his back. He had me to depend on, but with us, limitations had been put in place. I knew that the love he had for Ronnie in no way compared to what he felt for me. All I could say to him was, "You still have to live for you, and you have so much to live for. Your children need you, just like you needed Ronnie. Don't give up, because we love you so much."

Roc stayed in the living room all morning. I tried to find out who killed Ronnie and why, but I got no answer. I didn't press the issue, and when he was ready to talk, I was sure he would.

Ronnie's funeral was scheduled for Saturday. I had barely talked to Roc since he left on Wednesday afternoon to make the arrangements. When I asked if he knew who had killed Ronnie, he said no and refused to talk about it. Our phone conversations were short; he seemed to be so out of it. He invited me to attend the funeral with him, but to be honest, a big part of me didn't want to be there. I knew how much Ronnie disliked me. I felt as if going to his funeral would be very disrespectful. In no way was I happy about what had happened to him, and I truly wished that this whole situation had turned out differently. But I just couldn't relay those words to Roc. He needed me, and if the shoe were on the other foot, I knew he would be there for me.

I told Roc that I would meet him at the funeral. It was at the same church as the wedding. I walked into the church, dressed in my black linen short-sleeved dress that had a waist-length jacket to go with it. Pearls were around my neck and adorned my wrist as well. My hair was pinned up again, and I wore very little makeup. My black heels made me tall, but even so, I hiked myself up on the tips of my toes and looked over the many people in front of me to see if I could find Roc. I didn't see him, so I made my way into the sanctuary and took a seat in the far back. Ronnie's shiny black and chrome casket was already up front. On both sides of the church there were pictures of him. I swallowed hard, feeling so uncomfortable.

My eyes wandered around, taking in the hundreds of people who had piled into the church. The middle section was for the family, so the ushers started to bring in chairs to accommodate the crowd. Moments later, I looked to my right and saw Roc standing next to me.

"Why you didn't let me know you were here?" he said with a sad look on his face. His eyes were red and puffy underneath.

"I figured you would know I was here."

He reached out for my hand. "Come out here with me. The family ain't comin' in until last."

I wasn't family, but instead of saying it, I took Roc's hand. We made our way through the crowd, and as we went, people were rubbing his shoulder, telling him everything would be all right, and giving him lots of hugs. That made Roc very emotional, and every time we stopped to talk to someone, he squeezed my hand. I figured he thought I was going to let go, but I didn't.

Soon the funeral got started, and the long line of family members proceeded to go into the church. Roc and I were at the front of the line and were seated in the very first pew. I kept praying for God to give me strength so I could pass it on to Roc. His legs were trembling, and his eyes were glued to Ronnie's casket. Every few seconds, he'd let out a deep breath and sit back. Then he'd let out another and lean forward. He was very fidgety, and I reached for his hand to calm him. I held on tight and occasionally rubbed his back and patted his leg.

Midway through the funeral, the service was pure, deep torture. The cries in the church had gotten louder, the singing had choked me up, and one person after another stood up to tell how Ronnie had had such an impact on their lives.

"Y'all just don't know," said a young man as he stood in front of the church. He was crying his heart out. He pointed to Ronnie's casket. "That man right there, he took care of everybody. You could ask him for anything, and he would do it, no questions asked. We lost a hero, but I'm gon' be thankful that I got a chance to know who the real man was."

So many people in the church shared his sentiments and hollered, "Amen."

Roc tightened his fist and whispered, "Say that shit, man. Say that shit again." He rolled up Ronnie's funeral program, then tapped it against his hand. At one point, he seemed to calm down, and he reached his arm back to rest it on top of the pew. I looked up at him, but it was almost as if I were looking through him. This was a different Roc sitting next to me. A much colder one.

According to the program, it was now time to view the body. This was the part that I hated so much. With us being rather close to the casket, there was no way for me to avoid it. I prayed yet again for strength. The funeral directors opened the casket, and all I could picture in my mind was Roc lying there. From a short distance, I could see Ronnie laid out in a black pin-striped suit and burgundy accessories. Roc was staring at him again, and it wasn't long before the people in the church erupted with more hollering and screaming.

"Jesus Christ," one lady shouted, covering her mouth and damn near fainting.

I had never seen so many men cry in my life. A man dropped to his knees in front of the casket. "Why you leave us like this, man? Why?" he screamed. "You was supposed to be a soldier!" The ushers had to carry the man out.

One by one, some of the visitors kissed Ronnie, placed items in his casket, or fell all over it, in tears. Shouts of pain rang out, and when Roc dropped down to one knee, I stood up behind him. Several men came to his aid, trying to hold him up. Eventually, they had to carry him out of the church as well. I followed, wiping my tears and hoping that this torture would all be over with soon.

Nearly two hours later, it was. I got in my car at the cemetery and couldn't help but wonder where things would go from here, now that Ronnie was gone. Would Roc now become the head Negro in charge, or was this the right time for him to move away from the bullshit and be done with it? Just from observing and noticing all the people coming up to him, I wasn't so sure.

Chapter Twenty-two

I guess it didn't take long for my question to be answered, and just for the record, Roc had been fired from his job. His boss had come to me this morning, telling me that Roc had taken too many days off and had failed to call in to say why. I knew he hadn't been coming to work, and every time I spoke to him, he said that he needed more time to get himself together. Basically, he didn't feel like working, so he wasn't coming in. His Tuesday and Thursday visits had also come to a halt. The last time I'd seen him was at the cemetery that day. In no way did I want to pressure him, and when he asked for space, I gave it to him.

Besides, on my end, I had an even bigger fish to fry. Latrel had finally broken the news to me, telling me that he wanted to get married. I was livid, because he hadn't even finished college yet. He still had one year to go, but he refused to wait.

"What is the rush?" I asked, talking to him over the phone while I was on the treadmill at Gold's Gym.

"There is no rush. I've known her for a while, and I'm in love. We feel now is the right time to do it, and before we go back to school in August, we will be married. Either you're on board or not, Mama. It's going to happen, and I'm not going to argue with you about this. Just be happy for me, all right?"

"I'm trying to be, Latrel, but I don't understand why you can't just finish school first. That would make so much more sense. Give this relationship *thingy* a little more time."

"I'm not on your time. I'm on my time. Angelique agreed to marry me, and I'm not going to wait to do it."

"She's pregnant, isn't she? Why don't you just come out and say it, Latrel?"

"I would tell you if she was, but she's not. Look, I'm not getting anywhere with this conversation. I'll be home next weekend, and we can talk more about it. I have to get to class. Bye, Mama."

He hung up, leaving me fuming inside. In no way was I against him getting married, but Latrel needed to wait. He was moving way too fast. Just two years ago, he'd claimed to be in love with someone else. It reminded me so much of the situation Reggie had put himself in. I was concerned about Latrel following that path.

The weeks had flown by since the funeral. I'd been so sure that Roc would make some time for Chassidy, but he hadn't. Basically, he had cut her off. I didn't like it one bit. I was very upset with him, and even though I figured he was still going through a hard time, his approach was wrong. She had been asking about him, and I didn't have a legitimate answer as to why he, and Li'l Roc, had stopped calling and coming over.

Friday after work, I decided to go get my answer. I remembered the turmoil that going to his place had brought me the last time I paid him an unexpected visit, but I was prepared to deal with whatever. He wasn't my man, and this was all about how he intended to move forward with his daughter. I wanted what was in her best interests. If Roc had decided not to be a part of her life anymore, I needed to know that.

When I arrived at his place, I knocked but got no answer. I rang the doorbell; no one came to the door. I waited and then contemplated using my key. That would be such a bold move, and if the shoe were on the other foot, I would have a fit. Still, that didn't stop me from putting my key in the door and going inside. Just like the last time, the music was up very loud. This time, however, I called Roc's name to let him know that I was inside the house.

"Roc, are you in here? It's me, Dez."

I got no answer as I made my way up the steps, afraid to look into the living room and witness what I'd seen before. This time, the living room was empty, but it was a mess. Clothes were everywhere, smoked blunts were piled up in an ashtray, and empty beer cans, as well as liquor bottles, were all over. It looked like somebody had been partying and partying hard. I checked the dining room and the kitchen, but they both were empty. Two of the kitchen chairs were tilted back on the floor, and empty bags from KFC were on the table. I picked up the chairs, placing them back underneath the table. Afterward, I turned and made my way down the hallway to his bedroom. I felt very uneasy, and as I slowly walked, the floor squeaked loudly. Seconds later, I heard Roc's voice coming from his bedroom.

"If you make another move, I swear I'll kill you."

I stopped in my tracks, with an increased heart rate. "Roc, it's me. Dez."

I got no response, but as I inched my way to the door, I peeked into his bedroom. He was sitting up in bed. His gun was aimed in my direction, and when he saw me, he dropped it into his lap. The room was partially dark, because he had put up some curtains to cover the window. I turned on the light and saw that, just like the rest of his place, everything was a mess.

"What's going on, Roc?" I walked farther into the room. The smell of marijuana was potent. Roc's eyes were bloodshot, and I had never seen the hair on his head, as well as his facial hair, look so scruffy.

He scratched his head. I could hear how dry his hair was. "Ain't nothin' goin' on. Just chillin', that's all."

I sat on the bed, in front of him, looking around at his messy room. "It looks like something has been going on. Did you have a party?"

"Nope. If I had, I would've invited you."

"Don't do me any favors." I chuckled, but he didn't laugh. All he did was clear his throat.

"I . . . I'm not going to stay long, but I stopped by because you haven't called or come by to see Chassidy. She misses you, and I do too. Have you given up on your daughter? I know things haven't been going well with us, but I thought you'd at least still see about your daughter."

Roc rested his back against the headboard. "Yep. I've given up on everything. Ain't no place in this world for a man like me, so I'm here in my own space, doin' my own thing."

"So, in other words, you're hiding out? From what? Me? Chassidy? Who?"

"I'm not hidin' out. I just don't want to be out there right now. I like right where I am. This shit is peaceful, Ma."

"Well, I definitely don't want to interrupt your peace. I know how it is when you feel the need to be alone. I was the same way when I lost my mother, so I can understand how you feel." I touched the side of his face and rubbed it. "Just know that I'm here for you, and don't give up on life, okay?"

He said not a word, just stared at me, in a trance. I stood up, willing to leave Roc at peace. When it came to healing, people were on their own time and they dealt with the loss of a loved one how they wanted to. I figured Roc would come around, so I wasn't too worried. I gave him a hug; he barely hugged me back. Needing no answer as to why, I made my way to the bedroom door. I reached for the light and turned it back off.

"Dez," Roc said, halting my steps.

"Yes?" I turned to see what he wanted.

"I . . . I did it all for you. For you and Chassidy. I just wanted to let you know that."

My brows scrunched inward. "Did what for us? What did you do for us?"

I saw a tear roll down his face, and he swiped it away. I moved closer, asking the same question. Roc looked into my eyes and sucked his teeth.

"He was gon' kill you, Ma." He spoke tearfully. "You and my daughter, and I couldn't let him do it. I couldn't, Dez, so I had to make a decision. He was days away from doin' it, and when I found out about the letters and the phone calls from my boy Gage, I . . . I had to take action."

It felt as if cement had been poured over me. I couldn't move. I opened my mouth, but no words came out. Roc lowered his head and squeezed his forehead.

"Please forgive me, but I can't be around you and Chassidy anymore. It hurts too bad, and it reminds me of what I had done to him."

I looked at the gun in Roc's lap, realizing that he must have been over here contemplating suicide. What a messed-up situation to be in. There had been no doubt in my mind that Ronnie was coming for me, and no wonder Li'l Roc had asked if Roc had killed Ronnie. He'd known all along . . . He must have overheard a conversation.

This was so very tragic. I slowly sat on the bed and moved the gun away from Roc's lap. He began to tell me how he had Ronnie set up, and he described the paranoia he'd felt from doing so. He even let me listen to a tape that was given to him by Gage, in which Ronnie clearly described his plan to do away with me and Chassidy the day after my birthday. I was to be blown away at the front door, and directions had been given to do away with anyone else in the house and to make sure the little girl,

Chassidy, didn't live. I was stunned that Ronnie could be so cruel. It pleased my heart to know that he was now in hell.

I could see the pain Roc was in from making such a difficult decision. I put my arms around him, thanking him repeatedly for basically choosing our lives over Ronnie.

"Please don't be so hard on yourself," I said tearfully. "I am so grateful to you for what you did. One day you will realize that you did the right thing. Thank you, baby. Thank you. I love you so much. You don't know how much Chassidy and I need you."

I had a tight hold on Roc, but his hold on me wasn't so tight. He begged me not to tell anyone the truth and did his best to convince me that him not being in Chassidy's life was a good thing. According to him, there was no way for him to be the father he needed to be to her. And if anyone ever found out the truth about what had happened to Ronnie, we could all lose our lives. In no way did he want that to happen, so he asked me to please understand why it had to be this way.

"I will give you all the space and time you need, but you're not going to do this to us again, Roc. You promised me that you wouldn't give up on us, and I'm going to hold you to that promise. I will never repeat a word of this to anyone. At the end of the day, you made a choice that saved the lives of two people who didn't deserve to die. I know that losing Ronnie hurts, but it was a brave thing to do."

"Maybe so, but I'm not feelin' it right now. I really don't want to talk about this anymore. All we gon' do is disagree about Chassidy, and I have to do what I feel in my heart is best. Chassidy will one day get it. She's so young right now, and by the time she turns ten, she won't even remember who I am."

The thought of what he said choked me up even more. How could he continue to walk in and out of our lives so easily? My mouth hung open, and my throat ached from the thought.

"How can you say that? Every child needs their parents. If anybody knows that, it should be you. How dare you sit there and give up on her like that? I guess this is so easy for you, as it wouldn't be the first time you've done it. Chassidy loves you, and she has gotten to know—"

"What about you?" Roc asked. "Do you *really* still love me too, Dez? Ain't this got somethin' to do with you? This not all about Chassidy, so let's be real. What about us getting back together? You ended this shit with me over some pussy. Pussy that don't mean shit to me no more."

I looked down and fumbled with my nails. "I love you, but it's so hard for me to be with a man I don't trust. I don't want to keep being with a man who hurts me all the time. I appreciate all that you've done, but it's not enough."

He quickly fired back. "Not enough! I had Ronnie kill—" He paused, unable to say it again.

I stood and squeezed my forehead. I was so confused, and I debated with myself about what to do, as well as say. "I just don't know about us being together, Roc. That's a separate issue. Give me time, and I'll deal with it as it comes. Meanwhile, I hope you think about what you're saying about your child. Focus on being there for her. I can't tell you how much she needs you. She will always need you, and that's never going to change."

"I have thought long and hard about Chassidy. This is best for everyone. Even though you may not see it now, you will soon. Now, please. I got a headache right now, and I need my peace. Lock the door on your way out."

I threw up my hands in defeat. "Fine," I said, picking up my keys so I could go. I wasn't going to sit there and beg Roc to be a father to his child. Like so many other mothers, I could easily do this by myself. I should've known that it would come to this. *Stupid me.* And there I was again, having hope and faith about this situation turning out differently. I abruptly walked down the hallway, hoping that Roc would call my name to stop me. He didn't. Then something else hit me. My thoughts were sometimes late, but they were accurate. I went back into his bedroom.

"You're telling me all of this because you're leaving St. Louis, aren't you?" I asked.

He didn't hesitate one bit. "Yes."

"When?"

"Soon."

"How soon? Days, weeks, months . . . ?"

"Days."

I stood, shaking my head, feeling the huge lump in my throat that wouldn't go away, even when I swallowed. "And you weren't even going to tell me, were you?"

"No, because I knew you wouldn't understand."

I was stunned, angry, disgusted—all at the same time. This in no way made sense to me, but it clearly confirmed that Roc had love for no one. I reached into my purse, pulled out something that I knew would come in handy. I read Roc's own words back to him, hoping that he would reconsider.

"What is black love, and what does it really mean to me? For years, I thought that Black love represented drama and disrespect . . ." I continued to read and yelled the last words to him. "I hope black love don't give up on me, because I will *never give up on it!*"

I tore the paper to shreds, watching each piece slowly drop to the floor. "Like everything else, I guess that was a bunch of bullshit. Good-bye, Roc. Have a happy, fucking life."

Chapter Twenty-three

For the next several months, my life remained Roc free. He stuck to his guns, and it was confirmed by a very credible source that Roc had moved out of his condo and had left St. Louis. I felt dissed all over again, but I kept it moving. Like the last time, I threw myself into work, focused on my children, lost weight again, and put the past behind me.

Latrel's wedding was in late June, and by now he had my full support. I had completely changed my attitude, and if I couldn't get this thing called black love right, I was counting on him. He truly loved Angelique, and I was looking forward to her becoming a part of our family. I liked her mother and father a lot, and even though they were divorced, like me and Reggie, they still got along well.

The day of the wedding, I was a nervous wreck. Angelique wanted an outdoor wedding at Forest Park, and all the preparations had been made for it, but unfortunately for all of us, light rain was in the forecast. The sun was shining brightly for now, but I wasn't sure how long it would last. I prayed for God to hold off the rain for as long as He could, or just long enough for Latrel and Angelique to say, "I do."

Monica, Chassidy, and I got ready at my house, and Latrel and Reggie got ready at his place.

"I can't believe you are finally letting your son go," Monica said, pulling Chassidy's dress over her head. "And

I just knew you'd ask Latrel to be his best man, and I'm thankful he reached out to his best friend, Austin."

I threw my hand back at her, continuing to look in the mirror while glossing my lips. "I haven't let him go, and I will never let him go. I may play second fiddle for a while, but Angelique knows who the real boss lady is."

We laughed.

"I'm sure she does, and I must say that I'm glad she's a Democrat," Monica said, gloating.

"Uh, sorry to bust your bubble, but she's not."

Monica cocked her head back. "Then what is she? Latrel needs to call this mess off right now. He don't need to be marrying no woman who belongs to a Tea Party."

I reached over and patted Monica on her back as I whispered, "She's registered as an independent, so calm down, okay? And as far as I know, she doesn't belong to a Tea Party."

Monica playfully rolled her neck in circles. "And how do you know all of this?"

I put my hand on my hip and wagged my finger from side to side. "Because I already did my homework. Spent hours on the Internet, Googling her name and finding out everything that I could possibly find out about her. She did have a racy picture posted on her Facebook page, but everything else checked out."

"Ooh." Monica laughed. "You are so bad. I saw that picture too. Did you see that she had a judgment filed against her for not paying her credit card bill?"

My eyes widened. "Don't you tell me that, girl. Did you check her out too?"

"I sure did," Monica confirmed with a serious look on her face. "As soon as you told me Latrel was getting married to her, I got busy. She's pretty clean, but not paying your bills may not be a good sign."

"Are you sure it was her?"

"Let's go check and make sure."

We laughed as we rushed over to my computer, where we checked the information Monica had found.

"See? Right there," Monica said, pointing to the information given for a person name Angelique S. Branson, who owed $7,385.00 in credit card debt.

"Humph," I said with my hands on my hips. "Scroll down." Monica scrolled down, and I immediately realized that Angelique's middle name was Lashay. "Monica, that's the wrong person. Her middle name is Lashay."

"Is it?"

"Yes," I said, walking away from the computer, playfully swiping my forehead. "I'm glad about that. I damn sure didn't want my son paying for no big bill that she'd made way before his time."

"I know what you mean, but shame on us." Monica laughed. "Both of our asses were in big debt when we got out of college. If I recall, Reggie did have to pay for those Visa credit cards you racked up on, didn't he?"

"If you won't tell, I won't tell. Now, get your shoes on so we can get the heck out of here. You're going to have me late for my own son's wedding. You know I wouldn't miss this for the world."

The wedding was in progress, and Angelique's father had just given her away. She stepped up to Latrel, who looked handsome as ever, and linked her arm with his. Monica sat next to me, and Reggie sat behind us. He had brought another woman with him, and all I'd done was say hello. Monica saw that I was already getting emotional, so she slipped me some of the tissues in her hand. I dabbed my watery eyes, pleased by how happy Latrel looked, and smiled at Chassidy, who was the flower girl and just couldn't keep still. She was swaying from side to side, and every chance she got, she waved at me. I waved back, and several people laughed.

Then, all of a sudden, the lady who was sitting to my right moved. I looked up, only to see Roc take her seat. He was razor sharp. He was dressed in a black, single-breasted, tailored suit that traced his sexy frame. Two diamond-studded earrings were in his ears, and his hair was trimmed to perfection. Minimal hair suited his chin, and I would have loved to see him on the cover of *GQ* magazine. I swear, he could give Lance Gross a run for his money, but Roc would come out slightly on top.

"Glad I didn't miss too much," he said as he sat next to me. I watched him wave at Chassidy, and she smiled, waving back. She was about to run over to us, but I whispered and motioned for her to stay where she was.

Roc smiled. "Latrel would have killed me if I didn't make it." He looked over at Monica. "Hey, Monica. What's up?"

No doubt, we were both shocked to see Roc. Monica could barely get the word *hello* out of her mouth.

Roc cleared his throat and crossed one leg over the other. I looked at the sparkling diamond watch on his wrist and the two diamond rings on his finger, wondering what he'd been up to. My mind quickly got back to the wedding, and it remained my focus for quite some time.

As the wedding vows were being exchanged, everyone was taking peeks up at the cloudy sky. Dark clouds had slowly moved in, so the minister decided to hurry it up. Angelique and Latrel exchanged wedding rings, and after it was all said and done, they laid a big kiss on each other. The rain held off for as long as it could, and then it started to drizzle. I was glad, only because it helped to cover up the few tears that had fallen down my face.

"That was so beautiful," Monica whispered. "Shame on us for underestimating Angelique."

"No. Shame on you," I whispered back.

The minister shouted, "I give to you Mr. and Mrs. Latrel R. Jenkins."

Everyone stood and applauded as they ran down the middle aisle, shielding themselves from the rain, which was picking up. Latrel paused for a moment, mouthing that he loved me and nodding his head at Roc. I blew a kiss to him, sealed with approval.

Giving the wedding party time to leave, I held my tiny purse over my head, trying not to let the rain damage my hair too badly. A carriage and horse had brought Angelique to the wedding, but she and Latrel, along with the wedding party, were leaving in limousines. They rushed to the limousines and got ready to take the short drive over to the reception, which was at a nearby indoor banquet room. After everyone had got into the limousines, the guests started to leave. By now, the rain was coming down pretty hard, so everyone was rushing.

"I'll see you in the car," Monica said, squinting from the rain. She looked at Roc. "Are you coming too?"

"It depends. But I need to talk to Dez for a minute."

"Okay, but don't be long." Monica gave me a quick hug, then ran off to the car.

I continued to hold my purse over my head, but it did me no good. My hair was getting flat, and I could feel my heels sinking into the ground. As for Roc, he was completely drenched. He reached out his hand to move my hair away from my face and gazed at me with his lowered, hooded eyes.

"You look so sexy," he said, blinking his wet eyelids. "Damn, you're gorgeous."

"Too bad being beautiful has never stopped me from getting hurt. What's going on, Roc?"

"I'ma make this quick, but, uh, I just wanted to tell you that I moved, but not too far. I live in Kansas City, Missouri, now, and I wondered if you and Chassidy would consider movin' there with me? I'm ready, Ma. I am so ready to do this shit with you. I got my shit together, got a job, and lookin' forward to startin' a new life with you. I want you as my wife, and the sooner, the better. Tell me what you're thinkin'. Can we do this shit or what?"

I lowered my head, knowing that deep inside I still loved him so much. I had been miserable without him but had done my best to ignore the void in my heart. I felt like we had been to hell and back, but the time had come for us to stand still. I slowly moved my head from side to side.

"I'm sorry, baby, but your timing couldn't be more off. I believe that people come into your life for a reason, a season, or a lifetime, and your season is over. Obviously, you were never meant to be for my lifetime, and the way you continue to walk in and out of my life shows it. If I allow you to, you will continue to come and go as you please. Not anymore, Roc. You hurt me too bad this time, and I can't let you do it again. The one thing I regret is letting you back in. I could've prevented all of this from happening to me twice. I *so* wish things could've turned out differently between us, but the ball was always in your court, never mine. I truly wish you well, and take care of yourself."

I reached out to give Roc a hug. He didn't hug me back, but that was perfectly okay with me. I ran off, shielding myself from the rain with my hand and intending not to look back.

"Black love," Roc shouted. "No matter what, you can't fight it! It's there, Dez, and it's always gon' be between you and me."

I turned, just to get one last glimpse of his handsome self standing in the rain. I had to respond. "You're so right about black love, Roc," I shouted back. "It's out there, and I'm not giving up, because one . . . two men didn't get it right. Keep the faith. I hope you don't give up on true black love, either!"

I hurried to open the door to Monica's car and hopped in on the passenger's side. My eyes connected with Roc's as he continued to stand motionless in the rain. While it might not have worked out between us, I was so serious about not giving up on love. No matter what age a man was, or whatever age I was, black love was still out there. I was determined to find it.

Chapter Twenty-four

I remained Roc free for several long months, and I couldn't believe it was already mid November. Many days were up; some were down. I kept telling myself that I was content with the way things were, but I had to admit that I had some doubts.

Once I was dressed for work, I hurried to get Chassidy ready so I could drop her off at preschool. Every single morning she asked about Roc and about seeing Li'l Roc. All I could say to her was, "Soon."

"When, Mommy?" she asked as I pulled the purple shirt with Tinker Bell on it over her head. "When is he coming home, Mommy? You said it would be soon, but I haven't seen him in a long time."

I was too ashamed to tell Chassidy that Roc and I couldn't get our mess together. I told her he was on a long vacation, and once he got back, he and Li'l Roc would come see us. It didn't seem as though that was going to happen anytime soon, and I didn't want to break Chassidy's heart.

"His phone number changed, sweetheart, and I've been unable to reach him. I'll do some searching. If I get his phone number, I'll tell him how much you miss him, okay?"

Chassidy displayed a wide grin. Almost an hour later, I dropped her off at preschool and headed to work. While waiting at a red light, I tapped my fingers on the steering wheel, contemplating my next move. I had called Roc's number several times, but his phone was disconnected. Something inside told me to let go; then there was something encouraging me to pursue what I was feeling in my heart.

Like always, work was hectic. I kept busy. Since Mr. Anderson knew my vacation started tomorrow, he couldn't stop bugging me.

"Desa Rae!" he yelled from his office. My cubicle sat right outside his office, so yelling was unnecessary, and, more importantly, it seemed really inappropriate to me. It was something I'd gotten used to, so I didn't trip.

I rushed into his office. I was wearing a popping sheer peach blouse with ruffles around the collar and a fitted cream-colored skirt that ended above my knees. I'd accessorized my outfit with gold bangles on my wrist and a thick, shimmering gold belt around my waist, one that I'd gotten at Ashley Stewart.

"I apologize for yelling, but my intercom is broken." He reached out to hand me several papers. "Would you mind making copies of those reports for me?"

I left to make copies of Mr. Anderson's reports, then stopped by the lunchroom to get a soda. When I got back to his office, I stopped dead in my tracks at the doorway. Sitting in a chair in front of his desk was a young woman with long legs and eight-inch high heels. The tight skirt she wore barely covered her ass, and the flowing weave down her back made her look like a stripper. She tossed her hair aside and scanned me up and down, from head to toe. *Gold digger* was written all over her, and even though Mr. Anderson was a handsome black man, I could tell this woman was interested in his money.

"I have a meeting with Ms. Avery," he said. "And I won't require your assistance for the rest of the day. Have a wonderful vacation, and please close my door behind you."

"Sure," was all I said, and then I left.

When the lunch hour rolled around, I headed out to my car with the lunch I'd packed that morning, intending to eat and talk to Monica in private. While sitting in my car, I took bites of my tuna sandwich and downed a strawberry soda. The sodas were killing me, and I was doing my best to lose more weight so I could look good in a bikini. Monica and I were supposed to go to Jamaica on my vacation, but since money was tight, she had backed out on me. Yes, I was upset, but I understood her situation. She just didn't have the money, and quite frankly, I didn't have it to give. If I did, we would be out of here tomorrow. Instead of going away, I planned to give my house an old-fashioned cleaning and get ready for the upcoming holidays—Thanksgiving and Christmas.

"I know you're still mad at me," Monica said over the phone. "I really needed a vacation, Dee, but these kids done borrowed so much money from me, I barely have money for myself. That, along with my bills, ain't no joke. This economy has to get better, and since the rich are the only ones getting richer, I may have to start looking for a rich man to throw in some help!"

I laughed, but I was grateful that Monica and I both had been handling our finances on our own for years. "I'm not mad, girl. Disappointed, yes, but we'll go somewhere next year. Maybe by then we'll both be married to wealthy men who can help get us out of these ruts!"

"I agree. Wealthy, sexy, and good in bed. Don't know if those kinds of men exist anymore, and you know the last man I went out with, Chance, was out of control. The way he carried on made me take a step back. I'm afraid to date again."

"That was an awful experience," I said. "But don't give up on relationships. Somebody is out there for you. He'll come when you least expect it."

"I guess so, but I do get lonely sometimes. I'm not going to accept anybody, though, and you shouldn't, either. Maybe we should go out this weekend and see what's happening at the comedy club. We haven't been out in a while, and dancing, a good laugh, and drinking may be what we need."

"That may not be a bad idea. Besides, Chassidy is going to spend some time with Latrel and Angelique. They're coming to get her tomorrow, so I'll call you on Friday."

"I can't believe you've agreed to go out, but I'm glad you did. Who knows? You just may find another man like Roc. I can tell you miss him, Dee, and if you do, why don't you just call him?"

I wouldn't dare tell Monica that I had been calling him; I was too embarrassed. I had told her it was over, and I didn't want her to judge me. "Girl, I'm not thinking about Roc. I hope he's somewhere, living happily ever after. If he is, good for him."

"Uh-huh," Monica said, knowing me all too well. "I can't see you not thinking about Roc, and I don't believe for one minute that he hasn't crossed your mind."

I bit into my nail, wanting to tell Monica the truth. "Maybe just a little. I've been thinking about him a little, because I think I made some mistakes."

"If you're having regrets, call him. What can it hurt? You said Chassidy wants to see him. It's obvious that you do too."

I quickly changed the subject.

I happened to be shopping at Walmart the next day, and to my surprise, I ran into Roc's friend Bud. We chatted for a while, and when I asked him if he'd heard from Roc, he told me he had.

"Yeah, we talk every now and then. When Ronnie was killed, so many things changed. Several of our partners went down, and a few came up missin'. We never found out who was responsible, but I know Roc won't rest until he finds out what really happened. The last time we spoke, he was on a mission to do just that."

"I can only imagine. I wouldn't want to disturb his mission, but I would like to talk to him. Do you have a number where I can reach him?"

Bud didn't hesitate. He pulled a business card from his pocket and scribbled Roc's number and address on the back. He gave the card to me. I looked at the card and noticed that it was a St. Louis number.

"I thought he was in Kansas City. Didn't he move?" I asked.

"I believe he has a place in Kansas City, but he has a place here too. Go holla at him. I'm sure he'll be glad to see you."

"I hope so."

I thanked Bud for the information and returned to my car. Once inside it, I reached for my cell phone and dialed the number Bud had written on the card. My heart was racing a mile a minute. When I heard Roc's voice on the other end, my heart started slamming hard against my chest. My mouth was dry; I was barely able to speak.

"H-hello, Roc," I said with a stutter.

"Who dis?" he asked in a sharp tone.

"It's me. Desa Rae."

There was ongoing silence, then a deep sigh, which was followed by a click.

Chapter Twenty-five

I was so upset about Roc hanging up on me that when Monica called on Friday about going to the comedy club, I wanted to renege. She tore into me.

"You had me hyped about going on Saturday, and now you done changed your mind that fast? I guess I'll just go by myself, since you act like a little partying at a comedy club is a crime."

"It's not, and that's not what I'm saying. I was just thinking about the last time I went out with Roc. Things didn't go so well. I don't know if the club scene has changed."

"I don't know, either, but I'm willing to go out and have a good time. We don't have to stay long, just for a few hours."

I sighed but agreed to go because I hated to let Monica down. After all, we were both single, so what did we have to lose?

"I'll go, but you're driving. Pick me up around nine o'clock on Saturday."

"Will do. Now, what else is going on with you? I can always tell when something is bothering you."

"You know me all too well. I called Roc, but can you believe that he hung up on me? I want to call him back and cuss him out, but forget it."

Monica laughed. "See? You're better than me. I would call him back and get in his shit. What nerve does he have hanging up on you? I know he's not upset about how you walked away from him at Latrel's wedding, is he? What did Roc expect you to do?"

"That's what I want to know. He keeps disappearing, then showing back up and expecting me to be there for him, no matter what. What kind of mess is that?"

"I'm with you this time. Forget him. If he wants to act like that, who needs him?"

I was so glad that Monica had taken my side and was seeing things my way. The situation with Roc still irked me, though, so before I picked up Chassidy from school that day, I made a detour. I still had at least an hour and a half before I had to pick her up, so I decided to see what was up with the address that Bud had written on that business card, despite the fact that this meant going against everything I felt inside. If Roc had issues with anything I'd said or done to him, I wanted him to tell me face-to-face. It was ridiculous for him to hang up on me, and if the shoe were on the other foot, he would want some answers too. I had plenty of questions, so I pressed my foot on the accelerator and sped up.

When I arrived at the ranch-style home off New Halls Ferry Road, I became a bit nervous. Two SUVs were in the driveway, and the hatch on one of them had been lifted. The front door was open, but the screen door wasn't. The house itself looked to be in good condition, and the neighborhood was populated by blacks. I wondered if Roc was living with someone or if the house belonged to him. I didn't think that Bud would give me another woman's address, but when I saw a young chick who looked to be somewhere in her midtwenties to early thirties come outside, I figured that maybe he had.

She was an attractive young woman, a bit healthy like me, but her hair was cut short. I was glad not to see Vanessa, but I wasn't happy to see that the woman was pregnant. She looked to be four or five months along—she was definitely showing. I couldn't help but think how long Roc and I had been apart, and if my calculations were correct, it had been maybe seven months. Also, I wasn't sure who the woman was, but when she saw me parked across the street, she waved. I didn't want to look as if I was checking out the scenery, so I proceeded to climb out of my car to get the answers I came to get.

"Excuse me," I said, walking up the driveway with a smile. "Does Roc live here?"

Her seemingly nice demeanor changed, and her face fell flat. "Who wants to know?" she asked. Her eyes were all over me, and much attitude was written on her face.

I reached out my hand to shake hers. She looked at it and hesitated before she shook it. "My name is Desa Rae. I'm just an old friend of Roc's. I'm not here to cause any trouble. All I want to do is speak to him about our daughter."

She pulled her hand away and attached it to her hip. "Desa Rae? Are you one of his babies' mamas?"

Well damn! That didn't even sound right to me, but I guessed I was, especially if she was one too. Thinking about it, I now wondered what the hell I was doing there. I started to walk away—actually, I ran—but when I heard Roc's stern voice, my head snapped to the front door. Almost immediately, my heart slammed really hard against my chest, as if it wanted to get out. Roc looked dynamite, and since he had no shirt on, I could see that his chest was still carved in all the right places. The blackness of his silky skin was a beautiful sight, and the waves of his Caesar cut flowed well. His jeans hung low on his waist, showing his baby-blue boxers. He leaned against the doorway while holding the screen door open. I hadn't moved, and neither had the other chick, so he called out again.

"Tiara, come here," he said. "Come back inside."

Tiara rolled her eyes and closed the hatch on the SUV. She walked toward the front door but stopped before going inside. "See? This is what I was afraid of," she said to him. "I get tired of your hoes showing up at their leisure. I wish you would handle this."

Tiara pulled on the screen door and bumped Roc's shoulder as she walked into the house. He said not one word to her, but the smirk on his face showed that he really didn't give a damn. I'd seen that look plenty of times before. The one thing that I knew about Roc was he got a kick out of drama and could handle any woman who would bring it.

As I approached the door, the smirk on his face disappeared. His face was without a smile, and there seriousness was in his eyes.

"What?" he said. "What do you want? Before you tell me, though, let me just say that you are awfully bold, showin' up at my house and callin' me. This better be good, Dez. You got two minutes to get to the point."

Yeah, he was working me, but I tried to remain calm, especially since he had a point about me being pretty bold. Whether it was true or not, I was here, and I needed to get some things off my chest. His chest, however, had me screaming inside and creaming where I didn't want to be.

"It's kind of cold outside, so you may want to go back inside and put a shirt on," I said.

Roc sighed, let go of the screen door, and stepped outside. He crossed his arms across his bare chest, causing more muscles to bulge. *Damn!* I thought. This was so hard! My tongue was tied.

"A minute and a half, Desa Rae. Speak."

To stay warm and to calm my trembling, cold hands, I eased them into the pockets of my trench coat.

"I just wanted to see how you were doing and tell you that Chassidy really misses you. I have been trying to get in touch with you and haven't had much success. It's obvious that you're still upset with me for rejecting your invitation for us to move to Kansas City with you, but I think it's been so unfair to our daughter that you've made no attempts to be in her life. I've never asked you for much, Roc, but I never thought you would separate yourself from your daughter as you have. What's up with that?"

He sucked his teeth and stared at me as if I irritated him. "I told you what was up, and when I tried to make things right, you basically told me to go fuck myself. So don't stand out here and make this all about Chassidy, because if it was, you would've thought about her when I gave you an opportunity to. I don't know why you've all of a sudden had a change of heart, but my heart don't get down like that. Usin' Chassidy ain't workin' for me, either. If she misses me, you need to woman up and tell her why I'm not around anymore."

Roc's words and tone stung, but I did my best not to let my frustration with him show. "I'm not making this all about Chassidy, and I'll be the first to admit that I miss you too. But you know better than I do, Roc, that your timing at Latrel's wedding was off. I hadn't seen you in months and—"

He quickly cut me off. "So fuckin' what!" he shouted. "I was tryin' to get my damn life together, like you had asked me to. You were complainin' all the time about how I was livin', and when I attempted to do the right thing, it still wasn't good enough for you. I ain't havin' this conversation with you, Dez. Life goes on, Ma. The shit that went down between us is a wrap, and I ain't one to reflect or harp on the past. What could've been will be no more. And as far as Chassidy is concerned, you work it out and get at me when you do."

Now I was pissed. What in the hell did he mean by that? "Work it out? How? I don't understand the *slang* you're using, and you need to simplify your choice of words."

Roc uncrossed his arms and slowly inched forward. He stood face-to-face with me, so close that I could smell his peppermint breath and could see cold air coming from his mouth. "You can tell Chassidy that I miss her too, but you, Desa Rae Jenkins, can kiss my black ass. I hope that simplifies my words enough for you."

Without saying anything else, Roc turned, walked inside the house, and slammed the door in my face. My feelings were bruised, but I took a hard swallow, climbed back in my car, and left to get Chassidy. I would never, ever put myself in a situation like this again. If Roc ever wanted to be a part of our lives, he would definitely have to make the next move.

Chapter Twenty-six

Latrel and Angelique changed their plans and came to pick up Chassidy from school. They were off from school for the next two weeks and had plans to spend Thanksgiving with Angelique's mother and stepfather at their resort in Florida. I had to get used to being without my children on the holidays, and even though I viewed it as an opportunity for them to spend time with Angelique's parents, I still didn't like it. I figured Chassidy would be bored if she stayed here with me, and she probably preferred being with Latrel and Angelique. They had spoiled Chassidy rotten, and being with them would surely take her mind off Roc. I continued to tell her that I was unable to get in touch with him. I didn't know what else to say. My hope was that she'd stop asking.

On Saturday, Monica was right on time picking me up. Now I was excited about going out and had pushed what had happened with Roc to the back of my mind. That was until I sat at a two-seat table with Monica at the comedy club, waiting for the comedian, Fatz, to make his appearance. The club was crowded with people over the age of thirty-five, and the environment was pretty nice. The waiters and waitresses were very polite, and many of the partygoers around us seemed down to earth. We all joined in the conversation about the last comedian who had us cracking up.

"He was hilarious," said one lady who sat next to us at a different table. Her hand was on her chest, and she was smiling while shaking her head. "I almost spit my drink out, laughing so hard. And when he started talking about the *Maury* show, I could've died!"

Monica agreed. Even though I'd never watched the *Maury* show, what the comedian had said about it had made me want to tune in. I couldn't believe some women would lie about the father of their children. Didn't they know the only ones they would hurt were the kids? Either way, we were having a good time. I reminded myself to thank Monica for inviting me, especially when I saw an old flame from high school. His name was Darrell. I'd dated Reggie throughout high school and college, but I'd had a crush on Darrell for years. Of course, he looked much older now, but with a shiny bald head and a physically fit body, he was doable.

"Isn't that Darrell over there?" I whispered to Monica.

Monica knew how I'd felt about Darrell in the past, so she almost broke her neck as she snapped her head around to look behind her and catch a glimpse of him. She smiled and waved at him from afar, obviously realizing that it was him. I waved too, though I was unsure that he was looking in our direction.

"Oh, my," she said, turning to face me and speaking in a whisper. "It looks like he's headed over here."

"Yes, he is," I replied, as I saw him coming too.

When Darrell got to our table, he smiled and reached out to shake Monica's hand first. "What's going on, Miss Monica? How are you?"

She shook his hand, appearing to be happy to see him too. "I'm fine, Darrell. Looks like you are as well."

We all laughed. Monica was a person you could always count on to somewhat tell the truth. Darrell did have it going on from afar, but his suit didn't quite fit him as I had hoped. His shoes looked a bit worn, and as he shook my hand, I noticed that his palm was a bit rough. He was ashy too, but maybe I was being too observant. I was sure he saw some of my flaws too, and he could easily be thinking that I had put on some weight.

"Desa Rae Jenkins," he said. "Don't you look lovely . . . lovely as ever. I had to come over here to say hello. I'm so glad that I did."

His compliments were nice, and so was he. I had to realize that not every man was capable of setting it out there like Roc, and to be honest, Darrell wasn't bad looking at all. He pulled up a chair to sit at the table with us. Before I knew it, we were all talking about back in the day and I'd forgotten about how ashy his hands were. It wasn't anything a hint of lotion couldn't cure. Soon the comedian, Fatz, was onstage, and he had everyone cracking up. Darrell had lighter skin, and he was laughing so hard that his face was turning red. Monica's laugh was the loudest, but when a man behind us reached out, attempting to start a conversation with her, she turned to him and tuned us and the comedian out.

"So," Darrell said after he paid the waiter for our drinks. "What are you doing these days? Are you still married to Reggie?"

"No, I'm not. We divorced several years ago, but we do have a son. I work for Florissant Community College, as an administrative assistant for one of the bigwigs. What about you? What have you been up to?"

"I work as a customer service manager at Express Scripts. Been in that position for the past seven years. Never married, but I do have two kids. One just finished college, and the other is trying to start a business. I live in Maryland Heights. Are you close by or what?"

"I'm in O'Fallon. Not that close by, but this city is one big circle. You can get to any jurisdiction without long delays."

"I agree," Darrell said, looking at his watch. "It's getting pretty late. Would it be possible for us to continue this conversation in the car? I can take you home, if you'll let me."

Monica was still busy conversing with the other man, but when she heard Darrell ask to take me home, she turned her head. "Go ahead," she said, giving me a suspicious eye. "I'll be fine. I think I may have something cooking."

She winked, and I figured that she wanted to get to know the man she had been talking to a little better. With that, Darrell stood and so did I. I air kissed Monica's cheek and told her we'd talk tomorrow.

Darrell and I left together. He drove a GMC Terrain and politely opened the door for me to get in. Just from the conversation that we carried on in the car, and the memories that came back to me from high school, I started to feel better about Darrell. When he reached my house, he parked his truck in my driveway, still laughing at me for bringing up his unattractive girlfriend in high school.

"Hey, she was the best I could do. The young lady I was interested in was in love with Reggie, so I didn't stand a chance."

"Yes, I was in love, but I still had a teeny tiny crush on you too. But a crush wasn't enough, and here we are years later, talking about what could've been."

"Or what should've been," he countered.

We sat quietly for a moment. I really didn't know where to go with this, because the last thing I needed was to start another relationship, which I didn't have time for. Then again, maybe I wasn't being fair to myself or to Darrell. I knew I didn't want to spend the rest of my life alone, and if that meant I had to open up and give somebody a chance, so be it.

"Would you like to come inside?" I asked Darrell. I hoped he didn't think that coming inside would lead to us having sex, because I wasn't feeling up to that right now.

"Sure. I would love to."

Darrell followed me inside, and after I turned off the alarm, I stepped into the living room to join him on the couch.

"Would you like something to drink? I don't have much, but I do have some beer and wine coolers in the fridge."

"A beer would be great. Thank you."

As I made my way to the fridge, I couldn't help but think about how nice Darrell was. Actually, he was too nice. I was still in love with, and used to, bad boy Roc, and the differences between them were apparent. When I returned to the living room, I discovered that Darrell had fallen asleep. I started to wake him, but I figured the alcohol must have been too much for him. Somewhat tired myself, I went to the linen closet to get Darrell a blanket and then left him at peace.

As soon as I got to my bedroom, I sat on the bed and checked my messages from earlier. Latrel and Chassidy had called to say hello and to check on me. It was too late to call them back, so I would wait until morning. I then changed into my silk robe, lay across my bed, and fell asleep.

Several hours later, I woke up to hard knocks on my front door and the doorbell ringing. I also heard Darrell call my name, and as I squinted to look out the bay window in my bedroom, I couldn't believe my eyes. The same SUV that had been in Roc's driveway was now in mine, parked next to Darrell's truck. I couldn't see who was at the front door, but it was pretty obvious who it was.

I walked toward the front door, and when I looked into the living room, Darrell was sitting up on the couch, yawning. He had removed his shirt but still had on his slacks. His socks had the whole room funky. All I could do was rub my nose.

"Sorry," I said to him. "I think this may be my daughter's father, but he doesn't know she's not here."

Darrell didn't say anything. He reached for his shirt and started to put it on. I opened the door, and on the other side of it stood Roc. He was dressed in a leather jacket and heavily starched jeans. A white button-down shirt was underneath his jacket, and a silver rope chain with a diamond cross on it hung from his neck. I tightened my robe, attempting to cover the exposed sliver of my meaty breasts.

"May I help you?" I asked nonchalantly.

"Is my daughter here?"

"No."

He looked at Darrell's truck in my driveway and jerked his head toward it. "If she ain't, then who is?"

I took a few steps back in disbelief that he had had the nerve to ask who was in my house. "A friend. Now, if you don't mind, I'd like to get back to entertaining my guest."

Roc's eyes narrowed. I could sense his reluctance to leave. Little did I know that Darrell wasn't reluctant at all. He stepped up to me as I held the door open.

"Thanks for letting me stay," he said. He kissed my cheek and made his way out the door. "I'll call you later."

Darrell barely looked at Roc, but Roc sure as hell checked him out. He smirked a bit as he watched Darrell get in his truck and drive off. Afterward, Roc turned his attention to me again.

"Now that you're done entertainin', do you mind if I come in?" he asked.

I couldn't lie. I was happy to see Roc, but I'd be damned if I'd let it show. I pulled the door open, allowing him to come inside. The first thing he saw was the blanket on the couch. The pillows on the couch were smashed, and it looked as if Darrell and I had had an eventful night.

Roc wiped underneath his nose, then placed his hands in his pockets. He sniffed. "What the hell is that musty-ass smell? I know you ain't up in here doin' it like that. You can do much, much better than that nigga, can't you?"

Okay, so I was a little embarrassed by the smell, but Roc referring to Darrell as a nigga was out of line.

"He's not a nigga," I said. "And for your information, he's a very nice man. His feet may carry an odor, but it's something that I can live with."

Skeptical, Roc shrugged and walked to the couch to take a seat. He kept looking around, and then his eyes met up with mine.

"So what's up?" he said, resting his arms along the top of the couch. His sexiness had overtaken the room. His legs were open, and his eleven . . . twelve-inch hump, which had raised his jeans, was on display. "I've been thinkin' about what you said the other day. I came here to apologize for tellin' you to kiss my ass. I didn't mean to come off so harsh, but seein' you brought out a li'l anger in me."

I tightened the belt on my robe again, and then went to the other side of the sectional couch to take a seat. I crossed my legs, just so the robe could slide open and show my smooth, thick legs. Roc took a glance, but then he looked away, glancing again at the blanket on the couch.

"Apology accepted, but why are you looking at my blanket?" I asked.

He picked it up and shook it in his hand. "I'm checkin' for stains. Tryin' to see if that muthafucka makes you shoot juices from that twat like I do."

I rolled my eyes and tried to snatch the blanket from Roc. When I caught the corner, he pulled the blanket away from me, and as soon as I stood up, my robe fell apart. Roc could see my goodies underneath. He wound the blanket into a ball and tossed it across the room. Then he wrapped his arm around my waist and pulled me on top of him, leaning back. I grabbed his arm and tried to pull away, but he had a tight grip on me. I didn't bother to tussle with him; all I did was look down into his eyes.

"Why are you really here?" I asked. "And I advise you not to use Chassidy as an excuse, as I did somewhat when I came to see you."

"I'm here to see my daughter, but I'm also here to see if you want to get your groove back like Stella. Looks like I'm too late, especially since you got this other fool over here, dippin' and divin' into the goods."

"He hasn't dipped or dived anywhere. But how can you be so interested in me getting my groove back when you are getting yours back with Tiara? She is pregnant with your child, isn't she?"

"Tiara is good people, and yes, she is pregnant with my child. I'ma do right by her too, and I wasn't serious about comin' here to see what was up with us. While I miss the hell out of you, Dez, you hurt me like I've never been hurt before. I did a whole lot of shit for you. Made some changes that I haven't made for no one else. That doesn't even include what I had done to Ronnie and it still wasn't enough. I want us to be good friends, though, and I hope you'll be down with me comin' to see Chassidy again."

"She's your daughter, and I have no problem with you being in her life. I hope you are serious about doing right by the woman you're with, and if you are, why do you have me wrapped in your arms like this?"

Roc loosened his grip and eased his hands over my ass. He squeezed a nice-size chunk of it, then let out a deep sigh. I could feel every bit of his hardness pressing against me. I wanted to straddle him so badly and ride him, but I didn't want to appear anxious or desperate, especially since his intention was to do right by another woman.

"You wrapped in my arms like this because I will always have love for you," he admitted. "You ever hear of lovin' somebody who you just can't be with? Well, that's what's goin' down with us. I'm not turnin' back again, Dez. I don't think you want to, either. With all that I have goin' on right now, us tryin' to hook up again would be a big mistake. So allow me to do what I need to do as Chassidy's father, and let's keep all that other shit to the side."

I couldn't tell if Roc was serious, but it sure as hell sounded like it. I had no desire to change his mind. It appeared that he had some feelings for the chick he was living with, and wanted things to work out. I wasn't going to interfere, so it was wise for me to halt the drips from my coochie, remove myself from on top of him, and let him go. I did just that and made my way to the front door to open it.

"I couldn't agree with you more, Roc. Turning back does not seem like the sensible thing to do, but I am deeply sorry if you feel as if I was the one who hurt you. Maybe you'll have better luck with Tiara. I'm proud of you for wanting to do right by her. If it were me, you know I'd want you to do the same."

Roc rubbed the minimal, trimmed hair on his chin and slowly got off the couch. He stretched his arms, then yawned. "When can I expect to see Chassidy?" he asked.

"She won't be back until after Thanksgiving. You can stop by to see her then, but please do me a favor and call before you come."

He nodded and made his way to the door. His eyes lowered to my lips, but as my mouth started to water, he walked out the door. I closed it, wondering how long we would stick to the plan.

Chapter Twenty-seven

The plan was in place, for now, and Roc and I seemed to be sticking to it. I hadn't heard from him since the night he came to my house when Darrell was over. Had I thought about him? Absolutely. But Roc was right. If he had that much going on in his life, I really didn't want to be a part of it. And the whole thing with him having another child on the way truly bothered me, but it didn't upset me enough where I wanted to inject myself into the madness. I had to leave well enough alone.

The day before Thanksgiving, Darrell called to see if he could come over and keep me company. I told him the kids were still away, so he was welcome to come over. Monica had plans with her children, and even though she'd invited me over to join them, I didn't feel like leaving my house. Instead, I put on some soothing music and got busy on the few items I had planned to cook: a ham, stuffing, mac and cheese, and a peach cobbler. I danced around the kitchen with my apron on while listening to my girl Mary J.

I had stopped to stir my noodles in a boiling pot on the stove when the doorbell rang. I wiped my hands on my apron and headed to the door. My hair had a band around the front that pushed my curls to the back. I wore jeans and the BLACK GIRLS ROCK T-shirt that Monica had purchased for me last week. When I opened the door, Darrell had a brown paper bag in his hand.

"I brought us something to drink," he said. "Hope you like wine."

"Of course I do."

I invited him inside, and after several glasses of wine, great conversation, and delicious food, we chilled in my family room

"I'm glad you let me come over to see you, Desa Rae. I didn't have much to do today, either. I'll be going to my mother's house tomorrow, and I'm eager to see my sister, who I haven't seen in a long time. She's coming in tomorrow. I have to pick her up at the airport."

"I remember your sister. She was on the cheerleading squad, wasn't she?"

"Yes, she was. When I told her I'd been talking to you, she couldn't believe it. She thought you and Reggie would be together forever. I think most people who you ask will probably say the same. The two of you seemed inseparable."

"At one point we were. But as we got older, he went in another direction. My heart was broken, but I've learned to cope with it. Our divorce was for the best, and there isn't much that you can do when a man says that he's fallen out of love with you."

"I feel you, but what about your daughter's father? I didn't get a real good look at him, but from what I saw, he looked real young. You don't have that cougar thing going on, do you?"

"I don't know what the cougar thing is, but I do know that I found a man whose company I enjoyed. We had a child together, and the rest is history."

"Are you still seeing him? I mean, by his reaction, I sensed something still going on with the two of you, even though you told him you were entertaining."

"There is nothing going on between us. Prior to a few days before that, I hadn't seen him in months. I am looking forward to him spending time with our daughter, but that's it."

Darrell sipped from his glass of wine; I assumed he was thinking over what I had implied. The last thing I wanted to do was talk about Roc, so I got up from the couch and went to the kitchen to get more wine. Darrell got up too, and he offered to take the trash out that had piled up by the door.

"Thanks, Darrell. I appreciate that. That way I don't have to do it later."

I returned to the family room, and when Darrell came back in, he joined me and poured more wine. After he sipped from the glass, he moved closer and tried to kiss me. I turned my head.

"Not now, Darrell. Let me finish my wine."

He shrugged and backed away. "You look tired," he said.

"Very."

Darrell got on his knees and started to remove my house shoes. I laughed as he tickled my feet and massaged them. The massage felt pretty good, but when he eased his hand up my leg, I stopped him.

"What's going on with you, Desa Rae? Every time I make an advance toward you, you stop me. Are you not feeling me? If not, let me know. I don't want to waste my time."

"It's not that, Darrell. I do like you, but I'm not some oversexed woman who has to have sex with every man she meets. I know we've known each other for a long time, but I really don't know much about you, other than we went to school together. Besides, and to be honest, my heart is in another place right now. It may take some time for me to get over my previous relationship, so give me a little time, okay?"

"Well, at least I know I'm not doing anything wrong. I'm glad you told me your heart is elsewhere, because I don't want to waste much more of my time with this."

Darrell stood and got out of there so fast that I barely had a chance to say good-bye. I was kind of shocked too, and I wondered if I had said or done the wrong thing. I couldn't help but think that I might have just let a decent man slip away.

After Darrell left, I cleaned up my kitchen and put the food away in the fridge. I was truly exhausted and was ready to take my shower, get in bed, and read a book. My shower was so relaxing. As the water sprayed on my face, I scrubbed it with soap and water. My eyes were closed, but when I heard a noise, my eyes shot open. I stood still for a moment, trying to see if I'd hear the noise again. I didn't, but as soon as I turned off the water, I heard the phone ringing. I figured it was probably the kids calling me back. I'd planned on calling them before I went to bed.

I dried myself, moisturized my body, then changed into a comfortable cotton nightgown. I tossed my bath towel over my shoulder, intending to take it to the laundry room to wash it with all the towels that had piled up there. But as I made my way down the hallway, I was cut off by Darrell. He jumped out of my guest room and stood in front of me. My heart dropped to my stomach. I was so nervous that I couldn't even scream.

"What are you doing in my house, Darrell? You scared the shit out of me! How did you—"

The weird look in his eyes didn't feel right to me. His face looked like it had been carved from stone, and he didn't blink. I didn't say another word, and when I attempted to rush back into my bedroom, he grabbed the back of my hair. He pulled it so tight that I had to squeeze my watery eyes to stem the pain.

"What do you want?" I cried out as he shoved me into my bedroom. I reached up to pull at his hands, but they felt solid, like a rock that I couldn't move.

He spoke through gritted teeth. "I don't like how you tried to play me! I should take what I want, but it's going to suit me just fine to knock the shit out of you."

Darrell pushed me on the bed. Like a raging madman, he jumped on top of me. I swiftly kicked my legs and wiggled around like a flopping fish so he wouldn't be able to restrain me.

"Nooo!" I shouted. "Get the hell off me!"

Darrell used the back of his hand to slap me across the face. My head jerked to the side, and my left cheek burned. The blow was so powerful that it knocked me into reality. I wasn't sure if he was going to try to rape me, and I questioned my strength to get him off me.

"You're not going to get away with this!" I yelled. "Y-you can't do this to me!"

"Shut up!" he ordered, then head butted me. My brain felt rattled, so I squeezed my eyes to help ease the pain.

Darrell pinned my hands down on the bed, holding them so tight that I thought my wrists would crack. He seemed to get heavier and heavier, and I was running out of breath trying to force him off me. My next move was to distract him, and when I spat a gob of saliva in his face, he jerked his head back. I watched my spit slide down his face, and as soon as he wiped it, I kneed him in his groin as hard as I could.

His eyes opened wider, and his mouth dropped open. "Fuck!" he shouted. "You fucking bitch!"

I knew he wanted to reach down to soothe his burning balls, and as he thought about doing it, I kneed him again. This time he released my hands and rolled over on his back. He used both of his hands to hold his nuts and swayed back and forth on the bed. I didn't have much time before he came after me again, so I had to think fast. It was either the phone, which was ringing again, or my gun, which was tucked away in my closet. If I called 911, it would take the police time to get here. I didn't want to answer the phone, because I suspected it was my kids. Before I knew it, I was already off the bed and in my closet. I knocked several of my shoe boxes off the shelves and reached for my pistol, which was hidden behind them. A few seconds later, Darrell was standing at the closet door, staring at the trembling gun in my hand.

"Don't make me do this, Darrell!" I shouted, with tears streaming down my face. My hair was sitting wildly on my head, and my nightgown was ripped down the middle. With my titties hanging out and all, I now looked like the madwoman.

"Put the gun down, Desa Rae," Darrell said, inching forward. "I was just playing . . ."

I wanted Darrell out of my house or dead—didn't matter either way. He wasn't exiting fast enough for me, so I cocked the gun, closed my eyes, and pulled the trigger. The loud pop scared the shit out of me. My body jerked back, and I almost lost my balance. I wasn't sure where the bullet went, but Darrell moved so fast that if you blinked, you missed him. He was gone. I rushed out of the closet and followed him to the foyer, where he yanked on the front door and then ran outside, leaving the door wide open. He peeled out of my driveway, his tires screeching and rubber burning.

"Don't bring your ass back here again!" I yelled out to him. "Next time you may not be so lucky!"

I closed the front door behind me, thanking God that this situation didn't turn out in Darrell's favor. I was thankful that I had a gun. I had one only because of the threats I'd gotten from Roc's uncle Ronnie. While I didn't have to use it on him, it disturbed me that I had to use it on somebody I thought I knew.

I walked away from the door and went to turn on my alarm. I checked all my doors and windows, realizing as I went that Darrell must have left the back door unlocked when he took out the trash. I knew there was something about him that I didn't like, and that had little to do with my feelings for Roc. Being desperate for companionship was a dangerous thing. I realized that I had to be careful about the men I brought into my home. Chassidy could've been here. Darrell had proved that he was capable of doing anything.

I changed into another nightgown and reached for the phone to call the police. I wanted to report this incident and stop Darrell from doing this to another woman. He was straight-up crazy, and his charming ways were a bunch of bologna. I guessed it upset him when I didn't fall for it, and I felt deeply sorry for the women who had. The 911 operator said that she'd send a policeman right over, so I waited on the couch in the family room until he arrived. I also checked my phone to see who had been calling me. I didn't recognize the number, and when I checked my messages, there were none.

Less than ten minutes later the doorbell rang, so I hurried to the door and pulled it open. I had forgotten to turn off the alarm, so it blasted loudly. I was startled to see Roc. He stepped inside the house, and I ran to the kitchen to key in the code for the alarm. Roc came into the kitchen.

"I've been callin' you all day," he said with a frown on his face. "Why haven't you been answerin' your phone?"

Before I could say anything, I heard an officer's walkie-talkie. Roc heard it too. We both made our way back to the front door. The officer had stepped inside, and he had his hand on the gun in his holster. When he saw me and Roc, he gripped it tighter. I quickly spoke up.

"My name is Desa Rae Jenkins. I'm the one who called."
The officer looked past me, turning his attention to
Roc. "Who is he?" the officer asked.

I could see the puzzled look on Roc's face. It was an
angry yet serious look, and it alarmed the officer. "This
is a friend of mine," I said, touching Roc's arm and
looking at him. "If you don't mind, would you have a seat
in the living room while I talk to the officer about what
happened?"

I hoped that Roc wouldn't question me or say anything
to the officer. But he kept looking at me, and then he
asked how I had gotten the red mark on my face.

"I promise to tell you in a minute. Let me talk to the
officer first, okay?"

Roc nodded, but instead of sitting in the living room, he
made his way back to my bedroom. The officer and I remained standing in the foyer. I told the officer everything
that had happened with Darrell, and he took notes. Then I
took him to my bedroom and let him see the inside of my
closet, where I'd shot at Darrell. He saw the bullet hole,
which was on the lower part of one of the walls. My aim
wasn't worth a damn. I also showed the officer my gun.

"Is it registered?" he asked.

"Yes," I said, then showed him my registration papers.

The officer stepped out of my closet and glanced at
Roc, who was sitting on the bed with his arms folded
and his eyes focused on the TV. There was a little tension
between the two of them, and given Roc's past, I certainly
knew why. I was relieved when the officer made his way
back down the hallway.

"We'll put a warrant out for Darrell's arrest. Feel free
to call me if you need anything else. I will do the same if
additional information is needed," the officer announced
when he reached the front door. Then he gave me his card
and left.

I peeked through the window and watched as he sat in his car for about ten minutes, writing notes and looking at Roc's SUV. I was a bit nervous, but when the officer slowly pulled away, I felt better. I returned to my bedroom, where Roc was still sitting on the bed. He couldn't wait to ask, "What in the hell happened?"

I sat next to him on the bed, then told him what had gone down between me and Darrell. Roc's eye kept twitching, and he kept sucking in his bottom lip. After I finished telling him my story, he stood and put his hands in his pockets.

"Why you let that funky-feet muthafucka up in here, anyway? My daughter could've been here with that nigga. Don't you recognize a sly-ass fool when you see one? Are you that damn naive and desperate?"

Roc's words shocked the hell out of me. I couldn't believe how angry he was. He didn't have to diss me. I was the one who had come close to being beaten down by this fool, not him.

"I had some eerie feelings about Darrell, but since I've known him since high school, I didn't think he would do anything like that. The guy I knew had always been a nice guy, but I guess people change."

Roc shook his head. He looked disgusted. "Nice guy from high school, huh? What kind of shit is that? You damn right people change, but my problem is women like you, Dez. Y'all always goin' for the men who dress nice, who talk a good game, and kiss y'all asses. If he got a li'l change in his pockets and got a nine-to-five job, he's the best thing since sliced bread. Y'all want somebody to cater to yo' every damn need and do what y'all tell him to do. A brotha like me, on the other hand, can't get no play."

"That's not so, and you know it. I gave our relationship a chance, but you made a lot of mistakes too, Roc. Mistakes that—"

He quickly shot me down. "Mistakes? Naw, baby. I just wasn't perfect enough for you, remember?"

Roc was so upset with me that he turned to leave. I grabbed his arm and turned him so that he faced me. "Perfect men don't exist, and neither do perfect women. I've made some mistakes too, but you were the one who left me and Chassidy time and time again. What was I supposed to do, Roc? When you came to Latrel's wedding, what did you expect me to do?"

Roc peeled my tight fingers away from his arm. "You were supposed to give us a chance. You knew what I had done for you, Dez, but you walked yo' ass away from me that day and hurt the shit out of me. That pain was worse than what I had done to Ronnie. To do that to him and then have you turn your back on me . . . It wasn't a good feelin'. You'll never understand what I'm sayin' to you, because you don't want to."

Roc walked away, but I refused to go after him. This was too much; he was blaming me, and a huge part of me still blamed him. I was drained from all that had happened, and once I heard the front door shut, I got in bed. I tucked my body pillow between my legs, thinking about this long day, which disgusted me. My throat ached so badly; it was hard for me to swallow. Maybe I *had* been desperate and naive. Why else would I have let a man like Darrell come into my home? I didn't know, but one thing I was sure of was I felt so alone. The man I really did love was with another woman, and they had a baby on the way. Roc had no clue how much I still loved him, and at this point, I would've taken a man like him over a man like Darrell any day of the week.

As I was deep in thought, wiping my tears, I heard someone clear their throat. My breathing came to a halt, and I quickly lifted my head to see who it was.

"You should've gotten up to lock the door," Roc said, coming farther into the room. "I can't believe after what happened today, you would lie there without makin' sure your door was locked."

I never liked for a man to see me cry, so I hurried to wipe my face and sat up in bed. "I was getting ready to get up and check it."

Roc stood silently in front of the bed while looking at me. "I regret bein' so hard on you, and I'm sorry that you went through that bullshit today. If the police don't find that nigga, I guarantee you I will. He will never be given the opportunity to put his hands on you again, and his ass will pay."

I was sure Roc wouldn't listen to my recommendation, and I figured he would do something to Darrell behind my back, but I couldn't refrain from advising him. "I'm sure the police will find him, so please stay out of this. I don't want you to get involved, and we both can agree that you've already done enough to protect me."

Roc stood there in silence again. After a few minutes, he pulled his shirt off and tossed it on the leather recliner that sat near my television. "I'm stayin' the night with you," he said. "You look like you could use some for real company, and I don't want you up all night, worried about what happened."

Now, what made him think I was going to get some sleep with him in my bed? I was glad that he was staying. He left the room, then came back with ice wrapped in a towel. When he lay next to me, I felt very protected. Roc wrapped his arms around my shoulders, then put the ice pack on the side of my face. I rested my head on his chest, appreciating the nice gesture, as well as his good-smelling cologne. His jeans were still on, and his cell phone was ringing inside his pocket. He pulled it out and looked at the number.

"Do you mind if I answer this?" he asked.

I shrugged, feeling somewhat uneasy. I assumed it was a female.

"What up?" he asked. He paused, and I could hear the sound of a female's voice on the other end. "I'm with T-Bone and Gage right now. Don't know how much longer I'll be, but I'll hit you back when I'm on my way." He paused again. I could hear her talking; then there was laughter. Roc laughed too. "Yo' ass is crazier than a mutha. I knew you was gon' say somethin' about that fool, and when he go off on you, don't come cryin' to me." She spoke up, and then Roc did. "You know I will. But let me get at you in a minute. We need to make a move." I figured she told him she loved him, because he replied, "You'd better," and ended the call.

"Sorry about that," he said. "I wasn't tryin' to be disrespectful, but when she calls, I try to answer, especially with her bein' pregnant and all. She's had some complications, and I want to make sure she's all right."

"Sure," was all I said.

Lord knows the conversation didn't sit well with me, especially if Roc had found a woman he was genuinely happy with. It didn't seem like this chick brought the drama like Vanessa did, but there was one thing. He was willing to lie to her in order to be with me. If he cared so much about this woman, why was he not with her? I wasn't sure what his excuse was going to be in the morning, and as nice as she seemed right now, I was sure her tone would change.

As we lay in bed, I wiggled my fingers between Roc's and held his hand. I asked him to remove the towel, because my face was starting to feel numb. He placed the towel on the nightstand, then secured me in his arms again. I rubbed his chest while his hand meandered up and down on my back. Being with him felt so right. I wondered if he was feeling what I was feeling. He pecked my forehead a few times, trying to comfort me.

"If that nigga had hurt you tonight," he said, "I don't know what I would've done. I'm glad you had that gun, but I wish you would've blown his fuckin' brains out. I hate niggas who go out like that. If a woman don't want you, she just don't want you."

"I agree. But when she does want you, you'll definitely know it." I looked up at him and then lowered my eyes to his sexy lips.

"Don't even think about it," he said with a smile. "I told you we ain't gettin' down like that, and I mean it."

"Well, I guess this means that I'm in trouble again. Deep, deep trouble. Trouble that I'm always looking forward to."

"You are in trouble, but I'm not the one who is goin' to punish you. Now, get some sleep and erase those dirty thoughts from your mind. You ain't got jack comin'. Nothin'."

Roc was really standing his ground, and if he was trying to be all that he needed to be to another woman, I said that I wouldn't interfere. I dropped my thoughts and put my head back on his chest. Within minutes, I could hear myself, as well as Roc, snoring.

On Thanksgiving morning, I was awakened by the sound of grunting. I was still tired. Roc's phone ringing throughout the night had driven me crazy, and every time it rang, I'd jumped from my sleep. At some point he had turned it off. That had allowed us to get some sleep. I raised my head, only to see him on the floor, doing sit-ups in his boxers.

"Morning," he said, straining himself to speak. "Your bathwater ready, so get to it so I can get some breakfast."

I got out of bed and stepped over him. "Thanks for getting my bath ready for me, but you should be able to handle breakfast too, right?"

"Yeah, I can do that, so hurry."

As he continued with his quick workout, I got in the tub. A few minutes later Roc said he was going to the kitchen to make us some bacon and eggs. I thanked him again and was delighted that he was prolonging his visit.

Within the hour, I finished my bath and covered myself with a pink cotton robe. I then headed for the kitchen, and when I reached the end of the hallway, I could see Roc in the kitchen, cooking. He had a Bluetooth attached to his ear and was talking to someone. I couldn't hear his conversation, since his back was facing me, but I did hear him laugh a few times.

My eyes scanned the back of him, and I was unable to squelch my thoughts. The back of him was just as spectacular as the front. His muscles looked perfectly carved by a butcher, and his Calvin Klein cotton boxers hugged his meaty ass tightly. His thighs and calves showed strength. I didn't know how much longer I would be able to keep my hands off another woman's man. I tried to put myself in her shoes, but damn! I justified what I was about to do by telling myself that at least he wasn't married.

With that thought on my mind, I rushed back to my bedroom and removed my robe. I changed into a two-piece, sheer baby-doll negligee that was a soft mauve. The wire cups held up my healthy breasts, yet the sheer fabric showed my nipples. The matching thong with strings that tied at my hips revealed my goodies, which I knew Roc wouldn't be able to resist. I didn't want to seduce him like this, but then again, yes, I did. I removed the band from my hair and teased it wildly with my fingers.

After taking a deep breath, I made my way toward the kitchen, hoping that Roc wouldn't reject me. He was still on the phone. Several pieces of crisp bacon were on a plate, and he was in the process of scrambling some eggs. I inched my way forward, but always observant of his surroundings, Roc heard the floor squeak and quickly turned around. His eyes narrowed, and the conversation came to a halt. Before he could tell the caller to call him back, I removed the Bluetooth from his ear and placed it on the counter. I also turned off the burner on the stove.

"I'm not in the mood for breakfast," I softly said. "You?"

Roc stood there without saying a word. I helped him reply, especially when I removed the negligee and stood in nothing but my thong. He squinted and swallowed hard as he gazed between my legs.

"Sin . . . since you settin' that shit out there like this for me, I assume that you're sayin' you want me and that you don't give a damn about the other woman."

I slowly nodded, while looking into his eyes and trying to read him. "I do. I really do want you, and you're the only one who should care about the other woman, not me."

"If you do want me, then you know there are certain things about me that you have to accept."

I shrugged and held my stare. "Things like what?"

"Like . . . I get high, real high sometimes, and I'm not givin' up my marijuana."

"And? So what? Next."

"I curse a lot, and I will not refrain from callin' anyone that I want to a nigga."

"Say what you wish. No problem here. I won't say another word."

Roc snickered, then smirked. "I'm capable of causin' major damage to anybody who hurts me or causes disrespect to the ones I love. In some cases, the consequences may be brutal."

"What I don't know won't hurt. A snitch I will never be."

Roc nodded and reached out to grab my waist. He looked straight in my eyes. "I got some deep feelings for

Tiara, and I'm not tryin' to hurt her. She was down with me when you wasn't. She helped me somewhat heal from my situation, and my back will not turn on her, no matter what."

I pressed my breasts against his chest and placed my arms on his shoulders. "I'm not so sure about those feelings that you have for Tiara, and the only way you will hurt her is if you continue to deny your love for me. I'm the one who can help you truly heal from the hurt, and once I do, I hope you'll commit to never turning your back on me. So now that we've settled that little problem, shut the hell up with this nonsense and fuck me. Fuck me like you truly missed me, and get down on this pussy like we both know only you can do."

Roc couldn't say shit. I had left him speechless. He damn sure got down that morning, and for the record, he stayed for three days. Not once did he answer his phone to see what was up with the other woman, but you'd better believe that his phone rang like he was the owner of a billion-dollar business.

Chapter Twenty-eight

Chassidy had returned home. Latrel and Angelique had already made their way back to school, but they were due for another short break soon because of Christmas. This time, they were spending it with me. I was so excited. I had the entire house decked out with Christmas decorations, and with Roc's help, Chassidy and I had put up a nine-foot Christmas tree with colorful ornaments. She was so happy that Roc had been by to see her and he'd even brought Li'l Roc over. It was just like old times, but like always, there was always something or someone between us.

I never thought I'd be in a position where I would be well aware that I was sharing a man. In the past, I had figured that Roc was seeing other people, but what I didn't know didn't hurt. This time I knew it. I knew he had a baby on the way, and I knew he was living with someone else. Thing was, I'd never understood how any woman could find herself in this situation. I'd despised women who allowed a man to have his cake and eat it too, but there I was, going through the same thing.

At times I was okay with it, but many times I wasn't. Roc and I never argued about it, and to be honest, we just didn't go there anymore. Tiara's name was never brought up during our conversations. It was as if she didn't exist, but deep inside I knew she did.

Then there was Vanessa. She'd been his ride-or-die chick for many years, but then Li'l Roc mentioned that his mom was getting married. I assumed she had finally moved on, but there was something in Roc's eyes that didn't seem right when Li'l Roc mentioned the marriage thing. All of this was starting to get to me, but I kept my cool. Partially because of Chassidy. I also didn't want to find myself all alone again, but in a sense, I felt as if I was alone, because Roc was living with someone else. I questioned if I was settling for whatever, but after what had happened with Darrell, I was sticking with the man I was used to.

The police had informed me that Darrell had been arrested. They were charging him with assault, and that wasn't all. When I found out he already had several molestation charges against him, I could have died. I didn't realize the danger I had put myself in, as well as my daughter. *Never again,* I thought. *Never.*

There was a full house for Christmas. On Christmas Eve Angelique and Latrel spent the night in his room in the basement. Li'l Roc had Chassidy's room, Monica slept in the guest room, and Chassidy and I bunked together in my room. Roc left early in the evening and said he'd be back a little after noon on Christmas Day. Monica's new man, Shawn, came over on Christmas so I could meet him, and we all sat in the family room, talking and eating. With Monica's help, I had prepared Christmas dinner the day before. We had a full table and were thankful to God for our blessings.

"Yes, I'm grateful for all that God has done and will continue to do, but this has been a crazy year," Monica said, sitting next to Shawn and drinking eggnog.

"I agree," Angelique added. She was a petite little thing and was sitting on Latrel's lap. He was putting together a die-cast model car that Roc had gotten for Li'l Roc. "I'm so ready to graduate," Angelique continued. "And once we do, Latrel and I are moving out of Columbia, Missouri, and going right to Florida."

My eyes widened as she puckered her lips to kiss Latrel. They kissed, but that didn't bother me. However, the move to Florida was news to me. I hated when somebody hit me with something that caught me off guard. Lately, Latrel and I had been speaking at least twice a week. He had never mentioned moving that far away.

Maybe it wasn't the breaking news about Florida that upset me. It was almost six o'clock in the evening, and I still hadn't heard from Roc. He'd left yesterday, saying that he would be back no later than a little after noon on Christmas Day. Li'l Roc hadn't seen him all day, and neither had Chassidy. From what Li'l Roc said, Vanessa was getting ready to go on vacation with her fiancé. She hadn't even talked to her son today, and the least Roc could do was be there for him. Maybe I was the only one tripping, but things like that mattered to me.

My glass was empty, so I excused myself from the conversation and headed to the kitchen for a refill. On my way there, the doorbell rang. I went to the door, saw that it was Roc, and opened the door so that he could come in. Without saying anything to him, I turned to walk away. He grabbed my hand to stop me.

"Damn. Merry Christmas to you too," he said, puckering his lips for a kiss. I barely touched his lips with mine, and when he tried to hug me, I pulled away.

"I have company to get back to," I said dryly. "Merry Christmas."

Roc followed me as I made my way back into the family room after first refilling my glass in the kitchen. He already knew Monica and Latrel, but he had never been officially introduced to Angelique. She shook his hand, and so did Monica's man, Shawn.

"What's up?" Roc said, sitting on the couch near Latrel and Angelique. He and Latrel kicked up a quick conversation before Li'l Roc ran into the family room and jumped into his father's lap. He thanked him for the Christmas presents, and so did Chassidy. She was all over him too. He carried her into the kitchen, and when his phone rang, he spoke loudly to someone on the other end of the line. From the family room, we could all hear his conversation.

"Man, that's what that nigga get! They tenderized his ass . . . beat the shit out of him." He laughed. "I wish I had been there, because you know I would've put my foot in that ass too."

Roc's conversation was a bit much. And when he started talking about some cracker-ass white man who almost tore up his car, I'd had enough. I went into the kitchen and tapped his shoulder, as his back was turned. He spun around, looking as if I'd startled him.

"Can you please lower your voice?" I said, removing Chassidy from his arms. "These kids don't need to hear you cursing like that, and neither do my guests."

Roc cut his eyes at me, then got back to his conversation. He did lower his voice a little, but a few more "niggas" and "muthafuckas" did come out. Finally, he ended his call and sat at the kitchen table to eat. When he asked for some salt, I reached for it on the counter and then placed it on the table, in front of him. Before I could pull back, he slammed his hand on top of mine, gripping it tight.

"Don't you ever speak to me in that tone around other people, or when I'm on the phone. You haven't said two muthafuckin' words to me since I entered this house, and how dare you get at me over some bullshit?"

I tried to move my hand, but he squeezed it. "Let it go," I said in a sharp tone. "We'll discuss this later."

"Not on my watch, we won't. And just in case you don't understand what I'm sayin', I'm sayin' this is a done deal. Conversation over." He let go of my hand and shook the salt over his food.

My brows rose. I was clearly irritated. "I don't understand, and to hell with your watch. Obviously, it doesn't
have the right time, because if it did, you would've been
here at noon, like you said."

Roc ignored me and continued to eat his food. When I
proceeded to walk away, he called my name. I turned, and
he pointed his fork at me.

"If you want respect, you'd better give it. And if you
don't want to get embarrassed, you'd better walk yo' ass
out of here and not say shit else to me. That, I hope you
do understand."

I didn't understand why we had so many disagreements. Neither one of us was willing to let go of the
nonsense. At the end of the day, this was my house,
and he was in no way calling the shots. As far as I was
concerned, he had already embarrassed me with his loud
and obnoxious talking. All I'd asked was for him to hold
it down. He acted as if I'd told him to shut the fuck up.
I was getting ready to open my mouth, but the ringing
of the doorbell stopped me. I hadn't invited anyone else
over, but I wasn't sure if Latrel or Angelique had. I hoped
Latrel hadn't invited Reggie. I feared opening the door
and finding him on the porch.

Thank God that wasn't the case. When I looked out
the peephole, I saw Tiara standing on my porch. Her face
looked a little fatter than the last time I'd seen her, she
had a pug nose, and her eyes were puffy. I could tell she'd
been crying. Her hair was now in long braids. She wore
a heavy winter coat, but her belly was poking through it.
I wasn't sure if I should open the door or if I should go
get Roc to deal with his woman. But like I said, this was
my house, and it only made sense that I was the one to
handle this. She reached out to knock, and I pulled the
door open.

"May I help you?" I asked.

"Is Roc here?" she asked with a little snap in her voice.

"Yes, but please do me a favor and call him on his phone to speak to him. I have guests, and I really do not want things to get heated around here."

Her neck started to roll. "Well, I'm sorry for the intrusion, but as I see it, to hell with your guests. I need to speak to Roc right now, face-to-face. Tell him to bring his ass out here."

I hated arguing with women over men. Truly I did. But this fool was standing on my porch, telling me to hell with my guests and ordering me around. Either way, I refused to respond to her. All I did was shut the door. She rang the doorbell again, but I was already in the kitchen, where Roc was. Everybody in the family room was looking at me to see what was up, and even Roc asked who was at the door.

"Tiara," I said, with steam shooting from my ears. "She wants to speak to you. *Now.*"

Roc got up from the table, made his way to the door, and then stepped out onto the porch to confront Tiara. Latrel asked me if everything was okay, and I told him to chill out and take Angelique and the kids to the basement. I wasn't sure how heated things would get, but it wasn't long before they went from bad to worse.

"Fuck you, Roc," we heard Tiara yell. "You told me you were coming over here to see your damn daughter, but Durk told me you've been over here fucking this bitch! Then you got that tramp Vanessa blowing up my damn phone, saying the same shit! So I came here to see what the fuck is up. Are you or aren't you sticking your dick in this bitch? When you claimed that you were out of town for three days, were you with her or not? If you don't tell me the truth, I'm going to ask her! Come clean or else!"

When Roc knew he was wrong, he always spoke in a calm manner. He knew darn well that he couldn't defend his actions. "You need to calm down. To hell with what Vanessa said. She also said that you told her the baby wasn't mine, but you don't see me trippin', do you?"

"I'm calling Vanessa right now. I know she didn't lie on me like that. We can settle this once and for all!"

As Monica and I stood close to the front door, listening, we shook our heads.

"Sounds like somebody may need to call Maury," Monica said, laughing. "Girl, this is a mess."

"You're right, it is. And I'm going to put a stop to it right now."

I opened the front door, but by this time, Tiara and Roc were in my driveway, arguing. She looked over his shoulder at me, since I was heading their way. He swung around.

"Roc, if you need to leave, please go ahead and do so. It's getting pretty darn loud out here, and the two of you are causing quite a scene," I groused.

Roc ignored me. He told Tiara to get in her car and go, but she refused to do it. Instead, she moved toward me, and he held her back.

"So tell me, Desa Rae. What's up with you and Roc? Is he your man or what? If ain't nothing going on with the two of you, Roc, confront this bitch in front of me. If it's all about your motherfucking daughter, say so, *nigga*," Tiara hissed.

This was just sad and sickening at the same time. But I refused to let Roc off the hook.

"Go ahead and tell me, Roc. I'd love for you to confront me. I'm also surprised to hear that Tiara really doesn't know what's up. Should I tell her, or will you? Better yet, Tiara has one minute to clear my premises. If not, I'm calling the police to have her arrested."

Tiara clowned even more, and I couldn't believe it when Vanessa showed up to defend what she'd said. I figured that Vanessa was the one who had sent Tiara over here to begin with, so I settled this mess once and for all and called the police. I didn't give a damn who got arrested. All I wanted was for all of them to leave and to quit embarrassing me in front of my neighbors and guests. Needless to say, by the time the police arrived, Roc had fled. Vanessa and Tiara got arrested.

Chapter Twenty-nine

Christmas was ruined again. After Vanessa and Tiara went to jail that night, all Roc could do was what he did best—apologize. But I wasn't nearly as mad at him as I was at myself. I was a key player in all the mess that was transpiring. It was just a matter of time, I suspected, before Tiara confronted me again, and her insecurities let me know how bad her and Roc's relationship really was. Hell, he didn't even know if the baby she was carrying was his. I couldn't believe it, and all I did was sit back and allow all this crap to play out.

New Year's was over, and it was back to work for me. As I sat at my desk, I got a call from the school nurse about Chassidy. She was sick and needed to be picked up. I told Mr. Anderson that I had to leave right away.

When I arrived at Chassidy's preschool, I was surprised to see Roc's truck parked outside. I went inside and found him holding her. Her arms were wrapped around his neck, and her head was slumped on his shoulder. Her eyes were fluttering as he rubbed her back and spoke to the nurse. I walked up to Roc and reached for Chassidy. She climbed from Roc's arms into mine. I could feel how hot her body was.

"She is awfully warm," I said. "What's her temperature?"

"A hundred and one," the nurse said. "There's some type of bug going around. Some of the other kids have gone home sick with the flu. I'm sure she'll be okay, but we had to call you to come pick her up."

"I appreciate it," I said. "Thanks for calling, and we'll see you all when she gets better."

The nurse waved at Chassidy as she left. She was too ill to wave back. When we got outside, Roc told me to get in his truck so we could take her to the emergency room. As hot as she was, I agreed.

For the next three hours, we sat in the emergency room, waiting for the doctors to tell us what was wrong and what was needed. Chassidy did have the flu. She was given some medicine for her fever and an injection. After getting the shot, she cried herself to sleep. We left the hospital, and when we finally made it home after retrieving my car at the preschool, Chassidy was still knocked out. I felt so bad for my baby. I hated when she got sick, and I wanted to trade places with her. I helped her change into her nightgown, and I stayed in the room with her until she fell back to sleep. The medicine had her so drowsy that it wasn't long before she was out.

It had been a long day, and I was pretty sleepy myself. When I went into my bedroom, I thought Roc would be there, but he wasn't. I went into the family room, and that was where I discovered him lying on the couch, watching a basketball game.

"How's she doin'? Is she asleep?" he asked.

"I think her fever has gone down, but I'm not going to take her temperature again until the morning. She's knocked out right now. I can only imagine how terrible she must feel."

"She'll be okay. Don't stress yourself."

"I'm not. I need to type up a quick letter for Mr. Anderson and e-mail it to him. After that, I think I'm going to shut it down myself. Are you staying the night or going home?"

"I'm staying. Want to make sure Chassidy is okay in the mornin'. Tomorrow, though, I have to jet out of town to take care of some business for a couple of days. I'll be back late Sunday night."

I shrugged, and instead of inquiring about his "business" trip, I sat at my desk in the family room and scooted my chair up to the computer. As I started to type, Roc called my name. I turned around in my swivel chair.

"Yes?"

"Can we talk about some things? I want to clear the air. Been sensin' a li'l friction between us since Christmas, and I don't like where things are headed."

I really wanted to get Mr. Anderson's letter typed, but I was sure that if I told Roc the letter was more important, he would accuse me of not caring. Instead of typing, I got up and joined him on the couch. He sat up and rubbed his hands together.

"I'm not gon' keep pointin' the finger at you and tellin' you why I think this relationship keeps takin' turns for the worse, but I need to hit you with some facts. First and foremost, I never hid my relationship with Tiara or her pregnancy from you. You seem to think that I want to have my cake and eat it too, but the fact is you gave me the cake, so why shouldn't I eat it? Two, I do not know if the child Tiara is carryin' is mine. I have suspected some shit with her for a long time, but I don't like to come over here, talkin' about my madness with other women. I felt that we were gettin' along fine, and tellin' you about what I had suspected would've brought about questions that I won't have an answer to until she has this baby. Three, Vanessa and I are over. Done. It's been a wrap with us for some time now. I hope you ain't around here speculatin' about somethin' goin' on between us, because it ain't."

He paused for a moment, then continued. "Once again, I apologize for what happened on Christmas, but that shit was beyond my control. I didn't mean to embarrass you in front of your friends and family, but the damage has already been done. You think I'm a cold nigga who enjoys the madness with women, but what you witnessed from me that day is a man who don't give a fuck about women who dog me out, call me a nigga, and treat me like I'm a punk. You may think I get a kick out of that shit, but the truth is I don't. That's why I feel differently about you. That mouth of yours can get real slick at times, but I appreciate that you don't always cross the line."

Roc had said a mouthful. I wasn't going to dispute any of his facts, because all I wanted to do was finish Mr. Anderson's letter. I kept my response short. "Thanks for sharing, and your apology is accepted."

I got up and returned to my desk. As I typed Mr. Anderson's letter, Roc got up and went downstairs. I heard the stereo blasting music, but I tuned it out. After I finished Mr. Anderson's letter, I e-mailed it to him and told him to have a good evening. I then went downstairs to ask Roc to turn the stereo down a bit, but when I got there, I saw him lying on Latrel's bed with his arm resting on his forehead. He was staring up at the ceiling, deep in thought. His shirt was off, and the sheets covered his bottom half. I walked over to the stereo and turned it down.

"Are you sleeping down here tonight?" I asked.

"Yes."

"Why?"

"Because I want to. Besides, you actin' all funny and shit, so I'ma stay out of your way."

"I'm not acting funny. I'm just tired of the same old stuff, Roc. Tired of the same excuses, tired of dealing with your women, or should I say your Bad Girls Fan Club? And some of your facts didn't sit well with me."

"Nothin' I say sits well with you, Dez, and day by day you're pushin' me away. Don't be mad at me when I fall hard for someone else. I'm tryin' to show you that I care, and the last thing I want is for you to walk away from this with harsh and hurt feelings."

"The last thing I want to do is push you away, but if you develop feelings for someone else, I'm not going to cry about it. Besides, I'm sure if I continue to tell you how I really feel, that'll make you run, like you always do. So, for the sake of not hurting our daughter, I'll keep my mouth shut. I'm not mad anymore, just concerned. Get some rest and good night."

The next day Roc stayed until midmorning. After he saw that Chassidy was feeling much better, he left. Since he mentioned that he was going out of town, I didn't expect to hear from him for a few days. Actually, several days passed, and it wasn't until the following Sunday that he picked up the phone to call.

"How has Chassidy been doin'?" he asked. I could hear noise in the background. Kind of sounded like someone speaking over an intercom.

"She's doing fine. She's much better. I'm getting ready to take one of her friends home. She spent the night."

"Did they have a good time?"

"Of course they did. They kept me up all night, playing games and watching movies. I'm definitely not looking forward to returning to work tomorrow, but I must go make my money." I heard the intercom again and asked Roc where he was.

"I'm at the hospital. Tiara had a miscarriage earlier today. She'd been havin' some issues for quite some time. The baby didn't make it."

"I'm sure she's probably upset right now, and by the sound of your voice, I can tell you may be disappointed too. I appreciate you calling us. It's always good hearing from you."

Roc paused for a moment; then he spoke up. "I told you what was up with this baby, but either way, I feel guilty about all the shit that went down. A nigga do have a heart, you know? Tiara was under a lot of stress, especially since things didn't work out with me and her as planned. At the end of the day, she good people. I hate when shit like this happens to the ones who don't deserve it."

"I feel you, but don't be so hard on yourself. Do you really believe that the child was yours?"

"Deep down, I don't. But that don't even matter right now. I just want her to get well." Roc sighed and paused for a minute. "I'm talkin' too much about things that you don't care nothin' about, so I'ma let you go. Tell Chassidy I'll see her over the weekend. Maybe I'll take her and Li'l Roc to the movies."

"I'm sure she'll enjoy that. We'll see you soon, and whether you realize it or not, I do care."

Roc didn't reply. He just hung up. I couldn't believe that he had me pegged so wrong. I did care, and the person he was trying to make me out to be, I wasn't. I didn't think much of his comment and chalked it up as him being upset about the baby. If he was blaming himself, I was sure Tiara had him eating from the palm of her hand. For now, anyway.

I had given Roc space, even though he still made his rounds to spend time with Chassidy. She had invited him and Li'l Roc to come to her school play, which was on a Friday, at three o'clock in the afternoon. The teachers had made a really big deal about the play, and so had I. Chassidy was going to be a talking sunflower, and we had worked hard, rehearsing her lines over and over again. Latrel was supposed to drive in to see her too, but at the last minute he told me something had come up and he couldn't make it. When I questioned him about what it was, he accused me of being too nosy. I asked him if there was something wrong with his marriage and warned him about it affecting him at school. That was when he went off.

"It's the way you say things to people, Mama, and Roc is right. Your tone is shitty. You have a nasty attitude, and you're always trying to tell me what I should or shouldn't have done. I get that marriage is a big responsibility, and if I wasn't ready to take on those responsibilities, I never would've gotten married. Just back off. You were doing good for a while, but here you go again with a bunch of nonsense."

My eyes widened as he spoke. He must've been talking to Roc, because he sounded just like him. I was on the verge of telling Latrel off, but I decided against it.

"Whatever it is, Latrel, work it out. I told you that I'm not going to argue with you or Roc about your choices anymore, and I mean it. Good-bye, and I'm sure I'll see you soon."

I ended our call, furious because everyone was trying to tell me that my attitude stank. I guessed that menopause would be the next excuse, or that I was getting too old and didn't understand "young" people like I should. I got it very well, and I also knew more about my son than he thought I knew. He and Angelique had been having some problems, and he'd been unable to focus because of their middle-of-the-night arguments. Arguments about stupid stuff, which newly married couples often became embroiled in. My information about Latrel had come straight from someone Latrel had trusted over the years, someone whom he'd trusted more than me. Reggie. Reggie had told me what was going on, and while we didn't converse on a regular basis, he felt it was important for me to know what was going on with our son. I was always thankful to Reggie for sharing.

Chassidy's play took place in North High School's auditorium, which was across the street from her preschool. School had already let out, but many of the students had stayed to watch the play. I was so proud of my daughter. She had been rehearsing her lines in the car and knew all of them like the back of her hand. Her teacher had given her ten long sentences to memorize. I kept my fingers crossed that she wouldn't forget any of them.

As the auditorium filled in people, I wondered if Roc was going to show. I'd saved seats for him and Li'l Roc, because I wanted Chassidy to see us all sitting together. But as I watched the door, keeping an eye out for Roc and Li'l Roc, I got the shock of my life. Roc came through the door with a young lady trailing closely behind him. Not only was it disrespectful, but it was damn disrespectful. I bit down on my lip and quickly turned in my seat. I hoped that he hadn't seen me, and I figured he wouldn't have the nerve to come sit by me if he had. I was wrong. He excused himself as he stepped over four people who were sitting in my row and took a seat right next to me. The chick who was with him sat next to him.

Roc leaned forward and removed his puffy cream-colored leather jacket with the hood. It looked like something a rapper would wear, and so did his platinum chain. He laid the jacket across his lap, then turned his head toward me. "Li'l Roc couldn't make it, but, Dez, this is Raven," he said and left it there.

With her arms folded across her chest, and her long dark chocolate legs crossed, Raven leaned slightly forward. "Hello," she said with a forced smile.

Trying to be polite, I greeted her back.

I swallowed the baseball-size lump in my throat and kept my eyes on the burgundy curtains onstage, waiting for them to open. My thoughts, however, were all over the place. Roc had to know that this would infuriate me, but he obviously didn't care. My blood was boiling over, and I'd be the first to admit that I was very jealous. Raven was an attractive, fit woman. In order to compete, I had to work out more often. She looked like a Victoria's Secret model, yet she had curves in all the right places. Her adorable round eyes were hard to look into, and she presented herself as a classy young lady.

Roc's look was stellar too, even though I wasn't down with the hip-hop look. His cashmere sweater melted on his muscles, and his black jeans went well with his leather Timberlands. There was a diamond ring that I had never seen on his finger, and the diamond in his earlobe was glistening. His masculine cologne infused the space around us, but I could also smell Raven's perfume. I kept envisioning their near-perfect chocolate bodies pressed together while they were having sex. The thought of it hurt me, but what else was I to do but sit there and pretend that it didn't bother me?

Roc looked at his watch. "I thought the play started at four?" he inquired.

I was mad, so I didn't respond. Raven looked at her watch, then lifted his wrist to look at his. "You know you always set your watch ten minutes early. It's only five minutes after four, and nothing that I have ever attended started on time."

Roc reached out to pat her leg; then he rubbed it. She put her hand over his, squeezing it together with hers. He turned his head to look at her, and that was when she puckered her lips for a kiss. He leaned in to peck her lips, then looked straight ahead at the curtains.

Now, would I be wrong to get up and go sit some-where else? Nope. That's what Roc wants me to do. He was trying to get underneath my skin, but I wouldn't let it be known that he had. I sat there listening to them talk about going to dinner afterward and him staying the night with her. She giggled, and he laughed. He touched her leg, and she rubbed his. It was sickening. I was thankful when the curtains finally opened. Everybody clapped, and so did we.

The play took my mind off Roc and his woman. Chassidy, as well as the other preschoolers, put on quite a show. So many of them forgot their lines, even Chassidy. That was what made it so much more entertaining. The audience laughed as one of the teachers whispered the lines to them, and the preschoolers yelled them out loudly. Chassidy even scratched her head a few times and walked over to the teacher so she could hear what she was saying. At one point she bent down, trying to whisper to the teacher, as if no one saw her. It was one of those memorable moments, and when I looked at Roc, he couldn't stop smiling. I hadn't seen him hold a smile on his face for this long in a very long time. I guess the same could be said for me.

When the play was over, Chassidy and the other students ran to their parents. Chassidy ran right into Roc's arms.

"Daddy!" she said as he picked her up, then rocked her back and forth in his arms.

"You did your thing, girl. And you made your daddy real proud."

Chassidy was smiling hard. She reached out for me, and I took her from Roc. "I forgot my lines, Mommy, but I remembered them after the teacher told me what they were."

"Yes, you did. And you couldn't have done any better," I said with enthusiasm.

With Chassidy in my arms, we all moved toward the door to exit. Roc's hand was on the small of Raven's back, and I couldn't help but notice her perfect heart-shaped butt. I heard her tell Roc that Chassidy was so cute, but when Chassidy knew Raven by her name and thanked her for coming, I was taken aback. I wondered how Chassidy knew her but I didn't.

When we got outside, Roc told Raven that he was going to walk us to our car and go get his. In other words, he told her to stay put. She stood inside the double doors, watching as we walked to my car together.

"That was a nice play," he said to Chassidy. "Thanks for invitin' me. I want you to come to my truck with me, because I got somethin' I want to give you."

Instead of going to my car, we went to his truck. There was a balloon inside and a small brown teddy bear holding a red rose. Chassidy switched from my arms to his again. She was still smiling as Roc gave the balloon and teddy bear to her.

"Thank you, Daddy. You rock!"

He laughed, and so did I. "I'd like to think so too," he said. "If only *some* other people thought that way."

Doing what was the norm, I didn't comment. Besides, I was still worked up from him coming to the play with Raven. Roc drove us to my car and told Chassidy he would see her soon. He then drove to the front entrance of the auditorium and picked up Raven, and then they left.

On the drive home, Chassidy sat in the back seat, playing with her teddy bear. I watched her in the rearview mirror. I had a lot on my mind—her play, my conversation with Latrel, and Roc and his woman. I turned down the music and asked Chassidy how she knew Raven's name.

"She was with us at the movies one day. I remembered her name from then," she said.

"Did Daddy pick her up so she could go with you, or was that his first time meeting her at the movies?"

Chassidy scratched her head. "I . . . I think she met us at the movies."

"Did she go to dinner with you all?"

"No, but I think she's his girlfriend, because they kissed. I thought you were his girlfriend, Mommy, because the two of you are always kissing each other too."

I didn't know what to say. And shame on me for trying to pump my daughter for information. "He's not my boyfriend. We were just a couple."

I was surprised when Chassidy took my comment further. "If he's not your boyfriend, then how did the two of you make me? I thought a girl had to have a boyfriend to make a baby."

Honestly, I got tongue-tied. Chassidy had been paying way more attention to us than I'd thought she had. I didn't want her to believe that it was okay for boyfriends and girlfriends to make babies, or that it was okay for a boy to have two girlfriends. But that was how she viewed my situation with Roc. How was I to tell her that it really wasn't the right way, even though I had been representing that it was?

"Sweetheart, sometimes people have children out of wedlock, which me and your daddy did. Truth is, you should be married to a man before you have children with him, and he shouldn't be allowed to have two women. We'll talk more about that as you get older, but right now, all I want you to think about is being in more awesome plays, like the one you were just in, learning new things, and maybe even modeling again. You used to love having your picture taken, and I couldn't keep you away from the camera. What happened?"

Chassidy shrugged. "I broke my camera and didn't want to tell you. I do like taking pictures, and I want to be in more plays too!"

I was glad the subject had changed. I guessed my asking questions brought out something I hadn't prepared myself for. It was a wake-up call, letting me know that I had to be real careful about the messages I was sending to my daughter about relationships.

The next day Chassidy and I went to Monica's house to spend the day with her. Chassidy played with Monica's niece, Brea, in one of the guest rooms. Monica and I, however, were up to no good. I told Monica about Roc's new chick, Raven, and after I described her to Monica, she was dying to see who had been "getting a piece of the Roc." Those were her words.

The one thing we could count on was Facebook. If Raven was on there, hopefully she didn't have her privacy settings blocked so that we couldn't see her wall. I didn't know her last name, but if Roc was on Facebook, I was sure she was one of his friends. Under my log-in, Monica went to Roc's profile. Ninety percent of his friends were females, and you'd better believe they had been setting it out there for him. He hadn't commented much, but he did have plenty of sexy pictures out there that showed his physique, tattoos, and charming smile.

"Look at this hoochie here," Monica said, reading a comment from a picture of a female who had her back turned. Most of her ass covered the photo. I could barely see her face, but she was definitely putting her assets on display. She told Roc to check his inbox and his reply was, "Got it."

"I wonder what that was all about," I said.

But as we scrolled down his wall, there was much more. Again, Roc had responded to only a few, particularly to the pretty ones who were showing much skin. Monica clicked on the link to his friends, and we came across a photo of Raven. Monica clicked on it, and it allowed us to look through her pictures and read her wall. Her personal information was available too. In a matter of minutes, we found out that Raven's birthday was in April and she was twenty-nine years old. Her last name was Smith, and she worked at Ameristar Casino, as a blackjack dealer. She graduated from the University of Missouri and was also a model.

She had numerous pictures of herself in seductive positions, as well as simple ones that looked as if they belonged in magazines. Did she have to look that spectacular in a white swimsuit as she sat on Roc's lap? Her favorite activities included traveling, which she often did, and cooking. There was so much more about her available, but what stung the most was the numerous pictures of her and Roc. He was all over her wall. Friends complimented her "fine-ass man," and they seriously looked like a happy couple. From the outside looking in, it appeared that they'd been together for quite some time. At this point, I was speechless, and so was Monica.

She took a deep breath. I figured she had been thinking the same thing I had been thinking. Roc and Raven looked good together.

"How long has he been seeing this chick?" she asked.

I shrugged, regretting again that I was snooping. The saying "What you don't know can't hurt you" was fitting. "I'm not sure. But with all these pictures of him on her wall, it seems as if it's been a long time."

Monica started looking at the dates on the pictures, pointing them out to me. I had to walk away from the computer, because I'd gotten my feelings hurt. Monica turned around and told me that most of the pictures were recent, but there were a few that dated back to the summer of last year, when Roc claimed he was in Kansas City, getting his life together.

"It doesn't appear that he's known her for that long. And you know darn well that Roc would drop her in a heartbeat if the two of you got your act together."

"Whatever, Monica. It really doesn't matter, anyway, because he's not my man anymore. I don't want to spend my Saturday cooped up in your house, looking at pictures on Facebook and discussing Roc. Let's go shopping and take our butts to the Cheesecake Factory. We can take the girls with us. Reggie sent me some money for child support that was overdue. Since my bills are paid up, I have nothing to do with the money."

Monica shut down her computer and jumped up from her seat. "You don't have to ask me twice about going shopping and eating. I'm all for it, girl. Let's get going."

Monica hurried to change her clothes, we gathered the girls, and then we headed to the Galleria to shop. Being with Monica, Chassidy, and Brea took my mind off all that I was feeling inside. I couldn't help but thank God for my best friend, who was helping me cope.

Chapter Thirty

I needed to get away, even if it meant going to Columbia, Missouri, to be with Latrel and Angelique. This time, Latrel had invited Reggie and me to come to one of his basketball games. He hadn't played in several seasons, because during his second year in college he had torn ligaments and his leg hadn't healed. He had been on the bench more than anything, but Reggie had often visited to show his support. I was more excited about Latrel getting a degree in engineering. Angelique was getting a journalism degree, and they seemed to have a bright future ahead of them.

Monica had agreed to watch Chassidy for me, and as soon as I dropped her off, I made my way to Columbia. It was only a two-hour drive from where I lived, and the ride was very peaceful. Gave me time to think and take in the soothing music on the radio. The last time I'd seen Reggie was about six or seven months ago. I had promised Latrel that I would be on my best behavior. He didn't know that Reggie and I talked on the phone occasionally, nor was Latrel aware that we had been discussing him. I told myself that I wouldn't confront Latrel about anything that Reggie had told me, and I would definitely keep that promise.

Mizzou Arena was packed with basketball fans. I felt like I was at an NBA game; the place was so alive and rocking. Mizzou was winning the game, and Latrel had scored six points so far. He was a great rebounder, and it was another one of those moments when I felt so proud of my children.

Angelique seemed happy when Latrel scored too, and I watched her as she watched him. I could tell when a woman was genuinely in love; she definitely was. Her eyes lit up, and she was on her feet way more times than Reggie and I were. That made me feel good. My concerns about her were no longer an issue. I did, however, still have some with Latrel.

After the game was over, which Mizzou won, Reggie and I waited to greet Latrel. Latrel mentioned that he, his friends, and Angelique were all going out tonight, so Reggie and I decided to have dinner and drinks. We drove to a nearby bar, which was kind of crowded, thanks to all the people who had just come from the game. But we found a cozy booth in the corner. The bar was more like a wooden shack, and country music was playing. Many of the waitresses wore cowboy hats and boots. The food smelled pretty good, so we ordered hot wings and two beers. Before I could take a sip from my mug, my cell phone rang. I answered; it was Roc. I really couldn't hear, because of the music, so I excused myself from the table and went into the bathroom.

"I'm sorry. I couldn't hear you. What did you say?" I asked.

"I stopped by your house twice, but no one was there."

"Chassidy's with Monica. I came to Columbia to spend some time with Latrel. I'll be back Sunday night, so if you want to stop by then, that's fine. Just call before you come to make sure we're home."

"Will do. Tell Latrel I said what's up, and I'll get at you Sunday."

Roc hung up, and so did I. I hadn't thought much about him today. After seeing those hurtful pictures on Facebook, I had pushed thoughts of Roc to the back of my mind. Keeping myself busy helped.

After two plates of hot wings, several margaritas, and six or seven beers, Reggie and I were laughing and talking as if our lives hadn't missed a beat.

Reggie held up his frothy beer mug, which was filled to the rim. "What are we going to drink to now?"

I held up my margarita glass. "Let's drink to Latrel and Angelique staying together. Lord knows they are going to need all the prayers they can get!"

"Amen," Reggie said, clinking his glass with mine.

We laughed, and when several people started doing a country-western step dance, Reggie got up. I did my best to talk him out of it. Not only because he was half drunk, but also because he looked stiff as ever when he danced.

As expected, he made a complete fool of himself. The people in the room stood back and clapped their hands as he tried to do everything from the bump to the jerk. I covered my face in shame but laughed my ass off. It was just like old times, when things were going pretty well in our marriage.

"Reggie," I said in a whisper when he came close to me as he danced. "Sit down and stop clowning."

He took my hand and pulled me up from the booth. Yes, I was pretty messed up too, and after he twirled me around, I felt dizzy. I didn't know what the hell the bartender had put in our drinks, but it sure had me feeling good. So good that after the dancing wrapped up, we found ourselves back in his hotel room, ripping each other's clothes off. We couldn't stop laughing and feeling each other up.

Reggie gripped my ass as I straddled him with no clothes on. "Y-you don't know how long I've wanted to feel you like this again, Dee. I don't care what you say, baby. You are mine. You will always be mine."

I'm glad he thought so, because I didn't. And, make no mistake about it, Reggie was good in bed, but he was no Roc. The sex was to take my mind off things and pass the time.

The next morning we barely looked at each other during breakfast. Latrel could tell something was up, and he questioned us about what we'd done last night. Reggie looked at me, and I looked at him. We both smiled, and all Latrel said was, "Hell no."

Traveling back down memory lane always had repercussions. Reggie was trying to ease his way back into my life, but I already regretted having sex with him, especially without using a condom. He'd been jumping from one woman to the next. I should've known better, and when he called me at home the next day to talk about us, I reminded him that there was no us. After that, he tore into me.

"You'll never keep a man, because you don't know what is required to keep him. I don't see how Roc puts up with you, and I'm surprised that you've kept your hood Negro for this long. Especially since you were the one who used to cringe all the time and hold your nose in the air when I took you to my relatives' houses. You looked down on all of them, as if they weren't good enough. There is so much about you, Dee, that you need to correct. The last thing you should be worried about is Latrel. He's still young, and he's in the process of living and learning. You, on the other hand, are getting older. Look in the mirror and ask yourself if you're content with who you see. Personally, I think if you open your eyes wide enough, you'll start getting the picture. If I don't get a chance to speak to you on or before your birthday, have a good one."

Reggie hung up. His words had taken the breath out of me, and it was interesting to know how he felt. I slowly put the phone down. There was so much hurt inside of me, only because I couldn't accept the person the men in my life were making me out to be. I accepted that men and women viewed things differently, but why was

I being labeled the villain? What was wrong with being bitter toward an ex-husband who had treated me as Reggie had? Was it a crime that I didn't want the man in my life smoking weed, cursing all the time, sexing numerous women, and making a living by shaking and moving? I truly didn't get it. Maybe my approach wasn't the best, but did I *really* need to change my ways? I mean, why should I change myself for people who weren't willing to change for me?

The big day had finally arrived—my birthday. There was nothing really spectacular about it, but I was thankful to God for blessing me with another year. It seemed as if the holidays and special occasions always brought out the negative, so I decided to do the smart thing for my birthday this year and share it with my best friend. Monica's daughter was here from California, and she had taken the girls, Brea and Chassidy, out with her. Monica and I, however, were at a spa, getting a pedicure and manicure. She sat next to me in one of the comfy plush leather chairs, paging through a magazine, while an Asian woman worked her feet. I was on the phone with Latrel, who had called to wish me a happy birthday.

"Thank you," I said. "Monica and I are having a wonderful time. Tell Angelique I said hello, and I'll talk to you again soon."

"Real soon. Love you, Mother."

I returned the love and sat with a wide smile on my face.

"Who you thinking about?" Monica said, interrupting me. "Roc?"

I turned my head and threw my hand back at her. "Girl, please. I'm not thinking about him at all—just so you know."

Monica pursed her lips, wholeheartedly not believing me. I hated that she could read me so well.

Chassidy was staying overnight at Monica's house with Brea, and so as soon as I got home, I showered and changed into my nightgown. I tied a paisley-print head scarf around my head but left several curls hanging in the back. It was almost eight o'clock, and I couldn't wait to finish the last few pages of the book I was reading. No sooner had I started to get into the book than my phone rang. I looked to see who it was; it was Roc.

"Hello," I said.

"Just checkin' to see if you were home. I'm comin' over."

"You mean, 'May I come over?' You do have to ask."

He hung up, and even though I was annoyed by his actions, I did want to see him. I didn't bother to call him back to tell him not to come, but I tried my best to finish the book before he got here. It didn't him take long, because twenty to thirty minutes later, the doorbell rang. I got out of bed to go open the door. Roc came inside with a sly smile on his face.

"Why you lookin' all hood and shit with that do-rag on your head?" he asked.

"It's a scarf, but I'm sure a woman with a do-rag on her head would suit you better."

He shrugged. "She most likely would. But, uh, happy birthday. Is Chassidy here?"

"No. She's at Monica's house."

"Then go get your coat on so I can take you out to dinner."

"Dinner? I'm not going to dinner this late, and if I was, I wouldn't be going dressed like this."

He sighed. "Okay. Then go put your coat on, anyway. I want to show you something outside, and it's cold."

I hesitated but then went to the closet to get my coat. I hoped Roc hadn't purchased anything for me, because I still wasn't so sure where he was getting his money from. I never accepted any of his money, nor did I ask him for money to take care of Chassidy.

Shivering a bit, I followed him to his truck, which was parked across the street from my house. My house was near a dead-end street, and Roc's truck was close to it. The hatch was flipped up in the back, and when I looked to see what was inside, I noticed that the back seats were pushed down and two pillows were against the front seats. Wool blankets covered the carpet, and a wine bottle was chilling in an ice bucket, with two fluted glasses beside it. Pink and red rose petals had been spread throughout, and the smell of hickory barbecue was coming from two white foam containers. I smiled, even though I was freezing my butt off.

"I already know what you're thinkin'," Roc said. "But just so you know, thug men can represent romance too." He helped me climb into the truck. I sat Indian style, and after he lowered the hatch, he put the heat on full blast and lay sideways, one of the pillows propping up his neck.

"I never discredited what a thuggish man could do," I said. "And I'm sorry that you see yourself that way. Either way, this was a real nice thing for you to do. I guess you figured you wouldn't be able to get me to go out for dinner, right?"

"Let's just say I know you pretty well by now. Gettin' you to go to dinner with me would've been impossible. So I had to bring the dinner to you. I love the beef brisket sandwiches at Li'l Mickey's, and I wanted you to try it."

I opened one of the foam containers and was hit with a sweet-smelling, smoky brisket sandwich, which I couldn't wait to dive into. The meat was hanging over the bun, and I knew things were going to get messy. Roc gave me a plastic fork so that I could dive into it.

"This was so sweet of you," I said, forking up a piece of the brisket and putting it in my mouth. It was delicious. "Mmm, good. But you didn't have to do this. I wonder how your girlfriend would feel if she knew you were over here, going all out like this for me."

"I'm not sure how she would feel, but since you brought her up, I have to ask. Are you jealous?"

I looked at Roc with a straight face and lied. "Not hardly. If she's who you want, so be it. I wish you well, and as long as you're happy, I'm good. Besides, she's a beautiful girl. I'm sure her assets work in your favor, and most men would agree."

Roc cocked his head back. "Her assets? You think it's all about a woman's assets for me? Ma, you got me all fucked up. I couldn't care less about a big ass and succulent titties. While that shit makes my dick hard, it don't do much for my heart."

"Then what is it, Roc? What attracts you to Miss Raven? How long have you known her, and what's up with the two of you?"

I was surprised that he didn't hesitate to tell me. "She's good people. I met her while I was in Kansas City for those few months, but when I came back to the Lou, we went our separate ways. I kicked it with Tiara for a while, and you already know how that shit turned out with her. Surprisingly, when I took the kids to the movie that day, I saw Raven and we hooked back up. You and me had been havin' our problems, so I moved in her direction. I like her a lot, but she ain't no Dez. But Dez be trippin' too much for me. I realized that I will never be the man you want me to be. So as far as acceptance goes, I'm down with the one who loves and appreciates Roc for bein' Roc. Her fat ass has little to do with it."

"So, if her ass was flat, you'd feel the same way?"

"I don't do flat, but you know what I'm sayin'. You're tryin' to skip over all that I said and bring up what's not important."

"I get what you're sayin', but there is too much about you that drives me nuts. We've known each other for quite some time now, and I'm still not comfortable with who you are. You keep too many secrets. You don't tell me anything about your friends, family . . . work. How do you survive?"

"I don't tell you, because you don't ask. You couldn't give a damn about my friends and family, Dez, and—breakin' news, baby—I do work. On my time, I do. I also don't say much, because you are very judgmental. You have a cut-and-dry way of thinkin', and you believe your assumptions are always correct."

"Ninety-nine percent of the time, they are. And the only time that I've known you to do any work was when I got you a job. I'm not talking about the kind of work you're talking about, so tell me, where do you work?"

"I'm glad you finally asked," Roc said. "It's about damn time." He sat up and opened the armrest to get something out of the compartment. He also grabbed the small cake box that was sitting on the front seat. He tossed a business card to me. I picked it up and read what was on it. I saw ROC'S AUTO BODY SHOP AND CAR MAINTENANCE on the card, along with an address and phone number.

"The shop that I own is near Kossuth and North Taylor. You might have to bring your pistol if you ever come see me, but with it being dead smack in North City, I'm not sure your face or your purse will be found anywhere near the vicinity."

At least he was right about one thing—he definitely knew me well. I wouldn't be caught dead at an auto body shop in North City. Roc was brave to set up shop in that neighborhood.

"I can't argue with you there. Thanks for telling me. It's good to know that you're doing something productive with your time."

Roc cut his eyes at me. "More than you know."

He opened the cake box and pulled out two medium-size cupcakes with chocolate icing stacked high atop them. A candle was in one cupcake, and he used a lighter to light it. Once it was lit, he moved closer to me. He pecked my lips, then backed away. "Happy." He pecked them again, then back away again. "Birthday." Peck. "To." Peck. "You. Now, blow out the candle and make a wish."

I closed my eyes and made my wish. After I blew out the candle, Roc asked what I had wished for.

I held the cupcake in my hand. "Nothing spectacular. Just wished that when I smash this cupcake in your face, you don't get mad."

Roc tried to duck, but I smashed the cupcake in his face. The chocolate icing was all over his face. He didn't smile at all until I leaned forward to lick off the icing. I twirled my tongue on his cheeks and then stuck it into his mouth. As we kissed, our hands roamed.

"Let's go inside," I said in a whisper.

"Nah, let's stay right here, especially since I've learned to be creative and to work with the minimal space that I have."

I lay back, and Roc lay over me. Minutes later I found myself sitting between the front seats and holding on tight to them, as Roc was down low, making sweet love to my pussy. His tongue was so fierce that when I screamed from satisfaction, I was so sure I awakened my neighbors. Neither one of us cared. I turned on my stomach and enjoyed the feel of Roc's twelve inches disappearing inside of me as he held my cheeks apart. His thrusts were always to a rhythm that kept me on my toes, and the way he rotated his hips while digging deep into me was on point.

"I don't care what you say," he said, guiding my hips and pulling me back to him. "This pussy was made for me, specifically for me. And you need to do whatever it takes to keep this shit between you and me together. Somehow, someway, I want my black love back."

Truthfully, so did I, but I wasn't so sure how we could ever repair all the damage that had been done. My body felt so heated that I had a desire to cool off. I forced Roc backward, until we were halfway out of the truck, with our feet on the ground. I remained bent over, taking in all that Roc was giving to me. The cold air cooled down our naked asses, and it prevented us from sweating so much. We were definitely getting it in—had the back of his truck rocking for a while. There wasn't a man on this earth who could make me feel like Roc did. I wasn't sure if anyone was watching, but it was yet another memorable day that left me loving him more and more.

"I love the way you do this to me," I grunted while Roc played my clitoris like a violin and pushed in my folds with the force of his big dick. My wetness glazed his shaft, and he was in so deep that I could feel his balls smack my ass cheeks. It wasn't long before I felt his liquid and my hot lava flowing down my legs. Roc's body went limp. He laid his head on my back, and then his soft lips pecked me down my spine. I closed my eyes, savoring the moment.

"I love you," I mumbled while trying to catch my breath.

He continued to peck my back. "You always do, especially when you cum."

I slowly opened my eyes, then stared in front of me, thinking about what he'd said. He was right, but I didn't want to admit it. Maybe I was wrong for not expressing my love for him more often, but it was so hard for me to do that under the circumstances. I didn't want to appear desperate for this relationship, especially since he was with someone else.

We climbed back in the truck, wrapped our cold bodies in the warm blankets, and cuddled. Something about all of this felt good. Roc quickly fell asleep, and I lay there, awake. I played back many of the things he had said to me over the past several months, and realized that it was time for me to take a clearer look at myself.

Chapter Thirty-one

The past month and a half had been very busy. Latrel and Angelique were due to graduate from college, and we were all running around like crazy, trying to make sure everything went well for them. The things you did for your children . . . I didn't think any of them quite understood the sacrifices that had been made for them. Latrel was my priority, and so was Chassidy.

I had been so busy that I hadn't made much time at all for Roc, but to be truthful, he hadn't made much time for us, either. He'd been over to see Chassidy only about three or four times since my birthday, and when I asked him what was going on with him, he replied, "Nothing." I didn't have time to delve further for the truth, but I knew something was up. The nature of that something was revealed to me when Monica called while I was at work and told me to go to Raven's Facebook page. Monica stayed on Facebook more than I ever did, only because she had been networking to let people know about her event planning.

My face twisted from a bit of anger. "I couldn't care less about her Facebook page. I need to make some phone calls about the menu for Latrel's graduation party. I thought you were supposed to be helping me, but you're too busy on Facebook, looking at pictures of Raven. Come on, Monica. Please."

"Dee, you know darn well that I wouldn't call you about this unless I thought it was important. If you don't care

that she and Roc are engaged, then don't worry about it.
I'm just telling you what I saw. Take my information and
do what you wish with it."

Monica hung up, leaving me in complete, utter shock.
Engaged? Really? Not Roc. Had he lied to me in the truck
that day? He had made it seem as if his feelings for Raven
weren't all that. I knew the pictures I'd seen revealed
more than what he was willing to say. I was damn mad at
myself for accepting his lies, and it drove me crazy that
I could never really tell what he was actually thinking.
Damn him. His ass can go to hell.

I quickly called Monica back to apologize. She and I
rarely had a dispute, and I knew she was only looking out
for me. Her phone went straight to voice mail.

"I'm sorry. You know I've had a lot on my plate, but
that doesn't excuse the way I spoke to you. I love you
so much, and I appreciate you for making sure I have
a heads-up on everything. Call me back when you can.
Don't stay mad at me for too long, because I'll have to
hurt you if you do."

Monica called back a little later that day, and we reconciled our differences. She checked me about my attitude,
as everyone else had done recently. And right before
Latrel's graduation, so many things came to light. My past
conversations with Latrel, Reggie, Roc, and Mr. Anderson
caused me to stand before the mirror and take a good look
at myself. I saw a beautiful, full-figured woman with flaws
that were affecting me in so many ways. I was never one
to accept the negative things that were said about me, and
most of the time, I pushed those comments to the back
of my mind. I had a serious problem with listening, and
compromising with anyone was always out of the question.

The reason that Monica and I had remained good
friends was that I liked the fact that she agreed with me

the majority of the time. As my friend, she didn't want to be real with me, because she loved me so much that she wanted to protect my feelings. I got that, but I also knew that it was vital for me to hear others out as well. While I in no way held myself totally responsible for my failed marriage and relationships, I did start to hold myself accountable for a lot of things that had happened. In doing so, I was able to release that hint of bitterness that I held inside of me. I was able to see Reggie in a different light, and I realized that he'd made many of his choices because he felt that he was doing what was best for him. At this point, I had to do what was best for me too.

Graduation day was here. It was a long ceremony, especially with Chassidy moving around constantly, unable to keep still. There were minimal tickets available to the students, so even though Latrel had invited Roc, he was unable to come. I had also invited Roc to Latrel and Angelique's graduation party, but since Roc and Reggie didn't get along, Roc declined. I was kind of glad that he did, because the last thing I wanted was for someone to ruin my son and his wife's special day.

They were so happy. The plan was to move to Texas, not Florida, and get to work. Latrel had already been offered a job in engineering. It appeared that his career in basketball wouldn't be going much further. Angelique was planning to go back to school to get her master's degree, but she had interviews set up for a few positions in journalism. I sure regretted that they were moving so far away, but it was beyond time for my son to move on and live his life as he wished.

After the graduation was over, we headed to Boshee's, where the dinner and the dance were being held. The room was really elegant, and the food on the buffet looked delightful. Angelique and Latrel had invited plenty of their friends, along with lots of family. We had a blast. I was cheesing so hard when Latrel called me over to have my picture taken with him and Angelique. I stood in the middle as they proudly held their diplomas up high, cheesing right along with me.

"Let me hurry up and get this picture," Reggie said, snapping the photo with his camera. "We all know that Desa Rae won't be cheesing that hard for long."

Everybody laughed, but, you see, Reggie didn't have to go there. I promised myself that I'd be good, and when he asked me to dance, I didn't hesitate. The DJ had some hip-hop mess playing, but I did my best to work with it. On the crowded dance floor, I moved from side to side, while Reggie held back his suit jacket, trying to break it down to the floor. Latrel, his friends, and Angelique were cracking up at us. I ignored them, because they had no clue what real dancing was all about.

"I see you still can't dance," Reggie said, snapping his fingers while looking at me.

"And too bad you still don't know how to screw." I rolled my eyes and walked away. Good thing Reggie was laughing, because so was I. Monica was cracking up.

"Ooh, the two of you are vicious. Just nasty to each other, but I think that's because neither of you wants to admit that y'all still care."

Of course we cared for each other, but Reggie was not the man I wanted. Roc was. Latrel and his frat brothers were so outdone with the way we danced that they got on the floor and started stepping. Everybody crowded around to watch, but I sat back in my chair, thinking about how glad I was that this day would soon be behind me. Monday couldn't get here soon enough. It was time to do me.

***

On Monday I dropped Chassidy off at preschool around noon and went to Roc's house. When I got there, his SUVs weren't in the driveway. I knocked on the door, and no one came to answer it. The only other place that I suspected him to be was at his auto body shop. Lord knows I didn't want to go there. I debated with myself whether I should just wait to talk to him. I wanted to get so much off my chest, so I headed to his shop. I took Interstate 70 to the Kingshighway Boulevard and Union Boulevard exit, and as soon as I got off, I double-checked my doors to make sure they were locked. I knew it was considered a booshie move, but I wanted to make sure I was safe.

I stopped at a red light at the corner of Kingshighway Boulevard and Natural Bridge, where a man was selling candy. He lowered his head to my window, then knocked on it. I just looked straight ahead and waited for the light to change. It did, but I had to stop at another red light near a PX Liquor Store. Several men were hanging out outside the liquor store, with brown paper bags in their hands. I wasn't trying to go there, but drinking in a parking lot couldn't be considered work. Looking at it from another point of view, maybe they did have jobs. What did I know?

As I continued to look at them, I saw a dull gold Regal pull up beside me. The music inside the car was so loud that it made my car vibrate. The youngster behind the wheel had thick braids that ran past his shoulders. He glanced over at me, sucking his teeth, and then he winked. I quickly turned my head, trying to ignore him and doing my best not to show fear. I knew that the way I felt inside was stereotypical, but I couldn't deny that St. Louis was considered a high-crime area.

I couldn't wait for the light to change, but when it did, my GPS tracking system kept sending me in the wrong direction. I couldn't find Roc's shop for nothing, but I knew I was close. Unfortunately for me, I had to pull over and ask an older gentleman for directions.

"Are you from out of town?" he asked. "Everybody around here knows where that place is. If you go about two . . . maybe three blocks down, make a left. Keep straight, and then at the first street make a right. You should see Roc's place on yo' left."

I thanked the old man for giving me directions. I did as he'd told me, and as soon as I made a right, there was Roc's Auto Body Shop on my left. I could see the redbrick building from afar, as well as the sign with Roc's name on it. There were numerous black men, young and old, standing outside the shop. Some were talking; some looked to be working. Cars were parked everywhere, and car parts were on the side of the building and in front of it. It looked more like a nightclub than it did an auto body shop. And I wasn't going to lie—I was very nervous and tense. I prayed that Roc was inside.

I parked the car, and as I made my way toward the door, I regretted that I had put forth so much effort to look nice. I wore an off-the-shoulder royal grape top with gray, wide-legged pants. My hair was full of tight-hanging curls, and my peep-toe heels made me look taller than I was. One man who was power washing tires stopped to open the door for me. The other men's eyes stayed glued to me, as if I had dirt on my face.

"Damn, shorty," one of the men said. "How can a nigga like me help you?"

I clipped my lip tight, wanting so badly to respond, but I didn't want to find myself in trouble. Instead, I smiled at the man and kept it moving. I found more men inside, and a few women were standing around too. All eyes shifted to me, and a hefty man behind the counter with rotten teeth asked if he could help me.

I lightly scratched my forehead, trying not to make it obvious that I was wiping my sweat. "Is, uh, Roc here?"

"Yep," the man said, coming out from behind the counter. "Follow me."

I followed the man as he walked down a hallway stacked high with chrome rims and tires. He was stopped by another man, who asked where another person was.

"That nigga somewhere outside. I saw him about an hour ago with Romo and Gage. Check outside."

The other man nodded, then moved aside to check me out as I passed by him. "Umph, umph, umph. What a pleasure, what a pleasure. Today may be my lucky day."

Not quite. I forced out another smile and kept moving to the back. We walked through another area, where several customers were sitting. Small flat-screen TVs were on the walls, and comfortable blue chairs circled the room. There were two offices to the right, but the man walked me back to a huge shop area that was lined with numerous cars. Some of the cars were being painted, and some were being worked on. The man held the door to the shop area open for me and then followed me into the space. He looked around. Several men were working, and plenty of them were standing around, talking and laughing.

"Roc-kay!" the man shouted. "You in here?"

"Yeah!" I heard Roc say. "I'm over here!"

The man and I followed Roc's voice, which was coming from the vicinity of an old-school Cadillac that was being painted a shiny black. Roc was underneath the car, doing something, and the only thing I could see was his blue work pants, which were covered with paint, as well as grease stains. His black boots were busted up, and his shoestrings were untied.

"I'm not tryin' to interrupt you, but somebody is here to see you," the man said.

"I'm real busy right now, Craig, so handle that shit for me. Tell whoever it is I'm not here."

Craig was getting ready to say something, but I placed my finger on my lip, shushing him. I kneeled on the floor, then poked my head underneath the car. Roc's head was turned in the other direction.

I cleared my throat. "I know you're busy, but I came all this way . . ."

Roc's head snapped to the side, and his eyes bugged as he looked at me as if he'd seen a ghost. He quickly rolled out from underneath the car on a creeper with wheels on it and stood up. I swear, I had never seen Roc look so sexy. The white V-necked T-shirt he wore had grease stains on it and revealed the numerous tattoos that covered his arms. The tee stretched across his muscles, and he used it to wipe the sheen of sweat from his forehead. A smudge of oil was on his left cheek, and his hands were blackened with oil. He looked embarrassed, but little did he know what I was thinking. An orange rag was in his back pocket, so he used it to wipe his oily hands.

"Damn, Dez. I didn't know you were comin' down here. You know I don't like for you to see me like this."

"Why not?" I said, looking him over. If I could have pulled my clothes off and screwed him right then and there, I would have. "You . . . you look nice."

"I'm not sure about all that," Roc said, continuing to wipe his hands on the rag. The rag wasn't doing a good job, so he walked over to a deep stainless-steel sink to wash his hands. I followed him. "So, what brings you down here to my neck of the hood?" he asked.

"I wanted to talk to you about something important. Didn't want to wait until you stopped by the house, because Chassidy would be around."

Roc nodded, then pulled down a few paper towels from the dispenser to dry his hands. He told me to follow him, and we went back to the offices I'd seen by the second waiting area. He reached for a set of jiggling keys that were in his pocket and unlocked the door to one of the offices.

"Who the fuck turned off the air in here?" he said, walking into the junky office, which I could see through the glass window. Papers were piled high on his desk, and so were many auto books. A calculator was on there too, and so was a phone. There was also a picture of Li'l Roc and Chassidy hanging crookedly on the wall, and a picture of him and Raven. He saw my eyes on the picture, but he yelled out to one of the men in the waiting area, the one standing at a soda machine.

"Keith!" he yelled again.

Keith headed toward Roc's office, then poked his head inside.

"Find out who the muthafucka is who keep playin' with my air. It's hot as hell in here, and y'all got my customers and me in here burnin' the fuck up!"

It was rather hot in the whole place, so I understood his concerns. Obviously, Keith did too, because he got on the intercom and said, "Roc said whoever it is messin' with the goddamn air, leave that shit alone. If not, he gon' cut off yo' greasy, fat, crusty fingers! Troy!"

Everybody around us laughed. Personally, I thought it was very unprofessional, but what did I know? I sat in one of the metal chairs in Roc's office. He moved some of the books aside and partially sat on the edge of his desk. Before I could say a word, another man came in. He was chubby and had a scraggly beard. The name Troy was on his work shirt.

"Sorry 'bout that, boss. Just tryin' to save you some dollars, that's all."

"I dig that, but, man, you don't want us to die up in the mutha from heat exhaustion, do you? Leave my damn air conditioner alone and close my door. Tell these niggas to let me be for a while."

Troy nodded and closed Roc's door. He pushed the intercom button, then shouted, "Roc said to get to work and stop lollygaggin' around! Anybody caught slippin' will not be paid! He also said don't bother him for a while, unless it's in regards to m-o-n-e-y!"

Roc shook his head, and you could hear laughter again. "These fools are crazy. But, uh, what's up, Ma? I still can't believe you're here. You gon' have to pinch me. I feel like I'm in a dream."

I crossed my legs and playfully cut my eyes at him. "You're not in a dream, okay? I'm just concerned about a few things, and I really need to talk to you about us. But first, I want you to be honest with me about something."

"Shoot," he said, touching the hair on his chin. "What is it?"

I glanced at the concrete floor, then looked up at him and sighed. "Are you engaged?"

Roc licked his dry lips while holding his stare. "Who told you that?"

"It doesn't matter. Are you?"

I held my breath as he swallowed, looked out the window, then shifted his eyes back to me. "Yep. I am."

Hearing him say yes caused me to tighten my stomach. My heart had dropped somewhere below it. "When were you planning on telling me?"

"I was gon' tell you, Dez. I just didn't think it was important right now."

My eyes bugged. "Really? What would make you think that?"

"Because we really haven't been seein' much of each other since your birthday. You've been busy, I've been busy, and it seems like we don't make time for each other anymore."

"I get the feeling that you were never going to tell me. I think you were going to string me along and take all that you could from me until you couldn't take no more. And if I by chance found out, you were going to happily walk away and do your best to do right by your wife."

"See, there you go again, tellin' me how you think I do things. You don't know what I was plannin' to do, Dez. I told you that I was gon' tell you, whether it hurt you or not."

"Seems to me that it doesn't bother you to hurt me. You told me on my birthday that Raven was cool people.

How does being cool people turn into the woman you're going to marry? Out of all the things I've had to deal with, never did I think that I would be faced with you marrying anyone. You don't seem like the marrying type. I am stunned that after all we've shared, you feel as if you've found a woman who you want to share your life with."

Roc scratched his head and sighed. "You know what I found, Dez? I found the complete opposite of you. Like all these niggas you see runnin' around here, I found a woman who loves me like they do. Who appreciates everything that I do and who does not make me feel as if I'm some little boy with no direction. A woman who ain't afraid to come to my place of business and shoot the breeze with me and my crew. Who can walk into my family members' houses and kick game with them as if they just like her. Basically, one who prefers not to tear me down, and don't mind liftin' me up.

"I can go on and on, but the last thing I want to do is hurt your feelings. You and I both know that we've been tryin' to do this shit for a few years now. I got to shake and move, and too bad you didn't think I was capable of settlin' down. Thugs do that too, just in case you didn't know."

As Roc spoke, tears rushed to the rims of my eyes. Had I really been that darn hard on him? I wasn't tearing him down, was I? All that I'd been holding inside for months—maybe even years—was starting to flood me. This news about him getting married would've been less painful if he had pulled one of the daggers off his wall and sliced me in half. My breathing started to increase, and he could tell that I was about to lose it. He squatted in front of me as I dropped my head and closed my eyes to fight back my tears.

"Maybe I should've said somethin' sooner," he said. "But I don't know if it would've made a difference or prevented what you're feelin' right now. We tried, Ma,

and we both know this thing between us ain't possible.
Let's stop foolin' ourselves."

I swear, I was about to break down right then and
there. And in a matter of seconds, things turned from
bad to worse. I opened my eyes and saw Raven playfully
pushing the shoulder of one of Roc's workers as she made
her way toward Roc's office. Unlike me, she had a big,
bright smile on her face that seemed genuine. She said
hello to everyone who passed by her, and she rushed into
Roc's office as if she was delighted to see him. Her steps
halted when she saw him squatting in front of me. Roc
slowly stood up. My watered-down eyes were blinded by
the diamond that glistened on her finger.

"D-did I interrupt something?" she asked in a calm
manner.

"Nah. Dez was just leavin'. She was tellin' me somethin'
about Chassidy that has her a bit upset."

"Awww," Raven said, looking at me. "I hope everything
will be okay."

I couldn't even look at her. I knew Roc was trying to
spare me the embarrassment. Raven turned Roc's face,
giving him a short but juicy kiss. "I'm going to let the two
of you talk. I'll be . . ."

I stood up but left the tresses of hair that dangled over
my right eye in place. Needed them there to shield all the
hurt that could be seen in my eyes a mile away.

"You don't have to leave. We're done here," I said.

I walked by Raven and Roc without even looking at
them. As I hurried through his shop, my legs felt so weak,
as if I had just run a marathon. It felt like everybody had
their eyes on me. They did. I couldn't get out of there fast
enough, and for whatever reason, I surely thought Roc
would come after me. He didn't.

By the time I reached my car, I was a mess. I was so
choked up, because I knew this thing between us would
never be. I felt like a failure. I thought that if he saw how
much I loved him, things would be different. I thought

that coming down here would prove to him that I did
want to know more about the man behind my madness.
Why can't he see that? Why? I thought as I sat, full of
emotions, in my car. Then it hit me. Maybe he didn't see
it, because I had to tell him. The only time I told him
I loved him was during, before, or after sex. Maybe he
needed to hear me say it just because.

I wasn't sure if it would make a difference like he'd
said, but I had an urge to lay it all on the line. I hadn't
come this far to turn away or to let another woman have
the man I was still in love with. I took a few minutes in
the car to gather myself, and then I got out and headed
back inside. I walked with my head up and ignored the
many stares from those who just didn't understand. Troy,
however, attempted to stop me. He put up his arm to
block my passage as I made my way down the hall.

"Everything gon' be cool in there, ain't it? If not, I can't
let you go by me," he told me.

Yeah, these men definitely had Roc's back, but they
didn't have to worry about me. "Everything is fine. I just
forgot to tell Roc something."

Troy moved his arm, allowing me to go back to Roc's
office. Through the glass window, I could see him sitting
at his desk, with Raven sitting sideways across his lap. Her
arms were wrapped around his neck, but she loosened
them when she saw me come through the door.

I looked past her and gazed directly at Roc. "Yes. To
answer truthfully the question that you asked on my
birthday, yes, I am very jealous of your relationship with
Raven. And . . . and right now, all I can do is take you
back to this thing you once referred to as black love. Do
you remember black love, Roc? If you don't, I do. Because
black love makes what others may see as an impossible
relationship possible. Black love makes a woman living
with too high standards jump back to reality. The reality
is I love the hell out of you, Roc, and I am willing to accept
who you are.

"I will grow to love your family and friends as you do, because black love is about acceptance, not judging. I will not make you feel like my son. Rather, I will make you feel like my king and will not tear you down anymore. I hope you understand that sometimes black love can make you so bitter when you don't get it right. And when it shows up again, one may find oneself unprepared. I was unprepared for the man who had the courage to show me what black love is really about. That man is you, baby, only you.

"If, and only if, you have ever loved me, I want you to give us our final chance to get this right. Only if you can promise me no more heartbreaks and headaches, and that you can be a faithful man, I want you to take that ring off her finger and put a *new* one where it belongs. If you can't, allow me to shed my tears and leave me at peace. Keep that ring on her finger and always be thankful that we at least gave black love a chance. Neither of us can be mad about that." I paused for a moment to wipe the tears from my face and the ones dripping from my chin.

Roc sat in awe, and so did Raven. The whole place was quiet. You could definitely hear a pin drop. Having nothing else to say, I walked away.

Nearly everyone inside the shop was looking at me, and when I walked by one man, he held up his fist. "Let's hear it for black love. That's what's up."

I smiled, feeling good that I had gotten all of that off my chest. My emotions were still running high, but I couldn't help it. I wasn't sure what Roc was going to do, but the ball was now in his court. I started my car and drove down the street. Just as I was passing by Roc's shop, he rushed outside. He flagged me down, causing me to slam on the brakes.

"Open the door," he said as he walked up to my car.

Raven rushed outside just then, calling his name. He ignored her.

"Roc, please come here," she pleaded. "Don't do this!"

I opened my car door, and he squatted beside me. "Let me deal with this right now," he said. "I'll stop by to see you later. Calm down. You gotta trust me when I say everything gon' be straight."

I couldn't believe when he leaned in to kiss my trembling lips, but I damn sure kissed him back. Raven called his name again, and that was when he backed away from me. I reached for the door to close it but watched as he pounded his chest and kept his eyes connected with mine.

"Black love, au'ight? You and me." He pointed his finger at me. "You." Then he pointed his finger at his chest. "Me."

I nodded, and with that, I drove off.

I waited for Roc in the doorway after he called later that day to tell me he was around the corner from my house and would be pulling up soon. I bit my nails, nervous as ever about what he was going to say. I wasn't sure if he had broken Raven down gently or if he was coming to give me his final good-bye. Minutes later he pulled in the driveway with a blank expression on his face. He got out of his truck, and I slowly walked up to him with my arms folded across my chest. My eyes showed worry. Roc was well aware that I didn't want to come out on the losing end of this long battle.

"Who ya wit', Roc?" I hurried to say. "Tell me now. Who is it?"

He blinked his eyes and lowered his head to look down at the ground. A sigh followed; then he eased his hand into his pocket. I reached out and threw my arms around his neck, squeezing it tight.

"Yes," I said, kissing him and sucking his lips into mine. "Hell, yes!"

He cocked his head back and had a playful smirk on his face. "Wha . . . what are you sayin' yes to me for?"

I moved my head from side to side. "Don't play with me, because I know. I can feel it."

"Feel what?"

I paused and looked into his eyes. "Us. I can feel us."

Roc narrowed his eyes, then dug in his pocket again and pulled out a black suede box. I was hyped. I was on the tips of my toes, as if the ground were too hot to touch. When Roc popped the box open, I looked at the ring, making sure it wasn't one I had seen before. Thank God, it wasn't. I threw my arms around him again, and he hugged my waist. He nibbled on my ear and squeezed my side.

"You better make sure that you keep yo' promise on every last thing that you said to me," he teased. "And tomorrow you, me, and Chassidy gon' go to some of my people's houses so y'all can meet them. I don't want you gettin' all tense, either, and if you gon' be my wife, you gotta be down with my folks."

I leaned my head back to look at him. "I guess we have to start somewhere, right? I got you, fasho."

"I got you too."

Roc and I hugged as we walked inside my house together. I hadn't seen him this happy in a long time. I guessed the same could be said for me. Because after all of this, the one thing that I had realized the most was that black love wasn't about him having his way or about me having mine. No matter what age we were, it was about compromising and doing things that I was now able to do for the betterment of myself, and for the man I would soon call my husband. This time, he'd better get it right.